A Cruel and Violent Storm

By Don M. Esquibel

Thanks! Hope you
enjoy the book
—Don Esquibel

Published 2019 by Don M. Esquibel

ISBN: 9781793313546

Contact:

dmesquibel89@gmail.com
dmesquibel89@yahoo.com
www.facebook.com/dmesquibel89
Twitter: @dmesquibel89

Prologue

The night is dark and still, the sky unblemished by clouds and twinkling with an arrayment of countless distant stars. A gentle breeze caresses my face, its touch cool and calm and completely at odds with the nervous energy flowing throughout my body. All around me the shifting and murmuring of my family reach my ears, their fear and tension palpable, mounting my nerves ever higher.

Deep breath. In. Out. Have faith things will be alright.

To calm myself, my eyes trace constellations against the inky blackness. The Princess Andromeda—chained and left to the mercy of a monster...Just as my family are now at the mercy of the Animas Animals. Ursa Minor, the little bear where resides the North Star, Polaris—the star by which innumerable lost souls have been guided home. Home. A place of warmth and welcome. Of safety and belonging. A place I fought and sacrificed to reach, only to discover it a husk of what once was. Still, though my home may be shattered, my family remains unbroken. They have been robbed, blackmailed, coerced into believing no hope remains. But tonight, hope will be restored. Tonight, we strike back.

Faith. Faith. Just have faith.

My gaze drifts south, landing on the outline of the great warrior Hercules, slayer of the Nemean Lion, of the Lernaean Hydra, of a dozen other beasts who would rip and claw and maul without mercy those who crossed their path. I don't feel a warrior under the enormity of the night sky. I feel small. Weak. I feel a charlatan donning a mask so as not to reveal the cracks and fissures which run deep within. Nevertheless, beasts roam these lands. They are powerful, they are ruthless, and they have taken my kin into their den. So whether weak or strong, warrior or charlatan, I will face these beasts all the same. I will face them because of a promise made to create a life of peace for those I love. Because I live in a world where there are no heroes, no saviors, no line of defense against the beasts who seek to claim our lives as theirs. There is only us. Only men and women willing to sacrifice everything to keep those beasts at bay.

Swallow your fear. Wear the mask. Be the man your family needs you to be.

Midnight approaches. Soon I will be cloaked in darkness and throwing myself once more into the fray. I will fight and rage and drench myself in the blood of any beast who would keep me from my kin. And if in the end they claim my life, so be it. For before I fall they will know fear. They will know chaos. They will know a taste of the wrath that will one day be their undoing.

The door opens behind me, and I know the time has come. I close my eyes, take a deep breath, and once again step forward into the unknown. This was never the path I wanted—the path I would have chosen for myself. But it is the path that has been set before me. It is dark and twisted with seemingly no end in sight. Yet, I will see it through. Because only through this path do I have a chance to uphold my promise. Only through this path can I make my dream come true and leave this nightmare behind.

Chapter 1: (Morgan)

"Come back to me," she whispers. "Understand? You do what must be done, and then you come back to me."

In my mother's embrace I stand, her body half that of my own yet radiating a strength that feeds my soul. The room swirls in a whirlwind of anxiety and unease, tonight's actions leaving everyone an apprehensive mess. All except the fierce woman before me. She is the eye of the storm—the calm amid the chaos. She is the reason my family has survived thus far.

"I will," I promise.

Her hand's cradle my face and her eyes bore into mine: eyes I inherited and which seem to say a thousand things at once. I see pride and worry. Faith and hope. But above all I see love. I let it fill me, feeding me the courage I need for what is to come. She lets her hands fall and my father takes her place, wrapping me in a tight hug and squeezing me for all he's worth. As a child, I remember how safe I felt wrapped in his arms, certain that nothing and no one could do me harm so long as he was there to protect me. He was larger than life. My hero. His face is more lined than I remember, his hair more shot through with gray. He stands half a head shorter than me, his frame slighter than my own. Through teary eyes, he looks at me now and I have to fight the urge to look away, the admiration in his stare overwhelming. It's a humbling experience to see your hero look to you as you once looked to them.

"Be safe, son," he says. "I believe in you."

I turn now to Emily, her eyes so swollen it's a wonder she can see at all. She's been a nervous wreck most of the day, worrying over our plan and mourning her best friend. I hold her close while she cries silently into my chest. No words are spoken. Nothing needs to be said that we don't know already. Neither of us are new to weathering the harshness of this new world. I hold her till she lets go with a warning not to do anything stupid.

"Never, Princess," I say. She doesn't smile, nor do I. There is no humor in tonight.

It's strange to see Leon and Felix beside her, knowing they will not be joining me. Since this all began, they've never left my side. Everything I've faced has been done so with the confidence that they had my back. But they are more needed here. Our plan is too dangerous not to have contingencies. Should anything happen tonight, I need to know my family remains in good hands. I hug each of them in turn, a brief nod serving as our parting words. They are my brothers in every way but blood. We all know what goes left unsaid.

Grace is in my arms a moment later, shivering slightly out of fear. I can tell how badly she wants to stay brave, but she can't fight back the tears that fall when I squeeze her closer. The poor girl has been through so much more than anyone her age should ever have to deal with. Yet she perseveres, unwilling to let circumstance break her. She gets that from her sister. The strength they share is inspiring. But no one can be strong all the time.

"I'm gonna be ok, Gracie," I say.

"Promise?" she asks, voice thick.

"Promise," I assure her. "I'll be back before sunrise." *I will. I know I will.*

Grace quickly wipes her eyes and steps aside so I may greet her sister. Standing before the girl I love, it hits me just how real this is—how much I am about to risk. But what choice is there? Tonight is more than a simple rescue mission. It's about making my family whole again. It's about showing the Animals who took them that they are not invincible—that they cannot do whatever they damn well please without someone rising against them. Someone *has* to rise against them. If not, they will take and take and take, until their grip over this town becomes so resolute there can be no hope against them. As Lauren reminded me earlier, I am that hope. I am the promise of something better. That is my burden.

It feels so right having her wrapped in my arms. Everything is safe here. All of my fears forgotten as the warmth of her breath washes across my neck and her heart beats against my own. I don't want to let go. But eventually she releases me and suddenly I'm staring into an ocean of deep green as her eyes find mine. Would that I was a poet and could tell her all she means to me—that I could put into words what stirs inside my soul when she looks at me like this.

"I know, Morgan," she breathes. "I know."

Suddenly her lips are on mine and it is in this moment I realize what a fool I am. Of course I am lost for words. I always will be. Because love isn't something to be described, it is something to be felt—something to be experienced and shared with those who make life worth living. If ever there was proof of that, it's this.

I soak in the faces about the room, memorizing this moment forever in my heart. Through all the tension and angst lying upon the air, there is no mistaking the hope blooming between my family as they look at me. At times their belief in me is a weight on my shoulders—a cross to be carried. But at others, it is my strength. My drive. It is the fuel feeding the fire which blazes through me, burning away any lingering fear and doubt I may have held about tonight. I will not fail. There is still too much work to be done, too much life to be had. There is still a future for us. I have to believe that. And it all starts tonight.

"Stay alert and take care of each other," I say. "We'll be back by sunrise." Before I make my leave I share one last look with Lauren, allowing myself this quiet moment before it begins. As I watch her, she graces me with the smallest of smiles. A small gesture, hardly more than a grin and as fleeting as a whisper. Yet, above all else, it is what sets me at peace—what grants me the clarity of mind I need for tonight to succeed.

With a nod, I turn away and join my hunting party: Vince, Jerry, and Richard. Before we make our leave there is a moment we share, a feeling of camaraderie, of understanding that no matter how the night plays out, we will make through to morning.

"Let's head out," I say.

The hunt is on.

We move as shifting shadows, blending in with the darkness as we dart between patches of cover. My eyes flicker about for threats, my ears straining for anything absent our breaths and sighing wind. I will not be caught off guard again. I'm barely held together as it is, last night's events leaving me raw and wounded. I use that pain now to sharpen my senses, to keep a repeat from happening.

Richard takes point as we travel. At forty-four, he's near twice my age but in far better shape than I've ever been. I've been hiking the Colorado Trail for months. Richard served over twenty years in the Marines. Two years as a civilian and he's still fit as a fiddle. I don't know the man well, but I'm glad to have him on this mission all the same. He's a warrior. The horrors I've seen have been seen by him a hundred times over. He knows better than any of us the danger we face.

We crouch now in the brambles of a large hedgerow. A van slowly creeps along the adjoining street, barely visible, nearly silent. At the intersection, it turns and I let loose a breath of relief.

"The bastards stalk at night," Vince whispers.

"And the early morning," Jerry adds bitterly.

They both grow quiet and I know they're thinking of their sister, Julia. Early morning is when she and my cousin Trent were taken. Caught hauling water from an abandoned house whose spigot had served as their water source since the collapse. I can feel the rage flowing through them. I know it well. It is the same rage which flowed through me when I faced off against Clint and his gang. But I also knew how to tame it. To not let it run away from me. Rage can be a tool, a weapon. It can also lead to recklessness. To mistakes. We can't afford either tonight.

"We'll make it right," I assure them, tempering their emotion. "We just have to be smart about it. The plan will work."

We encounter no more patrols en route to our destination. In fact, outside of a wandering raccoon which nearly got pumped full of bullets after spooking Jerry, we encounter no activity at all. I'm not fooled. The population may have dwindled to a fraction of what it once was, but there are still plenty of people in the area. Behind locked doors, they wait out the night. Do they sleep? Do they stand guard? Do they feel the looming threat building in their backyard? Surely some do. But does that even matter if nobody is willing to stand against it? I shake the thought away. I need to stay focused on the task at hand. It's all that matters right now.

From on high, we eye our target. Lit from the light of a dozen fires, it sits on the opposite bank of the Animas River. The Doubletree. Once one of Durango's finer hotels, it now serves as the base of operations for the Animas Animals. It's a fortress. Sentries guard the entrances. Patrols walk its perimeter. As a deterrent to breaching parties, the sliding glass doors leading to guest patios have been boarded up all along the ground level. Witnessing the full scope of what we face, this suddenly feels more a prayer than a plan. Everything has to line up just right for us to have a chance.

"That's the ballroom, there," Vince whispers. The hotel is arranged in three sections: a central body consisting of the lobby and other accommodations, and two branches of guest rooms connected on either side. A large bank of windows at the center of the hotel marks the ballroom. Hidden behind the dark glass my cousins are held captive, joined by dozens of others who've been recruited against their will. So close, yet so many obstacles lay between us.

"Only a single patrol by the looks of it," I say.

"Arrogance," Richard spits. "They have the location. The manpower. But they're sloppy. They think because of their reputation, nobody can touch them." He turns to me, and I flinch at the glint in his eyes. He served in the military nearly as long as I've been alive. Retired or not, at least part of him still craves this. I feel a shiver dance down my spine, wondering if I might one day share such a craving. "Their mistake."

Slowly we traverse the backside of the hill so as not to be spotted by prying eyes. Beside the highway is a footbridge spanning the river and leading to the Doubletree. We find the way unguarded, just as they promised it would be. So much relies on what they observed the night Trent and Julia were taken. While I celebrated the feat of finally making it home, they scouted from nightfall to sunrise, making note of every detail they could. I just hope it's enough.

Across the bridge we leave the trail and make for the riverbank, using its slope to shield us from view. A strip of grass dotted with trees separate the hotel from the river trail. Fires burn in metal barrels across the expanse of grass, illuminating the area. But where there is light, there is shadow. We position ourselves accordingly. A patrol of three men approach from the north. They laugh as they grow closer, their weapons held loosely. Richard was right, their arrogance makes them sloppy, believing themselves untouchable. The fools. Nobody is untouchable.

Twenty yards out.

Ten.

They draw even, and from the shadows, we emerge. Hands cover mouths. Blades slash across throats. They never stood a chance. Warm blood soaks my hands as I drag my victim down the embankment. We strip the bodies of weapons and stow them inside the bag Vince had the foresight to bring. Every weapon, every bullet counts in this new world. At the water's edge, I take a moment to wash the blood from my hands, wondering how much more they will see in my quest to build a better life for those I love.

Doesn't matter. Has to be done.

We close the distance from the riverbank to the hotel in seconds. Flat against the ground we wait for a shout, a gunshot, an alarm that tells us we've been spotted. But none comes. When we are sure we've gone unnoticed we move into position for the next phase of the plan: infiltration. As the tallest, Jerry and I squat facing each other with our hands cradled before us. Carefully, Vince steps into our cradles while Richard stands close to spot him. Silently, Vince signals he's ready. With a grunt I straighten out and lift my arms as high as I can, Jerry mirroring my movements. Vince wobbles a bit but maintains his balance long enough to reach for the railing of the second-floor patio. He quickly picks himself over and throws down a rope after securing it to the railing. The three of us haul ourselves up and join Vince on the patio. We find the sliding glass door unlocked and the room occupied by two men. One snores heavily in his sleep while the second stirs to consciousness at our arrival.

"The hell is going—" Richard silences him before an alarm can be raised or a move made against us. Moments later the second man's snoring is silenced by Richards blade. The smell of blood is nauseating in the confined space. After all this time you'd think I would be used to it. We take the time to search the room, adding an AK, 30-30, and a revolver to our arsenal. Into the bag, they go.

We slip into the hallway, a handful of low lit lanterns spaced about creating a patchwork of light and shadow. We move swiftly, weapons primed and at the ready. Voices reach us as we near the end of the hallway, forcing us into the recess of a dark stairwell. Two men draw level and then they are past us, turning left at end of the corridor toward the lobby and main entrance of the hotel.

We enter the corridor, the antechamber to the ballroom on our left. Two guards cover the door. They sit facing each other at a small folding table, a deck of cards between them. Had they been more vigilant they might have heard us, might have noticed the shadows shift beyond their cocoon of light. But again their arrogance shows. Never did they dream someone could penetrate this far into their ranks.

Richard motions silently and I nod my understanding. On his signal, I unleash a crossbow bolt into the heart of one guard, while his tomahawk claims the life of his companion. Quickly, we snuff out the light and strip them of weapons. Behind thick drapes we stash the bodies, hoping to buy us time if a patrol sweeps the area. Either way, killing these men has put a ticking clock over our heads.

"Blades and silent weapons only," Richard whispers as we prep our breach. I hold the crossbow at the ready, my recently suppressed Glock holstered on my hip. The Animals might have cleared my family's store of guns and ammo, but they never found Richard's suppressors. They don't completely eliminate noise, but they mute it considerably. They're invaluable on a night such as this.

Vince and Jerry pull open either side of the double-door, and Richard and I advance. A wall of heat greets me, the air stagnate from poor ventilation and the amassed bodies throughout the room. A single lantern suspended from the ceiling lights the room. Mattresses line the floor in rows, nearly all occupied with sleeping captives. A guard stirs to my right, startled by our sudden entrance. A bolt claims his heart before he can raise his gun against me. Suppressed gunfire sounds beside me as I unholstered my Glock and continue my scan of the room. No shot presents itself. On the far side of the room, a guard lies dead, torso riddled with gunshot wounds. Two more lie dead to my left, one claimed by Richard's tomahawk, and the other by a pair of throwing knives. In seconds, we have cleared the room. But in doing so, we have awakened the captives.

It's a chain reaction, cries of alarm and confusion spreading along the lines until suddenly we find ourselves in a room filled with dozens of scared and desperate people. I strip my victim of weapons as Richard tries to quell their panic. But they are not calmed by his words, their voices growing more frantic as they notice the dead guards. This is a complication. We weren't anticipating half as many captives.

"Uncle Richard?" My head whips around at the sound of her voice. She rises to her feet, disbelief evident on her face. Julia, and beside her rises Trent. They're here. They're alive. If we can just make it back, this will all have been worth it.

Richard ignores her, continuing his effort to gain control of the room. "Quiet, everyone! You're gonna wake up the whole damn—" he's cut off by a crack of thunder.

"Shit!" I turn and spot Jerry clutching at his shoulder in pain even as he lunges to slam the doors shut behind him. Bullets rap into the wood, several shooting straight through and into the room. A man not ten feet away goes down with a gunshot to his stomach. Feet from Julia, a woman gets clipped in the thigh. It's chaos—screaming and crying and bodies flattening themselves against the floor. Jerry crawls my way, blood streaming down his shoulder.

No. Not again.

Flashes of last night return to me. Arm around her shoulder. Body hitting the dirt as she pushed me away. Running, praying, pleading with her cradled in my arms. Realization. Fearful eyes. Her hand in mine as her heart beat its last.

No! Not again!

"Richard, Plan B!" I yell as I help Jerry to his feet. "Vince, make a hole." I turn to Jerry, his eyes panicked as blood leaks past his fingers clutching his wound. I grab a sheet from one of the cots and cinch it tightly over it.

"Look at me," I say. I have to repeat myself before he does. "You're going to be alright, I promise. But we have to move. Now!"

The shooting ceases. Eyes look to me—to the controlled voice amid the chaos. Several rise as we rush toward the far side of the room, yelling and pleading and demanding to know who we are. They seek answers. Direction. I push past the mass of bodies with Jerry by my side, feeling heartless as I do so. I have nothing to offer these people. No plan, no guidance. In this room, surrounded by wolves on all sides, every second, every movement counts. Life and death are measured in the span of a breath, of a heartbeat. My heart beats for my family. Until the day we live in peace, anything I do must be with them in mind.

Richard hands me a lit bottle as I reach him, a second in his opposite hand. Jerry rushes to the corner where Vince makes ready our escape, Julia and Trent behind him. Voices sound from beyond the door, a dozen at least. Captives back away from us, some dropping back to the ground in fear of another barrage of bullets. We stand our ground, waiting. The doors burst open and they stream in, weapons raised. Richard and I act as one, our Molotov cocktails flying through the air and shattering against their first responders. Bodies are consumed in flames, their screams silenced as we draw our weapons and unload on the entrance. Shotgun fire and breaking glass sound behind us. Our clips run dry, and no sooner are we jumping out the window and onto the low roof of the cafe below.

Dozens of captives flow behind us, desperate to reclaim the freedom that has been taken from them. We hit the ground at a sprint as the night air is pierced by gunfire. Screams follow. I block it out, focusing instead on moving us forward. At 9th street, we leave the trail and cross the bridge spanning the river. We continue straight, up an embankment swathed in trees and bushes and emerge onto Cemetery Rd. We scramble up another embankment and push into the cemetery. Along the pathways we sprint, not daring to slow down until we reach the far edge of the graveyard. Here we pause, allowing ourselves a moment to catch our breaths and so Richard can assess Jerry's wound. Julia collapses onto her hands and knees, chest heaving with panting breaths. Trent stumbles another few feet before emptying his stomach behind a thick shrub.

"I can't believe you guys came," Julia says breathlessly, straightening herself out. Tears pool in her eyes as she finds Vince's face. He pulls her into his arms a moment later.

"Of course we came," he says.

I allow them some privacy and check on Trent who remains hunched over, clutching his stomach. "You alright?" I ask.

"Yeah. I'm good." He spits once and hastily wipes his mouth before straightening out. He looks at me now as if unsure of what he's seeing. "How the hell are you here right now, man? Your mom said you were visiting Emily when everything went black."

"I was," I say. "But we couldn't stay there, the place was absolute chaos. We had to get home. Besides, I knew there was a good chance I'd have to bail your ass out of some shit sooner or later."

He laughs. "Dick. But fair enough. I'll give you that one." I clasp his hand and swing my arm around him in a tight hug, feeling the tension loosen throughout my body. Then I hear a grunt of pain from Jerry, and I know we are not out of the woods yet. We rejoin the group to find Richard midway through patching Jerry up.

"Just a grazing shot," Richard assures him. "Tore a chunk out ya', but you should heal up just fine." A wave of relief passes over Vince and Julia at these words.

"Thank God," Julia says, hugging him tenderly as Richard finishes. "Thank God," she repeats.

Jerry squeezes her with his good arm. "You took the words from my mouth," he says. Watching Vince and Jerry embrace their sister takes me back to the trail. I know what it's like to fear the worse for your sibling—the mental toll it takes on you. I also know the overwhelming relief in feeling them in your arms, safe and alive despite everything. It's a heartwarming moment to witness from this side.

Julia lets go and throws her arms around me next. "It's so good to see you, Morgan," she says. "And Emily? Is she—"

"She's fine," I assure her. "She's going to be so happy to see you."

"Me too," she says. "But how did you guys get here? Have you been on your own all this time?"

"It's a long story," I say. "We should probably wait till we get back before it's told."

"Agreed," Richard says as he rummages through our bag of looted weapons. "But first things first." Trent is given a 12 gauge, and Julia the 30-30. They both appear comfortable with the weapons they're given, handling them easily. I'm not surprised. They've been with Richard for over two months. I'm sure they weren't the only ones who received a crash course in firearm training.

We pick our way slowly toward Rockridge, sticking to the forested hillsides blanketing the western edge of town. After what we pulled tonight, there are bound to be patrols in the area. I know men like them. They will not let tonight go unpunished, not when we've spilled the blood of their own. I can't say I would either if the tables were reversed. But I didn't start this. Tonight wasn't a choice, it was the lack of one.

We reach the crest of a slow rising hill, and below I spot a sight to make my blood run cold. Below travel a man and a woman, their furtive movements and constant glances behind them leaving me no doubt they are escapees from earlier. Down the block, an old Jeep slowly creeps along the adjoining street, on a clear path to intercept them. Before I can even consider what I'm doing I find myself yelling down to them.

"Clear the street! There's a—" Richard cuts me off, covering my mouth with his hand to silence me. I pry his hand away and shove him off me. "What the hell was that?" I seethe.

"Keep your voice down," he hisses. "It's already too late."

I look back down the hill to discover he's right. Headlights now flood the street, freezing the two with its harsh glare. It's hard to tell from this distance, but they look young, my age or not much older. But even from here there is no mistaking their fear as the Animals exit their vehicle and draw closer.

"Well, isn't this some damned fine timing. We were just getting ready to turn back when you two came waltzing through."

The voice grates inside my skull like nails on a chalkboard. Suddenly I'm no longer concealed in the darkness atop the hillside: I'm surrounded by blinding light, fear coursing through my veins as my loved ones take cover behind me. I'd know that face, that voice anywhere. My vision tunnels. Rage consumes me. My breathing comes in violent bursts like that of a caged animal. I turn in search of the duffle, desperate for a rifle that can reach out and end this man's life. Richard holds it, his stance telling me he knows exactly my intentions.

"It won't bring her back, Morgan," Vince says quietly.

"I don't care," I hiss. "That man deserves to die."

"Yes, he does," Richard agrees. He points behind me. "But you take a shot at him, and you'll be putting us knee deep in a pile of shit."

I follow his finger to see a blacked out van inbound from the south. It's headlights join the scout's and a half a dozen men pour out, creating a circle around the terrified escapees. They outnumber us over two to one. Even if I killed the sneering man, it would likely come at the cost of one of our lives, possibly all of them. I can't take that risk. My vengeance will have to wait.

I curse but nod my understanding. "You're right." I turn my attention back to the pitiful sight in the street, my anger still simmering under the surface. The captives have been brought to their knees, the sneering man pacing before them while twirling a knife in his hand. He's good with the blade. He bends now, using the knife's point to draw the woman's chin up and meet his eyes.

"I had high hopes for you, Sandra," he says. There's disappointment in his voice, genuine or not I cannot tell. She shakes with terror, a strangled sob stuck in her throat.

"Don't..." the man pleads beside her. Tears run rivers down his cheeks, his face tortured. The sneering man turns his way.

"Don't?" he asks, feigning confusion. "Don't what?" he traces his knife down her throat, toward her heart.

"Please," he begs. "W-we d-didn't know what to do. Guards d-dead. M-men with guns, y-yelling, shooting." He's barely coherent, too overcome with fear.

"What men?" The sneering man asks. "Who were they?"

"I d-don't know," he says. The sneering man adds pressure to his blade, drawing a droplet of blood just above the woman's collarbone. She screams, as does her companion. "Please! I don't know!" he yells, voice cracking. "They c-came for the two new r-recruits. The b-boy and g-girl."

The sneering man pauses, withdrawing his blade from the girl's throat and focusing entirely on the man. "The new recruits?" he asks. "The two we hauled in the day before yesterday?"

"Yes!" the escapee confirms. "H-heard her myself. C-called em' uncle."

The sneering man continues to stare at the escapee, his face an emotionless mask. Slowly, a smile cracks the mask, an amused chuckle issuing from his mouth. "Now *that's* some information I can use!" he says. "Please, stand," he insists, raising his hands. The two escapees shakily rise to their feet, the woman trembling in the crook of the man's arm. "I gotta say, you just saved the two of you a whole lot of suffering with that information. I mean, you've seen what we do with our enemies, right?" The escapee's nod in acknowledgment. "Childsplay compared to how we handle traitors...which is exactly what your actions tonight make you."

"Please," the woman begs. "Give us a second chance. We'll be loyal. I swear we will."

The sneering man lets loose a long breath. "Yes. I believe you would." He shakes his head. "But I'm afraid that time has passed."

"You s-said we w-wouldn't suffer," the man says.

"Don't worry," the sneering man assures him. "You won't feel a thing." The revolver is unholstered and leveled at the escapee's head a fraction of a second later. Two shots ring into the night, the man and woman falling in tandem to the sound, holes blasted through their foreheads. The sneering man holsters his gun and gestures triumphantly to his surrounding men. They look to him with ravenous eyes, the murder in the air making them hungry with bloodlust. "Looks like we got us a house call to make," he yells. The men cheer, eager for more carnage.

Into their vehicles they go, leaving us alone in the dark as they race north. Toward Rockridge.

Chapter 2: (Lauren)

A storm of emotions brews inside his eyes, so full of love and worry it almost hurts to witness. The room is flooded with nervous energy, his family barely holding it together. I know the feeling well—that chest tightening, stomach-churning kind of dread—the kind that only stems out of fear for those you love most. For as long as I can remember, that feeling was reserved for Grace alone. I remember nights cloaked in that fear, drowning in it. I remember carrying it inside me, an insatiable beast which fed off of every worry, every doubt, growing stronger as I grew weaker.

I didn't like the girl I was then: cold, unyielding, suspicious of everyone and everything. My world was small and closed off, room enough only for one. It had been like that for so long I didn't know any other way. It wasn't until he came into my life that I realized another path existed. These past months I have suffered hardships. Violence. I have taken the lives of men and witnessed the darkest side of humanity more times than I can count. But I also, for the first time in my entire life, feel as if I belong to something bigger than myself. Family, now, is more than just a word, an idea. More than the kind-hearted girl I have protected these past twelve years. He gave me that.

Standing here, I feel that old fear trace a finger along my spine, hear its silky voice whispering into my ear. But I am not the same girl I once was. I have opened my heart, filled it with love, felt the strength that comes by letting other people in. Now I am no longer smothered by that fear, it's weight no longer solely on my shoulders. To know I'm not alone in this, that there are people who care for me as I care for them, is comforting in a way I can't even begin to describe. Morgan was raised surrounded by this comfort, this love. It is the driving force behind all that he does: the reason we made it here, and what leads him to once again risk his life for others.

I wish he didn't have to go. I wish that I could go with him. But I know neither option is a possibility. He can't stay here, safe, away from the fight. It's not his way. And as he convinced me earlier, this isn't my fight to take.

"We can't risk it," he said. "This plan...it's delicate. So many things could go wrong."

"Which is why I should be there," I argued. "I'm tired of waiting where it's safe while you risk your life."

"I know you are," he sighed heavily. "But they're my family, Lauren. I can't stay behind...not when they're at the mercy of those men."

"I'm not asking you to," I said. "I just don't see why we can't face them together."

His hand reached out then, pushing back a stray lock of hair before lying against my cheek. "Because you're my family too. There's already so much at stake tonight, so many lives...I just don't think we should risk any more than we have to."

I relented after that. Still, it's hard knowing in moments he will walk out the door, carrying out their plan while I remain behind.

"Stay alert and take care of each other," Morgan says. "We'll be back by sunrise."

His eyes land on mine in all their intensity, filled with a tenderness that fills my heart with warmth. Sometimes I can't believe we've known each other so briefly—that only a few short months ago I was staring into those resolute, dark-brown eyes through the barrel of a gun, wondering if I could trust him. In the end, I gave him my trust, and with it, he gave me a home. Incredible to think the power a single choice can have. He grins slightly, and it's only then that I realize the smile I wear. It isn't until he nods and turns to join his cousins that it falls from my face. I watch them exchange a few words and then disappear into the dark, marking the beginning of what I know will be a restless night.

The house grows quite in their absence. Everyone seems in a daze, as if unsure of what to do with themselves. One by one they drift away, sinking into the couches and chairs where they will wait out the night. I wrap an arm around Grace and squeeze her close. My sister has always been sensitive to the emotions of others. This has to be taking a toll on her.

"You alright?" I ask.

"I'm fine," she says.

I know she wants me to believe that. So much of her childhood was spent with me hovering over her, trying to shield her from everything we grew up with. Still, she's heard things, seen things. Morgan once told me he couldn't believe how well she has coped with all that has happened. If he only knew the half of it. In so many ways, she was better equipped than most to deal with it all.

Felix walks up, an attempt at a smile on his face. "C'mon," he says. "We need more players."

"For what?" I ask.

"Monopoly."

Hours later, I am in the middle of the most depressing round of Monopoly ever played. But Felix was right, it has made the hours more bearable. Rolling the dice, buying property, passing Go; it gives us something to focus on besides what's happening beyond these walls. I sit beside Grace and Ray, Leon's younger brother. When I was introduced to Leon's family, I had to do a double take when I saw Ray. Except for the almond shape of his eyes, and slightly lighter skin, he could be a fourteen-year-old clone of his older brother. I've heard stories about his wild streak throughout the trail, but so far, I haven't seen a trace of it. I suppose surviving in this new world has tamed that wildness.

Emily sits across from me, her face pale, eyes lost. My heart breaks for her. I can only imagine the pain she must feel, how Maya's death must haunt her. I thought the world of Maya. I didn't know her long, but I feel like I knew her well. Her kindness in a world full of hate was a rare thing. But she wasn't my best friend. There are no memories of us outside these past few months. Those memories belong to Emily. I wish there was something I could do for her, but I know there is nothing to be done. Time is what she needs. I just hope we get it.

Leon rolls the dice and lands on Community Chest. "You win 2nd prize in a beauty contest," he reads from the card.

Felix smiles at that. "I'd hate to see whoever came in 3rd," he says.

Leon scoffs. "Well, we all know you wouldn't have even placed."

They continue to throw casual insults back and forth, their smiles never quite reaching their eyes, their laughs just a little too forced to be genuine. It's their way of trying to lessen the tension in the air, and it works to a degree. Their banter lasts as the game dwindles down, and is eventually abandoned altogether.

"I need to stretch my legs," I say, excusing myself from the table. Quietly, I slip past the living room and take the stairs, yearning for a breath of fresh air. Outside isn't an option, but upstairs I can open a window without fear of sound or light escaping into the street. I head for the same bedroom where I found Morgan earlier, only to find it's already occupied.

"I'm sorry," I say, already making to close the door again. "I didn't think anyone would be up here."

"It's fine, Lauren. Please, stay if you'd like." I'm hesitant, unsure if she's only asking out of courtesy. Then she shifts and the moonlight washes across her face, revealing those eyes which she and her son share, and I find my feet acting on their own accord.

"Thank you, Mrs. Taylor," I say.

She smiles. "I appreciate your manners. But please, call me Marie."

I return her smile. "I think I can manage that." I stand beside her now, the breeze from the open window soothing on my skin. I look out, amazed at all the homes before me. Morgan told me this area was full of wealth and I don't doubt it. Not every home is as grand as the one we're in, but they are all beautiful in their own way. Most have been abandoned, their owners either dead or moved on. In the end, their money didn't matter when the power went away.

The silence deepens, but I don't feel awkward in it. Her stillness, the way she carries herself despite all the strain she must feel, it all reminds me of Morgan. He always said his mother was the glue, the bond which held his family together. Just as he was that bond between us on the trail. I suppose he had to learn it from someone.

"I'm sorry if my family is a bit much right now," she says. "It's the tension. It's making everyone a little stir crazy."

"Your family's amazing," I say. "It's only tense right now because there's so much love between you all. That's never something to apologize for."

She graces me with another smile. "Thank you, Lauren," she says. "I think you're a pretty amazing young woman, yourself."

I'm caught off guard by her compliment. She's barely just met me, yet I hear the sincerity in her voice. "Why do you say that?" I ask, my words coming out more suspicious than I'd like.

"The way my son looks at you, talks about you. Everything you've done to get here. Not to mention the way I've seen you with your sister. How caring and protective you are of her? I'm a mother, Lauren. I know that kind of nurturing isn't something learned in a matter of weeks or months, but groomed over the course of years. That alone says a lot about you, that you've placed others needs above your own for some time."

I don't know what to say to that. The woman is more perceptive than anyone I've ever met, picking up on the most subtle of things. She reaches out and strokes my cheek once, her hand caring and gentle—the way a mother's touch is supposed to feel. Emotion swells inside me, a lump rising in my throat, the back of my eyes stinging with tears I've trained myself not to let fall. *Where the hell did that come from?*

"It's alright, dear," she says. "You don't have to say anything. Just know I mean what I said: you're an amazing young woman. My son is lucky to have you."

I return her smile. "I think we're lucky to have each other," I say.

She laughs, a warm, floating thing—like freshly laundered sheets pulled straight from the dryer. "Yes. You're probably right." She turns back toward the window a moment, exhaling a deep breath as she does so. "Well, I think I've hidden up here long enough. I should head back to the craziness." She squeezes my arm once before turning to leave. "I look forward to getting to know you, Lauren. I'll see you downstairs."

I stay a while longer, allowing the dark and quiet to calm my thoughts, steady my emotions. Now that she's left the room, I'm struggling to understand why her presence affected me as it did. Perhaps it's merely the air around her, how she commands the focus of the room without effort. There's no falseness to her, she's genuine in a way most people can't be. She's interpreted so much in such a short time. It makes me wonder what else she'll see, the layers she will peel back.

Finally, I make my leave from the room, shutting the door behind me. I pause halfway down the hall, a strangled sob to my right stopping me in my tracks. A soothing voice follows from behind a partially closed door.

"Shh. It's gonna be alright, Em." Leon speaks with a tenderness I've never heard from him before. My mind screams at me to keep walking, to give them privacy, but it's as if my feet are glued to the spot.

"You don't know that," she says. "We thought that last night too, thought we escaped them...and look what happened." Another sob sounds from behind my door and it helps me find my feet. The stinging behind my eyes sharpens, but I don't let the tears fall. I can't afford to let myself break down. Still, my mind starts steering toward those darker places, imagining all the things that might be happening outside. After last night and from what we've learned this morning, I know exactly what the Animals are capable of. And there were survivors from their botched attack—vindictive men full of anger and rage and who saw their friends die before their eyes. They will remember the man who stood against them, whose defiance sparked it all. And there will be no mercy for him should he be caught. He will suffer, and he will die, and—

Stop it! He's ok. He's too important not to be.

I foous on the immediate: the beating of my heart, the inhale-exhale of each breath, putting one foot in front of the other. I've had practice taming unsavory thoughts. When I make it back to the sitting room, it's to find Felix alone at the table. He forces a smile when he sees me.

"Monopoly must have worn them out," he says. I follow his gaze to find Grace and Ray asleep on the loveseat in the corner. Exhaustion finally caught up with her. I feel it myself, but sleep is still a long ways off.

"Understandable," I say. I take a seat opposite him. "You could probably do with some sleep yourself," I say. He looks like hell. The past 48 hours have been as hard on him as anyone. It was out of desperation that led him to take off in the dead of night for his uncle's farm. How full of hope he must have been when he finally arrived, excited to see his family after so long. I can't even imagine the pain he must have felt when he found the place so broken—the dark thoughts that must have consumed him as he wondered if the blood splattered on the floors and walls was the same blood running through his veins. To go through all that and then suffer the death of a friend right after? The strain of it all would have broken a lesser man. But despite his strength, I know how badly he must be hurting.

He shrugs the suggestion aside with a tired laugh. "I could say the same thing about you."

I smile in return. "You're not wrong," I say. I cast a glance at the clock on the far wall: 4:00 AM. Dawn grows nearer. Felix notices my gaze but doesn't mention anything. I know he's counting down the hours. I force some small talk, asking him questions about the town, about growing up here. It provides the distraction I need and keeps the quiet from settling in. But eventually I run out of steam and I find my mind wondering once again on what must be happening. And apparently, I'm not the only one. From the adjoining living room, a commotion reaches our ears, drawing our attention.

"Please, Jenna. Calm down," says a calming voice.

"Don't tell me to calm down! They should have been here by now!"

Morgan's cousin Jenna paces about the room, the strain of everything finally making her crack. Her mom, Virginia, tries in vain to settle her down, her words only adding to her tantrum.

"They got caught. Had to have," Jenna says.

"Sit down, girl!" barks Morgan's uncle, Will. "You don't know what the hell you're talking about!" His face flushes red with anger. The man has to be a nervous wreck. His daughter, Julia, has been at the mercy of the Animals for days. And now it is his son's who go to rescue her. I'm surprised he's kept it together this long.

"I don't take orders from *you*," she snarls. "What? Afraid I'm speaking the truth? You should be. If they haven't been caught, then where are they? Unless they got cold feet and are trying to save face by not coming back too soon."

Will rises to his feet, vein in his forehead bulging ominously. "I'm warning you: shut your goddamn mouth if you know what's good for you!" His voice has gone deathly quiet, filled with venom.

"You don't scare me," she says. "I'll say whatever the hell—" she's caught off guard as Will advances on her.

"Shit," I say. Suddenly Morgan's dad is between them, keeping Will at bay and yelling at him to calm down. Maybe he might have, but Jenna doesn't seem to know how to stop herself, yelling back, adding to his anger. More of the family rise to their feet, arguments rippling out like rings of water on a pond, completely unrelated to the fight between Jenna and Will. Mrs. Taylor tries to regain order, but her voice is lost in the shouting.

All the commotion has woke Grace and Ray who stand beside Felix and I—outsiders witnessing a family meltdown. There's shoving and pushing. Crying. Insults flying back and forth. This I understand. I've seen this scene before.

"Everyone shut the hell up!" Leon's voice booms from atop the stairs, loudly enough to pause the commotion. Heated glares race his way, as if all the anger in the room has shifted to him. But he continues before anyone can question him. "Trucks are coming up the road!"

Anger turns to fear. Panic. Darkness and silence fill the room as lanterns are extinguished and arguments die. Felix and I race to the closest window and carefully peel back the drape to see with our own eyes. Half the room follows suit, peeking out the corners throughout the front of the house. Headlights fill the street and I feel my blood turn to ice. My hand grips the revolver holstered on my hip out of instinct. Beside me, I can hear Felix chamber a shotgun shell.

First to emerge from the crest of the hill is a blue pickup, followed by a white van, a silver diesel, and finally a black scout. They park in a semicircle, headlights focused on Will's house. Men and women pour out the vehicles and spread out, circling the place. From the scout, another figure steps forward

"Shit," I whisper, recognizing him immediately.

He stares up at the house in contempt, his sneer twisted in hatred as he twirls a baseball bat in his hand. "Grunts," he yells out. To his right, a dozen men and women approach him. I take note of them immediately—of the resigned, disgusted looks on their faces. Some look to be mending injuries, others on the verge of tears. The sneering man's stare burns into them. "You say you're loyal. This is your chance to prove it. I want them alive if possible, but dead will work just as well." He jerks his head toward the house. "Go."

They obey, moving toward the house with their weapons drawn. They break apart into squads of threes and fours, focusing on different breaching points. Throughout the house, I hear silent curses and weapons priming. I squeeze Grace's hand and whisper it's going to be alright.

From the back of the house, I hear the kitchen's sliding glass door open and several bodies rush in. Heads whip from the drapes to the darkened kitchen, weapons held at the ready.

"It's us," calls a familiar voice. "We got em'"

Chapter 3: (Morgan)

My pulses races. Sweat pours down my face. I double over once inside, a sharp pain in my side as I struggle to catch my breath. Never have I ran so hard in my life. Vince Joins me, followed by Julia, and then Richard who helps Jerry along. They slide the door closed, and I find the breath to call out.

"It's us," I say. "We got em'."

We file into the living room where most of the family has assembled, the faint light from the street outlining their bodies. My Uncle Will rushes to us, sweeping Julia into his arms the moment we enter. Closely behind him is Jenna who launches herself into her brother's arms, a sob escaping her. I move past them when I spot Lauren in the next room.

"Hello, beautiful," I say, squeezing her tight. After the night I've had, all I want is to stay in her arms. But light from the street draws my attention. "What's going on?" I ask. I pull back the drape and take in the scene further down the street.

"They're clearing out the house," Felix says.

I clap him on the shoulder. "It's a good thing we're not there then, huh?"

It was Felix's idea to vacate the house. At dark, we packed everything worth saving from my Uncle's place and made for an abandoned house down the street. If tonight's plan failed and we were caught, there was a chance Vince, Jerry, and Richard would be recognized. The Animals would put two and two together, and they would go after the rest of the family. And if they were to catch me with them after last nights events, their revenge would be that much more brutal.

We watch as the men and women enter the house. Streaks of light dance between the windows as they search the place, finding nothing but empty rooms. Even from here their fear is unmistakable as they report back. The sneering man glares at them. "Well?" he asks.

Nobody seems eager to answer him. I don't blame them. Finally, a man in his late forties finds his voice. "Nothing, sir. They've abandoned the place."

The sneer leaves him as his face flickers in anger. His revenge has been stolen from him, and he can barely contain his fury. He raises the baseball bat and his captive flinches back. Beside the captive, my uncle's mailbox breaks apart with one hard swing. On the ground, he continues swinging until it turns into a pile of splintered wood and dented metal. Breathing heavily, he straightens himself out, turning slowly in a circle, eyes searching the area.

"I know you're out there," he yells into the night. "We could have had peace, could have built something together." He pauses, shaking his head. "But you've chosen violence. We will find you. You will pay for the blood you've spilled. And know this: your deaths will be long and painful. This, I promise you." He turns now to his men. "Torch it."

Men enter the house with gas cans. Minutes later the sneering man drops a single match, and flames leap to life on the ground and race into the house. The fire spreads quickly, and it's not long until smoke billows into the sky and the house is consumed in flames. I look to my Uncle Will as he watches his home burn. There's anger in his face—pain as so many years of memories turn to ash. But there is also resolve, acceptance. He squeezes Julia closer to him and looks to Vince and Jerry who stand to his left. He knows how much more he could have lost tonight.

The house begins to collapse in on itself as the first hints of light rise from the east. The Animals return to their vehicles, all of them filled with anger but for the captives whose relief is easy to spot. Before he enters the scout, the sneering man looks out once again, his eyes flicking about malevolently as if reasserting his promise. But eventually, he too enters the vehicle and the scout pulls away from the curb. It's not until they disappear past the crest of the hill, that we breathe easy once again.

There's a roar of triumph as my family celebrates our reunion. I smile and laugh, but it's hard to find joy when I feel so much blood on my hands. The Animals don't warrant my sympathy. But they weren't the only ones who lost people today. I remember that old man dropping to the ground with a gunshot to the stomach. I remember sounds of pursuing gunfire as we escaped through the smashed window with a score of freed captives. I remember a couple shaking out of fear as the sneering man sent a bullet through their skulls. Am I not responsible for those deaths?

Her hands find my face and force me to meet her eyes. "Get out of that head of yours," she says. She knows me too well. "Come," she says, leading me out of the room. "Sleep is what you need." Her words seem to make me aware of my own exhaustion. My eyes are heavy, feet like lead. Sleep is exactly what I need.

"Lead the way, McCoy."

The past two days catch up with me. I don't toss or turn. No nightmares grip my mind and rip me out of the dream world and into the real one. I sleep, deep and undisturbed. It's mid-afternoon when I finally wake. A cool breeze sweeps through the open window, carrying with it the sound of birdsong, a score of tiny, brown and white-winged birds flitting between branches of the cottonwood outside. Her head lays atop my chest, ear pressed against my heart which misses a beat when she looks up at me with those eyes of hers. No wonder I slept so well.

"Did I wake you?" I ask, voice scratchy from sleep.

"No," she says, nuzzling closer. "I've been awake for a while. I just didn't want to move."

Nor do I want her too. Everything about this moment is right: the warmth of her body wrapped around my own; the feel of her hair, smooth and dark as a midnight sky, flowing through my fingers; the sweetness of her lips as the dance across mine. This is what I fight for: these quiet, tender moments of peace with the girl I love. I could stay lost inside this moment forever.

"We should head downstairs," she says, though she makes no move to leave.

She's right. The real world waits on the other side of the bedroom door. There are plans to be made, problems to be solved. Worry and stress and fear loom ahead of us like a cruel and violent storm, its sharp winds howling in promise. We have weathered such storms from the beginning, and will continue to do so until those fleeting moments of peace can bend and stretch into hours, into days, until the winds calm and the clouds recede and we leave it all behind. But for now, I will hold onto this moment for as long as I can.

"Yeah, we probably should," I agree, planting kisses across her collarbone. "But we're not going to."

When we finally make our way downstairs, it's to find everyone in open debate about our options. Arguments are all over the place. Some over food and water, some over safety and security. The one common thread is the need to leave the area. Fear over Animal retaliation runs high. The problem remains: where to move on to?

"There are rumors about Mancos," says Ted, my Uncle Will's cousin. "I've heard they're unified, that they've secured their borders...maybe they would be willing to take us in."

Richard scoffs at the idea. "Heard the same rumor," he says. "Probably, most of the folks still around here have too. Even if it's true, gotta imagine we wouldn't be the first to think of joining them. They've probably been flooded with people trying to distance themselves from town. How will they be able to accommodate them? They're bound to be stretched thin already."

"We keep going round in circles," says Jerry. His arm has been patched up nice and neat. I suspect his sister's hand in that. After two years studying to become a nurse, I'm sure Jerry won't be the last person she treats.

"I don't see why this is so complicated," he continues. We have tents and we have gear. Let's get the hell out of here and hole up in the hills util we can think of a better alternative." Whatever patience he may have held at the beginning of this discussion has long since faded. The gunshot to his arm may have only been a grazing shot, but it still looms omnipresent in his mind. Another inch and it might have ruined his shoulder, blown apart his bicep. Another six, and it might have claimed his life. A second bout with the Animals is the last thing he wants.

"The hills are crawling with people, Jerry," Vince says. "You've seen it yourself." They've explained it to me too. Tracks, fires, voices. The collapse has turned the surrounding woods and hills into a beacon for many. Patchwork camps are not uncommon, dozens of people surviving together the best they can in the wilderness. It's made hunting and gathering not only difficult but also dangerous. With so many hungry eyes dispersed among the trees, getting a kill too far from home is a risky proposition: hauling a dead deer could easily make you as big a target as a live one.

"I'll take my chances with unorganized hunters any day over those bastards," he snaps back. His fear is unmistakable, and it spreads throughout the room.

"Maybe he has a point," says Kelly, Vince's fiance. She squeezes Vince's arm. "There's nothing to stop them from coming back...I don't want to be waiting for them if they decide to."

Vince squeezes her knee in reassurance. "We won't be," he says. "But there has to be a better option."

Lauren and I skirt the edges of the room and take a seat beside my parents. "How long has this been going on?" I ask.

"Too long," my father says. "It wouldn't be a bad thing if we actually accomplished something. But getting people to agree is like pulling teeth."

"I've already told you, I've got some friends up on the mesa," my Uncle Mitch says now. "They'll take us on, I know they will." His words come out slurred. Slow. I catch my mother's eye and arch an eyebrow in question. The small shake of her head is my answer. I look back at my uncle in frustration as he continues on in his slow voice, eyes wide and bloodshot as he tries to convince my family. Almost a year of sobriety down the drain.

If anyone else notices, they don't let on. Perhaps they don't want to add any more stress to everything we're already dealing with. I guess I can understand that. But if he continues using, something will have to be done. I haven't forgotten the man the booze and drugs bring out of him. That's the last thing my family needs. But his suggestion has me thinking.

"How are you holding up?" I ask Felix.

He stands alone beside the dining room window, staring out into the street with unfocused eyes. "I'm alright," he says, turning to face me. "But I should probably be asking you the same question. Vince and Richard were a little vague when they described what happened. I'm guessing there were some details they didn't want to worry the family with?"

The night flashes past. Bullets and falling bodies. Blood. Chaos. Men burning to death from fire thrown by my own hand. "You could say that," I say. "I can fill you in."

He shakes his head. "You're already going to relive it a thousand times," he says. "I'm not going to make you add another on my account."

I pause for a moment to gather my thoughts and push last night from my mind. "Where do we go from here, Chavo?" I ask him. Straight to the point, cut the bullshit. It's how our friendship has always worked.

A bitter laugh escapes him. "Obvious isn't it?" he asks. "We move your family out to my uncle's place. The gang never finds us. We find my family. And we all live happily ever after: a regular fucking fairy tale ending."

I'm thrown by the harsh sarcasm of his words. He looks away, and I know immediately he wished he could take it back. I don't know how to respond. I've been so caught up in my own pain, I forget how much others are hurting too.

"Felix..." I struggle to find words.

"I'm sorry," he says, ashamed. "You know I didn't mean that. I guess I'm not coping as well as I thought."

I lay a hand on his shoulder. "You never have to apologize to me, Chavo," I say. "We're all struggling to cope right now. You're doing a pretty damn good job in my opinion."

He attempts a smile. "Thanks," he says. "But there's some truth in what I said. Nobody's on the farm right now. I was actually going to mention it earlier but figured I'd wait on you. And judging by some of the suggestions I've heard so far, the farm is definitely our best move."

I grin. "Great minds. I was thinking the exact same thing. Besides, we're going to need to be out that way to start looking for your family. We've got to start working on that fairy tale ending of yours."

"It did sound pretty good, right?" he asks, with a genuine smile of his own. It sounded perfect, like the dream I hold in my heart when I look to the future. Is it really no more than that? A dream? A fairy tale I've painted in my mind? I push the thought away before it can take root. Fairytale or not, it is what keeps me moving forward: an oasis in the distance. If I'm to have a chance at all in reaching it, I can't allow myself to believe it a mirage. I have to have faith. I have to believe I will one day drink from its waters.

"We'll make it a reality, Chavo. Together."

We enter the main living room and suggest the idea. My family doesn't need much convincing. As Felix said, his farm is definitely our best move right now. It has a water well, prime hunting grounds to the north and east, and plenty of space to plant crops and greenhouses. I remember the seeds Elroy gave us along with his handwritten book on harvesting. Autumn has only just begun. Surely we can get something going before winter arrives. But more than anything, I think what really sells the point is the distance it provides between us and the Animas Animals.

"The location sounds ideal," Richard says. "Only thing we need to figure out is how to get there without drawing attention to ourselves."

Easier said than done. Even on the trail we didn't always go unnoticed, and that was with only a few of us. Now we're near thirty in number, most of whom are not used to hiking with heavy packs or constantly staying on alert for ambushes and attacks. It's going to be slow going, especially with our need to avoid major roadways. Add in the fact we will be traveling at night, and I don't see any way we can possibly make it to the farm by daybreak. I'm not the only one who realizes this either.

"What will we do come sunrise?" Leon asks. "We're going to be moving slow. No way we make it to the farm in one night."

"We'll have to figure it out as we go," Felix says. "Worse case scenario, we set up camp out of sight somewhere and wait out the day."

"Agreed," Richard says. "We'll see how far we get and assess our options later."

With that, we begin to hash out the route we'll be taking. The most crucial part is the first few miles as we try and leave the town behind. Fortunately, this neighborhood is surrounded by forest, making it easy to avoid the main entrance. But with the Animal's blood still running hot, we need to be careful. It only makes sense that they would leave at least a few men in the area.

"Assume we leave this area smoothly, how do we get to Florida?" asks my Uncle Will. "I don't want to use 32nd street to cross the river. We'll be too exposed."

"The river's low right now," my father says. "We should be able to cross it no problem. Head north of the bridge and cross out of sight."

"And once we're across, there's all that open land we can cut through. We can avoid 32nd street altogether," my mother adds. And past 32nd, forest surrounds Florida Rd. on all sides, giving us ample concealment as we travel. We just have to get there.

With a plan in place, the rest of the afternoon is spent preparing for tonight. We divvy up the gear between us and make sure everyone is armed to some degree. I know Richard will have given everyone a crash course in firearm training, but it's still strange to see with my own eyes. My sweet, Aunt Virginia, whom I've never heard say an unkind word about anyone, now loads a revolver at the dining room table. Grace and Ray sit with Richard's youngest daughter, Hailey, and T.J., my Uncle Will's nephew. Had the collapse never occurred, they might be counting down the seconds until the bell rang right now, eager to be released after a long day of school. As it is, even they have been armed for tonight's journey. We've made it clear that they are only to use their weapons if absolutely necessary—as a last resort if our backs are against the wall. I hope it never comes to that. None of them should have to know the terrible burden that comes with taking a life.

Only one of us will go unarmed tonight. I approach her now, lifting her easily into the air and spinning her round in circles as she squeals with laughter. "Stoppp it, Morgan!" she yells. I can't keep from laughing as I ease up on my spinning.

"You sure, Abe? Because your laughing tells me I should keep going."

She beats on my chest with all the strength her five-year-old arms can muster. "Quit calling me Abe!" she chides. "Abby, or Abigail. I've told you like, a thousand times."

"A thousand times?" I ask, spinning her around once more. I've missed her laugh. It still sounds the same as the day I left, untouched by all the bad that has happened around her. Despite all of the tension between me and my cousin Jenna over the years, it hasn't soured the love I have for her daughter. I'd do anything for this little girl in my arms. "You can't even count to a thousand!"

"Yes I can," she challenges. "One, two, three..." she continues on and I have to cut her off.

"How about I test you instead?" I ask. "What comes after fifty-nine?"

"Sixty!" she says, knowingly.

"Ok. What comes before two-hundred and twenty-six?"

"Two-hundred and twenty-five."

"Dang, you are smart," I praise. "I don't even think Leon knew the answer to that one," I add when I catch his eye. He flips me off behind her back, making me laugh. "Alright, final test: what comes after nine-hundred and ninety-nine?"

"A thousand!" she says, excited at proving me wrong.

I whistle in admiration. "It's official. You're a genius Abe...igail. What? I called you Abigail!"

I feel better after talking with Abigail, her innate goodness easing the ball of tension lodged inside my chest. As evening makes its presence felt, I make it a point to touch face with everyone throughout the house. I share memories and tell jokes with those I fought so hard to reach, and with each smile, each laugh, I feel that tension loosen further. There is still fear lingering in the air. It lingers in myself as well. There's no getting around that fact. But there is still so much to be thankful for, so many reasons to feel joy. I'm not going to overlook them—they are what will see us through this.

"You holding up alright?" I ask my mother. All day she's been seeing to the needs of others. Overseeing preparations, lending comfort, reassuring worried minds that everything will be alright. I've always said she was the glue which held my family together. That's truer now more than ever. And she's not the type to back away from that role, nor would she ever let others know the toll it takes on her. But I know the weight of it all must be substantial. I won't let her carry it all on her own. I need to be there for her now as she's always been for me.

She brushes my hair back and leaves her hand resting on my cheek, a small smile on her face. "I have you and your sister back," she says, simply. "I haven't been this good in months."

I feel a lump in my throat rise as she says this. Not so much for the words themselves, but for the sincerity behind them. "You know what I mean," I say, continuing to dig. "I see how much you put on your shoulders, how you always put your own needs last. I need to know that you're ok."

Her smile grows as she shakes her head, a breath of laughter escaping her. "You don't even see the irony, do you?" she asks. I must look confused because all she does is shake her head again. She draws my face close to hers and kisses me once atop my forehead. "Don't worry about me, my son. As long as I have air in my lungs, and my family is alive and well, I have everything I need."

I nod in understanding, knowing I'll get no other answer from her. "Ok," I say. "Just promise me you'll let me help you if you need it."

She draws me in for a hug, and for the tiniest of moments, I feel a child again: warm and safe inside his mother's arms. Leave it to my mother to lend me comfort even as I try to do the same to her. "I promise," she says quietly.

Not long after, the house is filled with the sounds of our imminent departure: zippers opening and closing; grunts and sighs as people heft their packs; the all too familiar sound of chambering rounds and clicks of safeties. Night has come. Time for us to make our leave.

"Remember the plan," Richard says. He addresses the family halfway up the staircase, drawing everyone's eye to him. He continues on, making doubly sure everyone knows their role. I find myself cringing. He's a career military man and he addresses us as such—like a commander laying out orders to his soldiers. I respect the man, and I know his experience is a tremendous asset, but I can practically feel his speech steal the air from the room.

"Do what you're supposed to do, and we'll make it out alive," he finishes. The unease following his words is glaring. Either Richard doesn't see what I see, or he chooses to ignore it. He descends the staircase, stopping to heft his pack and ready his weapons. People watch him with trepidation, shifting nervously from foot to foot. I can't let us leave the house in this state.

"It's alright if you're afraid right now," I say. Eyes shift to me, including Richard's who narrow in surprise. "We all know how ruthless these Animals can be. They've taken our food, our weapons, even two of our own until we took them back. Now they want our lives. They have guns and vehicles and outnumber us ten to one. They're dangerous. No sense in denying it. But despite all their power, there is one thing we have that they do not—something they don't understand and which can never be taken from us: Love. And please, don't scoff or roll your eyes at what I say. Love is what got me here—what gave me the strength to face so much evil on the trail and walk away from it alive. You gave me that."

I pause, taking a moment to look each of them over so they know I believe in what I say. I can feel their energy rise with my words, can see belief flicker inside their eyes. I feed off the momentum, driving my message home.

"I love each and every one of you," I say. "You are all my family, both by blood and by choice. There is no greater love than that. Put faith in it. Put faith in each other. And know that whatever we face, we face it together, as a family. We'll get through this. I believe that as much as I believe in anything."

Nobody speaks for a quiet minute as what I said sinks in. It's Vince who finds his voice first. "Amen, Captain," he says. He wears a smile and raises his hand in a mock salute. I find myself grinning in return, recognizing his praise through his sarcasm. More people sound their agreement, declarations of love and assurance issuing out of their mouths. I feel my heart lift as I watch it unfold, just as it did earlier when I spun Abigail in my arms. For the first time since I arrived, I feel as if my family is finally whole. Well, almost. But in this moment, it's as if I feel her presence beside me, a smile on her face as she watches us come together.

I know you're there, Maya. I feel safer already knowing you're with me.

"The night is young," I say. "Let's make the most of it."

Chapter 4: (Lauren)

Through the darkened hillside we walk. All around us, homes rise out of the ground like sentinels watching over this narrow valley. If only that were true. From below, I spot the remains of Morgan's aunt and uncle's home, a lifetime of memories reduced to ash. In the end, all its grandeur didn't matter. The strong walls and deadbolted doors may as well been made of straw when the big bad wolf came prowling. I only pray we survive long enough to create a house of brick.

As we move, I'm all too aware of the noise we make. Labored breaths, heavy footfalls, the general rustling of nearly thirty bodies moving through the night. It's impossible for a group this size to move silently. I know that. But I can't keep myself from wincing at every cough or snapping twig. Until we leave this area behind, my nerves are going to be sky high. Not that I'm alone in my anxiety. Nerves and fear swirl in the air around us, its presence more pronounced than the noise. Still, it's not as bad as it might have been. Morgan's words helped ease the worst of people's fears, giving them a sense of hope to cling to. It's what he does.

I walk beside him now, at the back of our long procession. It wasn't his first choice. If it were up to him he would be up front, scouting the route ahead and leading the way. As it is, that duty has fallen to Richard and Felix.

"I think it's best if you guard our six," Richard told Morgan earlier. *"You know how to handle yourself. I'll feel a hell of a lot better knowing you're there."*

There's logic in his argument. Enough so, that Morgan didn't fight the issue. But I have a feeling the move was more political than anything. Richard fancies himself in charge. It wouldn't do to have Morgan lead the way. Especially not after his parting speech from the house. Of course, I could be reading too much into it. And in any case, it doesn't much matter at the moment. We have more pressing concerns to deal with.

Soon we are past the houses, the street below dark and desolate as we leave Rockridge behind. I wonder where in the darkness the Animals lurk, waiting for us to reveal ourselves. I'm convinced they are out there somewhere, burning for revenge. But no shadows unfurl from the darkness, nor do any sounds reach my ear. Our precaution, it seems, has gotten us out of the hot-zone unscathed.

We never reach the hill's crest, but instead carry on horizontally, descending slowly till we dip into another neighborhood. My eyes flicker constantly as we hit the street, simultaneously searching for threats and to reassure myself that Grace is alright. She walks in the middle of our formation beside Leon's brother, Ray, and two of Morgan's aunts. Like everyone else, she is armed tonight. The .22 on her hip seems so out of place, a weapon of death on someone as kind as her. Could she really use it? My sister? The girl who collected flowers and wrote poetry until the collapse sent the world into this downward spiral? I feel nauseous just thinking about it.

We pass three blocks of ghostly houses before finding ourselves at the base of another steep hillside. I breathe more easily once concealed in the treeline, thankful they mapped out our route so well, keeping us exposed on the street only when absolutely necessary. If only we took the same caution last night. Maya might be beside us now if we had. My heart twists at the thought and I have to fight back the pressure building behind my eyes.

Forget the past. Focus on the future. The words spring in my mind, a well-worn mantra I adopted long before everything fell apart. It does for me what it always has: it keeps me moving forward.

Our progress up the hillside is slow and fractured. Three times we have to stop altogether to allow members of our party to catch their breaths. Each time, I find my patience thinning. I know it's not their fault that they are not accustomed to the weight on their backs, or hiking through this sort of terrain as we are. But there are still people out for our blood. And though the night may be dark and the hillside thick with cover, we are not invisible. A passing patrol might notice shadows shift above the homes they prowl, might decide to throw the spotlight up on the hillside on a whim. And there we'll be—deer caught in the headlights of a predator. It's not difficult to imagine what would happen then: running, bullets, people dying. It's all I can do but keep calm.

Finally, we reach the crest of the hill and stop for yet another breather. I walk forward until I reach the edge of the ridge. From where I stand, I have a decent lay of the land. The thin moonlight does little to accent the features of the town below, leaving me with only a vague feel of the place—like a painting only partially completed. Still, it's more than enough to highlight the vast difference between here and where I'm from. It's incredible. There's a raw beauty to this town the likes of which I've never seen. I look to Morgan who helps his Aunt adjust her pack. It must be devastating for him to see how far this place has fallen.

"She's sure is something, huh?" comes a voice to my right. I turn to see Morgan's father soaking in the landscape below. He looks my way with a quick smile. "The town, I mean."

"It's beautiful," I say. "So much different than the city. I wish I could have seen this place before the collapse."

He sighs lowly. "Yeah, it definitely had its moments. Growing up here, I guess it was easy to take it for granted. Never really thought about the fact that most people weren't surrounded by so much nature—that they couldn't go for a hike through the woods and mountains whenever felt like, or head to the river with a fishing pole and a tackle box, and throw a line out. All the years I jogged along the river trail, it never really occurred to me how unique it was: all the trees and flowers and plant life surrounding this path that stretched the entire length of town; looking over my shoulder and watching kayaks and rafts navigate the river, or people tubing lazily by." He pauses, a smile creeping onto his mouth. Morgan may have his mother's eyes, but he owes his smile to his father. "It definitely never crossed my mind that not everyone sat on their front porch with the love of their life, and watched the sunset each evening."

He grows quiet for a moment, reflecting, perhaps, on better days gone by. "Times change. People change. That's just life...But I never thought they could change like this." A deep silence follows his words, and I'm at a loss on how to fill it. I wonder what he sees as he stares over these darkened streets. Are they lit in memory? Does he see past the crashes and wreckage, and instead remember that simpler time before the world fell apart? It's easy to see the love he holds for this town. I can't say I've ever felt the same about Denver. Even before the collapse, I had always planned on leaving one day and never looking back. If it weren't for Grace, I'd have done so a long time ago.

I look over my shoulder once again to see the group stirring. I watch Morgan teasing his younger cousin Abby, see Felix hauling Grace easily to her feet. "Things have changed...but what's most important has stayed the same," I say quietly.

He tears his eyes away from the town and focuses on me. I get the sensation of being x-rayed as he fixes me with a penetrating stare. Then his eyes light up and his face splits into a smile. "Yeah, you're right about that," he says with an agreeing nod. "As my son said, there's no greater love than family. That includes you and Grace, now too."

Pressure builds behind my eyes once more at his words. I don't know where all this emotion has come from. That's a lie. It's this family, no doubt about it. I've only just met them, and already they've accepted me as one of their own. I've never known that kind of acceptance before.

"C'mon," he says, throwing his arm around my shoulders. "They're about to leave us behind." Even this is new to me, an affectionate arm around my shoulder with no pretense, no agenda—a casual, fatherly gesture he's undoubtedly done thousands of times. The old me would have shaken it off, would have slipped away somehow. But now I have no inclination to do so, feeling a certain comfort as he steers us back to the group.

We continue north atop the ridgeline until we come across a mountain-bike trail. We use it to descend the hillside, only leaving it as we near the bottom. Limiting our exposure on the street, we skirt around homes and buildings which string up along the way before we hit the edge of a townhouse development. A block down, we hit one of the town's main thoroughfares, easy to distinguish by the wreckage of dozens of vehicles littering its expanse. The sight is not unfamiliar but is still a harsh reminder. How many lives were lost in the span of minutes as EMP's tore across our world that day? Better that I don't know. Being here, surrounded by only a small fraction of that destruction is hard enough to comprehend.

Navigating the wrecks is a grim affair, and I think all of us breathe easier once we're past. The street is dark and still. Black windows stare at us like the eyes of watchful guard dogs, observing our passage in silent menace, daring us to come closer. Fortunately, it's a small neighborhood and it's not long before we're through it. I hear the river before I see it, the sound of flowing water easy to distinguish in the quiet. And then we're at the riverbank, its surface shimmering with silvery flecks.

"Never thought I'd be happy to see the river so low," Felix says. "Crossing shouldn't be a problem."

With that, we strip our shoes and socks, stowing them inside our packs to keep them protected and dry. The water is barely knee deep, but the stones lining the bottom make it a slippery crossing. Even as we take our time, a younger cousin and an aunt lose their footing halfway and are completely submerged. A small giggle escapes Abby as she rides atop Morgan's shoulders. Morgan reaches up and smacks her leg playfully, telling her it's not funny. But when he turns toward me he can't hide the grin he wears.

Once across, we roll on our socks and lace our shoes before continuing. We cut through a muddy field and then pick our way along the base of a small, steep embankment. It should keep us shielded from any prying eyes. As we draw nearer a small cluster of houses, we come across something we have yet to encounter tonight: signs of other people. Light flickers inside the house, shadows rippling through an open window on the second floor. The smell of wood smoke lingers on the air, coupled with the faint aroma of cooking meat. We give the house a wide berth, using the trees dotting the embankment as cover. Soon enough we are past and hit a county road.

I look to the right and receive a small jolt when I realize I've been here before. This is the same road we traveled as we entered town, the pawn shop and Exxon instantly recognizable. Was it only four nights ago? Things have changed so quickly. We were so full of hope then, caught up in the zealotry of arriving here after so long. How were we to know our plight was only beginning?

Continuing our strategy of concealment, we mirror Florida Rd instead of traveling it. Trees and hills, trees and hills, never have I seen a town so full of them. It makes avoiding the streets and buildings easy. Homes are spaced further apart the further we travel, more and more of which show signs of occupation. Perhaps the violence of town has not spread this far. If so, it's only a matter of time.

An hour on, we are concealed in a copse of trees, taking yet another breather. We've put in more distance than I thought we would, but we still have a ways to go. And with only a couple hours left till daybreak, we need to decide on how we proceed. Morgan leaves to confer with Felix and Richard, while I take the opportunity to check on Grace.

"How are you feeling?" I ask her.

She rolls her eyes. "I'm fine," she says. "I was on the trail just as long as you were. This is nothing." She's right. Tonight is nothing we haven't faced before. All the hardships and ugliness the trail threw at us was weathered by her just as much as me. Sometimes I forget how much she's grown.

"I know," I say. I lower my voice, making sure nobody looks our way. "Are you hungry? I still have half a protein bar from earlier."

She huffs, shaking her head. "Then you should eat it," she chides. "Seriously, Lauren. We're hardly eating anything as it is." She's not wrong. What little food Morgan's family had was stolen by the Animals the day his cousins were taken. The past few days we've been surviving solely off the provisions Elroy gifted us. But with so many people, already we are dangerously low. I only hope things turn around when we reach the farm.

"Hey, what do I always tell you?" I ask, attempting a smile. "It's my job to worry about you, not the other way around." She doesn't look amused, continuing to glare at me. "Fine. I'll eat it, ok?" I relent. "Soon as we get to the farm."

"Promise?" she asks.

"You can even watch me if you like," I say. She nods her head, satisfied. I don't allow myself to feel guilt at my lie. I'll save it, hoard it, make sure I have something in case things get really bad. I won't let my sister starve even if the rest of us do.

Morgan joins us, his face worried. "We're going to push through," he says before I can ask. "Farm's about five hours out. We won't make it by sunrise, but being so close, our best option is to continue on."

We do just that, eventually leaving the protection of the hillside and crossing Florida only to be swallowed by forest once again. Dawn approaches, the blackness slowly ebbing from the sky as we travel. We enter a small clearing, the air around us now an inky blue. Soon light will spill over the eastern horizon, chasing away any remnants of the night. Halfway through the clearing, my heart stops, a single, thundering gunshot shattering the silence.

On instinct we drop, roll, scramble for cover that isn't there. Guns leap into hands, eyes frantically searching for the shooter. But the light is low, and inside the treeline all is dark. For a long moment, it's as if somebody has hit pause over the scene. There's no movement. No sounds. Nothing. And then a voice rings out, eerie in the early morning gloom.

"What did we tell you pricks the other day?" the voice asks. "You assholes keep testing us and now here we are. What is it going to take for you to get the message? Do we have to kill all of you? Because that's about where we're at."

There's anger in his voice, but more than that there's aggravation. Either way, it's clear he thinks we are someone else.

"I'm sorry sir, but you have us mistaken for someone else," Morgan yells out. Before I know what's happening, he's squeezing my knee and rises to his feet. He walks forward, his hands raised and weapons left behind. "We have nothing to do with whoever you're having problems with. We're just passing through."

The voice scoffs. "Awful lot of you to just be passing through," he challenges.

"Big family," Morgan says with an attempt at humor. It doesn't sway the voice. He doesn't respond at any rate. "Look, I know how this must seem to you. Especially if you're having problems with other people, but I swear that's not us. We're just trying to relocate to my friend's farm. Figured staying off the road was a smart move...doesn't seem so smart right about now though."

The voice doesn't immediately answer, staying silent so long I half expect it not to answer at all. "How do I know you're telling the truth?" he asks. "How do I know you're not the same bastards who've been stealing from us?"

"I understand your dilemma," Morgan says. "Things have been hard on all of us. But put your fear aside for a moment really look at us. Do we look like we're about to try and raid somewhere?" Morgan pauses, allowing the voice the chance to answer. I wonder what the voice has gone through, what has led him to this point. What does he see when he looks at us? A ragtag coalition of people surviving this crazy world the best they can? Or does he see what he fears— predators after what is his?

"We have women...children," Morgan pushes. "We're just trying to survive the best we can."

Another long pause, tension lying over us all, thick and heavy. And then: "Everyone stand, and walk forward slowly," the voice says. "Anyone raises a weapon, we open fire on all of you."

Slowly, we rise to our feet and shuffle forward. I can make out the forms of men and women the closer that we draw, their silhouettes standing just inside the treeline.

"Eric?" Morgan's mother asks uncertainly.

I hear the voice curse, matching it with a thickset man with a furry beard. "Marie?" he asks. "Is that you?"

"Yes it's me, you beautiful bastard," she says with an incredulous laugh. "Now would you mind getting those damn guns out of our faces?"

The voice returns the laugh. "Stand down," he says. One by one they lower their weapons. "They're friends," he says.

Chapter 5: (Morgan)

I watch my mother work her magic. For as long as I can remember, she's had a natural charm—an ability to make everyone feel welcome. Even complete strangers, she would laugh and joke with them as if she had known them for years. Most of the time I had no idea one way or another. Half the town seemed to know her. I've shaken countless hands and been introduced to innumerable people whose faces I will never remember over the years. It doesn't surprise me in the slightest to be doing so again.

"You remember my kids? Emily and Morgan?" she asks.

Eric laughs. "Of course," he says, offering us his hand to shake. "You two sure have grown. Last time I saw the two of you must've been, what, ten years ago?" He looks to my mother for clarification.

"Sounds about right," she smiles. "That's about the time you and Denise moved to Texas. Speaking of which, what brings you to town? And Denise, is she..." Her voice trails off uncertainly. In this new world, the smallest questions can reveal hidden pain. But not today it seems.

His smile widens. "She's well," he says, guessing her unasked question. "She's back at the ranch with the kids. And as for being here? Just dumb luck, really. My sister's wedding was scheduled for the day after everything went to shit. Took us a while to even know anything had even happened. Had the bride and groom's families over at my brother's house for a barbeque. A sort of ice-breaker before the wedding, you know? But eventually, we figured out something had happened. We've been there ever since."

Despite everything I've been through, it's still strange to hear other people relive that first day. Only two months since this all began, and already it has become such a common question: *Where were you when the world fell apart?* Over seven billion people on the planet before the collapse and not a single person has been untouched by the fallout—the one common thread among all of us. I find myself thinking of his sister: a young bride, full of love, ready to commit herself for better or for worse. Will she ever know those better days? Or will they forever elude her?

"I would say at least you've been spared the craziness of town, but it sounds like you've had your own problems," my father says.

He nods, growing more serious. "We've had our share. People wandering mostly. Begging. It's not that we didn't want to help, but we're already dealing with enough. If we helped everyone, there would be nothing left for us." The pity in his voice is unmistakable, and I know he means it when he says he wanted to help. He shakes his head as if shaking the thought away. "But we've also had people try and take instead of begging. Most of the thieves haven't been too hard to deal with, but this last group is like a fly you can't swat. They've hit us almost every single day, for the past two weeks. They rarely get away with much, but every little bit hurts. Finally caught one of them two days ago, a young girl. Weren't sure what to do with her at first. Do we kill her? Hostage her? In the end, we let her go with a message to stop raiding us or next time we wouldn't be so lenient. They came back the same day. My brother took a shot and clipped one of them, yelling that they were warned. They didn't like that. Yelled back they would be back with a force. That's why we're out here, thought that was you."

"These thieves, were they well armed?" Richard asks.

"Not really," Eric replies. "Saw a couple rifles. Not nearly enough to go around."

"They've been coming in the early mornings?" Richard asks.

"Early mornings, dusk, midnight. It's always different. They like to keep us on our toes, I guess."

Of course they would. It's no surprise that people are targeting the countryside. I have done it myself while on the trail. But not every farmer and rancher are as kind as Elroy, and not every raider had the same intentions as we did. Eric's problems may be our own soon enough. I can only hope we'll manage to hold out as they have.

"This ranch, is it a big place?" I ask. "How are you keeping it protected? How many people do you have?" The questions tumble out one after the other, my hyperactive mind unable to help it.

"Why're you so interested in the specifics?" asks a woman about my mother's age. Her suspicion is clear, and she's not the only one of Eric's party to glare at me.

"I'm sorry," I say. "I know it sounds like I'm fishing for information, but it's not like that. I just want to know what I can expect when we get to where we're going."

"It's alright," Eric says. He nods to the woman as if to assure her. "Ranch is just over fifty acres, but we've scaled it back to a fraction of that. Not including the children, we have thirty-seven hands right now, four of which are always on sentry duty, checking our perimeter. Besides that, we have a few other preventive measures against thieves, traps and such. Still, it's a challenge keeping it secure."

I don't doubt it. Durango, while not a large city, isn't exactly the small town it once was. With barren supermarket shelves, and no deliveries coming into the city, what choice was there but to leave in search of sustenance? Thousands will have been displaced, combing through the forests and countrysides in hopes of filling their empty stomachs. I feel a weight settle in my own stomach just thinking about what lies ahead of us.

"My uncle's place is another couple hours from here," Felix says. "How active has this area been during the day? Do you think it's safe to travel?"

"Hasn't been too bad," Eric says, scratching the stubble on his neck. "Probably be a bit riskier than traveling at night, but I'd rather stay mobile during the day than try and hunker down." He pauses, a sudden uncomfortable look on his face. "I would invite you to wait it out at the ranch, but things...are a bit tense right now. Sorry. I just don't think it would be a good idea."

"There's no need to apologize, Eric," my mother says. "Really, we understand."

Eric nods. "Thanks," he says. "In any case, this spot is compromised right now. We should be heading back to the ranch and report back what happened."

"I don't think that's gonna be necessary," one of the men says. He gestures to the right, drawing our attention to the men trotting our way on horseback. I count eight of them, all armed, and none too friendly. Eric looks back to us. "Let me do the talking," he says, his tense face putting me on edge.

"Jake," Eric greets one of the men as they draw level with us. "We were just about to head back."

"Heard gunshots. Thought it best that we check it out." Though the man speaks with Eric, his eyes never leave us. I can feel him assessing us, taking in our guns, our nerves, our fear. We definitely don't give the best first impression. "Who are these people?"

"Their friends," Eric says. He points to my mother: "Marie and I go way back. They're not part of the gang that's been targeting us."

"Friends?" he asks. Finally, he looks away from us, skepticism written across his face as he stares pointedly at Eric. "And how do you know they're friends? Because you have a few memories with one of em' from back in the day?"

"Because I know the kind of person she is," Eric answers. "They're just passing through."

"Or that's what they said and are just waiting till you idiots turn your backs."

Richard laughs meanly. "Shrewd bastard aren't you? But unless you're also an idiot, one look should be enough to show you we're not about to try and raid you." I bite the inside of my cheek, barely able to keep myself from lashing out. Does he really need to stir the shit right now?

The man looks over at Richard, no sense of amusement about him. "You've got a big mouth," he says. "Anyone ever tell you that?"

Richard smiles. "Plenty," he says. "Have yet to meet someone who could make me shut it though." The challenge turns the tension all the way up to ten. I watch the man's fingers twitch as if longing to reach for the revolver holstered on his hip. All around him his men wait for a cue, a signal on how to react. Silently, my family shift defensively, the younger members being shielded by the others, everyone's grip tight on their firearms. A few wrong words and we've gone from cordial to being on the verge of ripping each other apart. Eric notices too.

"Jake, let it go," he says. "That one likes to talk, but I swear they're not trying to get one over on us."

"This one has a name," Richard says.

"This one needs to learn when to be quiet," my Uncle Will seethes. "Seriously, your goddamn mouth has been getting us in shit since we were kids. This isn't the time. Think of your daughters for Christ's sake!"

This alone seems to silence him. A brief flicker of shame ripples across his stony face, gone so quick I might mistake it for a trick of the light. But when he looks at his daughters, I can tell by the softness in his eyes I didn't imagine it. I remember overhearing my Uncle Will once say that the army was the best choice his brother ever made, that it had taught him to think before he acted. I can only assume this rash, hot-headedness is what he was referring to.

The man's nostrils flare as he huffs an angry breath. "Ok, Eric," he says. "I'll take your word on it. Being that you're such good friends, I'm sure you wouldn't mind seeing to it that they navigate our property safely. Wouldn't want them to wander across our crosshairs now would we?"

Richard manages to keep his temper in line and not take the bait. I'm grateful, though a part of me understands the anger. This man is definitely an asshole in his own right. Like Richard said, it should be obvious to anyone with a lick of sense that we're not raiders. That coupled with Eric vouching for us should be more than enough credit to convince him. Yet he chooses to goad us, creating animosity when there is no need for it. At least things didn't escalate further.

The horse riders depart with the rest of their people following after, leaving Eric alone with my family. He turns to us now. "Sorry about that," he says. "Like I said, things are tense right now. These damn bastards have everyone on edge."

"It's not just you," I say. "We're all dealing with a lot at the moment."

Eric nods. "Yeah. You're right about that."

We follow Eric as he leads us around his family's ranch. Atop a low hill, I catch a glimpse of the place: a large, single-story house; outbuildings; an open field with grazing horses. Men and women work in pairs and small groups, tending to the needs of the place in a practiced rhythm. As we shuffle down the backside of the hill, it's lost from view. Not long after, Eric comes to a halt some hundred feet removed from a highway. He apologizes again, and after a quick hug from my mother, wishes us good luck.

We move with haste, forgoing stealth for speed. After our altercation, we all want to get to the farm as quickly as possible. It's a quiet affair, everyone lost in their own thoughts. I'm not surprised. Though they don't say so, I can tell how shaken they still are. Even after the whole ordeal with the Animas Animals, most of them have little experience dealing with the violence of this new world. I've been immersed in it from the beginning. I know how ugly things can turn and how fast it happens. We were lucky Eric was there. We might not all be here if he wasn't.

We make it to the farm in under two hours, the fear induced fuel we had been riding crashing on our arrival. But there is still work to be done before we can rest. Slowly, we approach the farm from the rear, eyes searching for any signs of occupation. We reach the barn first, the sweet smell of hay and damp earth bringing me back to nights of drunken foolishness with Leon and Felix. I feel my heart clench. If these walls could talk, the stories they would tell.

After making sure the barn is clear, most of the family remain behind. I advance toward the house with Leon, Felix, Vince, and Richard. We peer through the open windows first, the scene inside turning my blood cold. As we enter through the kitchen, I know our search will yield nothing. Nobody would choose to stay here given the state it's in. Not unless it meant something to them.

"You and Richard should head back to the barn," I tell Vince. "We're not going to be moving into the house anytime soon." He looks around, taking in the wreckage solemnly. Vince may not know Felix as I do, but he's gotten to know him well enough over the years: through games of horseshoes on warm summer evenings, beer on ice, and burgers cooking on the grill; through early morning lift rides up Purgatory, skiing through fresh powder down Paradise and Upper Hades and all the other epic trails we'll never ski again. This shouldn't be his first impression of this house. Uncle Frank's large frame should dominate the room, his booming laugh making everyone feel welcome. The smell of homemade tortillas should permeate the air, Aunt Christina's smile as warm as the stack sitting on the kitchen counter. It should be clean, bordering on compulsive. It shouldn't be like this.

Vince nods once and leaves, Richard following after. Leon and I approach the living room where Felix stands motionless, a wonder he's kept his feet with the weight of so much grief upon his shoulders. How much worse this must all seem in the light of day, no darkness to hide the devastation. The front door is hanging off its hinges, a large crack in the center marking where it was kicked in. The furniture has been slashed and ripped, most of it overturned and stained with God knows what. Family photos lay scattered on the floor, their frames shattered, the memories they hold torn and covered in dirty boot prints. The walls show signs of a gunfight—bullet holes and clusters of buckshot tearing through the drywall—splatters of dried blood stained dark and ominous against the taupe-colored paint.

Felix stares at the blood-soaked floor, light from the shattered window throwing everything in sharper relief. Pools and smeared drag marks cover the hardwood like brushstrokes on canvas. It's been said that a picture is worth one thousand words. Perhaps that's true because seeing this has left me utterly lost for them.

"Thought I was exaggerating all the blood," Felix says. His voice comes out hoarse. Pained. "You know, with the shock of it all, and it being so dark and everything." He looks to us now, his eyes haunted. "I *really* wanted to have been exaggerating."

His voice quavers on that last bit, his legs shaky as he sinks onto an ottoman. How did he make it back to my parent's house after facing this alone? I doubt I could have done the same. Had our places been reversed, I would have broke—would have been crippled by the deep, dark places my mind would have taken me. Even now, my stomach churns with the emotions brewing inside me: anger and grief, vengeance and worry, a dozen others that erupt when I wonder what happened here, and more importantly, what happened to Felix's family. But I know anything I feel must be amplified one-hundred fold inside my friend. I need to stay strong for his sake.

I leave the room for the kitchen, knowing how hollow my words will be amid all this destruction. I search through the cabinets and pantry, finding the items I need. Outside I fill a bucket of water from the spigot, relieved to at least have a reliable source of water. I return to the living room to find Felix where I left him, his face buried in his hands and hidden behind a curtain of overgrown hair. Leon sits beside him, a hand resting on his shoulder. I set the bucket down and fall to my knees, Leon joining me when he sees what I'm doing. Wordlessly, we get to work scrubbing at the bloodstains with sponges and soapy water.

After a few minutes, I notice Felix watching our progress. He stares at me through red, swollen eyes, his pain etched deep into the worry lines on his face. But despite everything, he has not come undone. That lost, forlorn air which consumed him that morning at my parent's house does not shroud him now. He takes a deep breath, his nostrils flaring, and sinks to his knees beside us, soaking a sponge in the soapy water. He holds it in his hand a long moment, the suds slipping past his fist and racing down his arm. Slowly, he looks to me and then to Leon, resolve burning behind his eyes.

"You're still worth traveling down this road with," he says.

Chapter 6: (Lauren)

My heart broke for Felix when I stepped inside the house. Never have I seen a place so wrecked. The upturned furniture, the crumpled front door, the bloodstains on the walls and floor, it all painted a brutal picture of the dark deeds that took place. Emily and I joined the guys soon as we heard of the situation. Of course, hearing of it was one thing, seeing it was quite another. When I hugged Felix it felt weak and hollow, as if I were hugging a pillow or a stuffed animal. Physically he was here, but mentally, he was somewhere else entirely. I could only imagine the terrible thoughts plaguing his mind, all the questions he had no way of answering. Was he thinking of what happened to his family? Of what could have possibly happened here to create so much havoc? Or was he thinking not of the present, but of the past: of the warm, crystalline moments he and his family shared within these walls?

The five of us worked on cleaning the house until the late afternoon. Glass was swept, furniture re-arranged, but there is still so much left to do. As hard as we scrubbed on the bloodstained floor, there was no lifting it. The blood had soaked too deeply into the wood. Instead, we covered the worst of it with an antique rug Felix's aunt had insisted was far too beautiful to be stepped on, and which had been kept in storage for years, appreciating in value like a piece of art. I admit, it is beautiful: the intricate layers, the vivid colors, the tiny flaws in the hand woven stitching adding to its grandeur rather than taking away from it—like how music always sounds better on vinyl, the static and scratch giving it a flair that cannot be replicated or reproduced by digital means. It almost felt wrong to lay it on the floor: to cover something so ugly with something so beautiful. And though it's better than the alternative, I know none of us will forget what lies beneath.

At dusk we finally made our way back to the barn, tired and ragged. All of us except for Felix.

"I'll be alright," he assured us. *"I just need to be alone for a minute."*

Reluctantly, we agreed and joined the others, the gloom of the house following after us. That evening was quiet and somber. There was no celebration, no air of victory among us. It was as if we had accomplished nothing in our relocation. The magic farm—the place where we could start over and build a new life suddenly looked so very small. Twilight had barely asserted itself when nearly everyone settled in for sleep, nestling into their beds of straw, ready for this dreary day to end.

Their deep breathing and light snores sound from inside the barn, barely audible over the rhythmic singing of crickets. Morgan's arm wraps around my shoulders, the warmth of his body against my own warding off the chill to the night air. As it was so many nights on the trail, we keep watch over our sleeping group. I feel fatigue settle deep inside my bones as darkness settles in earnest. If I were to close my eyes right now it would be quite some time before they opened again. I'm exhausted. Sleep has been hard to come by these past few days, the brief snatches I manage filled with nightmares, memories, leaving me more tired than I was before. And sleep is still a ways away.

"Should we check on him?" I ask.

Morgan stirs beside me, letting loose a long breath as he pulls himself out of his thoughts. His mind is like a machine, constantly thinking, worrying, analyzing. He's always placed the needs of others above his own. It's that same selflessness which got us here. Being reunited with his family hasn't changed that. I don't know how he does it—how he carries the weight of so much on his shoulders. The least I can do is be there for him, to help carry the burden as much as he'll let me. It's the reason I'm here now instead of curled in my sleeping bag. Until he knows his friend is alright, he won't allow himself to rest.

"No," he says. "He needs some time to work through things. He'll come out when he's ready."

I nod, expecting as much. "I just wish there was more we could do."

He sighs. "You and me both."

He grows quiet, slipping once more into his thoughts. Being here must be nearly as hard for him as it is for Felix. The way he spoke of it on the trail, I know it holds a special place in his heart.

"You're thinking about them," I say after a while. "Felix's family."

"Yeah," he says. He pauses as if gathering the right words to answer. "His family...they were like my own. I practically lived out here during the summers in high school. I always liked how different it was from town. More simple. Quiet, you know?" He laughs, lost in a memory. "His Aunt Christina, she even bought Leon and me our own cots. Said if we were going to be there as often as we were, we might as well have our own beds."

I share his laugh. "Thoughtful of her," I say.

"Very," he says. "That's just who she was though. She had this warmth to her, this ability to make anyone feel welcome. She had some fire to her too, though. There were times when something set her off, usually one of her kids or Frank doing something or another to get under her skin, and she would start ranting and raving in Spanish, only to turn to me a minute later with a smile and some sassy one-liner that would make me laugh. His Uncle Frank was the same way, the true definition of a big ole teddy bear. He's as tall as me, but thicker, more powerfully built. I've only seen him truly angry once in my life, and I hope I never see it again."

He continues on for a time, sharing memories of this family he feels as close to as his own. He speaks of being rescued from the worst hangover of his life in the form of green chili and tortillas when Felix's aunt took pity on him. Of heated debates with Felix's uncle over football, and of early morning hunting trips. He tells of Felix's younger cousins: the eldest, Lena, who skipped two grades and was on track to earn a bachelor's degree in biology this winter at the age of twenty; Brianna, who at eighteen just graduated high school and had planned on enrolling in the Navy come fall; and Rob, thirteen with a knack for mischief, constantly looking to play jokes and pranks on unsuspecting people.

"They're still alive," he says a few minutes after talking himself silent. "I don't know who or what made them leave here, but I know they're still out there somewhere. Their story can't end in that house...not like that."

"I've been telling myself the same thing for the past few hours." Morgan and I both start as Felix solidifies out of the dark. He moves slowly our way, his eyes settling everywhere but on us. He glances behind him, toward the outline of his childhood home and shakes his head. "But I can't see them leaving this house. Even if they did try and join up with others, it doesn't explain what happened inside."

"You'll drive yourself insane trying to come up with the answers, Chavo," Morgan says. He stands and closes the distance between us and Felix. "But I swear, we're going to do everything we can to find them. We'll figure it out together."

Felix nods, finally meeting Morgan's eye. "I know, Moe. That's why you're my brother."

Morgan pulls him in for a brief hug and slaps him on the back. "You know it," he says. "And as your brother, I'm telling you to get some sleep. You look like hell."

"You give hell a bad name," he says, attempting a smile. "But I think I'm going to give it a bit. If I wear myself out enough, maybe I won't dream tonight."

I feel my heart clench as he says this, at the blunt honesty of his words. I don't blame him. After all he's been through, it would be only too easy for it to bleed into his dreams. A night of dreamless sleep is all he can hope for.

"But you two should go ahead and try and grab some sleep," he says. "I can keep an eye on things."

"Nah," Morgan says, brushing the suggestion aside. "You should know by now I don't sleep. I could stretch my legs though." He jerks his head to the side, indicating for Felix to follow him. "C'mon, Chavo. A zombie hunt for old times sake."

There's nothing forced about Felix's smile this time. "Zombie hunt," he says shaking his head. "Was life really ever so simple?"

The question brings with it a moment of silence, one in which we're all undoubtedly remembering that simpler time before things changed. I can't help but wonder what goes through their minds. Do they see their adolescent selves venturing through darkened fields, their worries low and their imagination high, facing off against hordes of the undead? Is it the laughter they shared on those nights that makes them smile now? I find myself smiling as well, not in my own memories, but in watching them remember theirs.

"Once," Morgan answers. "Maybe they can be again. For tonight at least."

Felix nods, his smile returning to his face. "You want to take point, or watch our six?" he asks.

Morgan slaps him on the back with a smile of his own. "Lead the way, Chavo"

I decline their offer to join the hunt. It's not my place to be with them right now. Besides, as tired as I am, it's enough of a struggle just to stagger toward my sleeping bag. Before I lay down to sleep, I reach into my pack and deposit half of the protein bar that was tonight's dinner, adding it to the emergency stash I keep for Grace. Ignoring the rumble of my stomach, I zip the pack closed and settle in beside my sister.

"Is Felix ok?" Grace asks, her words softened by sleep.

"He's fine, Gracie," I whisper. "Go back to sleep." Quietly, I begin to hum a gentle tune, my fingertips tracing up and down her slender neck, just as they did when she was younger. I hear her breathing deepen as sleep claims her, a smile curling on my lips at the sound. I'm not like Morgan. I don't have memories of zombie hunts or a past full of laughter and close friends. But I've always had Grace. As complicated as things were, this has always been simple: the love I hold for this beautiful, kind-hearted girl. Nothing will ever change that.

I wake to a nearly empty barn, Morgan and Felix the only other occupants. I stifle a yawn so as not to wake them. I have no idea what time they finally made it to their beds, but I have a feeling it was long after I fell asleep. They need all the rest they can get. Quietly, I dress and exit the barn. It's early. The sun hovers inches above the eastern horizon, its rays welcome against the chill of the morning. Despite the hour, there's a frenzy of activity about the place. To my right lies a small apple orchard, the string of trees stretching from behind the barn all the way past the house. A half-dozen people go about harvesting the fruit, picking at the lower boughs and using step ladders to gain access to the upper branches. Another group work in the garden, pulling weeds and seeing what can be salvaged. I notice Grace with them, listening raptly to Morgan's Aunt Virginia. The rest of the family I find in the house.

Everyone has thrown themselves into the restoration effort. Inside the kitchen, Vince's fiance and future mother-in-law assist his mom in cleaning and organizing the place. There's not a scratch of food, but I do notice flour and cooking oil and other usable items stacked on the kitchen counter. Every little bit helps. Passing into the living room, I immediately take notice of the difference between its current state and its state last night. The wall mounted flatscreen has been removed, as have the stereo system and floor speakers. There's no point in keeping them. I notice the busted in front door has been removed as well, one of Morgan's cousins walking through the empty entryway with two bags of trash to add to the pile we started yesterday. A loud *thump* makes me flinch, my hand gripping my revolver on instinct. Then I notice the source: Morgan's dad boarding up the broken window with Richard.

"Fast reflexes," a voice says behind me. I turn to find Mrs. Taylor wearing a smile, forehead glistening with sweat. She nods to my gun in explanation. "Your hand flew to your gun like you were born with it."

I feel heat creep up my neck, embarrassed. "Habit from being on the trail," I say. "I hated being exposed like that. My hand was always flying to my gun for one reason or another. It even got us dinner one night," I say, unable to keep from smiling as I remember the scene. "Heard something moving in the bushes as we set up camp. Moment the raccoon stepped into the open it had a bullet in it. Didn't taste half bad, to be honest. Much better than the squirrels Felix would sometimes bring in."

She shakes her head, an odd look on her face I can't read. "Raccoons and squirrels," she says. "I still have trouble comprehending what you went through to get here. It's a miracle any of you made it at all."

She's not wrong. There were dark times on the trail—times when all we had to go on was hope and faith. Yet somehow we pulled through. A lot of it was luck, but I know more than anything, it was because we stood together. Because we had each other to lean on when things were at their darkest. Sometimes I think back to that cramped break-room all those days ago when Morgan offered Grace and me the chance to join them. Saying yes went against everything I had taught myself over the years: *rely only on yourself, don't trust others, never admit you need help.* But I saw something in Morgan, sensed it—some ancient, deep-seated instinct that told me to trust him. I don't even like to think of what would have happened had I said no. There's no way Grace and I could have made it ourselves.

"Yeah," I say. "I just wish Maya was here to help us rebuild."

She nods slowly. "I know," she says. "She was such a sweet girl. Genuine and kind. It's not right that she's dead while so many wicked people still live."

"No. It's not." That familiar pressure builds behind my eyes, and it takes all I have to fight it back.

"But the important thing is *we will*," she says. She gestures to all the work taking place around her. "That's what this is all about. We can't bring her back, but we can at least build something she would have been proud of."

I nod. "How can I help?"

The place transforms throughout the course of the day. With everyone helping out, the house begins to look more like the home it once was. Bullet holes are patched. Bloodstains are either washed away or tactically covered up. We make it a point to tread carefully inside the bedrooms, throwing out only what is broken or useless. Still, it's strange going through a stranger's private space, unwittingly sifting through memories and catching a glimpse into their world. I sort through the clothes of Felix's cousin Brianna, the eighteen-year-old with naval aspirations. I fold the clothing inside her closet, curious of the stories stitched into the fabric—if she had a favorite pair of jeans, a dress that made her feel sexy, a faded sweater filled with holes and frayed edges, but so comfortable she could never bring herself to throw away. I have no way of knowing. When I'm finished, I carefully store the clothes away, hoping one day I get the chance to meet the girl they belong to.

Morgan and Felix join us later that morning. I find them in the living room as I return from adding yet another bag of trash to the heap gathering out front. Neither can hide the surprise on their faces. The house has come a long way since last night. Mrs. Taylor turns from her examination of the patched front window and spots them.

"I hope I didn't overstep my bounds," she says uncertainly. "I just didn't want you to wake up and—"

He doesn't give her the chance to finish her sentence, wrapping his arms around her in a tight hug. Tears silently stream down his cheeks and onto her shoulder. She pays them no mind, rubbing his back in a slow, soothing pattern perfected over years of practice. She whispers something into his ear, wringing out yet more tears. Morgan catches my eye and smiles, nodding toward the two of them knowingly as if he knew this scene would happen.

"Thank you," he says, finally unwrapping his arms. "You've always been good to me."

She smiles and lays a hand against his cheek. "You've always made it easy," she says. "We may not be blood, but I love you like you're my own. I always will." I feel a wet spot travel down my cheek and I hastily turn my head to wipe it away.

By the end of the day, the house has been returned to its proper state. Or as proper as it can be at any rate. The trash heap out front has been moved into a shallow ditch where we now set it ablaze. As it catches fire, I can't help but feel optimistic. I feel it flow between us as we watch the flames leap higher, and plumes of thick smoke billow into the evening sky. Each of us played a part in creating this moment, a moment we desperately needed. I can feel the bond taking place, the camaraderie building between us as we realize what we can accomplish together.

I feel his arms wrap around my waist, the warmth of his breath as he leans closer to whisper in my ear. "Have I told you that you look beautiful today?" he asks.

I roll my eyes but am unable to keep the smile from my face. "You just love spouting corndog lines don't you?"

"I admit, I do," he says, kissing me on the nape of the neck. "But not nearly as much as I love you." I can't help it, I burst out laughing and he joins in soon after. "Alright, that one might have been a bit much," he concedes.

"Just a bit," I say.

He turns me around so that we're face to face. His smile mocks me, but his eyes are warm and sincere. "But just so we're clear: *you are* beautiful, and *I do* love you. More than I could ever put into words."

I close the distance between us, putting all I want to say into a long, slow kiss. "You better."

I look back to the fire, watching as the debris from the house burn and the western horizon transforms into a patchwork of red and purple clouds. We still have much to do. I realize that. But standing here, surrounded by so many good people, I feel hopeful for the future.

Chapter 7: (Morgan)

"You realize we must look like a bunch of idiots, right?" Leon grunts.

"You'd think that after twenty-four years, you would be used to it by now," Felix says from up front.

What breath I can spare gets lost in laughter. Though Leon does have a point—pushing a stalled out, nearly six-thousand pound SUV, doesn't exactly make us look like scholars. But it's all for a purpose.

The garden at the farm fared better than we had hoped. There was some damage, made both by man and animal, but most could be salvaged. We've harvested some already: cabbage, brussels sprouts, broccoli, cucumber. And more will be ready in the next few weeks. Personally, I most look forward to the potatoes—paper thin slices fried in oil and sprinkled with salt. Before the collapse, nothing quite hit the spot for me like a bag of Lays and a Pepsi. Learning of the potatoes the other day has set off a craving I can't shake. It's been rough. Still, I'm thankful for the food we do have, little as it may be. But with nearly thirty of us, we're going to need a lot more. That's where the SUV comes in.

A dozen of us were out in the garden, brainstorming on how to grow more food. Thanks to Elroy we have seeds and a handwritten book full of information and techniques, but that only goes so far. My Aunt Virginia and Vince's soon to be mother-in-law, Leah, are the only two with any gardening experience. Felix knows a little from living here, but the garden was his aunt's domain. As for the rest of us, we have Elroy's notes and a prayer. We're going to need both if we're going to have a chance at surviving this winter.

There was a large section consisting of greenhouses—the different builds and how to maintain them. Page after page of information, but one thing became clear to us quickly: the majority of greenhouses in the book would take time and material to build, two things we are desperately short on. That's when my Aunt Virginia had the idea to convert vehicles into miniature greenhouses, the modern relics one thing available in abundance throughout the area. A clever idea, one we can only hope pays off in the long run. That brings us here.

Three days we have spent gathering a fleet to convert. It's physically demanding. The farm sits removed from major roadways, the neighboring farms and homes spread out far and wide. It's a great location as we try and rebuild, but it makes finding suitable vehicles difficult. Two teams have spread out from the farm to search—the first consisting of myself, Leon and Felix—and the second made of Vince, Jerry, and Ted. The rest of the family is back at the farm, gutting out the interiors of the vehicles we've gathered so far, and constructing raised garden beds to fill them. With any luck, at least a couple will be ready by the end of the day.

"Another quarter mile or so is the Begay's place," Felix says. "We should check and see if they know anything."

"You got the wheel," I call back. "Lead the way."

This will be the third home we've visited in as many days, fishing for any information that might lead us to Felix's family. The previous two yielded nothing we could use. Neither had left their property except to hunt, and in any case, had turned cautious of their neighbors. I get it. Trust was a fickle beast in the best of times. Today, it can mean the difference between life and death. Why check on a neighbor when doing so might get you killed? Who's to say Bill from down the street, president of the PTA, local handyman, all around good guy, wouldn't rob or kill you if it meant his family's survival? It's not pessimism, but the cold truth of the world we now live in. I don't like it, but it's the only logical way for us to start our search.

We leave the SUV at the entrance of a long driveway. Oakbrush lines the drive to the left, while to the right lies a large, overgrown lawn, stretching from the county road to the small house at the end of the drive. As we have with the previous two homes, we walk with our hands clearly visible and our weapons tucked away, trying to come across as non-threatening as possible. But the closer we approach, the more I get the sense that the place is abandoned.

Anyone still smart enough to be alive would have questioned our presence by now, yet we reach the front door without issue.

"Mr. and Mrs. Begay?" Felix yells, knocking on the front door. "Are you in there? It's Felix Chavez, Frank and Christina's nephew from down the road. I just had a couple questions if you have a minute." Nobody calls back. He looks to us and I nod quickly, guessing the unasked question in his eyes. He removes his Glock, and we do the same as he opens the unlocked door and steps into the house. They are holstered again almost immediately as we learn why our knocks went unanswered.

The Begay's were a quiet, older couple enjoying their retirement. And then everything went dark. You could almost mistake Mrs. Begay for being asleep if not for the smell of death about her. She looks peaceful, her eyes closed, hand still clutched in her husband's who sits beside her on the loveseat. There is nothing peaceful in Mr. Begay's death. A bullet has carved through his skull, throwing blood splatters on the couch and wall. It's not difficult to piece together the sad tale. Prescription bottles made out to a Mrs. E. Begay line the table, all of which are empty. Without her medication, she lost her life. Without his wife, Mr. Begay lost his will to live.

I don't know these people, but their walls tell a story of a couple who both loved, and were loved in return. Smiles frozen forever in time shine down on us from the many photos laying throughout the living room. Who are they, I wonder. Children? Grandchildren? Friends? Colleagues? All of the above most likely. Are any of them still alive out there, scraping and struggling to survive someplace far from their departed relatives? I'd like to believe so. I'd like to believe that at least part of this vast, smiling family still lives.

We clear the house of anything valuable. A shotgun, two bolt action rifles (a .22 and a .270), and the revolver that took Mr. Begay's life get added to our growing arsenal, as well as several hundred rounds we find stored in an ammo crate below their bed. These weapons, and more importantly, the ammo, are a huge score for us. Still, it leaves a foul taste in my mouth. The only thing that brings me any sense of peace is knowing they at least fell into our hands instead of others with dark intentions.

Outside of the weapons, we don't find much. Even with a healthy heart, I don't know how much longer Mrs. Begay and her husband would have lasted on their own. They kept no garden, grow no crops, and searching their kitchen yielded nothing but a can of green beans and a half-empty can of tomato paste. Perhaps it was kinder this way instead of the slow, grueling torture of starvation. Perhaps her death was painless—like slowly drifting off into a deep, dreamless sleep. I at least hope that was the case.

We bury them in the shadow of an old elm tree, its yellow leaves dancing in the breeze that sweeps through. It's quiet work, no words between us as we plow into the earth. After dumping the bodies and filling the grave, we stand in heavy silence. We didn't know these people. Even Felix only knew of them in passing. This isn't our place to be here, but there is no one else to stand in our stead. After a minute, Felix finally speaks.

"I don't know what comes after this life," he says. "But I hope you're happy, and at peace. Rest easy friends. Rest easy."

Short. To the point. It's more than fitting in this situation. We leave immediately after, stowing our looted weapons and ammo into the SUV before continuing down the road. It's only a mile or so to the farm, but the encounter with the Begay's has left me weary. My legs feel heavier with each step, a sharp stitch cleaving my side. But I push through it. At least I can feel this pain, can have the luxury of feeling exhausted.

As we pull into the farm, it's to find Vince, Jerry, and Ted dropping off their second vehicle of the day. Vince grins as we roll our SUV to a stop, asking what the holdup was. His grin falls as we recount what happened at the Begay's.

"So much damn death," he says, shaking his head. "I wish I could have just five minutes with that smug-faced bastard who was on TV that day, talking about saving us and creating a new world and all that crap. I mean, yeah, the world had its problems...but how is this any better? How can anyone justify doing this?"

I've pondered the same questions a hundred times over. It never leads to any answers. There is no justification for what they did to the world—for them to decide that billions of lives were worth sacrificing in order for their vision to come to pass. But the world has always known such men: the Hitler's and the Stalin's and the Bin Laden's, whose twisted minds could somehow justify their many acts of evil. The terrorists who did this might have had purer intentions than their peers throughout history, but their actions are every bit as cruel.

"He wouldn't have any answers for you," I say.

"No," he agrees. "But I could at least beat the pricks face in."

The response makes me smile. "Yeah. I wouldn't mind taking a swing or two myself."

Neither group heads out in search for more vehicles. Instead, the afternoon is spent gutting out the interiors of those we've already amassed and constructing the garden beds. It's hard work, made all the harder without the aid of power tools. We're only lucky Felix's uncle was old-school and kept more than enough hand tools to get the job done. His work shed is a craftsman's dream. Over the years I've helped him with a handful of projects around his place, and I can't remember him ever needing to buy anything but material. Everything we needed for the job was already there. The same holds true now.

Still, it's slow going. It will be a couple of days before everything's done—when we've collected and gutted all of the vehicles and planted the seeds we'll attempt to grow. It's strange to realize our survival may very well depend on the success of this project. It's just another reminder of how far things have fallen. I remember reading once that an EMP could send the world back to the 1800s in a matter of seconds. I know that now to be true. But until it actually happened, I never gave much thought to what that meant. I never really thought about the people who lived before technology reshaped everything: who never knew the world of supermarkets and fast-food chains and corner stores full of junk-food. All they had was what they could provide themselves. Now we're in their shoes. There are no soup kitchens or handouts waiting for us if we fail. We have nothing to fall back on. How harsh a world that a handful of seeds taking root could mean the difference between life and death.

As the afternoon cedes to evening, we find cause to celebrate. Two large garden beds have been erected inside the belly of a minivan, the first of our seeds planted into the soil. The significance of it isn't lost on anyone, and it's a good minute before we can do anything other than stare at the project. Soon after, we call it a day and retreat to the house. We sit together under the evening sky, at rest for the first time since sunrise. Like everyone else, I'm tired and hungry. What I wouldn't give for a steak dinner—a thick rib-eye cooked to a perfect medium rare, baked potato with all the fixin's, and freshly baked garlic-bread slathered in butter. Instead, I'm forced to make do with a meager portion of salvaged vegetables.

That's not to say I'm not grateful to have the food on my plate. I know how much worse things could be. The days after the wildfire were a raw misery, forcing ourselves along on aching, empty stomachs. It was only a taste of true starvation, but it was enough to last me a lifetime. My hunger will not go away with this food. It will linger inside me for quite some time to come. But my stomach will not be overcome with aches and pangs, nor will my mind be consumed with a desperate mania to find food. I'll rest, and talk, and spend time with those I love most in this world. As fragile as things are, I have it better than most. And I know that's something which must be protected.

As of now, the only line of defense between ourselves and intruders is the barbed wire fence surrounding the property. That needs to change. Richard and Felix spent much of the afternoon scouting the perimeter of the farm, thinking over defensive measures we might be able to apply. I ask them now what they've come up with.

"The best thing we have going for us is that we don't have a huge area to lockdown," Richard says. "If we fortify the roof of the house and post a lookout, we'll have eyes on 75% of the farm. Our biggest blind spot is behind the barn. All those trees and brush would make it too easy for a group trying to rush the place. I have a few ideas about some tension traps and some tripwires, but we're gonna need to clear most of the area out. We'll need the firewood before too long anyway."

A twinge of anxiety goes through me at the mention of firewood. I force it away before it can settle. Worrying over the approaching winter won't delay it. All I can do is stay focused and do everything I can to make sure we're as ready as we can be.

"What about the pastures?" I ask. "Both are wide open. Even with a sentry, a group could slip in unseen if it's dark enough."

"We thought about that," Felix says. "Even if they don't approach through the pastures, it's a prime location to scope out our operation. All that oakbrush past the fence is perfect camouflage."

"That's a lot of brush to clear out," I say. "Especially if we're already clearing out the area behind the barn."

"We won't have to," Felix says. "We'll use it to our advantage, lay down some nasty surprises for anyone sticking their noses where they don't belong. And if they somehow make it through and into the pasture, we'll dig out some pit-traps and lay down some tripwires—not like we have any animals to worry about. We can add an extra sentry at night if need be. Two sets of eyes are better than one."

We continue to talk over our defensive measures the remainder of the evening. Overhearing us, most of the family add their ideas and concerns to the conversation. It feels good to talk over this, to know we are taking action to protect ourselves. Since that first morning in Denver, I've been all go—constantly worrying and looking over my shoulder. It feels good to have somewhere that's worth protecting, to feel as if I belong somewhere instead of just passing through. I haven't had that feeling in a long time.

"Is it just me, or does it feel like we're building something here?" Lauren says into my ear. I can't help but smile as she rests her chin against my shoulder and wraps her arms around me from behind. That's exactly what it feels like.

"I did promise you."

"You did," she agrees. "That's why I'm not surprised that it's happening."

Chapter 8: (Lauren)

A week has passed since our arrival on the farm. We've been busy. Our days start early and don't end until evening, the slanted rays of the sun acting as our cue to call it a day. It's been hard work, but the place is finally starting to resemble a farm again. Whether or not we can call ourselves farmers, on the other hand, is yet to be determined.

"It's all in God's hands," Morgan's Aunt Virginia told me. *"Have faith that He will provide."*

I like the woman, it's the reason I smile and nod whenever she speaks of having faith in *"The Lord,"* which is often. God's not real. He's a fantasy, made up over the centuries by poor souls desperate for something to believe in. I learned that truth early—through countless nights spent on my knees, praying, pleading for His help, His protection. But always, my prayers went unanswered. So now I no longer kneel. I no longer look to the sky in vain. Anything I've ever had in this world was because I made it happen. This is no different. Anything we accomplish here will be because of us, not prayers whispered and disappeared among the wind. And to our credit, it does feel like we're accomplishing something.

Beside the garden sits our greenhouse experiment. As the only two with any real gardening experience, Virginia and Leah have been put in charge of the operation. Under their guidance, most of the amassed fleet has been gutted, and nearly half have been fitted with raised garden beds. We reference Elroy's black book frequently, planting the crops which have the best chance to produce this late in the year; beets and carrots and radishes among others. The more variety we plant, the better our chances of something producing. I hope it's enough, but the truth is, none of us know whether or not these greenhouses will work. But without a better alternative, we've no choice but to continue the course we've set.

I squat beside a halfway completed garden bed, my left thumb throbbing in pain. I blame the hammer, even though I know it's my own fault. But in my defense, I wasn't expecting a damn field mouse to brush within inches of my foot mid-swing. Mice have always been a phobia of mine; what with their dirty fur, and pointed teeth, and nimble bodies that can bend and squeeze through the tiniest openings. My skin crawls just thinking about them. And now I've gone and injured myself on account of one of those vile rodents. Emily can't stop laughing about it. The sound alone almost makes it worth the pain.

Maya's passing has affected all who knew her. As her best friend, Emily has been affected most of all. Her grief is easy to spot despite her best effort to conceal it. It's in the puffiness to her eyes and the shadows beneath them. It's in the hunch to her shoulders and the waver in her voice at times. Not a day has passed that I do not remember that night. Everything happened so fast, yet I remember it all with absolute clarity. I wish it didn't. All it does is remind me of how much worse things could have been.

Forget the past. Focus on the future. I repeat my mantra until that night dissolves in my mind.

"Go ahead, laugh it up," I tell Emily. "But I believe it was you who screamed like a little girl over a baby chipmunk in the tent."

That shuts her up. Beside her, Julia takes over the laughter. "Really, a baby chipmunk?" She asks her cousin. "I don't remember you being so squeamish. What happened to the girl who used to force me to hunt lizards and pick nightcrawlers with her?" She waves her finger and shakes her head in mock disappointment. "You've turned into a city girl on me."

"Ok, first off, I didn't scream," she says. "It was an involuntary shout of surprise at feeling something crawling up my leg."

This sets Julia off once more, her laughs occasionally punctured by snorts, which in turn, makes me laugh as well.

"And secondly," she continues, talking over us. "*You're* calling *me* a city girl?" she asks Julia. "Two words: rubber snake." The smile drops from Julia's face as it turns red out of embarrassment.

"Oh, C'mon, you can't say 'rubber snake' and not tell me the story," I say.

Emily smiles at her cousin and then turns to me, triumphant. "Sorry, Lauren," she says. "I can't give you the details. I'm sworn to secrecy. But I can tell you that it ended with me getting grounded for a week."

"Always the mark of a good story," I say. Though neither of them will share the rubber snake story, they do share others: stealing makeup from department stores when their mothers said they were too young to wear any; summer slumber parties, playing games, and pigging out on junk food, and falling asleep under a canopy of stars on the backyard trampoline. Born six months apart, they grew up together more sisters than cousins. All the important milestones of youth were shared together. Watching them reminisce now is like watching two best friends reconnect. It makes me wonder what it would be like to have a sister born months apart, instead of years. Would we have been like Emily and Julia? Would we have stories and memories to look back on—a past worth remembering? Likely not. It's better this way. Not all memories are worth sharing.

Stories and laughter continue as we finish installing our garden bed. Thunder cracks overhead as we carefully plant kale seeds in the soil. It's threatened rain all day, the sky painted steel-grey with splotches of purple-tinged storm clouds. Nothing has come of it, but as another clap of thunder sounds, it appears to be only a matter of time. I feel an anxious twinge in my stomach even though I know it's over nothing. Morgan and the boys know how to handle themselves. We've weathered storms far worse than this.

"We should be back by sundown," Morgan said. "But if we're not, don't worry. We'll be fine."

But I'm wired to worry over those I care about. Until they make it back, my anxiety will remain. Over the past few days, Morgan and Leon have accompanied Felix in searching for his family. So far, they've received no leads or information on their whereabouts. From what I gather, most people in the area seem on edge, fear of intruders and violence evident. More than a few have mentioned at least one encounter with groups raiding their places. Richard has been on a mission to fortify the place since hearing the news, but there is still much to be done. Every time the three of them leave the farm to search, the bitterness on Richard's face is easy to read. No doubt he believes they are more needed here, and I know he's not alone in his opinion. The hypocrites. Anyone in Felix's position would do the same—would cling to the hope that their family was still alive out there. I know I would. And as long as Felix clings onto that hope and continues to search, Morgan and Leon will be right there beside him. It's how their friendship works.

    While they have yet to find any leads, their trips haven't completely been in vain. Their searching has yielded weapons and ammo, farming supplies, and crazily enough, a dozen egg-laying chickens and a rooster. In each instance, the supplies were taken after finding the deceased remains of their owners. It's hard to feel grateful for these things given that fact. But we have to be logical, have to put our survival over our discomfort. It's the only thing that makes looking into Morgan's haunted eyes bearable, knowing those deaths affect him in a way they don't the rest of us. He has more empathy than anyone I've ever met: a quality that may be more curse than gift in this new world.

    The wind shifts, bringing with it the scent of rain and a sharp chill. It's the only warning we have before the deluge begins. We're soaked within seconds as we scramble to protect our work. Materials and tools are shoved into the interiors of vehicles we have yet to gut, while those who have been lined with beds are properly sealed. Once finished, it's a race of slipping and sliding bodies as everyone heads for the house. I, on the other hand, hang back to help Virginia maintain her balance on the suddenly slick ground.

    "Thank you," she says, clutching my arm. "When you get to be my age, taking a fall isn't something you can just shake off."

    "Don't worry about it," I say. "I'm not afraid of a little water." As we reach the house, Richard and his crew catch up to us, each of them as drenched as we are.

    "Damn the rain," he says as he steps inside the kitchen. "We're burning daylight."

I may not agree with Richard on much, but I share his frustration in having our workday cut short. I've lived in Colorado all my life. I know how quickly autumn can turn to winter—how leaves of red and yellow might litter the ground one day, and be buried under a foot of snow the next. And we still have much to do before then.

"How's the progress coming along behind the barn?" I ask.

He shakes his head. "Slowly," he grumbles. "We're already short on men. We can't afford to be short on time as well." It's all he says before following Virginia into the living room. I keep quiet, resisting the urge to bite back. His hints about Morgan and Leon wasting their time helping Felix is seriously annoying. If I didn't think it so important to keep the peace, I'd have said something already.

"It's really not that bad," Vince assures me. I turn at his voice, finding him sitting atop the kitchen counter, sweeping wet strands of hair from his eyes and smiling at my surprise. I didn't even notice him slip into the kitchen. "Uncle Dick has always tried his best to live up to his name. Best to take everything he says with a grain of salt." His smile widens and I find my own mouth curl in amusement. Outside his parents, Morgan has told me more about Vince than anyone else in the family—his laid-back older cousin with a sharp mind and clever tongue—who made everything look effortless, and whose personality filled a room. They may be cousins, but he's as much a brother to Morgan as Leon and Felix are.

"Noted," I say, taking a seat opposite him. "How are things really coming along then?"

He shrugs. "As well as can be expected, I guess. Shouldn't take too long to clear out the rest of the trees and brush. Then the real fun begins: boobie traps." He laughs. "Gonna lay out some tricks that would make Macaulay Culkin proud." There's a gleam in his eye at the prospect of mischief.

"Macaulay Culkin?" I ask, confused.

His eyes narrow. "Yeah," he says. "From *Home Alone*?" He must take my blank stare as an answer. "Seriously? You've never seen it? Kid gets left at home while his family is on vacation, and has to defend the house against two clueless crooks?"

"Sorry, not ringing any bells," I say. "But don't take it personally. I didn't watch many movies growing up."

He shakes his head. "All I'll say is that you missed out. There was just something about older comedies that spoke to me. Things always seemed simpler back then. Purer, you know?" His stares at the kitchen floor with a far-away look in his eye, and a small smile on his face, undoubtedly lost in a montage of movies he loved and will never see again. "Then again, maybe I'm just nostalgic."

"Maybe you just wish things could be simple and pure again," I say.

He meets my eyes, the ever-present glint of amusement momentarily lost in his. "Yeah, you're definitely right about that," he says quietly. He averts his eyes for a moment, a subtle grin spreading from the corner of his mouth. The glint is back when he meets my eyes again. "But have you ever heard my Uncle Gene's philosophy on wishing?"

The question makes me laugh. "About wishing in one hand, and shitting in the other?" I ask. He joins me in laughing.

"The very same," he confirms, and though it's not all that funny of a joke, it's a long minute before either of us catches our breath. "We're doing more than just wishing here, though," he says, voice serious once more. "Seemed like that's all we were doing for the longest time: wishing, just spinning our wheels trying to survive without actually getting anywhere. Then when things were at its darkest, there was Morgan: framed against the headlights like a POW about to be executed, and without even a flicker of fear on his face. It all felt like...I don't know, fate or something—the timing of everything you know? Now being here, after everything we've been through...it has to mean something, right?"

I remember speaking of fate with Morgan once, the morning he left to seek medicine in Salida: how I convinced myself he would return, simply because fate had destined it to be so. Only now do I see how foolish those thoughts were, to think the universe, as vast and powerful as it is, had a plan for us. It's all just chance. That's what it all boils down to: the chances we're given, and those we take. Morgan knew that even then. If I'm being honest with myself, I think at least part of me knew it too. But I suppose when you want something badly enough, your mind can make you believe just about anything. Who am I to take that away from Vince?

"It means everything," I say.

He shares a quick smile before getting to his feet. "I better check on my better half," he says. "She wasn't feeling so good this morning."

I make no move to follow him, instead, allowing myself the simple indulgence of an empty room. With so many of us, moments alone are hard to come by. I shift on the countertop, resting my back against the cabinet as I watch the storm rage through the rustic windows. The rain falls harder, it's melodic drumming against the rooftop picking up in intensity as its mist sprays against the glass. Flashes of lightning dance across the sky, deep claps of thunder echoing in their wake. I haven't seen a storm like this since the trail. I feel a shiver creep down my back at the memory of it: the numb, frozen fingers; the chill that reached down to the bones; wrapping Grace tightly in my arms beneath our damp and muddied sleeping bags, her body my only source of warmth. Now the winds have only grown more fierce, colder with the season. And Morgan and the guys are out there somewhere, facing the elements.

My stomach clenches on itself, that old familiar feeling of worry and anxiety coursing through me. I remind myself that they can handle themselves, but my mind has always had a tendency of running away with itself. *What if they were ambushed? What if they were shot at as they approached a homestead?* What if, what if, what if. The questions burn through me, and I have no way of answering them. Not for the first time, I wish I could join them in their search. In many ways, the danger wouldn't be as bad as the waiting. But there are too many reasons why that can't be. I need to do all I can to ensure Grace is kept safe—that means not taking any unnecessary risks. And as much as I love Felix, it's not my place to be with him as he searches for his family. Even if more of us were willing to help search, Morgan and

Leon would be the only two Felix allowed to join him. Like it or not, I'm stuck with my anxiety.

The sky grows steadily darker, the storm clouds swelling larger and more ominous. Out the corner of my eye, I catch a figure step onto the back porch, my hand reaching for my Glock out of instinct. It's not until a flash of lightning paints his face that I recognize Morgan's uncle, Mitch. A lit cigarette dangles between his lips, a look of relaxed contentment on his face as he takes a drag. He smokes it down to the filter before flicking it into the storm and enters through the kitchen door.

"Old habits, die hard?" I ask.

He starts at my voice. "Shit!!" he says, clutching at his chest. "I didn't think anyone was in here."

"Sorry," I say, amused at his jumpiness. "I didn't mean to startle you."

He looks around as if ensuring nobody else lingers in the shadows to surprise him. "No apology necessary," he says. "Truth is, I am a little jumpy. Feel like a frickin' teenager again, sneaking out back to light up a smoke. But if I don't, I'll have to hear my sisters bitch," he says, rolling his eyes. "Better to avoid that nonsense if I can."

"I guess," I say, surprised at the bitterness in his voice.

"I mean, I'm forty-three years old," he adds, continuing on his tirade. "That's twenty-one, two times over. I should be able to light up a smoke without feeling like I'm doing something wrong, you know?" I make a noncommittal grunt, at a loss for anything else to add. He continues on all the same. "I get that they want what's best for me," he says, grudgingly it seems. Then he shakes his head. "But they don't know everything. They think they do, but they don't."

I'm out of my element here. Mitch seems to have forgotten I'm in the room, his gaze drawn to the storm raging beyond the glass door. I want to say something, but I barely know him. For all I know, I'll just set him off again. Suddenly he snaps out of it, a look of embarrassment on his face as he looks to me.

"Sorry," he says. "You didn't need to hear all that."

"It's alright," I say. "We all need a good rant sometimes."

He forces a smile. "Yeah," he says. "Sometimes." He tugs on the collar of his sweater nervously a moment. "I'd better see if there's a fire going. Try and dry this out a little." He nods goodbye and turns toward the living room, tugging his sweater off as he does so. Just as he reaches the door separating the two rooms, a white bottle falls from the sweater pocket and rolls the length of the floor towards me. I look to the bottle back to him, his face ashen, eyes wide like a deer caught in headlights. I reach down and pick it up, the weight of it letting me know it's full of pills.

"Tylenol," he says. "Back's been killing me lately." He reaches for the bottle and I hand it back without raising an issue. He stuffs it firmly into his pant pocket, patting the denim outside securely. "Probably best we keep this to ourselves," he says. "Wouldn't want to make an issue over nothing." I'm not sure if it's a suggestion or a threat, his calm voice not matching his dark eyes.

The tread of running feet catches my attention. I turn in time to see Morgan run the length of the porch and fly into the kitchen, Leon and Felix behind him. They're breathless, each of them soaked head toe. I look back toward Mitch only to find he has already disappeared into the living room. Spotting me, Morgan straightens up and quickly closes the distance between us while Leon and Felix enter the laundry room to towel off.

"You're literally waiting by the door for my return?" he asks, grinning playfully. "How sweet." His brow furrows and his eyes narrow, perhaps sensing my lingering unease. "Are you alright?" he asks.

I don't know how to answer the question, unsure if I should mention his uncle's pills. I meet his eyes, the concern they hold rooting me to the spot. So much weighs on his mind these days—so much worry and stress. He's carried that weight since the beginning, and now, it's beginning to take its toll. I can see it in the rings under his eyes—can hear it in the tiredness in his voice. Just last night I woke him from yet another nightmare, the paleness of his face and cold sweat streaming past his brow, standing out vividly in my mind. Do I really need to burden him with this? Do I really need to give him more to deal with, when I myself don't know if there's anything to worry about?

"Of course," I say, forcing a smile. "I just find it funny how you say I'm waiting by the door when you're the one practically breaking it down to get to me."

A low chuckle escapes him. "They've yet to invent a door that could keep me from you, McCoy," he says. He places a brief kiss atop my forehead before meeting my eyes again, erasing any lingering unease. Nothing else matters when he looks at me like this—not our worries, not our fears, not our doubts. In these quiet moments which are both infinite and fleeting all at once, nothing matters but the two of us.

Chapter 9: (Morgan)

It's cold out this early morning hour, piercing winds howling in from the east where the sun still hides beyond the horizon. I put my hood up against the chill only to take it off almost immediately. It limits both my vision and my hearing, and I can't afford to impair either. There are bands of thieves and roving gangs scattered about the area. We've learned of their exploits from those we've questioned while searching for Felix's family. Hearing their stories has left me convinced that an attack on the farm isn't a matter of *if*, but of *when*. We need to be prepared for it.

It kills me to leave the farm as often as I do, knowing how much work still needs to be done. But I have an obligation to Felix. He's been my most loyal friend for as long as I can remember. Anytime I've ever needed him, he was there for me. No hesitation. No questions asked. Always, he's had my back. So long as he holds hope of finding his family, I have to be there for him. I won't abandon his side when I know he'd never abandon mine. Still, nearly three weeks of searching with nothing to show for it has been demoralizing, to say the least.

We started by checking in with their neighbors, and any family friends Felix knew of. Without any answers, we continue to widen our search, each place more unlikely than the next. Many of the homes have been abandoned, long since stripped of anything valuable. At others, only the decaying remains of their owners are left behind. Several times we've been deterred altogether, the sight of rifle barrels sticking out of open windows and the crack of warning shots keeping us from proceeding further.

On the occasions we have spoken with people, not a single person could recall seeing them since the collapse. *"They're dead, you fools." "Stop wasting your time and focus on your own survival."* They don't say as much, but I can see it in their pitying stares, can hear it in their fragile voices. I try my best to maintain hope, but it's becoming more and more difficult to imagine this story has a happy ending.

Our pace is a mix of caution and haste: caution because of the threats around us, and haste because of our need for time. Today, we venture further out than we've dared so far, past Oxford, near the outskirts of Ignacio. It's the reason we're out so early. Based on Frank's old road maps, we have a round trip of over twenty miles to cover. And with the days growing shorter and bad weather these past few evenings, we want to try and make it back well before dusk.

We pass Hwy 160 in silence. No matter how many times I see it, the wreckage that lines the road and ditches leaves me with a foul taste in my mouth. So many lives ended an instant, all for a cause only a few believed in. I wonder if those who did this ever regret their actions. Do they look at the chaos and destruction they created with pride? With a sense of victory? Is this the glorious rebirth they had envisioned for the world? One of violence, and brutality, and fear? Do they see the millions of deaths around the globe as noble sacrifices? The rapes, and starvation, and countless other depravities as necessary evils? I remember the euphoric glint that burned inside that terrorist's eyes as he delivered the message that forever changed our lives. Is this what he saw?

My thoughts are interrupted as we reach the crest of a small hill, the day's first blush drawing my eye as it spreads over the eastern horizon, a tide of orange and red splashing against the purple-tinged clouds. I pause, allowing myself a moment to soak in the sight of it—to relish the fact that there is still beauty to behold in this world. So much has gone wrong and yet the sun still rises. Life goes on. It's on us to make that mean something. I breathe deep, the crisp mountain air flowing through my lungs helping to calm the anger. We're going to be alright. So long as we have each other, we'll find a way to make it through.

"Are you positive we're heading in the right direction?" I ask a couple hours later.

"I think so," Felix says. He unfolds the map from his back pocket to consult it. He traces his finger along the route we've taken. "I've only been to the place twice before, but I remember it wasn't too far off 172. There was two, maybe three turns from that Baptist

Church...that would put it somewhere in this area." He circles a small area with his finger. "Either way, this road intersects with the church eventually. From there it shouldn't be too hard to find."

"I still can't believe we're about to check Connor Sawyer's ranch," Leon says with an edge to his voice. "Never thought I'd see that prick again."

I smile even though there is no love lost between Connor and myself. He's an obnoxious loudmouth with an innate talent for pissing people off. He always managed to avoid a fight though, fast-talking and backpedaling his way out before it came to blows. Except once. It was our Junior year and Connor made the mistake of bragging about the things he would do to the *little sophomore slut* he had been talking to moments before. It might have been better had it been me who overheard him talking about Emily. He would have still caught a beating, but I don't know if he would have ended up in the emergency room. I should have realized then how much my sister meant to Leon.

Needless to say, there has been tension between them ever since. It's something we can't afford to let flare up today.

"Neither did I," I say. "But we have to stay calm today. Don't give them a reason to start anything. If we end up in a standoff, I doubt any of us walk out alive." I'm repeating what we've already gone over, but it's an important point. Leon has always been the most hot-headed of the three of us. I'll bash the message over his head again and again if I think it might make a difference.

"I'm not an idiot, Moe," Leon says. "I know that. But if his family is anything like him, we need to be ready for something to go down. I mean he has what, three brothers? Have to figure he's not the only rotten apple of the bunch."

There's some merit to that. We've been at risk, to some degree, at every home and farm we've checked so far. But today is different. The bad blood between Connor and Leon complicates things. I only hope the collapse has made Connor grow up. Barring that, I hope his family are at least decent people. Either way, we need to be on our toes.

"What *is* his family like?" I ask Felix, the only one of us to have met any of them.

He shrugs. "Don't know them very well," he says. "His dad seemed alright, I guess. Kind of in your face. Cocky, you know? He goes way back with my aunt and uncle though. I remember him saying that my aunt's biggest mistake was choosing my uncle over him. It was like this long-running joke between them. Never did meet his wife—she died before I even moved here. Don't know any of his older brothers either, but I met the younger one. Forgot his name, but he seemed like a good kid: quiet, simple, kind of the exact opposite Connor."

"That's encouraging," I say. "Maybe Connor really is just the rotten apple of the bunch."

"Let's hope," Leon says.

An hour later we come across the Baptist Church, and I feel the hairs on the back of my neck stand up, the dark bank of windows facing us giving me the eerie feeling of being watched. I try my best to look for movement inside, but all I can make out are shadows from this distance. We cut across the parking lot, deserted save for a large white van by the front entrance, and a red Subaru at the far corner. The feeling of being watched stays with me until we're past the lot and starting down another county road.

True to his word, we arrive at the entrance to the ranch three turns, and one mile later. A large, single-story house sits at the end of a long driveway, two large pastures flanking the drive on either side. Beyond the house, I can make out the steepled top of a large barn and several outbuildings arrayed centrally to three more gridded pastures. A dozen plus horses graze in one pasture, while several cows lay in another. What else do they have here? Chickens? Pigs? Crops? They're in better shape than most. Certainly in better shape than we are. If Felix's family is here, what could that mean for us? Is it possible Connor Sawyer, of all people, could become an ally, a friend?

I shake my head. I'm getting ahead of myself. First, we need to find out if the family is here, and if not, whether the Sawyer's have heard from them. It's easier said than done. Twenty feet down the driveway, two trucks sit grill to grill, forming a V-shaped barricade for approaching vehicles. What gives us pause however isn't the barricade, which we could simply skirt, but the warning spray-painted in red across their bodies. "Trespassers Shot on Sight!"

"Not exactly encouraging," Leon says, mocking my earlier optimism.

I ignore it. This isn't the first time we've encountered something like this. But unlike before, we can't just turn around and hope for better luck at the next place. We need to figure out a way to seek an audience without getting ourselves killed. Before I can even ask if anyone has an idea, Felix has already made his decision. Quickly, he removes his rifle, sidearm, and extra magazines before laying them on the hood.

"I'll head down the drive with my hands up," he explains, taking off his shirt as he does so. "I'll call out my name, and why I'm here. They know me, know my aunt and uncle. They won't shoot."

"You don't know that," Leon says.

"What if it's not the Sawyer's who are running the place? What if it's been taken over by someone else?"

He brushes the concerns away. "Doesn't matter. We have to figure out one way or another. And based off this welcome message, I'd be shocked if they didn't have a lookout somewhere. They'll have seen us by now. Can't exactly sneak off and watch them from the bushes."

"There's gotta be a smarter—"

"We don't have time to debate this," Felix snaps. Whatever cool he's held throughout the morning is lost in an instant. "Look, I know it's a risk to walk out there unarmed. Stupid, even. But it's what I have to do. All this searching means shit if I'm not willing to take the risks to find them."

It's hard seeing my friend so desperate. He's hid it well, but now it comes rising to the surface. I know only a taste of the mania he must feel—that which consumed me so often on the trail until I was finally reunited with my family. And then the relief of having found them—to see them, feel them, hold them—it's something I can't put into words. Felix doesn't know that relief. I don't even want to think of the mess I would be if our situations were reversed. I'm sure I'd have done something far more desperate long before now. Which is why I accept his plan and don't raise another issue.

"We'll keep an eye out," Leon assures him, un-slinging his own rifle. I mimic him, ignoring the twist in my stomach, and take cover behind the trucks.

Felix pauses at the edge of the barricade, his face set. Determined. He looks our way quickly, confidence blazing in his eyes. "It's going to all work out," he says. Before I can so much as nod, he is looking down the long drive again. A moment later, he slips past the barricade and into the open. He walks with his hands splayed before him, shouting out his name and why he is here. Halfway down the driveway, the ranch's inhabitants make themselves known.

"That's far enough!" hollers a voice. I see no one, but I trace the voice to the house. Felix stops immediately.

"Mr. Sawyer?" Felix yells back. "I'm Felix Chavez, Frank and Chris—"

"Heard you the first dozen times," the voice yells back, cutting him off. "Only I'm not Mr. Sawyer. He's on his way from out back. You can talk to him when he arrives. In the meantime, I need your buddies back there to disarm and join you from behind the roadblock."

Leon and I look to one another, silently communicating how we should play this. He's as apprehensive as I am. Everywhere we've searched has had some risk involved, but not like this. Had this been anywhere else, Felix wouldn't have even walked down the drive in the first place. But he did, and now we're stuck between a rock and a hard place.

"No!" Felix says, making the decision for us.

A long, hard pause. "No?" the voice challenges.

"They're staying where they are," he says simply.

"I would advise against that," the voice warns. He sounds irritated. Annoyed. It's obvious he wasn't expecting to be challenged on this. "Right now I have you trained in my crosshairs and am trying to determine whether to trust you. Keeping them hidden behind cover doesn't exactly come across as trustworthy."

"Neither does threatening me by saying I'm trained in your crosshairs," Felix challenges. "Trust is a two-way street. Until I know that we can trust *you*, they're staying where they are."

Another pause, longer and colder than the first. "Remember your decision," the voice says.

Silence ensues the statement. The longer it stretches, the more I feel we've made a mistake. I scan the area for movement, strain my ears to pick up anything outside my own thoughts. Nothing. My eyes are drawn to my friend, an unflinching statue risking his life on the merest possibility that doing so might reunite him with his family. Flashbacks of the night Maya was killed come back to me, how I stood in the same no man's land Felix does now. A different fear grips now than the fear I felt that night—an impotent, paralyzing fear—knowing that any moment a bullet could take the life of someone I love and there's not a damn thing I can do to stop it. It's a slow torture. Waiting. Waiting. And then the front door opens.

Three men exit the home, the leader easy to spot even from this distance. His clothes are cleaner, his hair trimmed short and face stubble-free. Mr. Sawyer, Connor's father. Connor, for his part, is noticeably absent. Probably for the best. Mr. Sawyer smiles brightly our way, not a hint of worry on his features as he moves closer. A pistol sits holstered on his hip, more for show than anything. The assault rifles his men carry are all the firepower he needs. Unlike their leader, they wear no smiles, their eyes hidden behind dark sunglasses. I make note of it all: the weapons, their movements, everything. Sometimes the smallest detail can make all the difference.

"Felix!" he cries out, hands outstretched in welcome. "You're a sight for sore eyes, my young friend. An absolute sight!" He comes to a stop a dozen feet from Felix. "Friendly faces are too hard to come by these days."

"Thank you, Mr. Sawyer," Felix says.

"Please, call me Pete," Mr. Sawyer insists.

"Pete," Felix amends. "...It is good to see a friendly face."

Pete nods even as his smile shifts. "Always," he says. He takes in Felix's lack of shirt, at the general desperation washed across his face. His gaze lands on us, two strangers watching the exchange with our weapons held ready. "But I'm guessing you didn't travel all this way for a friendly visit."

"No sir, we didn't," Felix says. I can't see his face, but the apprehension lies thick in his voice. We've searched so many places already without anything to show for it. Felix knows our window is shrinking. If we don't find anything here, then where will we? "I'm looking for my family." He goes on to explain how we weren't here at the beginning of the collapse, briefly touching on what we've been through up until this point. "We've been searching for the past couple weeks, but nobody has seen them. I know you've been their friend for a long time...I thought they might have turned to you if they needed help."

The smile has long since faded from Pete's face, his mouth a hard, grim line. "That's a helluva story, son," he says. "But I'm sorry, I haven't seen Frank or Christina in months."

Even with his back to me, I can tell how hard the answer hits Felix. I can see it in the slump of his shoulders. In the hang of his head. So much must be running through his mind right now. This was our last, real hope at finding answers. Where do we go from here?

"I wish I had a different answer for you, Felix," Pete says. "I'm sorry."

Felix nods. "Thank you," he says. He straightens up and clears his throat. "Can you think of anywhere they might have gone to? Any mutual friends they might have tried, or any...I don't know, safe zones in the area?"

Pete shakes his head. "I'm sorry," he says. "Didn't have many mutual friends—none I can see them reaching out to anyway. As far as safe zones are concerned, I don't think there is such a thing anymore."

Felix nods again. "Yeah...You're probably right." He grows quiet a moment, as if suddenly unsure what to do with himself. "Anyway, thank you for your time all the same. We better get going though if we want to make it back before dark." He reaches out his hand to shake.

"You don't have to leave so soon," Pete says. "We're cooking up supper as we speak. You three are welcome to join us."

"I appreciate the offer, but we really do need to get going."

Pete nods. "Well...you take care of yourself," he tells Felix. "And if you ever need anything, you know where I am."

Felix's footsteps fall heavy as he makes his slow march back to us. He put so much hope in today. It's hard to see that hope leave him now. Tears don't well up in his eyes, nor do they grow cold in anger. Better that they did. To watch now as he shuts himself down, and his face forms an emotionless mask, is far worse.

"Felix—" I begin to say before he cuts me off with a shake of his head.

"I know, Moe," he says, voice thick. "I just need some time to process everything. To think, you know?"

I nod my understanding even though I remain concerned. Like a machine, he pulls on his shirt and readies his weapons once again. He takes point on our return trip, his own way of hiding his face from us. Leon and I share uneasy glances from time to time, each of us worried about our friend. I feel sick, a cold dread spreading throughout my body, yearning me to accept what I have refused to believe: that we will never find them. That they are truly gone.

It's a quiet procession, none of us much for words. As we walk, I can't help but feel as if something has changed. Without the low assurances and exchanges of hopeful optimism between us, it all feels too final. It feels as if we've failed. I continue to wrack my head for ideas, each one more hollow than the last.

To the north, giant thunderheads paint the sky in columns of white and gray, brooding in quiet promise. But we should reach the farm well before they reach us. We pass Hwy 160 once more, the wrecks on either side not darkening my spirits like earlier. A man can only feel so much at a time I suppose. From there, it's all autopilot, having searched these back roads the past few weeks: right turn, a sharp bend, and then two miles due north. Right turn, my eyes scan for movement. A sharp bend, my ears strain for threats. All is still. All is quiet.

Suddenly, Felix goes rigid, his hand reaching for his rifle as a crack of distant thunder reaches us. Leon and I follow suit, our rifles held at the ready.

Quiet.

Quiet.

And then I hear it: a distant boom, echoing across the countryside. Not the sound of thunder, but the sound of violence. Of death. A sound of terror ripped straight from my nightmares: gunshots. One look into Felix's eyes as he turns to face me, and I know there is no mistaking its direction. Due north. The direction of the farm.

Chapter 10: (Lauren)

It feels like I see his back more than his face these days. I watch it now even as it slowly disappears from my eyes, swallowed by the early morning dark. A sharp wind kicks up from the east, its icy breath penetrating the thin sweater I wear and leaving goosebumps along my arms. Still, I make no motion to retreat inside, the cold a welcome relief to the warm, stuffy walls. And despite the early hour, I'm not alone in rising.

"They already leave?" Julia asks.

"Yeah," I confirm. "They have a lot of ground to cover." I don't know the area, but I was shown the route they will take today. I don't know what's more worrying, the distance they must travel, or the bad blood between them and the ranch owner's son. A shiver overtakes me, more from nerves than the cold. *And so it begins,* I think to myself.

"It never gets easier, does it?" Julia asks me, pulling me from my thoughts.

"What doesn't?" I ask.

"The waiting. The worrying. All the dark thoughts that run through your mind while they're gone." Her eyes pierce mine. "It never gets easier."

I shake my head, understanding the feeling all too well. "No," I say. "It doesn't. If anything, it gets harder."

"I know what you mean," she says. "Kind of like you're only awarded so much luck. Like things can only go right for so long before they go wrong."

Her words are an echo of my own thoughts. Each time they return, safe and unhurt, all I can do is wonder when the time will come that they won't. I thought I was growing cynical, but it appears I'm not alone in my fears.

"Exactly," I say. "From my experience, something always goes wrong."

"Yeah," she says. It grows quiet, each of us lost in our own thoughts. Then silence breaks with a breath of laughter.

"What?" I ask, curious.

"Nothing, really," she says. "It's just nice to skip all the bullshit and speak honestly for once. That's why I like talking with you: you don't sugar coat your words and act like everything's going to be alright. I swear, it's like they've treated me with kid gloves ever since I got back—like they don't want to upset me by speaking about anything unpleasant. I mean I was abducted for Christ's sake. I had men grope me and tell me all the vile things they were going to do to me. I know as well as anyone how dark the world is. I'm not going to forget anytime soon."

Her voice grows harsh, bitter as she continues. When she's finished, I'm left without words, uncertain how to respond. I wasn't expecting half of what she said. She breathes deep and looks away, hiding her face from view. I don't think she expected it either.

"Sorry," she says, embarrassed. "You didn't need to hear all that."

I think back on these past few weeks, and I begin to understand her frustration. I've noticed how protective her brothers are over her, how her parents coddle and hover, as if afraid the Animals will arrive any moment to reclaim their captive. I may not know her well, but the girl I've gotten to know seems strong. Independent. I'm surprised she hasn't said anything before now.

"I may not have needed to hear it, but that doesn't mean nobody else should." I watch her mull over my words, nodding slightly till her mouth forms a small smile.

"Like I said: that's why I like talking with you."

"No sugar-coated bullshit?" I ask, sharing her smile.

"Exactly," she says with a small laugh.

"Anytime," I say. "Seriously. If you ever want to talk or vent or whatever. I'm here."

I see the gratitude in her eyes as they meet mine once again. "Thank you," she says. "Same goes for you. I'll be here."

I smile and say my appreciations even though I know the chances of me confiding in her are slim. She's a nice girl, and I know she means what she says, but I already know myself too well. Ninety-nine times out of one-hundred I would rather keep my issues bottled up than let them become a burden to others. It's an ingrained part of me.

A haze of blue light spills over the eastern skyline—an early precursor to the approaching dawn. Soon the sun will rise, and with it, the rest of the family. No sense in continuing to stand here, worrying. Time to embrace the day.

"C'mon," I tell Julia. "Let's check on the chickens. Maybe we'll have enough eggs to fix us some omelets."

Unfortunately, omelets are not in the cards for us. Even combined with yesterday's haul, there weren't enough eggs to go around. Instead, we make do with a handful of Brussel sprouts and half an apple apiece. It takes the worse edge off the hunger, but it burns away quickly as the day progresses. I work beside Emily, readying the farm's outer perimeter against intruders. With our greenhouse project well underway, defending the property has moved to our top priority.

With such a large area to cover, we keep things simple. We staple signs along the fence posts and trees trunks near the perimeter, warning intruders of deadly force if they enter the property. Once inside the property, things get kicked up a notch. We set traps. Some as simple as potholes meant to twist ankles and trip them up; others are more elaborate, designed to severely maim or kill. Most of the latter are laid out behind the barn and beyond the apple orchard—the areas thickest with trees and brush, and therefore, the most likely paths people would take if trying to conceal their approach to the house. As for the pastures, we're relying heavily on our lookout's ability to spot an approaching threat and raise an alarm. It's not without flaws, but it's a start.

I feel my hand begin to cramp as I staple another sign into the fence post. It's mind-numbing work. I know it must be done, but I can't help but feel I could be of better use than writing and stapling. I'd sooner help set up the *Home Alone* traps Vince spoke of, or disappear into the hills beyond the farm to hunt. But I know neither is likely with Richard in charge of the farm's defense. Not that there was a vote or anything. He just took up the role and nobody thought to question him. I could challenge the issue, but I don't see the point. Let him believe he's in charge. I can put up with these tasks if it keeps the peace and things continue to run smoothly.

Nearer the house, I watch Grace help tend to our greenhouses. She's shown a real knack for it. With everything planted, the day to day management has been taken over by Virginia. She's no farmer, but her care of our crops seems to be working. Stalks and shoots sprout from the various garden beds we've installed. Now, believing we could see a harvest before winter doesn't seem as far-fetched as it once did.

Virginia says something, and Grace tips her head back in laughter. I smile at the sight of them. They've grown close these past few weeks. Virginia has all but claimed Grace as her assistant, and she's taken it in stride. I'm thankful for Virginia: both for taking my sister under her wing, and for finding ways to keep a smile on her face. I've tried telling her as much, but she was quick to brush it aside, insisting it was her pleasure while smoothly reverting the attention to Grace, whom she sang praises of in kind. I swear, it's as if humility is ingrained in their family. Except for Richard of course. But then again, he's not a direct relation either.

"Your hand cramping?" Emily asks as she staples yet another sign.

I laugh. "Yeah. You too?"

"It's starting to," she says, flexing her hand to work it out.

"You're lucky," I say. "I've felt mine off and on since this morning. Almost felt like detention, writing all those lines over and over: Private Property. Do Not Enter. Deadly Force."

Emily laughs. "Is that a real thing?" she asks. "I thought that was only in the movies."

I'm not sure myself. I never went to the detentions I was issued and dropped out shortly after. I was never meant to be a scholar. That was supposed to be Grace.

"Trust me, it's real," Jerry chimes in. He works inside the fence line, digging potholes to trip up unsuspecting intruders. "At least it was for Mrs. Alger. Took her for German 1, freshman year. The problem was the class took place right after lunch, so I was tardy half the time. It was either write lines in detention or take a zero for participation credit. I took the lines, and applied for Spanish the next semester."

"Yeah, I can see how that would make you hate the subject," I say, amused.

"Nah, that wasn't it," Jerry says. "Nadia Hirsch and her family moved to Michigan over winter break. She's the reason I signed up for the class in the first place." He grins, eyes glazed over as if lost in memory. "She was definitely worth the lines."

"Should have known," Emily says, shaking her head. "I'm just glad I'm older than you. I mean, watching you hit on my friends definitely had its moments, but I'd have never lived it down if you had actually hooked up with them."

Jerry's doesn't say anything. His grin gives him away.

"Shut up!" She says. "Are you serious? With who?"

Jerry's laugh is a deep, fully bellied thing. I haven't heard it much since we've been here. Ever since the night they rescued his sister and cousin, he's been quiet. Withdrawn. I thought it was just his personality. Had I grown up with him, I would have known how unlike himself he's been. It's nice seeing a bit of his old self shine through.

"A gentleman never tells," he winks. "Besides, I've been sworn to secrecy. I mean, they were my sister's friends too, you know."

"Friends?" Emily asks. "As in more than one?" She shakes her head as he begins to laugh again. "Never mind. It's probably better I don't know."

She tries to sound disapproving, but it's not long before she too is laughing. Ray and TJ smile as they listen in. I can't help but smile myself at this moment of normalcy: of cousins ribbing one another over the past, their younger kin listening intently, wondering if the stories they hear are a foreshadow of their own to come. Only for Ray and TJ, that won't be the case. The world of high school parties and chasing after girls and acting without inhibitions will never be known to them. I feel bad for them all of a sudden. I don't know of that world either, but I also had never expected to. It's hard to miss what you never believed you'd have. Still, it's nice to share this moment. To pretend.

Then the moment passes, and the real world reasserts itself in all its brutality.

Jerry's laugh is silenced, its abrupt stop like a song suddenly losing its percussion. His eyes go wide with fear, with panic. The world slows. Someone is cursing, screaming. I reach for my Glock on instinct, swiveling my hips to meet the approaching threat. Too late. An arm wraps around my throat, cold metal digs against my head. A gruff voice yells into my ear, daring me to pull out my gun. Instead, I release my grip and it's unholstered by another's hand. A second voice commands Jerry and the boys to disarm and drop to their knees with their hands laced behind their heads. They comply. I feel a rope bind my hands behind my back. I chance a look at Emily, her face livid with angry tears falling down her cheek.

"You're a pretty one, aren't you?" my assailant asks me. I feel my skin crawl as he slowly tucks my hair behind my ear. I can smell his breath, sour and coated with alcohol. It's a familiar smell, one that sends a shiver down my spine. He leans close. "You be a good girl and do what you're told," he warns. "I'd hate for anything to happen to that pretty face of yours."

They order us to move. My assailant keeps close, using me as a human shield as we enter the pasture. Our sentry has finally noticed and raises the alarm. Our people hear it and frantically abandon their tasks to get into a defensive position, guns flying into hands as they run toward the cover of our greenhouses. It's all a blur, my eyes focused on my sister's scared face as she peeks over the hood of an SUV.

"*Get down, you idiot!*" I think to myself.

As if hearing my silent scream, Virginia pulls her back and takes her place. I watch her lean her rifle across the hood, the action so strange to see from her. Even stranger is the cold hatred etched into her features, the warm, matronly woman I've gotten to know nowhere to be seen. I shouldn't be surprised. She knows the brutality of this world the same as any of us. It was her son who was taken by the Animals, after all. It's not something she would soon forget.

Our captors aren't deterred, continuing to march in tight formation behind us so as not to provide a clear shot to the family. Only at the gate do we stop.

"I'm not one for speeches, so I'll keep this short," my assailant yells. "Here's what's about to happen: Y'all are gonna lay down your weapons, and two of my men are gonna enter the house and take some provisions. Bitch and moan all you like, I don't care. It's happening either way. The alternative is blood and bullets. People dying. Some us, some of you." He pauses for effect, shaking his head gravely. "I don't want that. So lay down your guns, and let's get on with it."

There's hesitation among the family. Indecision ripples between them as eyes are drawn one of two ways: to Richard, an ugly sneer on his face as he stares our captors down, grip on his rifle unwavering; and to Marie, her face angry and eyes fearful, never leaving her daughter. Of course, it's Richard who speaks first.

"Don't piss on my shoes and tell me it's raining," Richard yells back. "We lay down our guns, what's to stop you from killing us? And for that matter, how do we know your guns are even loaded?"

My assailant raises his gun in the air and shoots. My ears immediately start ringing, the shot loud and unexpected. "Is that answer enough for you?" he asks. The man pauses, allowing Richard the chance to answer. He doesn't. "Now for your first question, it's like I said: we try and kill you, and some of us get killed in the process. I'd like to avoid that. What you need to ask yourselves is if whatever's in that house is worth your lives or not. That's what this all boils down to." He pauses again, letting his message sink in. "So what's it going to be?"

"Everyone put down your guns," Mrs. Taylor shouts a moment later, laying her own rifle at her feet. "The bastard's right. Whatever they take isn't worth dying for." A few heed her warning, laying down their guns to avoid bloodshed. Others waver, taking their lead from Richard.

"Don't listen to her!" Richard yells back. "Drop your weapons and they'll just kill us anyway."

"You don't know that!" Mr. Taylor yells, backing up his wife. "They can't shoot us all before we retaliate. We fight, people are going to get killed. We comply, there's a chance we all make it out alive. It's the only choice we can make."

Someone else speaks out, and then another, and another, until there's a dozen raised voices yelling back and forth at each other. I can't keep track of what's being said or who said it. Hatred for these men flares through me as I watch the family turn on each other. I feel the inside of my boot glow hot with a cruel desire. I let it pass. I must wait. Waiting, however, is not on our captor's agenda.

A second gunshot sounds, effectively silencing the family's argument. "Let me simplify things for you," he says. "Either lay down your weapons or someone dies." He scans the hostages he's captured: Emily, Jerry, TJ, Ray, and myself. "We'll start with the little one." To my left, one of the men levels a pistol to the back of TJ's skull. "You've got ten seconds!"

He begins his countdown at ten, and most of the family have dropped their weapons by the time he reaches nine. He continues even as arguments commence, those who've dropped their weapons pleading for the others to see sense. One by one, weapons are lowered till only Richard remains stubborn in his opposition.

"You're making a mistake," he yells.

Five!

"For God's sake, lower the damn gun!" Ted yells, desperate now that his son faces death.

Four!

"They'll kill us if I do!" Richard insists.

Three!

Ted picks up his gun and levels it at Richard. "You don't, and I'll kill you myself!" he says. There's no bluff in his voice.

Two!

Richard looks to Ted, his surprise only matched by his anger. His glare is harsh as he stares down Ted and the family, still reluctant to let go of his gun.

One!

With a roar of frustration, Richard finally lays down his gun. A hard-edged moment passes as we wait for our captors to make a move.

"Wise decision," my assailant says. I can hear the smile in his voice, the contentment at having won. It's nauseating. "Now, just sit tight and this will all be over soon. I'm a man of my word. So long as none of you do anything stupid, nobody has to die today."

Two of his men slip forward and hop the gate, a duffle bag hanging over each of their shoulders. If looks could kill, they'd be dead a dozen times over as the family stares them down. Yet nobody reaches for their gun. Nobody makes a move against them as they enter the house. Minutes pass, the tension filling the air making time move slowly. It's quiet as we wait, either side opting to remain silent while the men loot the house. I'm thankful for that at least. With emotions as charged as they are, it wouldn't take much to set things off.

Finally, they re-emerge from the house, both of their packs bulging with looted supplies. I feel the anger rolling off the family. I feel it in myself. We've scraped and clawed and struggled for everything we have. Seeing the smug looks on their faces as they steal what we fought so hard for is a bitter pill to swallow. But I force it down. This loss will set us back, but we'll survive. This won't be the end of us. I repeat the facts over and over, reminding myself to keep calm.

They join us once again with a nod to my assailant. They must be satisfied with their haul. The bastards.

"Almost over," my assailant says assuredly. "Time we make our exit. We'll be keeping these five to ensure safe passage off the property. Don't reach for your guns. Don't move from where you are. We'll let your people go as soon as we are certain we're safe from retaliation."

I can sense the family bristle at this. That they've kept their anger in check so far is no easy feat. Even now they let it simmer, allowing their hateful glares to say what they won't allow their voices to.

"Alright then, you five turn around nice and slow," he orders. I turn as instructed, getting my first look at my assailant. His face is like an old strip of leather. Tough. Weatherbeaten. His eyes are dark, both in intent and color. They lock on mine and I fight with all I have not to show him the fear he searches for. He smirks as if amused by my defiance. "Let's go."

Slowly, our captors make their way back across the pasture. Their guns stay trained on us the entire way. It keeps the family in line. It also keeps us from trying any desperate bids for freedom.

"It really is too bad we must say goodbye so soon," my assailant tells me. His eyes probe my body, his twisted leer leaving no doubt of his thoughts.

"You could come with us, you know," he says. "I'd take care of you...so long as you took care of me." On either side of him, his men snigger and grin their amusement. I block it out, their cheerful smiles making my blood boil.

We finally reach the edge of the pasture, returning to where this whole ordeal was put into motion. The wind has scattered our stacks of flyers. They litter the ground around us, their warnings like a bad joke after this afternoon. How effective they were in keeping the wolves at bay. They stop at the fence line and order us to turn around as they pick themselves over. My assailant is last to move.

"Last chance," he says. He leans close, pressing his body against mine and speaking quietly into my ear. "You'll never be safe here. You realize that yes? I can give you a better life than this." He traces a greasy finger down my cheek and it's all I can do but remain still.

"What happened here today? It will happen again, mark my words. Deep down, you know I'm right." He pauses, continuing to brush his finger against my cheek. "So what do you think? Will you come with me?"

How deluded is this man? How could he possibly think that after everything he's done, I could possibly want to go with him? Perhaps he doesn't. Perhaps it's merely his last bit of fun, goading his victim before he takes his leave. I don't know. But the anger I've barely held in check comes spilling out my mouth before I can check myself.

"Go fuck yourself," I say. "Take what you've stolen, and leave. Don't come back. You do, and I'll kill you myself."

His laugh is a short, brutish thing. "Feisty," he says, tracing his hand through my hair. "But stupid." He grabs a fist full and forces my head back. There's a cruel amusement in his eyes. His smirk twisted. He pulls out a blade and traces it along my throat, drawing shouts of protest from my friends. With guns trained on them, it's all they can do. "Piece of advice: don't make threats unless you can carry through...for instance, if I threatened to slit your pretty throat if you disrespected me again, you would have to take me seriously. Right?"

He breathes deep, his breath creating a suffocating bog between us. I fight to remain here. To remain in control. But my legs begin to shake, tears build behind my eyes. My body betrays me. I feel paralyzed. Can't move. Trapped between now and then. The world swims in and out of focus. My heart beats hard. Fast. Too fast. Can't breathe.

There's a sound like muffled thunder. A spray of warmth splashes across my face, my captor falling to the ground with his head blown open. People scream. Scatter. One by one the rest of the captors fall. I watch it all from my knees. When did I leave my feet? I try to stand but am overcome with a sense of vertigo. Can't focus, my mind hazy. I hear my name as if hollered from far away. I turn and only then does the world make sense again.

Morgan is on his knees beside me. His face is flushed. Eyes worried. Panicked. It's sobering.

"Are you alright?" he asks. I don't think it's the first time he's asked.

"I'm alright," I say, voice shaky. I clear my throat. "I'm alright."

He hugs me close, and in his arms, I feel the tension leave me. But then I register yells, the sound of alarm around me. I turn to see Felix on his knees beside TJ, his body still, face covered in blood. Beyond him, the family sprints across the open pasture, Ted outpacing all but Richard.

"Is he?" The words barely make it past my lips, but Felix makes it a point to answer, more for Morgan's sake than my own.

"He's alive," he says. "He's alive."

Chapter 11: (Morgan)

Her head rests in the crook of my shoulder, my rough, calloused hand entwined with hers. She may think it's me who lends her strength, but without her touch, it's I who would unravel. We sit on the back porch, away from the others, the air in the house too tense and stuffy for me to handle. I breathe deep, the sweat and oils of her hair filling my nostrils. I should find comfort in the scent, in feeling the warmth of her body beside my own. But all I'm reminded of is a dirty hand yanking her head back, and a steel blade held against her throat. Worse, I'm reminded of the terror in her eyes—of the trembling of her body as she struggled for words. I've never seen her like that. Not my strong, fearless girl. It scared me. So much so that when I saw a clear shot, I took it. I put a bullet through that bastard's head without warning, without a plan, without any consideration of what was to follow. Now I think of TJ and have to repress a chill all over again.

He is lucky to be alive. Had the bullet struck an inch to the left, he wouldn't be. When I first laid eyes on him moments after the shooting, I thought surely he was dead: everyone surrounding him, face pale and covered in blood. As it is, he will keep his life for the price of an ear. Thank God. Or rather, thank Julia and Felix for their wits and quick action in time of panic. Together, they were able to stop the bleeding and save his life. I don't know how. They worked behind closed doors, Ted and Richard the only other occupants in the room. Even now, that cold dread is slow to fade. All I could do was think, *not again. Please, don't let another person I love die because of my actions.*

"It's not your fault, son," my father said to me. *"Nobody's to blame but the men who did this."*

Perhaps he's right. But I know his opinion isn't shared by all. I've become accustomed to Richard's glares, of his highbrow attitude and general unpleasantness. I expect nothing less from him. But when Ted left the room, the look he gave me was one of pure venom.

There was no mistaking the blame in his eyes as he saw me. I won't soon forget it. The worst part is that despite my father's words, at least part of me knows I deserve it.

The screen door creaks open, drawing my focus away from my morose thoughts. Aunt Virginia. She walks past Leon and Emily who sit in the twin rocking chairs beside the door, past Julia and Felix who emerged from the house not twenty minutes ago, desperate for fresh air, all the way to the far corner where Lauren and I sit. She takes a seat beside me with a long sigh, stretching her legs past the edge of the porch. After a minute she reaches into her pocket and withdraws a capped tube, inside of which holds a single cigarette. I watch her uncap the tube and roll the cigarette between her fingers with practiced ease.

"Still hear it calling your name?" I ask.

"I did today," she says, continuing to play with the cigarette. "Came damn close to answering too, if I'm being honest." She pauses, staring intently at the white stick in her hand. As if finding her resolve, she shakes her head and caps it back inside the tube that has been its home the past six years, ever since she learned she was to be a grandmother. "But then I reminded myself what it would cost me. Decided I couldn't do that to myself."

"That's good," I say. "Though I doubt anyone would have blamed you. Not after today."

"Yeah, it was one hell of a day wasn't it?" she says.

I agree, glumly.

"Grace doing alright?" Lauren asks.

"She's fine," Aunt Virginia assures her. "She's a sweetheart, your sister. Been talking with Ray most the evening. I think it's helping him cope with what happened earlier."

"That's good," Lauren says. "I should check in on her though. Make sure she's holding up alright, herself." She squeezes my hand once and then rises to her feet, leaving my side cold in her absence.

My aunt watches her leave with a smile on her face. "She's a right sweetheart herself," she comments.

The word barely scratches the surface of the girl I love. I would say as much, but even I have difficulty putting it into words. Not only that, there are more pressing questions on my mind.

"How's TJ?" I ask.

"Still asleep," she says. "Probably a good thing. He's gonna need a lot of rest in the coming days."

"And Jerry? Ray?" I ask. "How are they doing?"

"Hard to say with Jerry," she says with a sigh. "He's been so quiet as it is...this afternoon certainly isn't doing him any favors. We'll have to keep an eye on him. As for Ray, I think he'll be fine given some time. He's still pretty shook up though."

Of course he is. How could he not be given what he went through: assaulted, held at gunpoint, nearly seeing a friend die before his eyes? Not to mention the aftermath—the screams and panic, the smell of blood and death. He wasn't ready for it. Nobody ever is their first time encountering such things. I think of Grace, of all the dark deeds she's been victim to since Denver. That she's weathered it all and still has the capacity to lend strength to others says much about her. My aunt pegged it when she called her a sweetheart, though the girl is so much more than that. She's a fighter. A survivor, like her sister. Ray is lucky to have her shoulder to lean on.

"I think the same can be said of most of us," I say.

She nods. "Yeah. You're right about that." She shifts beside me, angling her face toward mine. I remain looking forward, knowing she wouldn't have sought me out like this without a reason. "That's why I came out here," she says. "Wanted to make sure you weren't beating yourself up too bad."

I force a smile. "Of course not," I lie. "Why would you think that?"

Her laugh is a soft, tired thing. Genuine, unlike my smile. "Because I held you in my arms the day you were born," she says. "And because from then on, I've watched you grow into the young man you've become. You've always been harder on yourself than anyone else could be—always took the blame even when it wasn't yours to carry. Grandma's vase, Uncle Joe's Mustang, the gardening shed.

You've been covering for your sister and cousins your whole life. You think we didn't know?"

Each incident she lists plays back in my mind, snapshots of that simpler time when the breaking of a treasured vase brought about a fear to chill your blood, and getting in a fender bender while joyriding an uncle's car felt like a death sentence. Instances that were never my fault, never my idea, but which I somehow ended up involved with. I don't know what compelled me to take the fall so often. I never really thought about it before. Everything always happened so fast, so quick, I just did what I thought best. Still, it's strange to know my actions didn't fool anyone.

"Why didn't you say anything?" I ask. "Why didn't my parents?"

She shrugs. "Sometimes we did. Mostly though we let you make your own mistakes, your own decisions. You learn from them the best that way. You may have been the one who received the groundings and the docked allowances and what have you, but trust me, that doesn't mean the others got away unscathed. There's punishment in watching others suffer because of your actions, a guilt that claws at your insides, knowing you're to blame for their predicament. Your sister, your cousins, they know that guilt. It's the same guilt that's eating away at you, even if you don't deserve it."

She delivers this last line with the air of a teacher arriving at their point. She's right of course. Whether I deserve it or not, that guilt has settled deep inside me, incessant—constantly reminding me of how bad things could have gone. An inch, maybe less, and I might have seen another person I love die before my eyes. I may not have raided the farm or pulled the trigger, but it was my rage which set the event in motion. Do I really deserve none of the blame? Or is this merely self-pity?

"It's alright, you don't have to say anything," she says after a long pause in which I struggle to respond. "Just know that what happened wasn't your fault. It may not feel that way, but it's the truth. You did what you did for the same reason you do just about everything else—to protect your family. In today's world, that's all any of us can do. Don't apologize or feel guilty for trying to do that."

Later that night, I'm awakened by Vince after a few hours of fitful sleep. Sentry duty. Wordlessly, I throw on my boots and make my way to our lookout tower atop the roof. Although nest would be a more appropriate term. It's a 4'x4' box made of thick plywood and metal sheeting. It's not pretty, but it does what we need it to do: provide a fortified space for us to hunker down and keep watch.

It's quiet out. Peaceful. The sky freckled with stars which will soon fade as morning draws nearer. A half-moon sits low to the west, casting a ghostly light upon the land. Vapor billows from my mouth with each breath, the cold air welcome after a night in the warm house. The wind rises, slicing through my layers, reminding me of the gales that chased us yesterday morning.

Yesterday. Hardly any time has passed since we set out, yet things feel so different from then. We knew the odds were against us when we went to the Sawyer's ranch. The odds haven't been in our favor for some time. But despite that fact, there was hope, small as it may have been. Try as I might, that same hope cannot be summoned now. Yes, guilt still weighs on my mind despite the assurances of others, but it's more than that. It's the fact that we were attacked—that a half dozen men were able to hold my family at their mercy and nearly got away with enough supplies that would have set us back weeks—time we cannot afford with winter drawing closer.

I dread the rising of the sun, of facing the changes I've felt in the air since I saw that blade pushed to Lauren's throat. Fear. The farm is swathed in it. Not since Rockridge has it gripped my family so thoroughly. In the weeks we've been here, that fear has slowly lessened over time. Each greenhouse, each fortification, each effort made to ensure our survival adding to the belief that this place might be the safe haven we've all longed for. And then yesterday happened. Not the Animals, but wolves all the same. Now that fear is back. All it took was a fresh reminder.

Despite my misgivings, daybreak will not be held at bay. First to disappear is the moon, it's trajectory finally sinking past the mountains to the west. Next goes the stars, thousands of sparkling lights petering out one by one until the sky unfurls into a curtain of cerulean blue. Light spills from the east, spreading all along the horizon. Our lone rooster crows it's morning song as activity stirs in the house beneath me. Paul, Leon's father, climbs the ladder and joins me.

"Morgan," he says in greeting.

"Mr. T," I reply. Were this the world before I might have asked him which fool he pitied today. He would have chuckled and answered with some reference I didn't understand, and I'd have smiled and laughed all the same, not because of what was said, but because I've always found humor in the nickname—at the vast difference between him and the A-Team star. Mr. T is thick with muscle, bearded, hair combed into an iconic mohawk. Mr. Thomas is of middling height, lean, bespeckled with a shaved head. Still, I haven't called him by his proper name in years. Leon's mother is Mrs. Thomas. But his father will always be Mr. T to me.

"How's Ray doing?" I ask instead.

"He's still pretty shell-shocked by the whole ordeal," he says. He sounds as tired as he looks. No doubt last night was a restless one. "We've talked, though. I think he'll be alright given some time."

"I'm sure he will be," I say. "It's a lot to deal with. Especially being so young."

He looks away for a moment, the early morning sunlight deepening the worry lines on his face, making him seem years older. "That's one of the worst parts about all this," he says. "My wife and I, your parents, we're already old. We've lived and loved, raised families, experienced what this world has to offer." He shakes his head solemnly. "But Ray? Leon? You?" He splays out his hands as if reaching a conclusion he can't put into words. "You're all so young...so young. You have so much life ahead of you. But with things the way they are, I'm afraid of what those lives will be like...afraid they might not be any longer than my own."

His words are proof of the fear I've felt spreading among us. Worse, it's warranted. I wish I could say something, do something to convince him all will be alright. But I can't even convince myself.

"We're here now," I say. "That's the important thing. We just have to take things a day at a time."

My words ring hollow in the air between us, my attempt at comfort falling flat with my lack of conviction. Mr. T nods all the same, averting his eyes as if embarrassed at having admitted his fears aloud. Awkwardly, I excuse myself from the conversation, suddenly eager to escape the roof. I hit the ground and make my way toward Lauren who's taken the liberty of collecting my morning ration.

"Thank's," I say. "How'd you sleep?" Despite her assurances, I'm still worried about her. The image of her at that asshole's mercy, terrified and trembling, won't soon fade from my memory.

"Better than you," she replies.

I force a smile. "That's not saying much." Indeed. Last night was filled with nightmares, all variations on yesterday's attack. I watched Lauren's throat slit open a dozen times. Watched bullets explode through the skulls of my family. Felt their blood soak through my jeans and stain my hands as I fell to my knees. My fault. All my fault. Twice I woke up, sweaty, confused, heart thrashing wildly against my chest. And then, like so many nights before, it was a gentle hand which calmed me—her fingers tracing along my jaw and weaving through my hair, her breath warm against my neck as soft words were whispered.

She reaches out that same hand now and draws my face to hers. "Get out of that head of yours," she says. "I'm alright."

I nod, accepting what she says with a deep breath. I've been wound so tightly the past 24 hours. I need to calm myself. Things can't be as bad as I've made them out to be. Another deep breath and I manage a smile, small but genuine.

"That's better," she says. Her lips find mine and for a brief moment, I don't have to focus on staying calm or remind myself that things will be alright. In that moment everything is. It's not until we break apart that I am brought back down to earth. Not immediately. Not until I've finished with my morning's ration and we sit chatting with Felix and Julia do I hear the commotion. Raised voices. Emily's.

Richard's. Turning heads and gathering bodies outside the kitchen door let us know of the source. I push through until I enter the kitchen.

"Rash and reckless," Richard shouts, the first words of his I clearly make out. His eyes find me and his voice turns sharper. "He's lucky he didn't get anyone killed!"

Emily's back is to me as she lashes back. "You're such a fucking hypocrite. Both of you." She points between Richard and Ted. "You're really going to stand there and act like you weren't as rash? Weren't as reckless? Ted had to put a gun to your damn head before you came to reason. Or have you forgotten?"

"I remember, girl," he snarls. "But ask yourself, did I fire the first shot? Was it me who decided to act without thinking, and nearly got TJ killed? No. It was him!" The eyes throughout the kitchen and those standing outside the door are drawn to me. Ted fixes me with the same cold stare he did last night, his anger and blame directed solely on me. I expected as much. What I did not expect was to see that same coldness reflected in the eyes of so many others. Less perceivable perhaps, but there under the surface.

It's not your fault. I've heard this repeated from the lips of my mother and father, my Aunt Virginia and Lauren. They would have me believe them because they believe my intentions pure. As if that somehow negates the consequences. Richard's words echo back to me and I nearly double over with the weight of my guilt. Not because of the words themselves, but because of the harsh truth that the others refuse to tell me.

I should say something. Defend myself. If I don't, Richard will take the opportunity to sow seeds of doubt in me. It's the game he's been playing since we set out from Rockridge. Only now, he finally has something tangible. Politics. I hated them in the old world and I have no time for them now. So I don't raise my voice. Don't speak my case. I turn my back and walk away, those gathered at the kitchen door parting for me without being asked. Lauren makes to come with me but I shake my head, stopping her. She doesn't understand but allows herself to fall behind. I don't understand either. All I know is that right now, what I need most is to be left alone.

Chapter 12: (Lauren)

The days grow colder, the slanted rays of the sun cooled by harsh winds which sweep through the valley in the late mornings and afternoons. Fires burn in the living room fireplace at night, turning the space into a giant dorm as many forgo privacy for warmth. The nights themselves are bitter things, the cold sharp, and penetrating. Leaves of red and gold litter the ground, the trees they once belonged to nearly stripped bare save for the thin patches desperately holding on against the inevitable.

Deep autumn. The season has settled over us like an overnight snow, the likes of which, I fear, are fast on their way. How long till we wake to a world of frost and ice—when the fiery hues of autumn lay buried under layers of white, and the promise of spring's first bloom seem impossibly out of sight? Either way, whether it be days or weeks, I can't help but feel we're woefully unprepared for what is to come.

I try to convince myself we will be, and for our part, we've done all we can to prepare. We've stockpiled a small amount of food and our greenhouses continue to show promise. Already we've harvested two vans full of radishes and turnips, and more have been planted in their place. The memory of Grace's prideful face when she and Virginia announced they were ready for harvest brings a smile to my lips. I only hope the rest of our greenhouses yield similar results. Our lives may soon depend on them.

Our defenses have been strengthened, both along the farm's perimeter and closer to the home. The house itself has become a fortress. All of the windows have been boarded up with plywood, strategically placed sniper holes spaced throughout. Guns are carried on us at all times, every magazine we have filled and at the ready. I tell myself it's enough: that the home's defenses will hold and keep us safe. We have the firepower. The bodies. Plans for even deeper fortifications. And yet, I'm not so easily assured. I can't help but feel we're putting all of our eggs into one basket, relying too heavily on our excess of bullets to keep the wolves at bay. I've voiced my concerns, but nothing has come of it.

"What else can we do?"

It's the question asked whenever I've brought it up: a question, admittedly, I don't have an answer to. Perhaps there isn't one. Perhaps making a stand behind our walls is our best option given the circumstances surrounding us. I don't know. And if I'm being honest, my biggest concern isn't so much our plans, but Richard's overwhelming influence in them. Since we were attacked, he's essentially taken over as the de facto leader of the family. Only Mrs. Taylor seems to hold any weight against him. But despite sharing some of my concerns, she has no more solutions than I do.

"I understand, Lauren," she said to me. *"But I don't know what other options we have. He's not an easy man to like, but he does have experience that we don't...until we can think of an alternative we have to have faith he knows what he's doing."*

Easier said than done. I can hardly think of the man without bitterness filling my mouth. For weeks, it was out of indignation on Morgan's behalf. Casting doubt on his ideas, voicing snide comments out the corner of his mouth, making him seem foolish when he would leave the farm in search of Felix's family. Now, such tactics are unneeded. The doubt in Morgan has already been planted, been spread among the family. Somehow, most of the fallout from our attack has landed on him. It's not anger they feel so much as disappointment, as if he were a child who ought to have known better. The hypocrites. How quick they are to forget the things he's done—the danger he's faced and the lengths he's gone to protect us. He's proven himself a leader yet they look at him as a fool. I suppose it doesn't help that he has done nothing to defend himself.

Something's changed in him. From the beginning, I was drawn by his presence, by the quiet strength he possessed. That strength has made myself stronger, better. It's what brought us here; on this small piece of land where we fight to build a future. It's something I haven't felt since we were attacked. I've tried talking with him, but he's always quick to brush my concerns aside, insisting all is well. If I didn't know him as I do, I might believe him: might let the forced smiles and false assurances convince me he really is alright. As it is, they only serve to highlight the opposite.

I work beside him now, helping to place barbed wire around our greenhouses. Sharpened stakes protrude from the ground at angles, lengths of barbed wire linking them together. The greenhouses themselves have been arrayed in a concave defensive line near the house, mounds of hard-packed dirt filling the gaps between bumpers, yet another line of defense we can utilize. Little by little, this once quiet farm has turned into something out of a war novel, the warm memories contained within the walls and echoing across the fields now buried under layers of fear and stress—of bullets and barbed wire. If Felix's family were to return today, would they even recognize the place?

I glance up at Felix in the watchtower, his face pulled into an emotionless grimace as he surveys our perimeter. He's pulled away even more than Morgan since we were attacked. When I think of Felix I think of a quick smile, of an easy demeanor and unfailing optimism. I haven't seen either since he called off the search for his family.

"It's been weeks...we've checked everywhere I could think of...what else am I supposed to do?"

I wish I knew, but I don't even know how to be there for him let alone answer that question. It's not just me. Emily and Leon seem as lost as I am these days, neither knowing how to help any better than I do. It's been demoralizing. I want to do something, anything, but I've been second guessing myself at every turn. Besides, I don't know that it's my place to bring up his family at all. I feel as if I know them from the countless stories I've heard: the kindly aunt, and jovial uncle, and cousins with all their quirks and traits. I can picture each in my mind's eye as one would imagine characters from a book. That's the problem. All I know of them is what I've been told, what I've imagined. I've never felt the warmth of his aunt's hand as we were introduced, or heard the deep-bellied laugh of his uncle after one of his famous one-liners. We're strangers. That's the simple truth of it. Better to leave it alone than overstep my bounds.

The afternoon passes quickly, focused as we are on our tasks. That and the fact that the days grow shorter. As has been our custom, we pack up for the day as the sun begins to set, returning to the house where awaits our paltry rations. Though no one complains, hunger remains with us long after the last bite, our constant companion. I haven't been able to save much of anything lately, our rations have been so small. The emergency stash I've kept for Grace is pathetic, enough for two days at the most. I eye my sister's small frame with deep worry, knowing how thin we are stretched with the approaching season. I need to figure out a way to save more.

Soon there is a call for quiet and the eyes and ears throughout the living room and kitchen fall on Richard. I roll my own eyes before they too seek him out. Every evening for the past couple weeks has been the same. Richard calls for order and proceeds to ramble on in his drone-like way on matters about the farm. It's part progress report, part rally speech, both of which fall short of the desired effect.

"We're making good progress on our defenses; We can't afford to get complacent; Always stay vigilant; Remember the procedure if we're attacked."

On and on he goes, oblivious, it seems, at the unenthusiastic response from his audience. He is trying though. Have to at least give him that. But he isn't one to inspire. The foreboding air among us remains as thick as ever. If there is any relief had from his speech, it's in it's ending.

"Well that was illuminating," Emily says, speaking lowly so only we can hear. It makes me smile. She doesn't like Richard any more than I do. Morgan doesn't share my humor.

"Not tonight, Em," he says tiredly.

"What?" she challenges. "Just saying, you'd think we were children the way he repeats himself every freaking night. It's annoying."

"And complaining about it isn't?" he asks.

Here we go, I think to myself. The bickering between them has steadily gotten worse. Emily has never been one to tame her tongue or keep her opinions quiet. She creates waves while Morgan has taken to avoiding them altogether, content to shuffle along with his head down and let others steer the ship. The two mentalities are natural deterrents of each other. Hence the bickering. It's as annoying as anything else.

It's not long before my mind goes numb and my eyes drift about the kitchen, settling on Grace who sits at the island with Ray and TJ, his overgrown hair strategically placed to cover his wound. Poor kid. He'll be deaf on that side for the rest of his life. Even so, he's lucky. Things could have been so much worse. That he's here, alive, smiling with his friends, is a blessing.

As if sensing my stare TJ shifts and turns my way, his eyes briefly meeting mine before looking past and settling on Morgan. I feel Morgan tense beside me. A strange look flits across TJ's face. Not anger. Not absolution. Rather, a look of confusion, as though he sees something he does not understand; something he doesn't know how to feel about. He stares for a second, maybe two, and then averts his eyes, that strange look still on his face. I squeeze Morgan's forearm, letting him know I am here.

"I think I'm gonna go try and grab some sleep," he says, standing abruptly.

"It's not even dark," I say.

He shrugs. "I know. Just tired, I guess." He looks as if he wants to add something, opening his mouth once before closing it. Instead, he forces a strained smile before crossing the kitchen and disappearing up the back stairwell. I don't follow. I want to be there for him, but a person can only be pushed away so many times before it takes its toll. I'm at that point now. Space is what we both need.

"I'm gonna get some air," I say. I exit the kitchen and step outside, the chill sharper now as the sun sinks. I settle myself onto the tire swing at the edge of the porch, the sky a deep purple above the apple orchard. Morgan and Vince built it for Abigail soon after we arrived, a surprise for their younger cousin to help lift her spirits. I find myself smiling as I remember the look that crossed her face when she first laid eyes on it—that kind of pure, unfiltered delight unique to children. The only one who might have been happier that afternoon was Morgan.

Despite the chill, I kick my legs and begin to swing, tipping my head as I lean back as far as I can, my hair flowing behind me in a long wave. The motion is a nostalgic one, flooding my mind with memories: a chubby-faced toddler playing in the sandbox with a pail and plastic shovel; a bold kindergartner, fearless as she stormed the playground's slides and jungle gyms; a smiling adolescent with a melodic laugh in the swing beside me, challenging me to see who could climb higher; all with the same deep black hair and dark emerald eyes. Parks were always an escape—a place I could take Grace and leave the real world behind for one of our creation—a place of magic, of wonder, a place where I could pretend everything was fine and we were as happy as the everyday people who explored the land beside us. Despite the ever-changing addresses and endless string of moving boxes, they were always there, a constant in my life when little else was.

Those days of pretending are over now, I'm afraid. The world is too wicked a place to delude oneself into believing otherwise. There's a reason for all the defenses we've erected: for the traps and barbed wire and lookouts surveying the land on the second floor. There's a reason why my Glock does not leave my hip and my AR is never more than an arm's length away. I let the swing slow down on its own accord, that familiar swoop in my stomach turning to stone as the moment passes.

The wind shifts and the sun disappears, plunging the temperature even lower. I shiver as the cold penetrates my sweater, ready to return to the house. Just then, a crashing thud sounds to my left. Silently, I leave the swing and take cover, AR aimed toward the work shed and distant apple orchard. Breath turns to vapor as I wait, resisting the urge to retreat to the far side of the porch and get someone. Felix will have retreated inside by now. I might be the only one in a position to identify the potential threat. I have to be patient.

Another thud, not as loud but clear against the quiet night. I squint, willing my eyes to see past the dark. Nothing. Nothing. And then, movement, the door to the shed opening and closing, a shadow of a man emerging from inside and staggering toward the house. He's unsteady on his feet, making no effort to conceal his movement. Still, I hold my ground, unwilling to give away my position. He's heading straight for the back porch, oblivious it seems to knee high strands of barbed wire looped across the gap between greenhouses and home. But then he stops and reaches into his pockets. I hear a click and a tiny flame erupts in the dark, briefly throwing his face into detail. Mitch. I let loose a breath that's part relief part frustration.

I shout a warning just in time. He looks down and spots the barbed wire he nearly toppled over. "Good call," he says with a laugh. "That would have blown a fat—"

"You're welcome," I say cutting him off. "What the hell are you doing out there alone, anyway? You trying to get yourself killed?"

He picks his way over the wire, laughing still. "Just enjoying the evening, darlin'. Same as you by the looks of it." He clumsily climbs the porch railing, losing his cigarette in the process. "Damn it," he says as he hastily bends to pick it up. He blows the dust off before proceeding to take another pull. A large cloud of smoke escapes his mouth with a content sigh. "No harm done."

He leans now against the railing, taking another deep pull as he surveys me. I feel a chill go through me as his stare lingers, reminding me of the dark tone his voice took when I discovered his bottle of pills the last time we were alone. With so much going on it had completely slipped my mind till now.

"So, what brings you out here?" he asks. "You and the nephew have a fight?"

I listen closely to his voice but detect none of the slur that coated his words that night in the kitchen. It's a moment before what said registers, catching me off guard.

"Why would you ask that?"

He shrugs. "Seems odd I guess," he says. "You out here, cold and alone. Morgan nowhere to be seen when you two are usually joined at the hip. Makes sense."

"We're good," I say, suddenly irritated by his questioning. Our relationship is none of his damn business. It's certainly not something I'm about to talk to him about. "I think I'll join him inside, actually."

I turn to leave when suddenly he reaches for me, his hand cold as ice as it locks around my wrist. I try and yank my hand away but he holds on till he's on his feet. "Whoa, relax girl!" he says. "I'm not gonna to hurt ya'."

I push against his thumb to break his grip, remembering the trick from hours of self-defense videos I watched online. I shove him hard against the porch railing, an amused chuckle issuing from his mouth. "What the hell are you doing?" I seethe.

His chuckle quiets, but the amusement remains in his voice. "You're a little hellfire ain't you?" he says. He takes one last drag from his cigarette and flicks it away into the dark. "Can Morgan even handle you?" he asks, shaking his head and exhaling a cloud of smoke.

I don't even know how to respond to that. "I doubt it," he says, answering his own question. He takes a step forward as I take one back. "Girl like you? You need you a man that knows how to stoke those flames higher, make them burn nice and hot. Nice guy's like my nephew?" He shakes his head dismissively. "Not in their nature."

"Step off, Mitch!" I warn as he continues to creep closer.

"I've seen the way you look at me," he says, unperturbed. "Don't pretend now." He steps within arms reach and I react instinctively, unholstering my gun and leveling it between his eyes which widen in surprise. I take another step back and this time he doesn't follow.

"Let me make myself clear," I warn, voice primal, pulse pounding with adrenaline. Still, I remain calm. I won't give him the satisfaction of appearing rattled. "Whatever looks you've deluded yourself into believing I give you? They're complete bullshit! I don't know if you're high or what. To be honest I don't really give a shit. You come at me like this again, and I won't hesitate to pull the trigger. Got it? So stay the hell away from me! This is the only warning I'll give you."

I keep the gun trained on him till I reach the door, only letting it drop as I turn the knob. Mitch watches me the whole way, a cold, subtle smirk splitting his face. He speaks just as I open the door, so low the words might have been meant only for himself. *Little Hellfire.*

I shut the door with a bang, drawing glances my way. Subtle. I ignore the stares and make my way across the room, trying my best to appear normal. Emily eyes me curiously, but I forestall any questions by feigning a yawn and wishing them goodnight.

"Your hands are freezing," Morgan murmurs as I settle in beside him. His voice helps settle the lingering tension I feel. His arm wraps around my shoulders and I let loose a long breath, releasing the rest.

"Stepped outside for a minute," I reply. "Temperature drops fast when the sun goes down."

"It's only going to colder," he sighs.

"I know," I say, the worry in his voice impossible to miss. My thoughts stray to the approaching winter, to our greenhouses, to the threats circling outside these walls. They stray to Mitch, our encounter still vivid in my mind. There are threats inside these walls as well. I want to tell Morgan. It almost feels a betrayal to keep it to myself. But with everything he's dealing with, I don't know how he'd react—the ripple effects it might have.

"We just have to be ready for it," he says.

My hand strokes the cold metal of my Glock tucked beneath my pillow, it's presence there a fixture since the first night of the collapse. I look back on that night, as well as all the nights that both followed and preceded it, and I feel my resolve harden. I won't allow myself to be cowed by the likes of Mitch. Never again.

"We will be," I say.

Chapter 13: (Morgan)

My face is numb with cold, the air charged with a wintery bite. It's dark, the days first light yet to peak from the east. Leon, Felix, and Vince accompany me. We hike to the steady rustling of leaves underfoot, the hillside we climb thick with trees and large shrubs that grow starker by the day. It won't be long till the smattering of yellows and reds fade and fall as autumn cedes to winter. Long have I dreaded the season of snow and cold. It's brewed on the horizon for some time, dark and ominous. I've watched it stalk closer day by day—felt the warmth of the sun fade under fierce gales and rolling clouds, watched lightning dance across the sky and thunder ring loud in my ears. Only now it looms above us, angry and violent, the sky above a darkened shade of steel, twisting and unfurling in promise. The deluge is upon us, and staring it full in the face has me very, very worried. All any of us can do is continue to prepare the best we can. But it's hard to feel hopeful when already we've suffered setbacks.

In the last week alone we've lost over a quarter of our greenhouses to the cold. It's a tough loss, we're stretched so thin already. Heat sinks have been added to those that remain, the idea being that the trapped heat will be released during the night. It's not an ideal solution, but without power, it's the only chance we have.

In the meantime, our rations grow smaller. The hollow pangs clawing at my stomach are a constant presence. I think back on my travels along the Colorado Trail, on those desperate days that followed the wildfire. I've known hunger greater than this, but I fear it may be just a matter of time until I'm reminded of that desperation or, God forbid, I surpass it. And this time there will be no hidden farm teeming with crops and resources, no kindly old man like Elroy willing to help us in our darkest hour. All we have is us. This farm and whatever we can scavenge along the way. Which brings us here, to this frozen hillside when even the sun still sleeps.

With winter upon us, we're going to need more than a hope and a prayer over our remaining greenhouses. And with game near the farm as scarce as it is, we are forced to expand our hunting grounds into the forested, rolling hills east of the farm. Felix leads us, his knowledge of the area always an asset. Still, these are not the same hills they once were, and though our quarry has led us here, none of us are fooled into believing we are the only predators abound. There's a reason we've never ventured further than a mile into these woods before now.

The day breaks unaccompanied by the sun which lays hidden behind an overcast sky. I eye it with unease, a long hike home soaked and freezing is the last thing I want to deal with. I force it from my mind. We're out here regardless. No use in worrying over something I have no control over. I return my focus to my surroundings, eyes scanning for movement, ears tuning in on the sounds beyond our breaths and rustling leaves. I do so in search of threats as much as I do for game. We pause as we approach two adjacent hillsides, taller than those around them, their slope rising quickly and steeply.

"There's a small pond on the other side of these hills," Felix says, a small smile gracing his face. "You should remember it well," he tells Leon. I find myself smiling as well. Suddenly my mind takes me away from these cold winds and dreary sky, away from the worry and stress to a time when neither existed. It was the summer of my 13th year, the sun bright and bold in the afternoon sky as we explored the hills on ATV's. It was a dry year, turning the pond in question into little more than a mud pit, the shallow water barely reaching halfway up our tires. We took full advantage and raged through, drifting and sliding and covering ourselves with mud with reckless abandon. It was an afternoon like so many before it, the three of us together, living in the moment, completely unaware how precious and golden those days were. And then disaster struck for Leon.

He was making a pass through the mud when he braked a little too hard, turned the wheel just a little too sharp and upended his ATV, sending him sprawling into the swampy mess. I remember feeling the momentary concern for him closely followed by the hilarity as he quickly stood up, unhurt and completely soaked through with mud. Though he didn't get injured, the pond did its damage. I laughed with Felix on the bank of the pond until Leon's curses died down and he grew quiet. I called out, asking if he was alright. He didn't answer for the longest time, his back to us and his head hanging. Eventually, he turned around, holding out his phone in explanation. Ruined. His first phone, a birthday gift from his parents, not even a month prior. He was in shit deeper than the mud he currently stood in and he knew it. Leon ended up having to wait till Christmas before his parents gave him a second chance at a phone, and in the years that followed he was sure to take much better care of them.

"Crazy that a fried phone could ever feel like the end of the world," Leon says. His smile is forced as he looks around. Is it because of what the world has become? Or is it in looking back at the boys we were that fills his eyes with such sadness? Both I'd imagine.

Felix clears his throat after a pause. "Anyway, figure we split up from here," he says. "Moe, you and Vince take the right ridge. Leon and I will take the left. Both sides should offer plenty of sightlines. As good a place as any to hunker down for a bit."

"Good luck," I say as we part. Vince and I ascend at an angle to combat the steep rise. My legs tire quickly, calves and hamstrings burning in protest. I'm weaker than I was on the trail. Body thinner, the paltry diet and hours of physical work leaving me taut as a piano wire. It's reduced my stamina to shit. We tackle the hill in sections, taking several breaks to catch our breath and check our backs. When we reach the top, it's in relief to momentarily rest our legs. We space ourselves some sixty feet apart and settle in.

The pond below is more full than in my memory, the storms over the past months swelling it up. It sits close to the base of the adjacent hillside where Leon and Felix are posted, at the edge of a small clearing surrounded by sparsely set trees. As Felix said, it's a good place to hunker down. I sit with my back against a tall pine, eyes scanning below hoping, praying for movement. But the forest remains still and silent save for the occasional bird going to and fro between branches and sky.

Time passes slowly, made worse by the dull ache in my stomach. I study the terrain with quiet intensity as if I could see what's not there if I just focus hard enough. Worry eats away at the back of my mind. I look back at these past few weeks, at the tension that's taken root between my family. I may not solely be to blame for that, but I can't deny my share. I've messed up, made mistakes. That's why today's so important. We have to bring something back. It's a mental need as much as it is a physical one. A meal—a real meal of grilled meat after what we've grown accustomed to could go a long way—could give us hope to cling to long after the calories have been spent. This could be the salve we need to get back on track. We just need a little bit of luck.

But the morning stretches toward the afternoon without a sign of game. The sun still hides, the sky above churning slowly, thickening into a deeper shade of gray. Were this the old world we'd have deemed this hunt a failure by now—would already have started hiking back toward camp for lunch and a beer. How different this hunt is from those of my past: the difference between hunting for sport and hunting for survival. Turning back empty handed isn't an option, not while the weather holds and night remains hours away.

I look toward the adjacent hillside where Felix waits, debating if I should get his attention and suggest finding another area to scout. And then the air is pierced by the deafening boom of a rifle on my right.

"Damn it!" Vince curses.

"What was it?" I quickly make my way to him.

"Buck," he says, adrenaline coating his voice. "Big bastard too. I hit him but he didn't drop. Took off over that null." I follow his finger to the smaller hill in the shadow of our own. "We can track him down. He can't get too far before he bleeds out."

We signal to Leon and Felix and set out, scampering down the hill after our quarry. We reach level ground and sprint the short gap between hillsides. A quarter of the way up the hill we pause, blood splattered against the fallen leaves marking the spot where the deer was shot. It swims before my eyes and I have to close them against the sudden bout of lightheadedness. *Control the breathing. In. Out. In. Out.* The feeling fades and I open them again.

"You alright?" Vince asks.

"I'm good," I say, shaking it off. "Let's go."

We follow the blood trail with renewed vigor, the prospect of meat allowing me to fight against my protesting body. At the crest, we pause in search for our prey. No movement catches my eye, the forest thicker on this side. Silently we descend, our movements slow and measured as we are forced to scan for signs of the buck's passage. I'd feel better if Felix were with us, his tracking skills much better than our own. But he and Leon have yet to catch us. We're on our own for now.

"Blood," Vince says. He's gone to a knee and rubs it between thumb and forefinger, dying it red. "Must have passed—" He's struck silent by the sound of a gunshot. Wordlessly we brace ourselves against two close-growing trees, our rifles un-safetied and held at the ready. My heart beats loud in my ears as I strain to hear past the silence. *Buh-bump. Buh-bump.* Not three beats later another gunshot shatters the quiet. I curse, unable to tell where the shots are coming from. Surrounded by hills, the sound is hard to pinpoint, hard to gauge the distance.

"What do you think?" I ask.

"Push forward," Vince replies. "Buck has to be close. We have to track it, you know how badly we need the meat right now."

I do know. It's that knowledge which has kept me from retreating already. There's risk in moving forward. But I think of the amount of blood we've followed. How much farther could it have traveled? Surely the buck would have bled out by now, right? I think of the ruined crops we were forced to scrap and of those which still remain in danger. Another hard freeze could take our situation from bad to critical. The thought of my family, starving and desperate as winter settles around us is enough to make up my mind. It's a risk we must take.

"We should wait for Leon and Felix," I say.

"There's no time," Vince says, his tone changing, desperation creeping into his voice. "Those shots could be close. We have to move. Now." I'm unconvinced, but Vince isn't about to let my indecision stop him. "Wait here if you want. I'm going."

Before I can say or do anything, he leaves his cover and darts forward. Cursing, I follow. I can't let him go off on his own. We proceed with our rifles half raised, ready to fire at a moment's notice. Adrenaline rages through me. Every sound is amplified. Each shape at my peripheral making me do a double take. Another splatter of blood coats the side of a bush and we pick up our pace. My pulse quickens. Logic says we have to be close.

"There!" Vince says, voice buzzing with excitement.

I see it. It lays motionless some forty feet to my right, half concealed by brush. I approach with the deer cautiously, ready to put it down should it have some life left in it. It doesn't. Vince turns to me and I can't help but smile.

"Good work, cuz," I say, slapping him on the back. We haven't had a bounty like this in some time, surviving off of small game and whatever we could scavenge. A buck this size will go a long way. It's exactly what we needed.

"Just glad we found the thing. Bastard had some fight in him." He sounds as relieved as I feel. He leans his rifle against a tree and unsheathes his knife. "Time to get bloody." Vince goes to a knee to begin dressing the kill. He pauses, knife hovering over the corpse.

"What's wrong?" I ask.

He looks up, worry replacing the excitement that shone in his eyes moments earlier. "He was shot more than once," he says. A sinking weight fills my stomach at his words. The gunshots we heard. We're not alone in tracking the buck. And if we beat the other party here, they can't be far behind.

"Shit," I say, shouldering my rifle and unholstering my Glock. "We have to move. Grab a leg and let's drag it out."

Before either of us can reach out to do so we hear it—breaking twigs, the tread of fast-moving feet on fallen leaves. Our rival party approaches. I strain my ears in vain to identify their number but it's impossible to tell. It's not until they are nearly upon us that I see them. They move like shadows shifting in and out of sight, a half dozen at least, using the density of trees to cover their advance. They fan out into a semicircle formation with us at the center. Vince and I brace ourselves against tree trunks on either side of the buck, pistols out. The gun is of little comfort. If it comes to a shootout, we'll lose. Stupid. We should have waited for Leon and Felix. Better yet, we should have turned back when we first heard the gunshots. We took a risk and it backfired. Now we're facing the consequences.

I peek behind my cover and count the gun barrels facing us, seven in all. Bad odds. My mind races a mile a minute, desperate to figure a way out of this. Nothing comes to me. We're pinned down and outmanned.

"Whatever ideas you're cooking up over there, forget them." The voice rings out cool and languid as if the speaker already grows bored of the situation. "Fact is we're not all that interested in you. All we want is the deer. You lay down your guns nice—"

"The deer is ours!" Vince yells out, cutting the voice off. I stare at him in disbelief. Does he not realize our situation? The voice remains silent a beat, perhaps regaining his composure after unexpectedly getting cut off.

"What's that now?" Annoyance has crept into that bored voice, reminding me, oddly, of a school teacher irritated at a student for speaking out of turn.

"I shot it first. Tracked it. Reached it before you did. By all right's it's mine!" I understand where Vince is coming from: the desperation to bring back food, the injustice of having something so valuable snatched right from under him. But he's letting his emotions blind him of the reality we're facing. Right or wrong, we're not walking away with the deer. He just doesn't see it. Those surrounding us know this truth, and that knowledge is heard in their mocking laughter.

"By all rights, you say?" Another voice, this one deeper and full of cruel amusement. "Child, where have you been? What's right hasn't mattered in some time."

"And in any case, the deer fell by my bullet," the original voice adds. "Which means that *by right,* it belongs to me." Vince makes to say something but the voice steamrolls him. "Enough! The deer is ours, end of discussion. What I'm offering you is the chance to walk out of here alive. I've done enough killing these past months. I really don't want to add you to that list. So take my offer and leave. Right now. Don't raise your guns against us, don't try and take what's ours. Just leave. You have five seconds to decide."

Vince is about to open his mouth when I too cut him off, earning a scowl from him. "How do we know you won't just shoot us when we leave our cover?" I ask.

"That's a risk you'll have to take. Not like you have any other options. And you're out of time...So what's it going to be?"

He's right. Our options are either fight and die, or retreat and possibly live. There's no choice between the two.

"Alright," I yell. With a prayer, I leave my cover and begin backing away. Vince stares at me, anger and disgust written all over his face. But my retreat leaves him with no choice but to follow. I eye the gun barrels staring at us with a stomach twisted in nerves, waiting for their bullets to tear through my body and take me from this world. But the moment never comes. The guns remain steady and threatening until we leave them behind, the forest swallowing them back up. Still, it's a good ten minutes before I breathe freely again. The moment is short lived as Vince wheels on me, finally letting loose his frustration.

"Why the hell did you back down so easily?" he asks.

I stare at him a moment in disbelief. "Are you serious?" I ask. "What choice did we have?"

"We could have stood our ground," he says. "We could have negotiated to take back at least some of the meat. We had options but you threw them all away."

I sputter for a response. "Were you somewhere else just now?" I ask. "What about that situation makes you think we should have stood our ground? They had seven guns on us, Vince. Seven. There was no negotiating with them. If we tried, I doubt we would be here now. We definitely wouldn't have any meat. Why would they give us anything when they had all the leverage?"

He shakes his head and spits on the ground. "Guess we'll never know now, will we?" he asks. Before I can respond he shoulders past me and it's only a whistle to my left that keeps me from shoving him back. Instead, I turn and see Leon and Felix emerge from the treeline and jog my way.

"Holy shit! Talk about dodging a freaking bullet," Leon says as they reach me.

I shake my head. "You saw what happened?" I ask.

`Felix nods. "Yeah. We were almost to you when we heard those guys crashing through the trees. Decided we should keep out of sight, try and get to a better vantage point in case things turned south. We never found one—not a good one anyway. We're lucky they let you walk."

"Tell that to Vince," I say, unable to keep the bitterness from my voice.

They look to Vince who already has climbed halfway up the hill, his back to us. "He just needs to cool off," Felix says. "He'll come around."

"Can't totally blame him though," Leon says. "That buck would have made a huge difference."

Don't I know it. The same anger that's built inside Vince resides in me as well. I swallowed it because I had to, but that doesn't mean it's gone. Just thinking of all the meat we might have brought back makes returning home empty handed all the more difficult. But I remind myself that focusing on that anger won't change anything. The dye has cast. I have to shake it off and move past it. Easier said than done.

Vince's sour mood permeates the air as we travel. Even keeping my distance I find it hard to ignore. Every few dozen feet his glare lands on me, the blame reflected in his eyes. It's a test of my patience to remain silent, and they are quickly wearing thin.

"You know you might have actually spotted another deer if you didn't glower at me every ten seconds!" It's at the outskirts of the farm that I finally snap, my frustration getting the better of me.

Vince's eyes widen in surprise before quickly narrowing again. He forces a humorless laugh. "Yeah, maybe," he says. "We also could be carrying some meat back right now if you didn't balk the first chance you got."

"Really? This shit again?" I ask. I should let it go. Arguing will do nothing but make the situation worse. But right now I'm too angry to care: at Vince, at having the deer snatched away from us, at the unforgiving world we live in. I couldn't hold my tongue right now if I tried.

"I was the only one of us who was using their brain. What the hell would you have had us do? Start shooting? Butcher seven men all so we could take home a fucking deer? Cause that's where it was heading. They weren't backing down, and if we didn't, bullets would have started flying."

He sneers at my words. "You're a damn physic now, are you? You know all this would have happened?" He shakes his head. "Ever think that they wouldn't want to die over a deer either? That maybe they would have let us go with something rather than let the bullets fly?"

"You wanna know what I think?" I ask. "I think you're starting to sound a lot like your dear Uncle Richard. Letting your hot head dictate what you say and do without thinking it through first."

"Yeah? Well, you wanna know what I think?" he asks. "I think you backed down earlier because you were afraid. Because you weren't man enough to call their bluff." He snorts in disgust. "I've known you my whole life, cuz. I never would have taken you for a coward."

I lose it. All the stress, all the anger I've felt building inside me the past few hours, weeks, months, boils over. I launch myself at Vince as if he were my enemy and not the man I grew up with—the one who's had my back since training wheels and who's always felt more brother than cousin. In this moment, I'm blind to that fact.

I crash into him but he's ready for me, absorbing the rush and wrapping his arms around me to stop my momentum. We grapple, each trying to bring the other to the ground until I manage to sweep a leg and we both go down in a tangle of flying limbs. First I'm on top, and then him, trading punches back and forth as if we were in a cage match. Leon and Felix don't interfere as we tear into each other, letting us get on with it.

Insults fly back and forth as breathless grunts, each of us growing winded. I hardly hear him, the rage still riding hot inside me. I don't know how long it lasts. It's not until I'm pulled off him and hear my father's voice that I come to my senses.

"That's enough!" he seethes. "What's the matter with you two? You're cousins for Christ's sake!" My Uncle Will assists in breaking us apart, holding his own son back.

"What the hell's going on?" Uncle Will asks.

Vince violently shakes him off. "Ask him!" It's all he says before picking up his rifle and storming past the small crowd that has gathered.

Uncle Will watches Vince walk off a moment before turning back toward me. Now that I'm no longer resisting, my dad lets me go and looks to me as well, waiting. I shake my head, shame replacing the lingering anger I feel.

"I'm sorry," I say. "Things just got out of hand." I meet my mother's eyes and immediately have to look away, the hurt and disappointment too much for me to handle atop everything else.

"I'm sorry," I repeat. I don't even know who I speak to: my mother, my father, Vince. I suppose it doesn't matter. What matters is that I let my emotions get the better of me—that I did what I accused Vince of doing and acted with a hot head instead of thinking first. I messed up. Again. And I can blame Vince, and the hunters in the woods, and the bastards who set this all in motion all I like. But the truth is, this is all on me.

That's the only thing that matters.

Chapter 14: (Lauren)

When it rains, it pours. A cliche, but one I've found throughout my life to be true more often than not. Something bad happens and it is immediately followed by something else, something worse. Problem after problem, setback after setback. You try so hard to get ahead, to move past it, only to find it unshakable: your own personal cartoon rain cloud shadowing your every move. Eventually, it begins to take a toll on your psyche. It can make you want to give up, to stop trying: the voice in the back in your head telling you things will never get better. I know better than most.

I grew up hearing those poisonous words. I know that voice as if it were my own. Were it not for Grace I might have lost myself in all that darkness—might have let myself be broken by circumstance and wound up a statistic. She was always the light I needed, the hope I could cling to. But that was back when it was just the two of us, when all my fears and worries revolved around her. That's no longer the case. And as wonderful and uplifting as it's been to finally feel the warm embrace of family, it comes with a price. That price is the worry churning inside my stomach, the dark thoughts whispered in the back of my mind. I know better than to listen to that voice, but I find it harder to ignore as the hits keep coming.

Things have been tense for weeks. Given what we've been through, that's hardly surprising. What with being raided, and held hostage, and TJ getting his ear shot off. Factor in our scarce diets and lost greenhouses, and it's easy to understand the growing worry among us. Sitting here with winter at our doorstep, our outlook has never looked more bleak. But more than the threats circling outside the farm, more than our sparse food supply and approaching season, what has me most concerned is the tension between ourselves.

The close-knit, caring family I first met in Rockridge has fractured. The love among them I once thought unbreakable has collapsed under the weight of outside pressures. It's been simmering under the surface for a while, but it wasn't until Morgan and Vince came to blows that it completely boiled over. Now, there is no sense of trust, no unity between us. New grudges arise and blossom daily. Old fights are dug up and brought to light rather than remaining buried. Insults are thrown. Tempers flare. Each day the gulf between us seems to grow. If it weren't for Mrs. Taylor, everything likely would have fallen apart already.

When arguments escalate and people's voices grow loud and cold, she's there to ensure they don't spin out of control. When the weight of everything becomes too much for someone to carry, she's there to help them through. She's the lone bridge among the family— the one person holding everything together. She reminds me so much of Morgan. Or rather, she reminds me of how he used to be.

I'm worried about him. He's been off kilter ever since we were raided, but his fight with Vince has only made him retreat further into himself. Before he tried to hide it under false optimism and strained assurances, forcing himself to smile and pretend all was well for our sake. Now he no longer pretends. He wears his heart on his sleeve, all of the worry and stress and fear inside, clear for all to see. Something has broken inside him, and I have no idea how to fix it.

"You need to talk about whatever this is you're going through," I said one night.

"What do you want me to say, Lauren? The world's gone to shit. I can't keep pretending like it hasn't."

"Pretend? So that's what you've been doing this whole time?" I challenged.

He wheeled on me then. *"That's exactly what I've been doing! Pretending like I knew what the hell I was doing. Pretending that I could keep us safe—that we could all make it through this if we just tried hard enough. It's all been one giant fucking ball of pretend, make-believe, the desperate wishing of a child! I can't do it anymore. I won't. It's too painful."* He looked away quickly, hiding the tears which leaked from his eyes.

"You're 'pretending' got us home, Morgan," I said, willing my own tears back. *"It's what lead us here."*

He shook his head. "Yeah," he said, voice full of cynicism. "And look how well we're doing. Maya's dead. TJ's had his ear blown off. The greenhouses are hanging on by a thread... Shall I continue? Cause I can go on."

"So that's it then?" I asked, anger stirring inside me, seeping into my words. "The world's too harsh a place, so why try and fight it? After everything we've been through, everything we've done, you're just going to give up?"

It was as if my question stole the air from his body, he deflated so quickly. "I haven't given up," he said quietly. Finally, he turned to face me, his eyes raw and honest. "But I can't be that guy anymore. I can't be the one making the plans, and calling the shots, and forcing myself to smile so that the others don't lose hope...I just can't."

I didn't know what to say to that. I still don't. Somewhere along the line he lost his way, and I don't know how to help guide him back. I have to find a way though. The tension between the family may have been building for a while, but it was only after we were raided that things were escalated, the same time that Morgan's guilt and self-doubt robbed him of what made him the man he was. I don't think that's a coincidence.

Morgan says he can't be the one to make the plans, to call the shots. In short, he claims he can't be the one to lead. But I've seen what's happened with others at the reins, and I see the end they will steer us toward if something doesn't change. I just have to get Morgan to see it too.

I watch now as Morgan and Felix step off the back porch and begin their rounds. We've set dozens of animal traps throughout the area. Most days we at least get something out of them, rabbits and squirrels and such. Not much meat to them, especially once it's divided among all of us. Still, it's helped see us through. Although that too is beginning to dry up as critters brace themselves for the approaching season. Something needs to change before they completely burrow away. I watch till they disappear from view before turning back to the task at hand.

"And to think, I used to complain about having to haul my stuff to the laundromat across the street," Emily says, flexing her fingers. I understand where she's coming from. I used to hate the four block walk to the laundromat back in Denver. Now I only wish it could be so simple. Like all things, laundry has become a more difficult task in wake of the collapse. There are no more washing machines or dryers, only tubs of steaming water and our bare hands, scrubbing clothes with improvised washing boards and ringing them out the best we can manage. It works the hands something awful. Out of practicality, we've limited our washings as much as possible, only doing so when it could no longer be avoided. We're at that point now, our last wash nearly three weeks ago. I try not to think too much on that fact as I plunge my hands into the soapy water beside Emily and Julia. Somehow the task has fallen on the three of us each time it needs to be done. All women of course. For some reason, I don't' think that was an accident.

Julia shrugs when I mention it. "It is what it is," she says. "All the chores around here suck in their own way. At least we don't have to scavenge or chop wood."

Emily huffs. "Give me an ax. I'll chop wood any day over this," she says, holding a pair of soapy boxers gingerly by her fingertips.

I laugh. "My thoughts exactly," I say.

Although I must admit, as tedious as hand washing clothing for over two dozen people can be, it has its moments. The long process of scrubbing, and wringing, and rinsing is done so with a constant flow of conversation. Stories are recounted in vivid detail. Idle gossip is passed in low voices and subtle smirks. Laughter is had. Given everything we deal with, all the burdens we carry on our shoulders, it's uplifting to still find humor in the world. Indeed, there are times I get so lost in stories or my own laughter that I forget our troubles altogether.

Growing up I didn't have much in the way of friends. I had co-workers, and before that, classmates I would force smiles upon and engage in the kind of polite small talk so popular in the world before. It just wasn't in the cards for me. I could offer them neither the time nor support required of friendships. Things changed on the trail. That feeling of camaraderie, of belonging, finally took root. Morgan, Emily, Leon, Felix, Maya: they gave me that. Now I feel those roots expand and entwine with others: with Julia, with Vince and Jerry. And though my worry and fear grow alongside them, I know they are more than worth it.

One thing I've learned since this all began is that the drive to keep going is as much about the lives around you as it is your own. After all, what does anything in this life matter if there is nobody to share it with?

After hanging the clothes to dry, the remainder of our afternoon is suddenly clear until they've done so. I'd sooner be given another task. It feels wrong not having anything to do—to sit idle with so much daylight left. But with our defenses erected and a plan of action in place in should we be attacked, there is less to be done than when we first arrived. We won't be alone in finishing up early. Sure enough, over the next couple of hours, people finish their tasks and gravitate our way. Most head inside, seeking shelter from the whipping winds that have kicked up. Leon joins us on the porch though, as do Grace and Ray a little while later.

Despite my best efforts, I can't help but glance their way curiously. The two of them have clicked since Rockridge, and they only grow closer as the weeks pass by. I watch them now as they rock together on the porch swing, a Rubix-cube held between them. They've been trying to solve it for the past two weeks, never managing to fill more than one side a solid color. Not that they seem to mind all that much, smiles and suppressed laughter echoing between them as they work. A strange apprehension fills me the longer I watch them, my eyes zeroing in on their body language: at Ray's hand sliding over her's, of Grace brushing the hair from her eyes and stealing an appraising look while he focuses on the cube. There's an attraction between them, and I don't know how to feel about it. This is uncharted territory for me.

I continue to steal glances their way until Morgan and Felix emerge from behind the barn, drawing my focus onto them. Even from this distance, I can tell they didn't have any luck with the traps. If the empty sacks on their hips didn't give it away, the slump of their shoulders and grim expressions certainly would. I'm not the only one to notice.

"Nothing?" Leon asks as they reach us.

"Not a thing," Felix answers. "Empty. Every single one of them."

It's a blow, one which we all feel. Our only shot at a halfway decent meal tonight now depends on the success of Richard's hunting party. He left early with Vince, and Jerry. They've yet to return but given the hour, they should be back soon. All of us are aware of the danger of staying out past dark. Richard, for all of his flaws, knows not to take such a risk in the wake of everything else.

"Need a hand?" Morgan asks me.

"Sure," I reply, gauging that the clothes are dry enough.

We wave off Julia and Emily as they rise to help, insisting we got it. Morgan is even worse with idle time than I am. The least I can do is provide him with a tedious chore like folding clothes, forcing him to focus on a single task and keeping his mind from wandering.

"Any tracks at least?" I ask

He shrugs. "A few," he says. "There's still small game in the area, we're just having a bad streak right now. We're bound to get something sooner or later, though. Just have to keep at it."

He tells me what he thinks I need to hear. But what I take away most isn't the words he says, but the doubt with which he speaks them. It's as if he's trying to convince himself as much as me. Only I don't think either of us are fooled. He opens his mouth to add something only to immediately close it, his body tensing. I don't ask for an explanation. I hear it too. We move with practiced efficiency, wordlessly drawing our guns and seeking cover while Grace and Ray enter the house to alert the others. We're lucky nearly everyone has finished for the day. Only Richard and his hunting party are unaccounted for.

We wait as the commotion dies down, the quiet heavy in its absence. Behind us, I hear those inside getting into position—windows sliding open, muffled curses, bullets chambering. The prelude to battle. I can practically feel the fear reverberating through the wall, our last attack still vivid in people's memories. But we're prepared in ways we weren't then. Our fortifications will hold. They have to.

"Hold Firo!" calls a familiar voice from the brush. Still, the voice alone does little to put us at ease. It's not until they emerge, safe and unbound do we finally lower our weapons. Yet there is still cause for unease. With them are two men, one in his early forties with overgrown hair and bushy beard, and the other maybe fifteen or sixteen, his eyes hidden behind thick glasses and his face riddled with acne. It's they who lead the procession, their hands bound behind their backs where Richard and Vince aim their pistols.

"Found them lurking in the brush," Richard says as he reaches us. Most of the family has assembled around us by now. Though they are bound, there is no mistaking the fear still radiating amid the family—the apprehensive staring as if the men were rabid animals, snapping and snarling against their restraints.

"Were they armed?" asks Mr. Taylor.

"Had a .22 rifle and a couple knives," Vince answers. "They're about out of ammo though. Everything else was just camping gear." At that, Jerry produces two hiking packs for us to see.

"What does this mean?" Virginia asks, looking to Richard. "They can't have meant to attack the farm, could they?"

Before Richard can answer the bearded captive answers. "We weren't trying to attack anyone," he says. "We were just..." His voice fades mid-sentence as if suddenly losing the nerve that made him speak out in the first place.

"You were just what?" Richard presses.

The man averts his gaze, hiding his face behind a curtain of dirty, matted hair. "We were just scoping the place out...seeing if there might be some food we could nick." His voice quivers as he answers, as much out of shame as out of fear.

"Oh, is that all?" asks Will scathingly. "Well no harm, no foul. As long as you were only trying to steal what little food we have from our mouths, it's all good. Can't imagine there's a problem with that."

"I'm sorry," he says. "I know how shitty that is to do to you...but what else am I supposed to do? We were camping out inside the hospital, about a dozen of us. We didn't have much, but we were carrying on. But last week we were attacked. They came at night, fast like, guns blazing. Me and my boy were the only ones who made it out alive, nothing but the .22 and the clothes on our backs. But it's been rough going. Neither of us has had anything to eat in over three days...like I said, we're desperate. Desperate enough to resort to this..." His voice breaks on that last bit, a deep sob wracking his entire body. "I'm sorry," he repeats. "But I couldn't just sit by and watch my boy starve to death."

Beside him, his son cries freely. Not in mournful sobs as his father does, but quietly, his head hung in resignation. It's as if he's been read a death sentence. It's a sad sight, one which makes me both realize how much we have to lose, and how fine a line it is between us and the two captives—that we are not immune to the kind of misfortune they've suffered. I can't find it in my heart to hate. All I feel is pity. Pity, and worry that we might one day be in their position. But not all feel as I do.

Hate. Fear. Mistrust. These and more shine in the eyes of the family: emotions that dwell deep within them, cancerous seeds that have been planted by pain and circumstance, watered by the likes of the Animas Animals, by the raiders who held us at gunpoint and blew off TJ's ear. Now they grow like vines, spreading and twisting in their hearts and minds, razor-sharp thorns keeping the pain of what they suffered fresh in their memory. What room is there for empathy amid such an overwhelming presence?

Ted snorts derisively. "Good story," he says. "I'd imagine I would say the same if I were caught in your situation. The only problem is, how do we know it's not a bunch of bull shit? How do we know you weren't scoping the place out so you could come back later tonight with a posse and slit our throats while we slept?"

His words resonate among the family. Even those few who may have sympathized with the man must be second-guessing themselves. He has a point after all. Memories of the night we met Eli and Jolene come back to me. How badly I felt for that squalid family as they stood by the fire, waiting for us to pass judgment. We fell for the trap they had set, one which might have come at the expense of our lives had we not wriggled out before it closed. They weren't wicked, just desperate, doing what they believed they had to out of fear and the manipulation of the cruel men they served. That was months ago. The world has only grown more desperate and cruel in the days since.

The man shakes his head vigorously. "Please, I'm telling the truth," he pleads. "There's no posse. There was never any plan except trying to smuggle away some food. You have to believe me!"

The man looks around desperately, eyes frantically searching for an ally as a drowning man would look for a life preserver.

"Perhaps it's best if we discuss this in private?" Mrs. Taylor suggests. "Vince, Jerry, if you wouldn't mind..." She gestures toward one of our barricades. However, it's only after a nod from Richard that they move the captives away.

"He could just be telling us what we want to hear," Will warns, soon as they're out of earshot. "How can we trust him?"

"How do we know he's not being honest?" asks Mrs. Taylor. The focus shifts to her as it often does when she speaks. "I mean two men, one hardly more than a child, and armed with a .22 and a handful of ammo? Not exactly a strike team. Seems to me that a desperate father and son looking to steal some food is the more likely scenario of the two."

Nods of agreement are had at that. Even the most distrusting of the family can see the sense in what she says. Richard, however, remains unimpressed with the argument, countering before anyone can have the chance to mull it over. "So what do you suggest?" he asks. "That we take their word for it? Just let them go, free and clear?" The heavy skepticism in his voice makes it obvious what he thinks of the idea.

"I don't see many alternatives," she answers unflinchingly as she meets his harsh glare. "What would *you* suggest?"

A small smirk crosses his lips, cruel and humorless. "I suggest we find the truth," he says.

"And how do we do that?" she challenges.

"I have a few ideas," he says. "Give me an hour in the barn with them, and we'll find out just how honest he's been."

Though his words are vague, none of us are lost on what they imply. Torture—that dark deed stained throughout human history—a tactical tool used and justified in times of dire circumstances. Have we really come to this? I study our two captives: the father who looks broken, watching us with pleading eyes; and the son, shaking and shivering out of fear, eyes so swelled with tears it's a wonder he can see at all. I feel my stomach twist in disgust at the idea of him screaming in pain, suffering all to ascertain their honesty.

I look to Morgan who looks as troubled as I feel. He opens his mouth as if to speak, only to immediately close it again. His eyes linger on the captives a moment, face creased uneasily. He wants to say something, I can tell. Yet he remains silent, averting his eyes and staring fixedly at the ground. He's not the only one to do so. Despite the anger and mistrust, nearly everyone looks troubled at such an ugly prospect. But like Morgan, they do not speak up. They do not condemn the notion. His mother, however, has no qualms voicing her contempt.

"You can't be serious?" she says. "That's your brilliant plan—to beat the truth out of them? And what happens if at the end they were telling the truth after all?"

"Then we let them go," Richard says. He turns, speaking now to the entire family. "I'm not suggesting we work them over with a screwdriver and a blowtorch, but we need to apply some kind of pressure. It's the only way we'll know for sure. It's the only way we can let them walk out of here and know they aren't a threat to us." Though the unease remains, I can all but see the grim resignation dawn on them—accepting that this is the only way forward.

"We're better than this," Mrs. Taylor says fiercely, eyes sweeping over her family. "There has to be another way." Nobody seems prepared to offer an alternative. I don't have one either, but I can sense the way things are breaking and I can't remain silent. I have to at least say something.

"She's right!" I say. "We can't do this. If we're wrong, how will we be able to live with ourselves? Do you want to live with that guilt? We just...we have to find another way."

Silence ensues for a long minute, though I don't need half that to realize my plea has done nothing to turn the tides. "Does anyone share their opinion?" Richard asks. Few do. Mr. Taylor and Virginia both try and appeal to them as well, but it quickly becomes clear we are in the minority.

"Say something!" I hiss into Morgan's ear, voice low so only he can hear me. If he speaks, people will listen. They always have. But when he turns to me, I'm reminded of how much he has changed. This is no longer the man who invited Eli and Jolene to camp beside us on the trail; who later gave them the chance at redemption by joining us after taking out Clint and the men who coerced them into doing their bidding. So when he shakes his head, eyes filled with guilt he must be drowning in, I know what will come to pass.

"Who are you?" I ask. I see something ripple across his face as I ask this, but I'm too far gone to care at the moment. Without waiting for a reply, I turn from the sad scene and make for the house, unwilling to be party to what is about to occur.

Chapter 15: (Morgan)

The day is dismal, unforgiving winds coupled with intermittent showers of frozen rain assaulting the land, beating on the roof, its icy breath seeping through the tiniest cracks and fissures. From horizon to horizon the sky smolders a shade of thick smoke, depriving us of the sun for the past three days. For the most part, the family has stayed confined to the house, venturing outside only when necessary. Trails of churned mud mark our most frequented routes, the most trodden being that between the back porch and the greenhouses. Somehow they continue to hold strong, though I know I'm not alone in worrying they won't make it to harvest. It's a worst case scenario I don't even want to consider. Each time I do, all I see are slow, painful deaths for me and my family.

Dreary though the cold and rain may be, it's nothing compared to the gloom that has settled over my family. Since greenlighting Richard to interrogate the father and son who were caught lurking on the outskirts of the farm, there's been a dark energy among us. I feel it as I would a sickness—a disease slowly writhing through my veins, sapping my strength, leaving me to wallow my own moroseness. It's a feeling shared throughout the household, and while some fair better than others, not a single one of us are untouched by its effects. Even Richard with all his cock-sureness and bravado has been dejected since that night.

I was witness to what occurred in the barn, to the tactics Richard employed in his search for the truth. I always pictured torture as they showed in the movies: of hot knives slicing through flesh and cauterizing wounds, of pliers extracting molars and removing fingernails. Blowtorches, saws, hammers, all tools of the trade. But now I know such methods aren't a necessity. Sometimes all it takes is a bucket of water, a towel, and a few well-placed punches.

"Who are you?"

Lauren's question stuck with me all throughout Richard's interrogation. I replayed it over and over again: the bitter sadness in her voice, the disbelief in her eyes, the way she shook her head, face twisted, not in anger, but in disappointment. It was painful in a way I can't put into words, not merely in seeing the girl I love look so crestfallen, but knowing I was responsible for it. As I watched water cascade over the bucket's lip and soak the towel draped over the man's face, his body bucking and heaving against his restraints—as I watched Richard paint the man with bruises, and saw tears fall freely from his son's eyes—all I heard was Lauren's voice: *Who are you?*

The truth is, I don't even know anymore. And that's what hurts most of all.

In the end, Richard concluded that the man was telling the truth. They were released, the man only able to walk with the aid of his son. I watched them limp their way off the farm and disappear into the dark, alive but forever maimed. Still, they have a chance. At least that's what I tell myself. The truth is, we may as well have killed them. We may not have taken their lives, but we broke their spirit. And in this cold world, that in itself is a death sentence.

Lauren has barely been able to look at me since that night, avoiding me whenever possible. Can't say I blame her. I've avoided mirrors long before then. And though guilt remains on my part for condoning what occurred, I can't suppress the feeling of resentment building inside me.

Who am I? Who are you *to ask such a thing?*

I love her, but she thinks too highly of me. Expects too much. How can she not see how flawed I am? How can she look past all the mistakes I've made and still think I know what's best? She says I am the reason we made it home. She's wrong. Luck got us home. Luck, and an old man who showed mercy when few would have. In the short time I knew him, Elroy earned my respect in a way few ever had. When I think of a leader, it's men like him that come to mind—strong and wise and generous—the kind of man I once aspired to be, but whom I now feel as distant from as the old world is to this new one.

I'm not the man Lauren believes me to be. I never was. I was only ever a boy faking his way forward—wearing the mask of a leader until I could no longer breathe under its smothering weight. That's what scares me. I love Lauren more than anything, but I fear she has only fallen for my mask. What will happen when she finally realizes this? How can I hope for a girl as strong as her to accept that I am only a shade of the man she thought I was?

I watch her now through the window. She sits alone, swinging gently on the back porch as the sky unleashes yet another torrent of frigid rain. Condensed breath billows from her mouth, quickly dispersed in the wind. She looks frozen. Not from cold, but in thought. Through glazed eyes, she stares across the barren pastures, face blank and unreadable. While most of the family vie for spots around the living room's hearth, she endures the cold for a moment of quiet. Does she do so to escape the house, and the gloom within? Or is it merely to escape me?

"Penny for your thoughts?"

I shake my head slowly, my gaze remaining on the swinging girl. "I'm not sure you'd want to hear them," I say.

He breathes a huff of laughter, the kind reserved for simple amusements. "That depressing, are they?" he asks.

Finally, I tear my eyes away and turn around. My father looks at me with a tired smile, split, it seems, between concern and amusement. Then I see his eyes flicker past me and through the window. He nods in understanding before shifting his eyes back to me.

"Ahh," he says, exhaling slowly. "Should have known."

"It's nothing," I say, folding my arms across my chest.

He huffs again, amused. "From my experience, it's rarely 'nothing' when it comes to women," he says. He takes a seat at the kitchen table and nods to the chair across from him. "Humor me."

I sit with a heavy sigh, mentally drained from the past few days. My father assesses me from across the table, and I have a hard time meeting his eyes, afraid of what mine will reveal. He must have questions, must have sensed the tension between Lauren and myself. Yet he remains quiet, giving me time to find my voice.

"Do you ever feel...I don't know...lost, I guess?" I ask.

The question leaves my mouth before I can fully think it over, draped in the uncertainty I've carried for so long. I feel like I need to explain, but I find myself afraid to do so. For weeks I've struggled against these feelings, bottled them up, buried them. It's not easy bringing them to the surface.

"Of course," he says. "We all do from time to time."

I shake my head. "No," I say, positive he doesn't understand. "I'm not talking about feeling lost like I don't know what's going to happen tomorrow or next week. Or, I don't know...that I'm not sure what the right thing to do is. I mean *lost*. Like you don't even know who you are anymore—like you've gone your whole life as one thing, and then somewhere along the line, that person died without you even noticing. And now you're this whole other person you don't really know, don't really understand, and you're only just realizing it."

I let loose an exacerbated breath and run a hand through my hair. "I don't even know if that makes sense," I say. "That's what makes this so damn frustrating. She looks at me and I can tell how disappointed she is; like I'm failing to live up to the expectations she has for me. She has these notions of who I am, who I am supposed to be, and it's just not someone I can be right now. But she doesn't get it. Nobody does. I wake up every day feeling like I've already failed her, failed everyone...I'm tired of failing."

Finished, I rest my forehead against my fists and close my eyes against the pressure building behind them. I thought admitting these things would make me feel better, but all I feel is exhaustion.

"In what world have you failed us?" he asks softly.

A short, bitter laugh escapes me. "Look around you," I say. "Who dragged us out here? Who convinced everyone we could start over—that we would be safer away from town? I did. And you all took my word for gospel rather than the bullshit that it was. I didn't know what was best. I still don't. But for better or worse, we're stuck here: freezing and starving, over a quarter of our greenhouses lost, waiting to see what becomes of us, scared to death that we'll be attacked, that we'll be killed. Hoping and praying. Hoping and praying. It's like that's all we have left to us: this naive notion that we can survive if we just wish hard enough. We're all fools, and I'm the biggest fool of all. I promised us a new beginning...but I'm afraid all I've done is delay the end."

I can feel the tears building and I want to scream at myself for being so weak, for letting my emotions run away from me like a child. My father watches me now without a hint of the amusement he had when he first arrived, worry lines creasing his frowning face.

"Morgan..." he says, the word dragging on and on as if suspended in time, voice filled with a concern so heavy I feel as if I'll buckle beneath its weight. Suddenly I find myself on my feet, shaking my head. I know where this is headed. I know the platitudes and assurances he'll tell me and I can't stand to hear them. Not now.

"It's alright," I say. "I just need some air."

I stumble toward the door and wrench it open, only remembering Lauren's swinging form after I've shut it behind me. She turns at the sound, eyes scanning everything from my pale face to my balled up fists, letting her know the state I'm in. I can tell the moment it hits her, how her eyes round and features soften. But I'm too caught up in anger and bitterness to feel any of the warmth or comfort she has to offer.

"What's wrong?" she asks.

"You're talking to me now, are you?" I find myself lashing out. "Well, no need to worry. I'm just, what was it you said the other day? Wallowing! Yes, that's right. Just feeling sorry for myself, and wallowing in my own self-pity. So please, feel free to go back to giving me the cold shoulder like you've been doing for the past three days. Go back to blaming me for what happened to that father and son—to being angry for falling short of your expectations."

I see fire ignite in her eyes. "I don't blame you for what happened to those two," she says. "But you're right, I am angry. Angry and frustrated that you're so damn arrogant! You take in every failure, every mistake, every single bad thing that's happened to us and swallow it as if you were the one responsible for it. Some assholes decide to attack the farm, it's your fault you didn't see it coming. A greenhouse freezes, it's your fault you didn't figure out a way to heat it. And it doesn't matter what anybody says or does, there's no convincing you differently because you alone control our fates, right? If we live, it will be because you saved us. If we die, it will be because you failed us. It's all up to you: our last, great hope. Jesus, get over yourself!"

Part of me, deep down, hears the truth behind her words. But the heat of the moment is too overpowering for me to accept it. I'm caught up in the riptide that is my anger, its current drawing me in with a force I can't battle.

"You just don't get it, do you?" I ask, voice colder than the wind swirling around us. "Everything I've ever done is for my family. Every choice, every action, it was all for them. Only I'm just now realizing how little it all amounted to: how far we are from where I thought we would be. Do you have any idea how hard it is to look at my family and see how scared they are—to feel their fear claw at my heart so deeply it feels like it's about to be torn to shreds?"

I shake my head, and when I speak again my words come colder still, my tongue an icy whip that can only maim and injure.

"Of course you don't. How could you? They're not your family!"

There's a moment between the words leaving my mouth, and my brain fully processing what I've said. Then the moment passes, and I feel as if I've been jerked out of a deep sleep. I want to take it back. I want to apologize. Better yet, I want her to go on the attack again: want her to yell, curse, rage, lay into me with every foul thing she can think of. Have her punch me, kick me, claw me. I don't care. Anything would be better than this cold silence—than the stunned, wounded look of betrayal she fixes me with.

"Lauren..." I breathe her name in one long exhale, hoping the words I need to mend this emerge. But nothing comes, and her name fades among the wind. Reeling, I make to close the distance between us, desperate to do something. But she stops me before I've made more than a single step, holding out her hand to halt me, her eyes flashing in warning.

"Don't," she says. Her voice is an assassin's blade: quiet as a whisper and razor sharp. She's shaking, though from what I can't tell.

My stomach churns in disgust. How could I have been so careless toward the woman I love most? Her past remains a mystery yet I know, deep down, that she was raised without the warmth of family— without that feeling of unconditional love and acceptance I had always taken for granted. But she's felt it among us. First on the trail, and now on the farm. I can see it in the effort she puts forth in everything she does, can hear it in her voice when she speaks of those she cares for. That warmth now lives inside her, a flame amid the darkness. Finally, she knows what it means to belong to something bigger than herself. And here I am, telling her she doesn't understand; that she was never actually part of the family at all.

I want so badly say something, do something, but I'm frozen to the spot. Her eyes bore into mine and I force myself to meet them, praying she can see how sorry I am. She shakes her head, and I know that whether she can see it or not, she's not ready to forgive.

"Don't follow me," she says. She moves past me, and it's only with the greatest restraint that I do not reach out to her. She steps off the porch and into the freezing rain, so desperate is she to distance herself from me. Yet I don't call her back. I don't stop her. I remain rooted to the spot, staring silently at the empty swing as it continues to sway gently in the wind, wondering just how badly I messed things up.

Chapter 16: (Lauren)

The rain hits like a shower of stinging needles, yet I hardly feel it. Tears pool inside my eyes, restricting my vision to shapes and shadow. I move toward the largest of them, stumbling half blind in the gale. I lose my footing and fall to my knees, soaking my pants through with frozen mud. Cursing, I haul myself up and stagger into the shelter of the barn. The air inside is cold and damp, filled with the earthy scent of dirt and hay. But at least it's dry, and more importantly, it's empty.

Distantly, I'm aware of the effect the rain and cold are having on my body, of the way my arms instinctively cross my chest as shivers and shakes take hold of me. I feel numb, emotionally more than from the cold. A musty horse blanket hangs on the wall which I drape over myself before settling down on a hay bale. It helps, but I find myself shaking worse than ever as I sit here.

Don't cry, you stupid girl.

Fight it.

You're stronger than that!

Only I'm not. I can't keep the dam behind my lids from breaking, or stop the streams of hot tears cascading down my frozen cheeks. I hate that I've allowed myself to be reduced to tears. I promised myself a long time ago that the days of crying over what others said and did to me where over, that I would never allow myself to be put in such a position again. But on the other hand, the position I find myself is one I never expected to be in. Strangers. Enemies. You know to keep your guard up in such company, to expect the worse. You don't expect to be blindsided by the one person you trust above all others. I guess the old adage is true: that those you love have the power to hurt you the most.

"They're not your family!"

I try not to dwell on it, but the words repeat over and over in my mind. Slowly, the tears stop and the numbing disbelief gives way to anger. I don't even know who I'm most angry at. It would be easy to blame Morgan: to rant and rave and call him a hypocrite. He told me he loved me. He called me his family. So how could he just as easily tell me I couldn't possibly understand—that his family is not my family regardless of how much I've come to care for them? But I know, deep down, that what he said was true: that I don't understand. My memories of these people can be measured in weeks and days. I know nothing of the lives they lead before. I only know the after. And though I do care for them, I know our bond has been one of necessity, one forced upon us by circumstance. For that reason alone, I could never care for them as Morgan does. The anger remains, but it's directed mostly at myself. After all, it's not Morgan's fault I looked too far into things. I should have known that just because they felt like family, didn't actually make us family. But maybe that's for the better.

The combination of cold air and rain-soaked clothes are starting to take a toll on me. I think longingly of the fire blazing in the living room hearth, of changing into something dry and curling up under the thick comforters covering the beds upstairs. But to do either would require going back to the house, would put me face to face with Morgan again. I'm not ready for that. Instead, I make do with wrapping the horse blanket tighter around myself until the worse of my shivers subside.

I lose track of time out here. My mind feels numb, thoughts out of focus. I don't even feel angry anymore. Just tired. I feel my eyelids begin to flutter closed. I'm not asleep, yet not quite awake either. I'm in between, the dream world and real world blurring. I hear the sound of approaching footsteps squelching through the mud. I open my eyes wide enough to confirm it's him. There he stands silhouetted against the open entrance, face lost in shadow. I turn my face away. Of course, he followed. I'm surprised he's waited this long.

He approaches slowly, footsteps cautious as if I were a wild animal he doesn't want to spook. But he doesn't speak, nor do I. He sought me out. He can be the one to break the silence. His mud covered boots stop at the corner of my vision, droplets of water beading off him and falling to the ground. Still, I don't turn to face him, keeping my eyes fixed on the earthy floor. He pauses, then sits beside me on the hay bale, his arm snaking around my shoulders and squeezing me close.

I exhale a long breath as I sink against his touch, pressure building behind my eyes. For once, I don't try and fight it. I let it out: the anger, the guilt, the frustration, all the things I usually suppress, it all comes pouring out of me. I can't do this anymore. Whatever walls Morgan and I have built around each other these past weeks need to come down. If there's one thing I'm certain of, it's that we need each other to see this through.

"I don't want to fight anymore," I say, voice thick.

"I knew you would come around."

My body stiffens. Blood turns to ice. The words linger in the frosty air, the triumphant sneer in his voice curling my stomach. I try to break free but his arms are a vice around me. Desperate, I stomp on his foot with as hard as I can. He grunts in pain and swears, his grip on me momentarily going slack. It's the edge I need to wriggle myself free and gain my feet. I make toward the entrance, hand flying toward my holstered pistol, but he's already recovered from my attack, bearing down on me once more. My hand closes around the pistol grip just as his hand clamps around my wrist. I twist and struggle with everything I have. My pistol clears the holster and I pull the trigger, aiming for his leg. I miss. I shoot again. Miss. With a violent jerk, he forces my hand upward even as I fire twice more, both shots missing by inches.

"Enough!" he yells, spit flying from his mouth, voice full of rage. He uses that rage now and slams me against the wall. The air leaves my body, but somehow I hold onto the gun. He slams me again, the back of my head meeting the wood with a hard thump, and I feel the gun fall from my hand. I'm dazed, a deep pain radiating from the back of my skull as the fight leaves my body. Gently he lowers me to the ground.

"I didn't want it to be this way," he says, voice almost tender. He strokes my hair and I feel myself shudder at his touch.

"Please...no..." My voice comes out as a whimper. I can't move, his body too heavy atop mine. His face looms above me, the look in his eyes filling me with a cold dread. I know those eyes:

hungry, dark, cruel. They are an echo of a past I thought I had escaped. Those nights of tears and pain return to me, past and present overlapping with one another so that my concussed mind can barely keep them apart.

I'm on a twin bed, eye black, the taste of blood in my mouth from my bleeding lip.

I'm on a cold dirt floor, mouth dry, face slick with frozen tears.

Above me shine an arrayment of faux stars, their glowing bodies giving me something to focus on, a distraction from my reality.

Above me, there are no stars, no light, only a leering face staring down at me. There's no escape from this reality.

"Mitch..." I plead.

"Ooooh," he breathes. He draws nearer, so close I can feel his stagnant breath wash across my face. "I love the way you say my name." He brushes the hair away from my face and kisses me lightly on the forehead.

I try and wriggle free, but I can't budge him, can't free my arms pinned to my sides. All I manage is to make my head pound harder. He smiles at my feeble attempt and I have to close my eyes. I channel all my energy in making my mind go blank, to retreat deep inside itself. But I'm still too aware of all that's happening. I can still feel him. Hear him. Smell him. I feel paralyzed—feel as if I were trapped in a nightmare, unable to move, shout, defend myself. I can see how this will end, and I'm powerless to stop it.

"Don't worry," he says. "I'm going to take good care of you."

He fumbles with my belt and then hastily yanks my pants down till they reach my knees. His belt comes next, his breaths growing fast and loud. The sound of a zipper. Cold hands on my hip. Fingers playing with the edge of my underwear. A muttered curse, surprised. Alarmed. My eyes open to see him turn quickly toward the entrance, eyes wide, panicked. Not a moment later he's lifted off my body, a dark blur crashing into him in a violent rush.

I shuffle backward while simultaneously trying to pull up my pants and making sense of the scene playing out before me. It's not easy, my vision full of shifting shadows, ears full of swearing and fighting. A dark figure approaches me and I recoil, my danger meter overloaded.

"It's me, Lauren," calls a familiar voice. "It's going to be alright." Folix kneels beside me, looking me over. His eyes land on my unfastened pants resting halfway up my thighs and I hear him inhale sharply. "The dirty bastard," he says in an angry whisper. I barely hear him, my eyes drawn toward another familiar voice—one I barely recognize, contorted as it is in rage.

Morgan has Mitch pinned to the ground, curses flying from his mouth in an endless torrent as he rains down punches, merciless in his fury. Mitch tries in vain to protect himself, his hands doing nothing to stop Morgan from bashing in his face. Three more dark figures rush into the barn, and it takes all of them to pull Morgan off. Even then they can barely hold onto him, desperate as he is to continue his assault.

"Morgan," I breathe. Only at my voice does he cease his attempt to get at Mitch. A moment later Felix stands and Morgan takes his place, a deep sob released from deep within him as he sinks to his knees. He wraps me in his arms and I can't believe I could have ever confused Mitch's touch for his.

"I'm sorry," he says, voice raw and wounded. He's shaking, overcome with emotion. "I'm so fucking sorry."

"I'm safe now," I whisper. It's all I can think to say, the only thing I feel in this moment as I lose myself in his embrace.

I wake in a fog of confusion and dull aches. My thoughts sluggish, head tender. Focus. One thing at a time. A soft bed. Thick blankets cocooning me in warmth. The storm has passed. Sunlight streams through the window for the first time in days. It's early. The house quiet. The light creeping along the walls glowing with the golden tinge of morning. Deep breathing. The feel of another's hand cradling my own. I turn my head to look, a small throb beating in the back of my skull as I do so. Must close my eyes against the pain. Open them once more to find Morgan, slumped over and fast asleep on the chair he's pulled beside the bed. My eyes land on his busted knuckles, the sight of them reminding me of what happened.

I squeeze his hand, the pressure rousing him awake. He lifts his head sleepily, eyes bloodshot, rimmed with dark bags beneath. I doubt he got more than a few hours sleep. He sees that I'm awake and he snaps to attention, the last vestiges of sleep gone in an instant.

"How are you feeling?" he asks, voice thick and constricted.

"Shitty," I reply, deciding to go with honesty. My mind is too fuzzy for much else right now. He tries to smile, but the effort proves too difficult for him, his mouth set in a slight frown.

"I'm sorry this happened," he says. He covers my hand with both of his, holding on as if afraid I'll disappear should he let go. "I'm sorry for everything." He speaks now not only of what transpired in the barn but of our argument which preceded it. I hear it in the guilt in his voice.

"We both said things we wish we could take back," I say. "I don't blame you. It's nobody's fault but Mitch."

He tenses at the mention of his uncle, a cold anger radiating under the surface. "I still can't believe he did that. I mean, he's sort of always been a screw-up. Drugs and alcohol. Theft. Trespassing. That sort of thing...But this?" He shakes his head. "I never would have thought he was capable of something so heinous."

"He's family," I reply. "Nobody wants to think their loved ones capable of such things."

"No," he says, voice suddenly harsh. Raw. "He's not family; not anymore. He's lost that privilege." He scoots closer, squeezing my hand tighter. "*You're* my family. You're the most important thing I have in this world. I'm sorry if I ever made you doubt that." His eyes bore deep into mine with a quiet intensity, imploring me to believe him. It's a look I've seen him give before: in Denver, when he offered Grace and me the chance to join them; after returning from Salida, beaten and exhausted, when he first said he was in love with me; the night after the forest fire, when he said he would never lose hope things could get better, and that he would die trying to create a future we deserved.

Each time I've put my faith in him, and each time he has delivered. I'd be a fool not to believe him now.

I bring his hands to my lips and kiss them gently. "I've never doubted you," I say, my turn to make him believe me, "I just wish you wouldn't doubt yourself."

He stares long at our entwined hands, brow heavy, furrowed in thought. Slowly, a small smile spreads across his lips, lightening the gloom that has settled in his features. "Even after all you've been through, you're more worried about me?" he asks. "Your strength is inspiring."

His says this with such certainty, as if there could be no debating the fact. It makes me wonder what he sees when he looks at me. Not the truth. That much I'm sure of.

"I'm not as strong as you think," I say. He's given me everything. Heart and soul. I've never been strong enough to do the same.

"What do you mean?" he asks. "Of course you are." I grow quiet. Can't meet his eyes. Even now I'm afraid to go there, to break the facade he's created of me. "Is this about Mitch?" he asks. "Because you don't have to worry about him. He's never going to touch you again."

I shake my head. "I'm not worried about Mitch," I say. "I stopped being afraid of men like him a long time ago." Confusion ripples across his face at my words. He wants the truth. I can feel the questions burning inside him—those he's always had, but which I made him swear never to ask. I love him, but I've never trusted him enough to reveal what lies hidden in the darkest corners of my past. I suppose I haven't changed as much as I thought I had. That secluded, mistrusting girl I once was is still a part of me. She exists still, hiding in that darkness, whispering, reminding me to keep my guard up—that to trust is a mistake and that the only person I can rely on is myself. And I know she will remain there, a voice I can't mute, a shadow I can't shake, not until I trust someone enough to let them inside that darkness; to go against every instinct I've engraved in my psyche, and allow myself to be completely vulnerable in the eyes of another. If I can't do that with Morgan, I'll never be able to with anyone.

I sit up straighter, ignoring the throb flaring in the back of my head. A nervous twinge flutters inside me, a thousand trapped butterflies spreading from my stomach throughout my body. My heart beats faster. Mouth goes dry. I've faced so many challenges since the world fell apart, but in so many ways, this is the hardest. Finally, I meet his eyes, the love and concern in his stare helping me find my voice.

"Do you remember when I asked you not to question me about my past?" I ask.

He studies me for a long moment, curious, but also wary. The implications of my question are not lost on him. He may not know the truth, but the man's not stupid. He knows enough to surmise that my story isn't a happy one. Only now, he's about to find out just how unhappy.

"I remember," he says.

"Thank you for keeping that promise. But it's time you knew the truth." I take a deep, steadying breath. It's time to trust, to have faith. "What happened last night...it's not the first time I've been attacked like that."

Chapter 17: (Morgan)

The dam has broken. In streams and waves, the truth pours out of the girl I love. It's crushing. Long have I wondered about the ghosts of her past—how terrorizing they must be to haunt someone as strong and brave as her. Seeing them with my own eyes, I now realize just how strong she truly is. Still, I can tell how much each revelation costs her. I want so badly to wipe the tears from her eyes, to hold her in my arms, to tell her it's all going to be alright. More than anything, I want to take her pain away. But I can't. All I can do is sit quietly. Let her squeeze my hand. Force myself to stay strong as she continues her confession.

She tells me of life with a bipolar, alcoholic mother. How, as a seven-year-old, she found herself caring for the needs of a baby sister because her mother couldn't be bothered with it. Soup kitchens. Charities. Stealing. She kept them alive by any means necessary, the disability checks her mother received mostly being commissioned to support her addictions. There were good days, she said. Days when her mother would smile, and laugh, and one could almost pretend they were a normal, happy family. But for every good, there were twice as many bad. Yelling, crying, beatings. They were the foundation she was raised on.

Eviction notices were not uncommon, nor were the stints in shelters while they were between places. But wherever they settled, their home would turn into a railway station of bad company—dealers, addicts, friends, lovers—sometimes it was impossible to distinguish between them. Public parks and libraries became her refuge: a place she could take Grace to escape the madness at home. Life had never been fair to her, but she made the best of it. It wasn't until her mother brought home a man named Steve, that things turned from bad, to worse.

She was fifteen years old when he moved in. It took less than a month for him to "accidentally" stumble into her room one drunken night. It took only another week for him to find his way to her bed. Her mother refused to hear of the accusations, choosing to turn a blind eye to what was occurring right in front of her face. Or perhaps she couldn't see past the haze of alcohol and drugs Steve kept a steady flow of. She didn't know what to do. She had no family. No friends. There was the police, but even the thought of it terrified her. The scrapes healed. Bruises faded. But the threats Steve had planted in her head; the violent, heinous promises he made to her should she ever think to turn him in, were the scars that would not heal. And even if the police could protect her from him, she and Grace would surely be placed in the system. There, they could be separated, a notion that scared her as much as any threat Steve made against her.

"Maybe it was selfish of me, keeping her in that environment. But she was my whole world...I couldn't lose her."

She grows silent, tears leaking from her eyes. I want to say something, do something, comfort her in some small way. But I know the best thing I can do for her is to listen. To give her as much time as she needs to tell her story.

"So I didn't do anything," she says. "I let it continue. At night, when that door creaked open, and I felt his weight on the mattress, I forced my mind to go blank and black everything out until it was over. That was without a doubt the worst year of my life. If it weren't for Grace, I wouldn't have survived it. I'd have killed myself—would have swallowed a bottle of my mother's pills and let the darkness have me. But for Grace, I endured it. I kept fighting for the both of us."

She grows silent once more, though it's different from before. Her eyes harden, grow cold. An unforgiving anger building inside her. "It wasn't until he started looking at Grace that I knew I had to get us out of there. I knew if we stayed, there would be a day when looking wouldn't be enough for him. But before I could do anything, I needed leverage. So I created it. Videotaped him in the act one night. Played it for him. Threatened to turn it over to the police if he tried to stop me and Grace from leaving. I also warned him that a friend had a copy of it and that if anything happened to either of us, they would ensure the tape was delivered. It was pure bullshit, I didn't have any friends. There was nothing to stop him from beating me, killing me, and I know he so wanted to. But he didn't. I guess the fear of being labeled a child molester and being sent to prison was enough that he didn't dare call my bluff.

"The next day Grace and I left. My mother didn't even put up a fight when I told her. 'Two less mouths to feed,' she said. By then she was so far gone into drugs I doubt she'd have even noticed that we left in the first place. That was over three years ago...I haven't seen her since."

An image of a sixteen-year-old Lauren enters my mind. A girl half my size but with a strength worlds beyond my own. I see her standing firm against her tormentor, risking everything to protect the one person she loved. The courage it must have taken to do that is incredible. I often wondered how she adapted so well after the pulse hit, how the chaos that ensued didn't seem to faze her as it did the rest of us. Now I know. She had already seen the darkest side of humanity. Faced it. Endured it. Chaos was nothing new to her, only to us.

"And Steve?" I ask after a minute or so of quiet, voice hoarse from misuse. "What became of him?"

She starts, and it's a moment before my question seems to register. "My threat held him in check for the most part," she says, finally. "Still, he couldn't resist the impulse to let me know he was around. He would show up to my work sometimes. He'd sit either at the bar or another section and just sort of leer and smirk at me—like we were the only two in on a really funny joke. He never spoke to me though. Never tried to hurt me...at least not until the day of the terrorist attack."

"When your tape no longer mattered," I say, disgusted. She nods in confirmation. The dirty bastard. As the world fell apart, and most people could only think of how to keep themselves and their loved ones alive, there were others who relished the opportunities now before them. To rob, rape, kill without fear of recourse. To a man like Steve, it meant the opportunity to finally break the girl who dared threaten him all those years ago. But I'm still missing something.

"But...you say you saw him that day..." I ask, my question trailing off at the end. But even through the confusion, a foggy picture begins to take shape in the back of my mind.

To my surprise, a small smile graces her lips, the sight of which so at odds with the ominous dread I've felt throughout her story. She lifts her eyes to mine, those green depths I adore suddenly aglow as she squeezes my hand with both of hers.

"I did," she says. "So did you." I continue staring into her eyes, searching for the answer behind the words. Slowly, the picture comes into focus as I realize the truth.

"Those men we killed; the ones who attacked you and Grace that first night...that was *him?*"

More tears shed as she nods, though there is something noticeably different about them. These are not tears of pain, but of gratitude. Of joy. The only kind I've ever wanted to see from her.

"I knew I was going to die that night," she says. "Either that or I would wish I were dead. Even now it's all a haze to me: just a blur of crying and pleading and being manhandled. I don't even remember starting, but at one point I realized I was praying. It surprised me as much as anything. I hadn't believed in God since I was a little girl, praying her heart away for a better life only to watch them go unanswered. But that night, I found myself turning to the sky. Not for myself: they could do with me as they wanted as far as I was concerned. I only prayed Grace might somehow be spared...and she was."

She's moved to the edge of the bed, her hands cradling my face as I look into her eyes. "I don't know if God heard me, or if He's even real or not. All I know is that in my darkest hour, when I had abandoned hope and all seemed lost, you came bursting into my life. Things like that don't just happen. Whatever force that led you to me, it happened for a reason. I'm sure of that now."

I feel a chill sweep across my body, hardly believing what I've just heard. I always felt that meeting Lauren was more than mere coincidence. I mean, for the terrorists to strike on the day that they did, and for us to go through all we went through in our scramble for supplies, only to end up in that dingy accounting firm, so close to where Lauren and Grace were taken? It always seemed like there was something more at play, something bigger than myself. I've never been one to hold much stock in God or fate, but when I consider how Lauren entered my life and the role she now holds in it, I find myself wondering if it were not all indeed part of a grander plan.

"On the trail, when you asked me if I believed in fate...all this was going through your mind?" I ask, remembering that emotionally charged night before I set off for Salida.

"There were a thousand things going through my mind," she says. "But yes. It all stemmed back to this: to you finding me."

I stop fighting the tears that have built behind my eyes, letting them fall without restraint, without embarrassment, letting them bead down my cheeks and roll across Lauren's fingertips.

"We found each other," I say, sweeping the hair from her face. "You understand? I don't know how. I don't know why. To be honest, I don't care one way or the other. Whether this was all part of some intricate, cosmic plan, or if we just lucked into it: it doesn't matter. What matters is that we *did* find each other. I am yours, and you are mine. That's all I need to know."

I pause for a moment, gently brushing away the fallen tears from beneath her eyes. "You have me on this pedestal because of what happened that night in Denver, for saving you and Grace. But you've saved me more times than I can count. Whenever I was drowning in self-doubt and felt suffocated by my own dark thoughts, it was your voice that pulled me to the surface—that breathed the air back into my lungs. You told me once, that we couldn't have made it here without me...but don't you see? *I* would never have made it this far without *you!*

"I want to thank you for trusting me with the truth. That you've endured so much evil in your life, yet haven't let it poison you against the world is amazing to me. I wish more than anything those things had never happened to you. But you know better than I do that there's no erasing the past. We all have demons, some of us worse than others. All any of us can do is move on from them, refuse to let them dictate the rest of our lives. I know that's hard at times. We just have to put our faith in each other: in the belief that better days lie ahead. Maybe not today, maybe not tomorrow...but one day we'll look back on all of this and smile. Those days are coming, my love. I swear they are."

This time, it's she who wipes the tears from my eyes, filled as they are from so much emotion swelling inside me. I see that same emotion staring back at me as she shakes her head, a small smile playing about her lips.

"I never doubted it," she says. She draws my head forward until we meet in a soft embrace, the sweetness of her lips mingling with the saltiness of my tears. She pulls back, and levels me with those eyes I could get lost in. "But it's nice to have you back."

Hours later I sit at the kitchen table, heart heavy with what I know I must do. To my left sit my mother and father, to the right, Uncle Will and Aunt Virginia. Directly across from me is Richard, who, for once, does not look at me in challenge or mockery. That alone speaks volumes to the situation. Others fill out the room, sitting on stools or else propped up on countertops. But all eyes are drawn towards the table. Here a decision will be made.

"How is she doing?" My father asks in deep concern.

"As well as can be expected," I say. Indeed, the courage and dignity she's shown today is incredible. Had she not told me the truth, I might once again wonder how she came to be so strong. As it is, I know too well.

"I still can't believe what happened," Aunt Virginia says, her voice pained. "I mean...he's our brother." She looks first to my Aunt Claire, whose face remains cold and unyielding. But it's her eyes that give her away—the way they swell at the mention of her brother. My mother, by contrast, cannot hide how troubled she is by the whole ordeal.

"He's always been a fuck up," my Uncle Will says bluntly. Even now, there's no sympathy in his voice. No forgiveness. Only a bitterness he's always harbored in regards to Mitch. "Always

something with him: '*I need bail; I got fired; can I borrow a few dollars'*
Claire and I paid his way through two different rehabs, and never saw
even a penny's repayment. And that itself wouldn't bother me if the
man could just stay clean. But no. Without fail, he'd start doing that
shit again. Hell, he's still a damn junkie! Even with all we're dealing
with, he still finds a way to get his fix." He makes a noise of disgust.
"Huffing paint thinners and lighter fluid, I ask you!"

That was the defense that was used. Mitch claimed to be so
high after inhaling those toxic fumes that he wasn't in his right mind.
That it was all a big mistake. It's for the best that I wasn't present while
they questioned him. I doubt I could have heard his desperate pleas
without launching myself at him and finishing the job I started in the
barn.

"He's had his issues," my father agrees. "But what he tried to
do with that girl...that's something else entirely." The room ripples with
nodding heads and echoed sentiments. Even Uncle Will inclines his
head in agreement. None of us saw this coming.

"It's a shame, alright," Richard says. "As if what he did wasn't
bad enough. Now we have to decide what to do about it."

Silence follows his words. Not that what he's said comes as a
surprise. We all know why we're here. But to know what needs to be
done and actually doing it are very different things. Nobody seems
eager to start things off, myself included. For Lauren though, I do so.

"Family or not, high or not, nothing excuses his actions last
night," I say. "He followed Lauren into that barn for a reason. He knew
exactly what he was doing. I just thank God that she was able to put
up a fight. If we hadn't heard those gunshots go off...well, we wouldn't
be having this conversation for starters. I'd have killed him with my
bare hands. You wouldn't have been able to stop me." I pause, taking
a moment to look about the room, allowing everyone to see the
seriousness in my eyes before I speak again. "I can't live under the
same roof as the likes of that."

I wait as the family absorbs what I've said, their faces grim as
the air we breathe. It's as Lauren said: nobody wants to believe their
loved ones capable of such things. And despite what I told her, despite

all that he's done, he's still loved. Cause though I can't get the images of last night out of my mind, or stop the fits of rage which accompany them, he's still my uncle. He's the man who snuck me into the R-rated movies my parents didn't want me to see; who would make me banana splits for breakfast after exhaustive nights of video games and pay-per-view. We'd build bonfires and roast marshmallows in the summer, go sledding and sip hot chocolate in the winter. He was always up for an adventure, and I loved him for it. I wish it didn't have to come to this. But the truth is he's no longer the man from my memories. The drugs and harshness of this world have stripped him from all that made him the man I once admired. Now, he's a man I don't know—a man that can't be trusted. And in a world where trust means everything, I can't allow such a man in my life.

"I agree," Richard says, an ugly look on his face. "I don't give a damn what he says about not being in his right mind. I have two daughters to think of."

Uncle Will casts a meaningful look at Julia who sits on the middle island beside Emily, his eyes hardening. "Yes," he says. "The man must go."

Around the room rises a chorus of agreement. Although, there are some who remain troubled with the idea, namely my mother, Aunt Virginia, and Aunt Claire. His sisters. It comes as no surprise that those who knew him best would have the most difficulty with this decision. To them, he's still their little brother. The boy they grew up with still lives inside their memories. I cast a furtive glance toward Emily, trying to imagine what it would be like to cut her out of my life forever. I can't. For the life of me, I can't imagine a scenario where I would be forced to. Yet, that is the burden my mother and aunts have been tasked with.

My Aunt Claire is the first to accept it. "Agreed," she says quietly, clutching my uncle's hand and hastily wiping the tears that have formed. "If he's capable of what he did...well...who knows what else he might be capable of."

"But is there no other way?" My Aunt Virginia asks. She looks around the room as if someone might offer an alternative. My aunt has always had the biggest heart of anyone I knew. I hate seeing the pain this causes her, knowing this decision weighs on her in ways it does not the rest of us. Where Mitch is the youngest of my mother's siblings, Virginia is the eldest. As such, much of the responsibility of raising Mitch fell to her after my grandmother's untimely passing. In many ways, Mitch is as much a son to her as he is a brother. I feel another flare of anger at Mitch for what he did. It should never have come to this.

I turn my attention now to my mother, the one person at the table who has yet to speak. It's impossible for me to get a read on her, her face an impassive mask, eyes focused on her interlocked fingers. My father sits beside her, hand squeezing her shoulder, but offering no more input. I'm not the only one who studies her now. One by one the gaze of the room hones in on her, waiting for her to break her silence. If she can feel the eyes on her, she doesn't show it. Doesn't allow it to distract her. But finally, it seems, she reaches a decision.

"He has to leave, Vee," she says. Her eyes are for Aunt Virginia alone. "He's our brother, and I'll always love him. But he's never going to change. He was always an addict, always a liability. We all knew it. Accepted it. After all, he's still family...But this time he's crossed a line he can't come back from. It may seem harsh, cruel even, but we can't afford to let him stay. If he does, he'll be the cancer that eats away at us—that will destroy us in the end. There's too much at stake to let that happen. We've built too much to let him set it all on fire."

Silent tears trace Aunt Virginia's crumpled face. With my mom on board, the decision becomes resolute. There's nothing that will change the outcome. Still, she tries. "If we do this, we may as well just put a bullet through his head. That's what forcing him from this place will amount to: a death sentence. A man can't live alone in the world anymore."

A tremor of emotion flashes across my mother's face, the first sign she's shown of the turmoil she must feel. It's gone a moment later, the stoic facade she's maintained through this ordeal in place once more. Only in her eyes does she waiver, tears she won't shed trapped deep inside   But she doesn't take back her claim, nor does anyone else. Dirty a deed as it is, it must be done. Virginia finally realizes this.

She stands abruptly, heat rising in her cheeks. "So be it," she says. With that, she strides across the kitchen and disappears into the adjacent living room where some of the younger cousins sit, no longer wishing to take part in this.

"She has a point you know," Richard says. "Might be best to take him out now."

My father looks at him incredulously. "You can't be serious?" he asks.

"Why not?" he challenges. "It's like Virginia said: nobody can live on their own anymore. And if by some miracle he does survive, how do we know he won't want revenge? We'll be looking over our shoulders for the rest of our lives."

He turns, appealing to those he knows he can convince. Sure enough, Ted nods his head in agreement, echoing the sentiment that we'll always be looking over our shoulders should we let him go. More nods will follow the longer this plays out. What's worse, I know Richard has a point in his argument: that it's the only way to guarantee no retaliation will be made against us. Still, I can't bring myself to agree with his plan. Killing is a brutal, yet inescapable part of living in the world today. I know only too well. But that shouldn't make the taking of a life any less difficult. In a world where we are called upon to act as judge, jury, and executioner, we must exercise great caution with such power, lest we lose ourselves to it. He may deserve death for what he's done, but it would be a mistake for us to take such action. To do so would destroy this family as surely as allowing him to stay would.

"My mom's right," I say, speaking up as my mom finishes condemning the idea. "Look, I know what he's done and I know what he's capable of. But killing him would be a mistake. It's all well and good to talk about taking a life, but few in this room have actually been forced to do so. You don't know what it's like to relive those moments over and over in your head, or see the faces of those you killed haunt your nightmares. Be grateful for that. It's a burden I wouldn't wish on anyone. And make no mistake, it's a burden you'll be taking on if you allow this to happen. It won't matter what justification you paint it in or assurances you tell yourselves. You'll never be the same after. Is that what you want?"

My message hits home. First my mother, then my father voice their support, echoing my words that it would be a mistake to execute Mitch. Aunt Claire is the next to agree, closely followed by Uncle Will who nods his agreement after meeting his wife's eyes. One by one, the room follows suit till all but Richard and Ted oppose. Richard eyes me but doesn't try to sway the others.

"The road it is," he says, conceding. "So how do we go about this?"

The night is an uneasy one. I lay awake for most of it, lost in my own thoughts as Lauren sleeps, her head peeking out from the mass of covers piled on the bed. Neither the twin bed in the far corner nor the rollaway cots that have been placed end to end are occupied. For the second straight night, we are granted privacy. For the second straight night, I watch over the girl I love, her face peaceful, lit by the glow of a single candle burning low on the end table. Giving what she went through, I'm grateful she can sleep so soundly. The same cannot be said for me, however.

Sleep claims me in gaps and stutters, haunted memories weaving in and out my dreams, making me wake with a start. Each time it's the same process: confusion; racing pulse; eyes frantically searching the shadows of the room; find Lauren who remains fast asleep, mind untroubled; remember to breathe; in, out; remind myself it was only a dream; fight the urge to drift off again lest the cycle start anew. It's out of relief when I wake to find the shadows gone and the first rays of the sun filtering through the window pane.

"You never came to bed," Lauren says.

I rub the remaining sleep from my eyes before finding her. "You needed to rest," I say, standing briefly to kiss her good morning. "You wouldn't have got any if I had." She nods, needing no further elaboration. My sleeping patterns are well known by now.

"I tried to wait up for you last night, but I just couldn't keep my eyes open," she admits. She pauses "So...what happened?"

"He's out," I say. "Should happen within the hour, I'd expect." It feels surreal to say out loud. I know it has to be done, but the thought of watching him walk off the farm is one that brings me no joy, only a dull sadness it had to come to this.

"I want to be there when he does," she says. I go to argue, but the look she fixes me with makes me relent. I won't fight her on this.

Half an hour later we join the others downstairs. Not surprisingly, the dour mood from last night seems to have carried over into today. People's faces are glum, as are their morning greetings. There's nothing good about this situation. After a few minutes, my mother and Aunt Virginia emerge from the back room where Mitch has been confined to. Though she tries her best to compose herself, I can tell how much this hurts my mother. I can see it in her red, swollen eyes. Aunt Virginia, on the other hand, wears her pain openly. I don't know which is worse.

Mitch comes next, hands bound behind his back, closely followed by Richard and my father. The look of stunned disbelief he wore last night has long since faded from his features. I watched as my mother broke the news of our decision to him. He didn't seem to register then, staring at the wall with unfocused eyes, refusing to look at her. He understands now, alright. Tears fill his eyes as he looks around desperately, searching for a rescuing hand to pull to safety. None will come.

"Please. Don't let them do this to me!" he pleads when he finds Aunt Virginia. "I'm your brother!" A tremor passes her face, but she does nothing except shake her head and disappear into the next room, too overcome with grief to continue watching. He must sense that his last and final hope has left, as the pleading quickly gives way to anger.

"Is this what family means to you?" he spits even as he's forced along by Richard and my father. His eyes land on me, narrowing in hate before switching onto Lauren. His lip curls in disgust. "You're going to side with a whore over your own flesh and blood?" he challenges scathingly.

I move forward without thinking, rage flaring inside me at his utter lack of remorse. How dare he meet her eyes? How dare he speak to her? My hands curl into fists, eager lay into him again. But then her hand is on my shoulder, and her voice reaches me through the blood pounding in my ears.

"Don't," she says. "He's not worth it."

I stop my advance, my breaths short and agitated as I try and calm myself. Focus on her words, on the feel of her warm hand. Slowly, my hands unfurl and I let them fall to my sides. Once they do, she squeezes my shoulder and steps forward, her eyes like frozen emeralds as she surveys her attacker.

"Call me what you like, Mitch," she says. "It means nothing. Everyone here can see the man you are, now. That's why you're alone. But I want you to know that I don't hate you. You disgust me, yes...but I don't hate you. I know you'll never own up to what you did, cowards never do. Just know that it won't ever happen again. I'll see you coming, and believe me when I tell you that I shoot to kill. Fair warning."

Mitch stares her down with malevolent eyes, but Lauren stands her ground and refuses to look away. Ever since her attack I've been worrying over her as if she were something delicate—something that *needed* to be protected. In this moment I am reminded of exactly who she is. She's more than capable of fighting her own battles. Indeed, it's Mitch whose the first to look away, his stare now directed at me.

"Nothing to add?" he snarls.

"You're dead to me," I say as indifferent as I can manage. "Why waste words on dead men?"

His face twists in an ugly sneer as he looks about the room, sowing as much hate and guilt as he can. Many stare daggers right back. Others cast their eyes at the floor, the ceiling, avoiding his gaze altogether. His eyes linger on my mother, her face once again blank and unreadable despite the currents of emotion that ripple within her. Finally, he turns back toward Lauren and myself, damnation burning in his eyes—a look of unforgivable betrayal I will not soon forget.

Wordlessly, he allows himself to be guided out of the room by Richard and my father. Once past the threshold he stops and looks back at the assembled family one last time.

"Family," he says, making a mockery of the word. "Once it meant something." He spits on the ground. "I see now, it no longer does." Richard and my father have heard enough and push him roughly along. "Remember, this was your choice. Your choice!" he yells even as he's forced away. Eventually, he stops struggling and allows himself to be steered without resistance. I watch as they leave the farm and then disappear from view altogether, a leaden feeling of worry settling in my gut as they go.

It's a gamble letting him walk. His hot temper and cold words proving just how much so. And as I stand here, I begin to doubt whether we made the right choice. Around me, I can feel that same trepidation rising from my family. Soon that feeling will expand and coalesce into that deep gloom that has been our companion these past weeks. It's a cycle I've seen play out again and again—all the misplaced anger, and anxiety, and mistrust spreading from one person to another until we're all affected, suffering it alone because we chose to divide ourselves rather than band together.

United we stand, divided we fall.

Once I thought it no more than a pompous cliche, the sort of thing said by politicians wishing to sound patriotic and inspire the electorate. Now I feel a fool for not heeding its warning even as my family fissured and split before my eyes. I was too busy playing the victim, burying myself under the guilt of my mistakes, my failures, creating layer after layer of excuses I could hide behind, convincing myself it was for the best—that I could no longer be the man people looked to. But the deep spine truth is that I was too much of a coward to own up to those mistakes and failures, terrified of making more. How was I to know that in itself would be a mistake? Well, I'm done hiding. Flawed as I am, afraid though I might be, eyes are still drawn to me. The time for pretending otherwise has passed.

"He's wrong," I say, breaking the chilled silence. "About family no longer meaning anything. It means everything. It's the only thing that makes living in this cruel world worth it."

For the first time in weeks, I feel the full attention of the family fall on me in all its intensity. Assurance. Unease. Doubt. A full spectrum of emotions stares at me as I look about the room, that old feeling of duty once again falling on my shoulders. It's a feeling I refuse to shy away from, embracing it as I did when I first stepped foot onto the Colorado Trail all those months ago. So much has happened since then. So much has changed. The only constant being the love I hold in my heart for the people around me. I don't know if I can be the man they believe me to be. But I do know that they deserve a hell of a lot more than the man I've been.

"It would be easy for me to stand here, and list all of the bad shit we've been through since all this started. There's no shortage to choose from. Then I could go on and say that we only made it through because of each other and that if we just keep trying, we can pull through this too. There's truth in that. It's what we've done since the beginning: struggle, persevere, survive. And yeah, it's kept us breathing. But is that really all this boils down to? Banding together for protection, doing whatever it takes to survive another day?"

I pause, shaking my head. "There's so much more at play than that. I mean, why endure so much pain if you can't find joy with those around you? Why suffer so much violence if you can't feel at peace among those you love? All this time, I've held these grand aspirations about the future. I built it up in my head into this perfect, unattainable dream—this time and place where we would want for nothing and could live out our days in peace, protected from the outside world. Everything I've done since making it home has been in an effort to make that happen. But I was a fool, so caught up in my vision of the future that I overlooked everything I already had. That was a mistake. Because despite all the things I didn't have, I still had you..."

I have to stop, suddenly overcome with emotion as my thoughts drift to Lauren and the hell she endured throughout her life. I always knew that not everyone was lucky enough to have been born into a family like mine. But it took her story to remind me just how lucky I was. How could I ever have taken so much for granted?

"I'm sorry I didn't appreciate that more. Believe me when I tell you I won't make that mistake again. Of course, I still dream of better days. We have to. But we can't lose sight of what's most important: that no matter what challenges we face, we face them together. Hold onto that. Put your faith in each other. We do that, and maybe one day we'll live to see that brighter tomorrow. And if we don't, find comfort in knowing that as cold as the world might grow, you will never be without the warmth and love of family...I love you all. If you don't believe a word I said, please believe that."

My words are not magic. They do not lift the skepticism entirely from the room, nor do they heal the many wounds we've inflicted upon each other these past weeks. Only time can do that. But standing here, I can't ignore the feeling that a major shift is taking place. I feel it too—that energy, that spark—that fervor which grips the heart and stirs the soul in moments such as this. And as Lauren slides next to me, her hand fitting seamlessly inside my own, I feel hope blaze through me as it did when we sat watching the sunset over Rockridge once upon a time.

I can't help but smile. For the first time in I don't know how long, I finally feel like myself again.

Chapter 18: (Lauren)

Fat white flakes fall from the sky. Their progression slow. Movement lazy. As though savoring every second of their journey from heaven to earth. Icicles hang from the edges of the rooftops, the greenhouses, all along the railings of the pasture fence. The world has transformed overnight. Shoveled paths lead to the latrines, the well, the barn— all the areas of the farm we need frequent access to. Everywhere else remains unblemished. Snow blankets the fields, clings to the boughs and branches, the hillsides surrounding the farm the picture of a winter wonderland. To the north and west, mountains stand frozen and imposing, encased in ice and snow. Long has this day loomed before us, always in the back of our minds as we toiled away in determined preparation. Now, that day has arrived. Winter has come in all its fury.

And yet I smile.

Morgan and I kneel beside one another, three giant snowballs of varying sizes taking shape by our hands. Around us are an arrangement of seemingly useless items: sticks, rocks, and a threadbare scarf among others. They'll be put to use soon enough. Abigale walks toward us now, her head barely clearing the largest of our snowballs. She notes our progress, unimpressed.

"Really?" she asks, impatience in her voice. "Vince and Kelly are almost done." I look behind her and see that she's right. Already they have advanced to adorning their scavenged decorations.

Morgan laughs. "This isn't a race, Abe," he says. "This is serious business. Don't want to rush it."

I throw a lump of snow at the back of his head, making the little girl laugh. He wheels about, yelping at the sudden cold. "Quit calling her Abe," I warn. Catching her eye behind Morgan's back, I wink. Morgan sees it and grins.

"You shouldn't have done that, McCoy," he says with a deep sigh. He gathers a lump of snow in his hand and carefully molds it into a ball. "Five seconds," he warns

"Five". I raise an eyebrow in challenge.

"Four." Refuse to move.

"Three." Cross my arms.

"Two." Smile, seeing what he does not.

"One." Burst out laughing as he's caught unaware.

From behind, Abigail launched her own offensive, dumping a handful of snow down Morgan's back. Like a scene from a comedy, he hops up, howling at the sudden cold. Soon other laughs join mine and Abigail's: Vince and Kelly from a little ways away, their project momentarily forgotten; Leon, Emily, and Felix who are busy readying the smoker for today's meal; other relatives who have been drawn outside to indulge in the season's first snow. It's a minute before Morgan can remove all of the trapped snow. When he does, his eyes turn to Abigail with a grin. He holds up his hand, his fingers splayed wide.

"Five," he says. Unlike me, Abigail bolts. She doesn't get far, even with the headstart Morgan allows her. "Think you're funny, do you?" he asks, scoping her into the air. "Is this funny?" He attacks her sides with his fingers making her writhe in his arms as she shrieks in laughter. Morgan lets up his attack, allowing her a moment to catch her breath.

"No more," she says, breathless. "I'm sorry, Morgan."

"You don't want me to tickle your ribs anymore?" he asks.

"Please, no!" she says.

"Alright," he says with a sigh. She lets out a breath of relief as he sets her down. Then his grip tightens on her and he takes her to the ground, his fingers this time aiming for her neck. If anything, her shrieks grow louder. "What?" he asks. "You didn't say anything about your neck."

This moment, watching Morgan with Abigail, hearing the laughter ringing in the air, I can't help but be amazed at how quickly things have turned around. It's hasn't even been two weeks since Mitch was forced from the house, yet the atmosphere couldn't be any more different. The bleak, dispirited air that had plagued the house for weeks has all but lifted. In its place rises hope. Belief. A renewed energy flowing among us. Morgan would never claim credit, but his words were the catalyst for that change.

He reminded us all what many had forgot—that the bonds of love and family are the most important things in this world. It's a message that struck at the heart of those who listened. They've responded in kind. Now, it no longer feels as if we live in a house divided. The discord, the blame, no longer rippling under the surface of every action, every word. The unity we lost gets restored more and more with each passing day. Standing here now, witnessing it all come together, I feel my heart swell, knowing this is always how it should have been.

Eventually, Morgan shows mercy and lets Abigail go. Ten minutes later, we are arranging our snowman's lopsided smile and crowning him with an old straw hat atop his great domed head. Seeing we're finished, Abigail begins her inspection. Slowly, she circles our creation, examining it with a look of great concentration on her young face. It's all I can do to keep from laughing.

"C'mon, Abby," Vince says as he and Kelly join us. "No need to give them hope. We all know ours is better."

Morgan laughs. "Who are you fooling?" he asks, looking over their own snowman with a sour look. "Yours is looking skinny as you these days, Vin. Couldn't have fattened him up any? Or at least made sure it stood up straight? It's leaning so bad, one good wind will probably knock it down."

"Yeah?" Vince asks. "Well, at least ours doesn't look like an obese farmer. The straw hat really caps it off nicely. All that's missing is a can of chew and a pair of overalls."

I can't help but smile as Kelly rolls her eyes, nodding to the two of them. Competition and jibes. From what I've been told it's formed the basis of their relationship since they were Abigail's age. Leave it to the two of them to keep the spirit alive in something as trivial as snowman building. Even so, I'm glad they've mended things. I know how heavily their rift weighed on Morgan. It's good to see them revert back to their old selves.

"I've made my pick," Abigail informs us a minute later. Morgan and Vince stop their back and forth, growing quiet for her announcement. Smiling, she turns to Morgan and myself, declaring us the victors. Without warning, Morgan lets loose a loud cheer and proceeds to hoist me into the air and throw me over his shoulder. My surprised shout quickly turns into a squeal of laughter as he begins to spin circles, making my vision go blurry and head go dizzy.

"What gives, Abby?" Vince challenges as Morgan finally sets me down. "What's wrong with ours?"

"Morgan's right, it's too skinny," she says seriously. "And yours doesn't have a hat. They're supposed to have hats."

Vince's indignation lasts throughout the afternoon, aided in part by Morgan's bragging. I laugh at the two of them, knowing it's all in good fun, an act they play off one another. But also because on some level, I know they both really wanted to win.

"I mean, sure, ours was a little slim," Vince admits that evening. "But it was the only way the vest would fit. And you can't deny, that vest was guap as hell."

Kelly places her hand over his with a small laugh. "Let it go. It's over."

"It's never over with this one," he says, nodding across the table to Morgan who laughs and offers a shrug in agreement. He lets the issue drop, the arrival of Leon and Felix drawing his attention away. My mouth waters, the smell of cooked meat a fragrance I haven't enjoyed in some time. Richard came through huge for us yesterday, bringing down a large buck during an afternoon hunt. Combine that with our recent harvest, and for the first time, we have a small surplus of food. It's nothing crazy, but we shouldn't starve anytime soon. That knowledge alone gives us a peace of mind we haven't known since this began.

Thick slices of venison are served with an assortment of mixed veggies. It's a meal the likes of which we have not had in some time. Tomorrow we will return to rations. But tonight we allow ourselves to indulge, a feeling of celebration about the place. Halfway through our meal, Vince rises to his feet, a look of wild disbelief on his face as he stares down at his beaming wife. He turns and shouts for quite, that same disbelieving smile on his face.

"Sorry to interrupt, but it's just come to my attention that my beautiful fiance is currently carrying my child," he says in a calm, polite voice. It disappears a second later. "You hear me?" he says, voice rising to a shout to be heard over the family's roar of surprise. "WE"RE HAVING A BABY! I'M GOING TO BE A DAD!".

Wine is poured. Stashes of whiskey and vodka unearthed. I laugh more than I have in ages, a feeling of great contentment washing over me. An evening like this is exactly what my soul needed. Good food. Good conversation. A mellow buzz flowing through me, making every joke more hilarious, every story more entertaining. I watch Vince grinning like a fool with his ear to Kelly's stomach, speaking to his child despite Kelly's instance that the baby has yet to develop ears. I don't ever want to leave from this table. Everything about this moment is gold. If only there were a way to capture it, preserve it, make it stretch on and on toward infinity so we might live in it forever. Yet even as I wish it, I know all too soon it will pass, the same as every golden moment that has come before it. All I can do is enjoy it while it lasts.

"Huh?" I ask, only just recognizing a voice trying to get my attention.

"Are you drunk?" Emily asks, amused.

"Of course not," I say, surprised to hear the slight slur in my words. "Well...maybe a little," I concede.

"Keep a secret?" she asks. She doesn't wait for a reply before leaning closer, her mouth hovering inches from my ear. "So am I," she whispers. Immediately she bursts into a fit of giggles, the likes of which I've never heard from her, causing me to join her.

"Oh Lord," Leon says from Emily's opposite side. "Em's got the giggles."

"Right on schedule," Felix laughs. "Surprised it hadn't happened sooner."

"And what do you two have against giggles?" I ask in Emily's defense.

"Nothing," Felix says. "Giggling Emily is hilarious."

"It's the next couple phases you need to watch out for," Leon says. "The: *I love everybody, emotional drunk stage—*"

"Closely followed by the: *hiccuping, uncontrollable crocodile tears stage,*" Felix finishes.

"Don't listen to them. They're just being assholes," she says as they continue on, citing various examples of these stages from parties past. She takes another sip of her wine. "Besides, you already know I love you, right? That's not the drink talking either...from the heart...I really do."

"I love you too, Em," I assure her, a lump rising in my throat. Drunk or not, Emily is not one to mince words. She boldly wears her heart on her sleeve, unapologetic in her words and actions. So when she tells me that she loves me, I know she truly means it. And she's not yet done, wrapping her arms around me and drawing me close, our faces squished together cheek to cheek.

"I always wanted a sister," she admits, lowering her voice so only I can hear her. "I love Morgan...but it's just not the same...you know? Wasn't till I went off to college that I knew what it felt like." Maya. Tears fill her eyes as she speaks of her lost best friend—the first time I've heard her mention her since the burial. "I fucking loved that girl. She was all heart. All love...I miss her so Goddamn much." I feel wetness on my cheek, whether her tears or mine I can't tell. Probably both. It's a minute before she composes herself enough to continue. "But life goes on. This world might have taken my sister away from me...but I feel like it gave me another." She kisses me on the cheek and squeezes me tighter. "I'm so glad I have you in my life. You ever need anything, I'm here for you. My sister."

Both of us have to wipe our eyes when we part, much to the amusement of Leon and Felix who immediately take notice. Soon the bottles stop flowing. Yawns punctuate the air. The table slowly empties around us. Eventually, Morgan and I make our way into the crowded living room, the upstairs bedrooms having finally been abandoned. Wending our way through the rows of mattresses and sleeping bodies, we reach our small cot. As I lay down, I can't remember the last time I felt so at peace, head sinking into the pillow, the feel of Morgan's arms around me, the warmth of his breath on the nape of my neck.

For once, sleep comes easy for Morgan, his breathing deepening within minutes as his mind shuts down. My own eyes grow heavy. The drink in my system melting me to the bed like butter on toast. So comfortable. So tired. Still, I fight to stay awake. Today has been like something out of a dream—a taste of that future someday Morgan has spoken of. I'm not ready to let that go. But even as I fight, shadows creep on the edges of my vision. Darkness settles. And the thoughts drain from my head as sleep claims me.

I sit, surrounded by loved ones on the slope of a small hill. It's a warm night, the sky above an endless expanse of stars and velvety darkness. I breathe deep, savoring the smell of lilacs drifting on the air, enjoying the feel of grass beneath my bare feet. Among us, there is a feeling of expectation. Excitement. It builds the longer we wait. All in quiet. Our bated breaths the only sound to pierce the silence. And then it happens.

Streaks of light rise in the sky above, their colors vibrant, their glow bright. Silver, red, green, blue. They climb up and up until they burst, painting glittering arcs, sparkling webs, dazzling flowers, all against the black canvas that is the night sky. Boom, boom, boom. The sound of thunder echoes with each explosion, the noise loud from our position on the hillside. Fireworks. I thought they were part of a world that no longer existed. But here they are.

More rise. Their intervals shorter, their patterns more intricate. I'm immersed in their beauty, in the sound of the percussion. It's not until the smell of smoke tears through the scent of lilacs that I sense something's wrong. Fire spreads below, caused, no doubt, from the falling sparks raining down from the sky. The flames eat up the hillside, grass and shrubs and trees consumed and reduced to ashes. What's worse, nobody seems to have noticed but me.

I try to speak, yell, warn them. But I can't make a sound. I leap to my feet, trying to pull them up, to make them tear their eyes away from the sky and see the approaching threat. Nothing works. All I can

do is scream my silent scream. All the while the flames draw nearer.
Fireworks explode overhead, beautiful as ever. Boom. Boom. BOOM.

I wake to a room full of confusion. Panic. There are cries, screams, shouts for quiet. All around people are scrambling to their feet, reaching for boots, for weapons, their bodies lit with a fiery glow. I bolt upright, searching for the source of the flames, positive they have chased me from my dreams. But there is no growing inferno threatening our lives. Only the glow of the low lit fire on the far side of the room. Then what the hell is going on?

Boom.

The sound reverberates through the house, echoes off the walls. Shouted orders from our sentry follow, warning someone not to make another move or the next shot goes through their heart. Before I can register anything else, Felix is flying up the stairs and Richard is yelling instructions, readying us for a siege.

"You have your gun?" I ask my sister from the cot beside our own. She nods, determined not to reveal any of the fear I know she must feel. "Good. Keep it ready and stay away from the— " I cut myself off as Felix bursts into the room, face panicked. Without a word, he crosses through the room like a rushing bull, roughly pushing people aside and falling deaf to the curses and questions flung at him. Morgan and Leon are out the room moments later.

"Stay here," I instruct Grace, already moving toward the kitchen along with Emily and Vince while Richard rushes upstairs for a better vantage point. Vince is first out the door, holding up a fist for Emily and me to pause.

"They're bringing somebody in," he says, staring out into the dark.

"Raider?" I ask.

He shakes his head. "Don't think so." He squints and then curses. "Christ. He's just a kid." He steps aside as Felix and Morgan reach the door, the arm of a skinny youth draped around each of their shoulders. Vince was right. He's just a boy: one so pale I might have mistaken him for a corpse if not for the violent shivers that rack his body. He's soaked, dressed only in a thin fleece and jeans, the amount of snow and frozen water caking his clothes suggesting he's fallen several times. Tougher than he looks to have kept getting up. Who is he? Where did he come from? More importantly, why is he alone? Before I can voice any of these questions, Morgan begins issuing instructions, Felix's attention solely on the boy.

"We need to warm him up." He speaks rapidly, turning to each of us in turn. "Lauren, blankets and dry clothes. Vin, call off the alarm and make sure we have some space. Em, a pot of water and some sugar—there should be some in the pantry. Get it to Leon, he should have the camp stove going already." None of us challenge our directives. Dashing into the living room I snatch Felix's bag and two thick blankets from his mattress near the stairwell. Vince follows after to address the family. "Everything's fine," he assures them. "Nobody's trying to attack us." It's all I hear before re-entering the kitchen where Morgan and Felix have already stripped the youth of his clothes. Felix hastily ruffles through his bag, unearthing a hoodie, sweatpants, and a pair of wool socks they quickly dress him in.

"Everything's gonna be alright, Robbie," he says, wrapping one of the blankets securely around his shoulders. "You're safe. You're home."

Suddenly it all clicks. Felix's mad rush from the house. The soothing voice. The concern burning in his eyes.

"He's a wild-child if there ever was one," Felix once told me. *"All go, all the time. Absolutely fearless."* He grew silent for a long minute, the small smile on his face slow to fade. *"That's a good thing though...He's going to need that courage now more than ever."*

I've heard the stories. Seen the photos. Watched Felix struggle with the burden his family's unknown fate. Now, after all this time, here he is—living proof that at least part of that family survives. Rob: the energetic, younger cousin Felix spoke of so often.

"Felix." He speaks, voice hoarse, words barely slipping past his chattering teeth. "I--I tr--tried. H--had t--to..."

"Shh," Felix says. "Save your strength. We need to warm you up." As if in response to this statement, Leon and Emily re-enter the kitchen. Leon carefully pours the steaming contents from the pot into an empty coffee mug before handing it to Felix. "Slowly," Felix says holding the cup to his cousin's mouth, Rob's hands trembling too badly to do so himself. "Too much, too quick and you'll cough it right back up."

Tension fills the kitchen as we wait, Felix never leaving his cousin's side as he helps him finish the remainder of the pot. Words of comfort pass between them as Felix works, a tenderness to his actions I've never seen from him before. I can't even begin to imagine the thoughts and emotions that must be brewing inside him. Because even as he hugs his cousin close and assures him all will be well, there are still questions that need to be answered.

After a while, his teeth stop chattering. His shivers cease. And though he's still pale, some of the color has returned to his face, making him resemble more of the boy whose photos still adorn these walls.

"I knew you would come back," Rob says. "Told em', if anyone could find a way back, it was you."

Felix reaches his hand to his cousin's shoulder, squeezing it gently. "I made it back because I had something worth returning to." A sob escapes Rob at these words. He hangs his head, hiding his face behind a curtain of overgrown hair. "I know it's been a long night, Robbie, but I need you to tell me what's happened. The rest of the family, are they safe? Are they..." He doesn't complete his second question. I don't think he can bring himself to voice his greatest fear into words, not when he might finally know the answer.

"I don't know," Rob admits. He looks up again, his eyes haunted, filled with pain. Slowly the story is told. It was his mother and father's frantic shouting that woke him the day our lives changed forever. He sped into the living room to find his parents staring transfixed at the TV, scenes of horror and mayhem being broadcast from all corners of the world. And then everything went black.

"Mom was still freaking out, but it's like the blackout settled dad down," he says. "He knew what had happened, explained it to me and mom. He said he had to get to Lena and Brianna before things got out of control. Looked like something out of a damn nightmare by the time he was finished loading up: Tac-Vest; Assault Rifle; 12 Gauge; pistol on his hip, and another strapped to his ankle. Never seen him look so scary before. None of the cars would work, but the old Polaris started right up. He told us to lock the house up nice and tight, and not to open up for anybody until he returned. Said he should be back by nightfall, morning at the latest...That was the last time I saw him."

The scene plays out in my mind's eye as he tells his story. The fear he must have felt watching his father drive off the farm, dressed for war. And then the long wait that followed: day fading into night, night ceding to the dawn, morning passing by in fear and worry, all without hide nor hair of his father's return. And I have a feeling the story only grows darker.

"He never returned?" Felix asks. Outside he doesn't let it show, but the news has to come as a blow to him.

Rob shakes his head miserably. "We waited," he says. "Must have been two, maybe three weeks. Never came back. Lena and Brianna never showed up either. It was just me and mom. In the early mornings, we'd haul water and tend the garden, the rest of the time we locked ourselves inside. Dad told us how bad things would get, how desperate people would be without food. He said to wait, so that's what we did. We didn't know what else to do."

"You say you waited for three weeks...what happened after that. Why did you leave?" Felix asks after a pause.

Rob looks away, attempting to hide his face once more behind his overgrown hair. "Was my fault," he says, voice thick. "We slept in shifts, one of us awake in case something ever happened. I dozed off one night, woke up to mom shaking me awake and the sound of the front door being smashed in downstairs. We could hear them moving around, four, five voices at least. Didn't have a choice, had to get out of the house before they found us. We were gonna lay low in the barn, see if they decided to move on, but one of them spotted us before we made it. Didn't even shout a warning, just started shooting. Lucky for us he was a shitty shot. But after that, we had no choice but to run."

He looks up again, tears in his eyes. "I'm sorry, Felix," he says. "I shouldn't have fallen asleep. If I was awake, I might have been able to stop them or scare them off at least. We might have still been here when you got back."

Felix reaches out and squeezes his shoulder once again. "Don't punish yourself," he says. "You have no way of knowing what might have happened if you tried to stop them."

More tears leak from Rob's eyes. "Yeah," he says. "But I also know what wouldn't have happened." He pauses, and I can practically hear Felix's heart thump against his chest in the silence that ensues. "We didn't know where was safe. Most of the friend's mom could think to reach out to were either back in town or lived too far away. She was afraid of town ever since dad left and didn't come back. There was only one place she thought might be safe."

"Pete Sawyer's ranch..." Felix says, voice barely above a whisper. Rob nods his affirmation. Felix stands, hands balled into fists at his sides. He shares a look with both Morgan and Leon, anger flashing dangerously in his eyes. After a deep breath, he returns his attention back to Rob. "Tell me everything."

He does. He tells of them arriving at the ranch early that next morning, exhausted and desperate. But where they had hoped to find safety they instead found captivity. Pete Sawyer, long-time friend, pounced on what must have been a dream come true for him. Christina had always assumed it a joke when Pete would claim her biggest mistake was choosing Frank over himself. She assumed wrong. After years of lusting after her there she was, completely at his mercy, no law or husband to protect her.

He would keep them alive, he promised. But for a price. The same terrible price countless women have been forced to pay since the dawn of time—one which a mother like Christina would willingly pay to ensure the life of her child. And though Rob was spared, life under the Sawyer's regime wasn't easy. Used as free labor, all of his duties were supervised to prevent him from escaping the ranch. Still, he tried, especially in the beginning. Bruises, scars, seven tiny cigarette burns in the shape of a smiley face stand proof to the punishments he received in doing so. It wasn't until Pete threatened to punish his mother in his stead that the attempts stopped.

"I fantasized about attacking Pete a thousand times," he says. "Beating him with a shovel or stealing a gun from one of his men. But I knew the second I tried anything like that I would be killed. Even then, I almost tried. The only thing that stopped me was thinking about how it would break mom. I hated what that prick was doing to her...but I knew it would hurt her a thousand times more to see me killed. So I kept going, for her. But it was without any real hope either of us would survive much longer."

He wipes the tears from his eyes, finally able to meet Felix's again. "And then there you were. I could see you from the house. I tried to break for the door, tried to yell out, but they knocked me out before I got close. When I woke up my head was throbbing. Pete was in a rage, ranting, warning me not to do anything stupid. But it didn't matter what he threatened me with, I knew the truth. I knew you made it home."

It's Felix who has to wipe the tears from his eyes this time. "I gave up," Felix admits, his words full of remorse. "I stopped searching. We checked so many places, talked to so many people. And all this time you were..." He stops abruptly, a guilt-ridden sob stuck in his chest. "I'm sorry, Robbie. I never should have gave up on you."

"Don't be sorry," he says. "Knowing you were alive is what kept me going. All this time I was waiting for the right moment to escape. Tonight it finally happened. The ranch has been fighting off attacks the past couple weeks, some gang based out of Ignacio. They've been doing it gradually, stealing here and there, trading gunfire back and forth with Pete and his crew. They attacked again earlier, must have been twenty men at least. It was my chance. He couldn't afford to keep someone on me, he had lost two men already that week. I tried to get mom out. He had her locked in his bedroom with one of his men. The moment I peeked my head through the window he saw me, would have blown my head clean off if mom didn't knock the gun sideways. She screamed for me to run, so I did. Didn't stop until I made it home. I knew I had to find you, knew you were the only one who could get her out of there."

Felix hugs his cousin close, bringing his forehead to his. "Don't worry, Robbie," he says, rage building behind his words. "I'll bring her home."

Chapter 19: (Morgan)

A storm rages around me. Gone is the languid snowfall that kept us company while we built snowmen, and laughed around the dining table, and lost ourselves in a moment of normalcy. I should have known it wouldn't last—that the calm would give way to the cold winds and fierce flurries we now move through. Snow falls thick and fast, hiding the surrounding landscape behind a swirling white veil. My vision is restricted to feet in front of me, shapes apparating suddenly into being before being swallowed back up again. I have no clue where we are, how far we've come. All I can do is keep my eyes on the two figures ahead of me and trust that Felix can navigate the storm.

He sets a furious pace, fueled by the same fire that burns through my veins. It sparked the moment I laid eyes on Rob, soaked and freezing, barely able to stand. Throughout his tale, I felt it grow and spread, appalled at what he described. I can still see the scars, the bruises. I can see the twisted smiley face burned onto his forearm and the urge to kill overwhelms me. And that's not even the worst of it.

"Mi hijo, que bueno verte!"

I hear the words as clearly as if she were here beside me. Rarely did Christina Chavez call me by my name. No. It was always *mi hijo.* My son. And she welcomed me into her home as such, treating me as she would one of her own. It was within her walls that I learned you don't have to be blood to be family. *Mi otra madre.* My other mother. I remember the smile she wore when I first gave her that title, the way her laugh filled the room with warmth, with love. That's the image I always remember of her: smiling, happy. But it's not the image that plagues me now. I see tears, pain, misery. I see the kind-hearted woman I love like my own flesh and blood broken and suffering at the hands of someone she thought a friend.

I shake the image away. I can't afford to let my rage run away with itself. Not until she is safe. To distract myself, I recount the plan we came up with based on what Rob told us of the ranch's layout and defenses. It's rough at best. Truth is, it's tough to know what to expect, especially considering the place was under attack when Rob escaped. But it's not as if we have a choice in the matter. Leaving Christina behind is not an option. I only hope the storm lasts. It's the biggest advantage we have.

"How much farther?" It's the first words she's spoken since we left, providing me with a much more thorough distraction than our shaky plan.

"You promised me. Are you a liar?" The question twisted my heart, knowing she was referring to the promise I made on Elroy's farm so many months ago—that I would not stop her from joining me on occasions such as this—that I would leave that decision up to her. The moment I looked into her eyes I knew there was no persuading her. Her mind was set. Determined. Fighting would accomplish nothing but waste precious time. So I relented and kept the promise I made. But that doesn't stop the fear that rises as I see her beside me.

"Not far," I say. "At this pace, we should be there soon."

Felix comes to a halt shortly after, the outline of the Baptist Church visible through the storm behind him. Leon and Emily join us a moment later. My sister's presence worries me as much as Lauren's. I'd have kept both of them from this if I could. But as headstrong as Lauren is, it's nothing compared to Emily. Over two decades of butting heads with her has taught me that. *"You're not the boss of me. I can come if I want to!"* For a moment the fierce young woman before me vanishes, replaced by the girl she once was. How strange to realize they are one and the same—that the heart which beat in that little girl, beats inside her still. Where did the time go?

"Ranch is just over a mile out," Richard says. "Remember, just as we discussed..." The old military veteran takes charge, and I wouldn't have it any other way. Unlike Lauren and Emily, his decision to join us was completely unexpected. I was sure he'd be against the idea—that he would point out the obvious gaps and flaws in our plan, and tell us that it was too dangerous—that it would be foolish for us to risk our lives with so much unknown to us. But the caution was never preached. Instead, he laced up his boots, hugged his daughters, and was the first to follow Felix into the storm. Knowing what he can do, his presence is a welcome one. Still, I can't help but wonder what could have possibly driven him out of the warmth and safety of the house. Was it really all about helping us save a woman he doesn't even know? Somehow, I doubt it.

We set off again, our pace slower, more careful than the mad rush we used to get here. Remaining vigilant however proves difficult. While the storm remains our biggest advantage it's not without its own faults. An army could be hidden in the mist and falling snow, and we'd have no way of knowing until we were practically on top of them. Factor in the known gang roaming the area, and it's all I can do to keep my calm. As we move I put all my focus into the sounds around me, listening for anything that might alert us to the presence of others. None come. Howling wind and treading snow are the beat to which we march.

"This is it," Felix says. Behind him, Richard sets to work cutting through the barbed wire with a pair of bolt cutters. Felix points past the fence as if he can see more than a dozen feet beyond it. "House should be on the other side of the property. Stay alert, especially around the outbuildings. If there are any lookouts, that's where they will be."

The adrenaline mounts as we enter the snowy field, numbing my worries, my fear. There's no room for either right now. We stick close to the fence line as we move, the wooden posts and snow accumulating along the base offering at least an illusion of cover if need be. We reach the corner of the field without incident, Richard cutting through the strips of barbed wire as he did earlier. Our escape route if things go south.

We leave the field and enter the heart of the ranch. Richard leads us, hand signals serving as words. Here the snow has been disturbed, the tread of dozens of feet leaving trails criss-crossing over one another in every direction. Suddenly, Richard holds up his fist to halt our progress and goes to a knee. We mimic his actions. Straining my eyes, I see what has his attention, the shape of a small outbuilding just visible ahead of us. After a minute he stands, and we set our course on the building. There are no windows and only one door which sits ajar, a smear of blood coating the metal handle. Richard signals his plan and we situate ourselves accordingly. He holds up three fingers. Two. One.

I kick in the door and flatten myself against the wall. No shot follows. Felix lies on his stomach, the flashlight attached to his rifle sweeping through the dark interior. He gains his feet.

"Two bodies," he says grimly. We don't investigate further. As we move toward the house more bodies turn up. A man with a bullet through his forehead. Another on his back, arms and legs splayed as if struck down while making snow angels. There are women too, two of whom appeared to be making an escape, their bodies lying just short of the fence. Splatters of blood stand out vividly against the snow, turning into pools the closer we get to the house. The battle seems to have reached its peak in the shadow of a huge barn. There's over a dozen bodies, each death more unpleasant than the one beside it. In the barn itself, more bodies are found, one vastly different than any we've seen today: it's still alive.

"What happened?" Richard asks, taking a knee. The man isn't long for this world, blood soaking his shirt and pooling into his lap. He'll soon bleed out. It's a miracle he hasn't already.

"The bill came," he says shakily. I don't understand, but Richard nods his head solemnly. "It always does in the end," he tells him. I don't see Richard draw the blade but I hear it find its mark. A gasp of pain. His fist clawing at the ground. And then he goes still, the light leaving his eyes.

We scout the house from here, scopes trained on the darkened windows for any movement within. Felix is restless. I can feel the nervous energy coming off him as the minutes pass, the struggle to remain patient becoming increasingly more difficult. I relate only too well, that same struggle waging war inside me. My body yearns for action but my head reminds me to stay calm, to slow down. My head wins. This close to our goal, we can't let our emotions outweigh logic.

After ten minutes without movement, we make our move. I exit first with Felix, striking for the left side of the house. My heart thumps wildly in my chest as we move across the open ground, eyes drawn to the shadows beyond the windows, convinced I'm about to see a muzzle flash, hear the sound of approaching death. But no shot comes. We make it to the house unharmed. Leon comes next with Emily, followed closely by Richard and Lauren.

"Just as we discussed," Richard whispers. "Stay low and—" His words are cut short by a scream of pure agony from within the house.

"What the hell is that?" Leon whispers. The sound reaches us again, and I feel a chill creep down my spine no storm could bring.

"Doesn't matter," Felix says, paler than he was only a minute before. "Stick to the plan."

We proceed toward the front of the house, keeping as close to the wall as possible to minimize our visibility from inside. Three windows dot this side of the house, each of which Richard checks through the reflection of a small mirror. The first two prove empty, belonging to a bedroom and bathroom respectively. Before we've even reached it, I know the third will be a different story. The sound of raised voices grows louder the closer we approach, punctured once more by that pain riddled scream. Richard uses the mirror to scout inside. After a minute he holds up eight fingers, one for each of the people he's counted. He passes the mirror to Felix who studies its reflection, eyes narrowed in an almost manic intensity. Finally, he lets the mirror drop, the grimness of his face not encouraging.

"They have some poor bastard tied up in there," Richard whispers. We've retreated to the first window we cleared so as not to be overheard. "I have no idea what their end game is, but I saw the tools they were using...if they're trying to coerce him somehow, he'll break sooner than later."

"And Christina?" I ask, eyes only for Felix.

"Didn't spot her," he says. "Still, she could be somewhere else. I mean, look at the size of this place." I don't miss the worry in his voice. He's trying to convince himself more than us.

"What about Mr. Sawyer? Connor?" Leon asks.

A dark look passes Felix's face. "They're leading the interrogation," he says. "They're in their element."

"Which makes this the perfect time to strike," Richard says. "They're never going to be more vulnerable than they are right now." He's right. The longer we wait, the more time they have to pull themselves together. Better to catch them with their pants down.

"What's the plan?"

The screams ring loud in this enclosed space. It echoes off the walls, the floors, the sound of anguish making the hairs on the back of my neck stand on end. Even worse are the sobs, the pleading. But if there was ever mercy in the hearts of his tormentors, it has long since passed.

"Please! I'm begging you...no more." A scream of pure misery adds to the hatred boiling inside me.

"Beg those you killed for forgiveness." Cold wrath coats Mr. Sawyer's words. "They give me the word to stop, and I will. Until then..." Another twisted scream, soon followed by another, and another still. I can all but hear the hope leave his body, each act of violence stripping away his humanity a little more each time.

Mean laughter reaches my ears, closely followed by the portentous voice I remember from my school days: one that, even back then, seemed to find joy at the exploitation of others. Connor Sawyer always did have a certain cruel vanity about him. He can only have grown worse in the wake of what's happened. The collapse has had the unique ability to turn good men bad, and bad men into monsters. The sudden image of a broken father and son limping away in the distance fills my mind, their faces haunted, the weeks that have passed doing nothing to mute their pleading which still echoes in my mind. It's a truth I know only too well.

The man murmurs something I can't quite make out. A squeal of pain immediately follows.

"Speak up!" Connor says. "I can't hear you over your whimpering!"

"Just kill me!" the man yells. "I've told you everything...just finish it." No hope remains in the man's voice. He knows his end has come. Perhaps he's known from the moment he was captured. Perhaps even earlier. Perhaps he knew from the moment his ears were filled with the sound of gunfire, and the bodies of his friends fell around him, their life's blood weeping from open wounds as they breathed their last, and he could do nothing but push forward, returning fire as if by killing those responsible for their deaths he could somehow avenge them, honor them, as if they hadn't already left this ugly world behind. Then again, perhaps the fight has simply been beaten out of him. Perhaps all he wants now is to die with what dignity he has left.

Connor laughs, relishing his victim's pleading. "Kill you?" Connor asks as if the notion were completely ridiculous. "Why on earth would we kill you? You're far too much fun to let die! Besides, what if more of your friends decide to come looking for you? We'll need you to show them what gracious hosts we are. Don't you agree?" Another scream sounds after the man refuses to answer. "I asked you a question!"

"Enough!" Mr. Sawyer snaps. "This is supposed to be about retribution for those he and his people killed. This isn't for you to get your rocks off. Try feeling a little bit of grief and stop treating this like a fucking game!" Unlike his son, pain riddles Mr. Sawyer's words. Twisted though he may be, I can hear how much the deaths of his men weigh on him. The knowledge, of course, changes nothing. His blood will still spill. But hearing the humanity in his voice reminds me that none of us are all good or all bad. And that while it's alright to hate him for what he's done, it's on me to stop that hatred from twisting me into the very thing I despise.

"*I'm* treating this like a game?" Connor challenges. "I've warned you since the beginning that we needed more security! I told you it was only a matter of time before we were attacked. But would you listen? Of course not, cause you always know best. You want to blame someone for what happened, look in the mirror!"

"You forget yourself boy!" Mr. Sawyer yells. "Talking to me like this is your God damned house. Who the hell you think you are?"

"Just admit that you were—"

Connor stops speaking mid-sentence, a disturbance from the driveway silencing the fight between father and son.

"PETE!" Felix's voice cuts through the walls like an icy whip, the anger behind his words cold as the storm raging around him. "Show yourself, you lying piece of shit! Face me like a man unless you're so much of a coward that you only feel powerful standing up to women and children!"

The tension builds as confusion erupts among the Sawyer clan. I close my eyes, blocking out the details of the room, focusing solely on the sounds taking place around me. Mr. Sawyer and Connor arguing once more. The familiar cadence of weapons priming and bullets being chambered. From somewhere deeper in the house, a child crying. Then, finally, two pairs of feet approaching from the back of the house, the commotion up front drawing them away from their posts. So far so good.

"No gun. No backup. What the hell is he playing at?" Mr. Sawyer's may be a lot of things, but he knows something's not adding up.

"Told you letting him walk away was a mistake!" Connor says. "Let's just kill the spick now. Be done with it."

"Of course that's your solution!" Mr. Sawyer snarls. "Shoot first, think later. Try using your brain for once: he's alone, he's unarmed. Doesn't matter how angry he is, he's not going to risk doing anything that might threaten his aunt's life!"

"COWARD! I'm waiting!" Felix's goading comes at just the right time, causing Mr. Sawyer to lose what little cool remained of him.

"Enough of this. Connor, end it—he won't last much longer anyway. *You*, help keep things quiet back there. The rest of you, with me. Spread out and stay behind the barricades. Never know what he might be hiding up his sleeve."

If only you knew.

New sounds reach me. A pair of feet moving swiftly down the hall and disappearing with the slam of a door. Choking and coughing.

The creak of the front door and the tread of people exiting the house. Quiet. And then, our cue.

"Felix? What the hell's the meaning of this?"

Slowly, Richard pries open the door an inch or two, noise muted by Mr. Sawyers voice. From his pocket he withdraws his mirror, scouting ahead as Felix responds.

"Don't insult me by pretending you don't know the answer to that question. I'm here to bring my aunt home. I'm not leaving without her."

Richard pockets the mirror and with a nod over his shoulder, we move.

"I hate to tell you this son, but she is home. She belongs to me now."

We approach slow. Silent. Only the tortured man strapped to the wooden chair remains behind. His throat has been slit open and blood covers his entire front. Connor granted his wish after all.

"I don't want to have to kill you, Felix," Mr. Sawyer says. "We don't have to be enemies."

At the front door, Richard uses the mirror to scout ahead once more. Silently, he relays what he sees and lays out his plan for Leon and myself.

Connor laughs. "Yeah, Felix," he says, mockingly earnest. "We can all be one big, happy family!"

Felix's eyes find mine as we make our move, a grin splitting his face that wipes the smirk off Connor's.

"I already have a family," he says. "Unfortunately for you."

Death stalks through their ranks—silenced rounds buried into the backs of skulls and larger caliber bullets ripping through exposed torsos. It's pure carnage, their men caught between our strike team and snipers concealed in the snowfield. Most are dead before they even know what's happened. Few manage to turn in time to see us among them, guns halfway to their shoulders before being shot down. Even fewer manage to get shots off, their bullets eating into the dirt at their feet or else flying clear over our heads. In the end, only two survive, both of whom are completely incapacitated by their wounds. We leave them where they are. Their lives are not ours to take.

Felix strides forward, his anger cold and quiet as he stares at the wounded men. Even as he bleeds out, Connor Sawyer manages to sneer contemptuously. "Spick," he says in greeting. He spits bloody phlegm at Felix's feet. "The little bastard found you then, huh?"

Felix responds by pressing his boot onto the bullet wound in his lower abdomen. Connor screams in pain, unable to help himself. To his left, his father makes to launch himself at Felix. Richard has him restrained in seconds.

"He has a name," Felix says. "Roberto, Chavez."

"Sorry, don't speak wetback," Connor says. He screams as Felix presses his foot harder onto his wound.

"Say his name," Felix says.

"Smiley," Connor says, forcing a laugh through his pain. "Look at the mark I left on his forearm if you don't believe me."

Felix kicks Connor in the stomach, making him double over from the pain of it. Mr. Sawyer groans as he struggles against Richard's grip. I feel a dark satisfaction pulse through me at their suffering. They are far from innocent. They deserve this pain and more for the acts they've committed. But then I see the look on Felix's face, the cruel glint flashing in his eyes as he lands another kick. I see tears pool in Mr. Sawyers eyes as he watches, helpless—a wicked, twisted soul, yes—but still a father watching his son in pain. The vision of another father and son enter my mind for the second time today, reminding me of the thin line we tread and how easily we can lose sight of it.

"Chavo!" I say as he rears back for yet another kick. He stops and lifts his eyes to mine. "Remember why we're here." Slowly, the glint leaves his eyes. He nods.

"You're right," he says. He turns his attention now to Mr. Sawyer. "My aunt, where is she?" he asks

Mr. Sawyer looks up at Felix, face twisted ferally, his contempt a force onto itself. Yet he doesn't lash out. Perhaps he wishes to save his son from more pain. Or perhaps he simply realizes no good can occur from doing so. "In the house. First bedroom past the kitchen."

Felix waits, allowing Mr. Sawyer the chance to add something should he chose He doesn't. "I didn't want any of this," Felix says. "This is all on you." He pulls out the pistol strapped at his back and fips off the safety.

"Wait!" Mr. Sawyer pleads, raising his hands defensively. It's the only word he manages before Felix fires, once through his outstretched hands, and again through his forehead. Connor screams and curses, his skin pale as a corpse. He makes to stand, but his knees give out and send him back to the ground. It's a pathetic sight. I'll always hate the man for the things he's done. Yet I can't help but pity him in his final moments.

"His name is Roberto, Chavez," Felix says, turning now to Connor. "And you didn't break him." Connor slumps to the ground beside his father, a twin bullet buried through his forehead. He stares down at the pair of them for a moment, the raw hatred from earlier cooled into a grim acceptance.

After a minute, Felix looks up. "Almost done."

I follow Felix back into the house. Past the kitchen, we reach the door Pete mentioned. Felix turns to me and nods, his face equal parts fear and longing. I pull out my Glock and return the nod. Moment of truth.

We enter what must be the master bedroom. Wooden walls. Plush rugs thrown over hardwood floors. A fire flickers inside a stone covered fireplace, flooding the room with warmth. Opposite the fire sits a king size bed, in front of which stands the Sawyer's last line of defense: a girl, roughly my age with fiery red hair, and a teenage boy, pale with fear.

"Stay back," he warns, lifting a shaking shotgun. "I'm not afraid to shoot." A lie. If his hands didn't give him away, the tremor in his voice certainly would.

"Put the gun down," Felix says. "I've had enough bloodshed for one day. That's not the reason I came here."

"And what exactly is your reason?" the girl asks. Unlike the boy, she holds her shotgun steady. Whatever fear she might feel she hides it well, betraying not a flicker of unease. Given the circumstances, I have to respect that.

Felix is about to respond when the door behind him opens and out steps the woman whose face I know as well as my own mothers.

"It's ok, Ruby," she says. "He's my nephew."

The girl looks to Christina, her eyebrows raised. "This is Felix?" she asks, her eyes shifting back to Felix. There's a familiarity between the two that I didn't expect. Even more unexpected is for the girl's gun to drop at Christina's nod. The boy is only too eager to follow suit and let his gun fall.

The danger passed, Felix drops his gun and closes the distance between them in the span of a heartbeat. "Estoy sonando?" she asks, her body hidden from view as Felix squeezes her tight. A sob escapes him at the question.

"It's not a dream, Tia," Felix says. "It's not a dream."

My heart swells. The whereabouts of his family have weighed on my friend's shoulders for far too long. To see him reunite with part of it fills me with nothing but joy.

"I knew you were still alive," she says, looking him up and down in an appraising sort of way. "I felt it in my bones."

Felix looks away at that, swallowing the lump in his throat before reapplying: "I wish I had the same faith in you," he says, tears leaking out his eyes. "I'm sorry, Tia. I never should have stopped looking for you. I should have come back, should have kept searching. If I had, maybe I could—"

She puts her hands on either side of his face, making him stop mid-sentence. "Hush, child. You're here now. Eso es todo lo que importa." *That's all that matters.* Felix nods, sinking against her touch as if he were a boy again. A minute later it's my arms wrapped around her, and then Leon's, tears and words of endearment flowing freely between us. Felix introduces her to the rest of our rescue party. She greets them all the same, hugging them close as if she's known them for years. It's always been her way. From the shadows of the private bathroom emerge more people. First out is a woman in her early thirties, a boy no older than two held in her arms. Behind her comes several children: a boy and a girl around nine, and an older girl who's maybe twelve. All have hair a shade of red except for the toddler whose hair is a dark blonde.

"Quienes son?" Felix asks.

"They're friends," she says. "Surely we can use more, yes?"

I share a look with Felix and I know he too has read between the lines. He knows his aunt's heart better than I ever would. Before either of us can question further, Christina beckons them forward and begins introducing them one by one. Heath Sawyer, Pete's son, and Connor's half-brother. Ruby and Scarlett Sawyer, cousins to Heath. Scarlett's children: Sara, the twelve-year-old, and twin siblings Noel and Brice. And the toddler in Scarlett's arms: CJ, short for Connor Jr.

Felix's smile falters at learning CJ's name, a guilty flush rising to his cheeks. It goes largely unnoticed, but I know my friend. The blonde hair, the blue eyes, his father's features live on through him—a father he won't remember and whose blood stains Felix's boots. Connor may have deserved to die, but being blindsided like this has to be hard on him.

"Good to meet you," I say, giving Felix a moment to collect himself.

"We heard the gunshots," Scarlett says. "Does that mean they're..." she spares a quick glance at her children. "You know...that they're gone? All of them?" She looks to us eagerly, as if we were the bringers of news she has longed to hear. It catches me by surprise.

"They're gone," I confirm. "All of them." She looks to her sister, an unmistakable look of relief passing between them. "You don't seem troubled by this."

Ruby laughs humorlessly. "This was a long time coming," she says. "Those bastards deserved whatever end they got." I can tell by the silence among my friends, that I'm not the only one caught off guard. "What? You thought we would be angry, that we would want revenge? Please. You did us a favor."

"How's that?" Felix asks.

"They killed our father, for starters," Scarlett answers. I don't know what I was expecting, but it certainly wasn't this. "They called it an accident, but they killed him. He saw how wrong this place was, pushed against Pete to change things. This place would have been so much different with him in charge. Instead, they snapped his neck, and said he fell from the hayloft in the barn."

"Yet you stayed?" Richard presses. "Even with your suspicions?"

"What would you have suggested we do?" Ruby asks, heat rising in her cheeks. "That we pack our bags and go? That we take the kids and try and make it on our own?" She fixes Richard with a challenging stare. "What choice did we have but swallow the bullshit and stay?"

"They speak the truth," Christina says, coming to their defense. "They're good girls, good kids. We can trust them."

"Is that right?" Richard asks. He looks now to Heath. "Can we trust you? Even after what we did? I mean, that was your father and brother, right? That doesn't rub you the wrong way? There's not even a part of you that want's to level that shotgun at us and pull the trigger?"

"That's enough!" Christina stares sharply at Richard. "I've already vouched for these people. You think I do so lightly? I've been kept here against my will for four months! I know the way of the world just as well as you."

Richard inclines his head in acknowledgment. "Of course you do. You understand then my questioning—my need to be absolutely sure we can trust these people. I mean, you do intend for them to return with us, right? You'll forgive me then if I need more than your assurances before I stand by and let them under the same roof as my family."

"And you'll forgive me if I remind you that the roof you speak of belongs to me," Christina says, her words clipped and waspish. It's a new tone for her, forged, no doubt, over the past few months. "Don't misunderstand me, you have my deepest gratification for what you've done for me today. And of course, you and your family are more than welcome to stay under my roof for as long as you wish. But don't think for a second that you have the authority to tell me who is, and is not welcome in my own home."

Richard doesn't look swayed, and oddly enough, I find myself siding with him. I don't doubt the hardships Christina has suffered. And though those hardships have changed her, I still know the heart that beats within. It wouldn't surprise me at all for her to grant pardons to those who don't deserve them. How can we really know if he is made of a different cloth than his father and brother?

"It's ok," Heath says. Christina makes to argue but he pats her gently on the shoulder, a familiar, reassuring gesture that stops her from interrupting. He stares between us, gathering himself before speaking. "I understand your concerns about me. That's how it always plays out in the movies, right? The hero's family gets killed but he survives, setting him on a path of revenge." He laughs bitterly. "That's not what this is. I might share their last name, but believe me, there was no love lost between us. My mother raised me. I saw Pete only a handful of times growing up, and that was fine by me. I was always a bit of a disappointment as far as he was concerned. Then I came out of the closet when I was fifteen and he really didn't want anything to do with me.

"Only reason I'm here was because the state forced me to. My mother, she...she passed a little over a year ago. Didn't have a choice but to come here after that. When things went dark I was set to leave. Whatever was waiting for me outside couldn't be any worse than what I had to put up with for the past year. I stayed for him." He looks to CJ. "I know the kind of men Pete and Connor were. I could suffer this place if it meant I might be able to shield him in the process. So to answer your earlier question: no, it doesn't rub me the wrong way. As it so happens the only men I've ever had the urge to level a shotgun at are already dead."

I believe him. The emotion in his voice, the affection in his eyes as he looked at his nephew too genuine to be faked. And I'm not the only one. The rest of us accept what he told us as the truth. Even Richard nods and offers his hand to shake.

"I apologize," Richard says. "But I had to know."

The boy takes it. "I get it," he says. "Knowing who my family is, I expected nothing less."

A light awkwardness ensues, each of us quiet with our own thoughts. I clear my throat, drawing the attention to myself. "Well, shall we get started then? I have a feeling there are some supplies around here we could put to use."

Ruby smiles. "I can think of a thing or two."

Chapter 20: (Morgan)

The storm has passed and night has fallen when we finally return to the farm. Beneath a cloudless sky, the family gathers, our arrival drawing nearly everyone from the warmth of the house. I can see the awe, the disbelief. Can't say I'm surprised. Six of us set out this morning, nothing but our weapons and the clothes on our backs. Now I dismount from one of our newly acquired ATV's, flashing a smile I cannot feel, face numb from the cold. And I'm only the head of the procession. Behind me, truck doors open and engines go silent. From the trailers come snorts and stomping, their occupants eager to be released. A second ATV coasts to a stop beside me.

"All clear," Richard says, cutting the engine and unmounting. "No pursuers."

"Good," I say. "We've had a long enough day as it is."

A rare smile splits his face which I find myself returning. Long barely scratches the surface. I'm exhausted, operating on next to no sleep over the past forty hours or so. But a warm cot isn't far away, and the spoils of our operation are more than worth the fatigue.

Rob is the first to reach us, breaking free from the gathering crowd and throwing himself into his mother's arms as if he were years younger. When he straightens, I'm surprised to see he stands taller than she does. When did that happen?

"Thank you," he says, sobbing into Felix's chest. "Thank you." He repeats himself again and again, so overcome with emotion he's at a loss for words.

"You don't ever have to thank me, Robbie," Felix says. "You're family. There's nothing I wouldn't do for you."

Theirs isn't the only teary reunion. Richard's daughters are engulfed in his arms moments after he unmounts. Leon's mom trembles as he hugs her, his arms seemingly the only thing holding her together. When I hug my own mother I feel a great, shuddering breath leave her body, as if she can only breathe freely now that we've returned. Before I can think anything of it, she's moved on to my sister and Grace takes her place in my arms. Behind them, my father hugs Lauren as he would his own daughter. We've been gone less than a day, yet it seems so much longer than that.

Eyes eventually study the caravan we've arrived in and the family who stands beside it. The Sawyer family observe us cautiously, wary to move any closer. Once again, it's Rob who's first to greet them, breaking free from Felix and making a beeline for Sara, Scarlett's eldest daughter who moves forward at the sight of him.

"I told you," he says, voice still shaky as they cling to one another. "Do you believe me know?" I have no idea what he told her or if she believes him, but watching them, seeing the care and concern they hold for one another makes me believe that bringing them here was the right decision. Inspired by the display, I begin to make the introductions.

"For those of you who don't know her, this is Felix's Aunt Christina," I say. "It's her home we've been living in these past months." I make it a point to emphasize that last bit. Christina deserves nothing less than the respect she's owed. Predictably, it's my mother who greets her first.

"It's so good to see you again," my mother says, embracing her in a brief hug. "When I heard what happened..." she pauses, her words falling off. "Anyway. Thank God you're such a strong woman. Welcome home."

"Thank you, Marie," she says. "It's good to be back." She turns and beckons the Sawyer's forward. "These are friends of mine. They each made these past months infinitely more bearable."

There's awkwardness as the two sides meet, everyone assessing, analyzing, trying to get the measure of one another. Not that I expected anything different. Anyone who's managed to survive this long knows the importance of remaining cautious around new people. And considering the encounters we've dealt with, it's only natural for one to grow guarded. It'll take time. But seeing the warm smile on my mother's face as she shakes hands with Scarlett and

Ruby, Christina by her side, introducing herself to my Aunt Virginia, I have faith things will work themselves out.

"We have a fire going inside," my mother says. "Come. It's freezing out here."

My mother ushers Christina and the Sawyers into the house, Aunt Virginia and Richard's daughters following as well. The rest stay behind, eager to take a closer look at the supplies we've brought.

"Holy shit," Vince says, realizing just how much cargo we're hauling. Holy shit about sums it up. When we set out this morning, all that mattered to me was getting Christina out safely and returning her home. It never crossed my mind we would be returning with so much more. Working vehicles. Medical supplies. Crates of food. And that's just the tip of things. Richard and Leon hop into the bed and unload one of the storage crates.

"Bastards were sitting on a gold mine," Leon says, opening the latch and revealing the contents inside. Several people curse, making me smile. I had the same reaction. My father withdraws one of the stacked boxes which fill the container and opens it. He clicks on a small flashlight to read the cover: Federal, 5.56x45MM.

"How many rounds is this?" Uncle Will says.

"Didn't get the chance to run inventory yet," Richard says. "This wasn't the only crate they had." He gestures to the four remaining crates, each stacked full of ammo.

"Seriously?" Vince asks. "What other calibers?"

"You name it," Richard replies. "7.62, 9mm, .45 ACP, .22 LR, 12 gauge shotgun shells. The place was like a damn sporting goods store."

"How the hell did they get so much ammo?" my dad asks, more to himself than to us.

"Traded apparently," Felix says. "Gave most their livestock in return for the ammo, a working truck, and one hundred gallons of gasoline."

Uncle Will curses. "Must have been a hell of a lot of livestock." He looks over to the horse trailers attached behind both trucks. "But I can see they didn't trade everything." People come forward, peering inside for a closer look at the stirring animals. Four horses occupy one trailer, six pigs in the other.

"Anyone else have a sudden craving for pork chops?" Mr. T asks, staring at the pigs with hungry eyes.

Leon claps his dad on the shoulder with a laugh. "Don't worry, Pop. There are two males and four females. With any luck, we'll have plenty of little pork chops running around before long."

The wind kicks up a notch, reaching through the layers I wear. "As nice as it is to admire all this, these trucks aren't going to unload themselves," I say. I drop down the tailgate of the second truck and remove a crate of food. "Shall we?"

An hour later I am setting down a final duffle bag with an audible grunt. Inside is a mixture of rifles and shotguns taken from the ranch. We made it a point to bring back every firearm and round of ammunition we could find. Whether it was hauling crates of ammo up from the cellar, or prying a rifle from the frozen fingers of its fallen owner, we left no stone unturned in our search. Some might find scavenging as we did macabre, disrespectful, but I feel no qualms about it. We'll make better use of them than the dead.

The living room is more crowded than ever, the addition of Christina, Rob, and the Sawyer's stretching it's capacity to its limit. They were offered private rooms, but like us, they chose warmth over privacy. That in itself speaks volumes: it's no easy thing these days to trust someone to watch over you while you sleep. It's as good a sign I could have hoped for this first night.

Less than 24 hours have passed since I was violently ripped from my sleep and forced to leave the cot I now sink into. It seems longer, my mind and body completely spent from all that's happened. I don't even have the energy to wish Lauren good night. My eyes close the moment my head makes contact with the pillow. Seconds later, or so it seems, my thoughts vanish entirely, my mind drifting away into a dreamless sleep.

For weeks I dreaded the approaching winter. I feared the ice and cold. I feared scarce game and low provisions. I feared I was doomed to watch my family freeze and starve—that despite all our work and sacrifices, it wouldn't be enough to survive the unforgiving season. But that was before Rob showed up in the dead of night, setting off a series of events that changed everything. It's surreal how quickly our fortunes have turned.

I stare at a full pantry, stocked to capacity with the food we brought from the Sawyer's ranch. If I were to open the cupboards in the kitchen behind me, I would see a similar sight. Canned goods, packages of pasta, huge sacks of rice and beans. Wicked as Pete Sawyer was, the man knew the importance of preparing for the worst. Have to at least give him that. If we're careful, we should have enough food to see us through to spring. That alone is a huge relief. I won't soon forget the desperation I felt over the summer. The hunger pangs. The headaches. The mental toll you face when you're starving and don't have a clue of when or where your next meal is coming from. They're the kind of things that stick with you.

The heat at my back is another new feature of the room. A small, wood burning stove sits against the opposite wall, filling the room with warmth. A good idea on Richard's part who foresaw how it could be put to use. All we had to do was remove a window to accommodate the chimney pipe and seal it up with some plywood. Now, the two largest rooms in the house are heated, allowing us to spread out a bit from the overcrowded living room.

Outside I watch as Leon, Emily, and Ruby make their way back from the barn where the horses and pigs are being housed. Better them than me. I'm still sneezing after yesterday. Hay has always wreaked havoc on my allergies. Worth it though to haul what we did from the abandoned farms in the area. Should be enough to feed the horses for a while at least. As for the pigs, Ruby believes one might be pregnant. One can only hope. Just the thought of bacon makes my mouth start to water.

My gaze drifts to Richard and Felix who oversee another round of firearm training, mostly for the benefit of the younger family members. Grace is among the attendees, soaking in every word being said and practicing the motions being taught. Rob is also in attendance, handling the different weapons with ease. None of this is new to him. I have the feeling his true reason for being out there has less to do with practice and more with the redhead standing beside him. Sara, whose attention is wholly focused on her task, fails to note the sidelong looks that I see. I can't help but smile. Seems like only yesterday Rob was launching sneak attacks on me with toy swords and nerf guns, his laugh infectious as I would chase him and pin him to the ground. Strange to see the look of puppy love on his face.

The group moves on to target shooting where airsoft guns replace the real ones. It's not ideal, but with bullets as valuable as they are, it's the best we can afford. Should the time come when they need to use the real thing, they will at least have some shooting practice under their belts. They take it in turns, one person shooting while the rest observe. I'm impressed as I watch on. There are few who are wild with their aiming, but most are decent shots. Rob, of course, outshines the group, hitting the center of the targets time and time again. He turns to smile at his cousin who is quick to return it. But as Rob turns away I notice the smile falter, his features forming into a solemn mask I've seen too often these past few days.

I don't understand it. I thought having his aunt and cousin back would help heal the void he's felt since arriving home. To everyone else, it might seem that way. In their company, he's nothing but smiles and laughter. Upbeat. Confident. But I can look past the pretense and see the role he's playing. It's one I've been forced to play myself: carrying on for the sake of moral, pretending like all is well even as you're breaking inside. I know that look, know its burden. I won't let Felix carry it alone as I did.

As evening gathers, I accompany Felix to check on the animals and lock up the barn for the night. The grounds are still and quiet, empty but for us two. If the cold weren't deterrent enough, the smell of tonight's supper easily ensures our privacy.

"We haven't really talked much since we got back," I start. "You doing alright?"

Felix looks at me strangely, my question catching him unexpected. "Yeah, man. Why wouldn't I be?"

"I don't know," I admit. "Just seems like something's eating away at you."

"You're seeing things," he says. "What could possibly be eating away at me?"

"Again, I don't know. Why do you keep answering my questions with another question?" He stares at me for a long moment. Shields up. Defiant. I stare back, unwilling to break the silence. It's on him to make the next move.

"I gave up on them," he finally says. It's as if the words steal the air from his body, from the room. Them. His family. Suddenly it all makes sense.

"You did all you could, Chavo," I say. "There's no way you could have known the truth."

"Yeah, that's what I keep telling myself. But they're just platitudes. It doesn't help. Doesn't change the fact that they were alive and I assumed them dead—that they were suffering and I wasn't there to protect them."

He breaks, crushed beneath the weight guilt he's tried so hard to bury. I sit beside him, hand gripping his shoulder. No words are spoken. Anything I could possibly say would only ring hollow in his ears. I wait. I share his pain in silence until he's ready to continue.

"I never thought I would see them again," he says, wiping his eyes with the back of his hand. "I should be ecstatic right now. I should feel blessed every time I see their faces. But whenever I'm with them it just feels...off. Like something's missing."

I can sense where this is heading. If I'm being honest, I had a feeling it might be leading this way since Christina and Rob returned home. Felix gave up on his family once. He won't do it twice.

"When do we leave?" I ask

He meets my eye, and I know he knows that I've guessed his intentions.

"This isn't like the ranch, Moe," he says. "You saw what it was like in town. Things could only have gotten worse since then."

"Your point?"

"My point is that going in there is like walking into the lion's den," he says. "One slip up, one wrong move and (he snaps his fingers) it's over, just like that. I can't ask you to risk your life for this."

He doesn't believe he'll come back. I can hear it in his voice. And knowing my friend the way I do, I know that won't stop him from going. After finding his aunt and cousin alive, he won't give up on the rest of his family so long as there's the slightest chance they too might be alive out there. If that means walking into the lion's den, that's exactly what he'll do. But damn him if he thinks I won't be there to make sure he walks out.

"Do you remember what you told Leon and I, the morning after we made it to town?" I ask. I don't give him time to respond, gripping the back of his neck and bringing his forehead to mine as he once did to me. "You called us your brothers—told us we were worth traveling down the road of life with." He sniffs loudly, tears leaking out the corners of his eyes. "Nothing's changed. If this is the road you're taking, bet your ass I'm not letting you travel it alone."

He nods, pulling back slightly. "Thank you," he says.

"You never have to thank me, Chavo," I say, repeating the words he spoke to Rob. "You'd do the same for me."

After dinner, I inform the family of our plan to enter town and search for the rest of Felix's family. In the master bedroom, my friend does the same with his aunt and cousin. It's best this way. Whatever her reaction, Christina deserves privacy as the full weight of our decision sinks in. I don't imagine the incredulous faces around the room would do her any favors. They don't understand. That much they make perfectly clear.

You can't be serious. Think of the danger you'll be putting yourself in. They've been gone for months; if they haven't returned after all this time...

There are different variations, but basically, it all comes down to the danger of entering town, and the difficult task of tracking down Felix's family, assuming, of course, that they are even still alive. It's nothing I don't already know. I'm fully aware of the odds and risks involved with what I've agreed to.

"I've told you all before: there is nothing I wouldn't do for those I love," I say, cutting through their protests. "Did you think I was lying?"

"This is bigger than that, Morgan," my father says. "I love Felix like he was my own, but what you're talking about is madness. What are you going to do, knock on every door in town and hope they'll answer?" He shakes his head, angry, frustrated. "It's madness."

I hear the fear in his voice as he tries to convince me to stay. I would say it's a fear I understand, but in my heart I know that's not true. I have no sons, no daughters. I know nothing of the exhilaration one feels when holding their child in their arms for the first time. I know nothing of the highs and lows, the innumerable feelings that come with raising a child. All I know is the love of a son, the love of a brother, and somehow I've been trapped between the two.

"I understand why you want me to stay, and I love you for that," I say, turning my attention back to my father. "But if you don't see why I have to do this, I'm afraid I can't explain it to you."

Only he does see it. I can tell as his arguments die in his chest, the truth finally sinking in: there will be no persuading me. My mind is set. I have to look away after a moment, hating the hurt in his eyes. I turn instead to my mother who sits beside him. Unlike my father, she has remained silent, impassive throughout everything I said. She always was the more reserved of the two, more difficult to read. She was also the one more likely to let us test our strengths, to make our own decisions and learn from our mistakes. *"It's your life,"* she would tell us. *"I can't tell you how to live it."* Whether or not she agrees with my choice, I cannot tell. But when she meets my eyes and tilts her head to me, I know I at least have her support. In this moment, I couldn't be more grateful for it.

"When do we leave?" Leon asks. Like with my mother, unspoken looks serve as the communication between Leon and his parents. There is no calling him crazy or begging him to stay. Both Mr. and Mrs. Thomas accept his decision in silence, his father squeezing his shoulder, his mother his hand.

"Midnight," I say. "We want to make it to town well before dawn."

"Sounds like it's going to be another long night." My stomach clenches at the sound of her voice. I expected to hear it long before now, but that does nothing to numb my worry. I chance a look at my father, her words the boot that crushes him. We would both keep her from this if we could, but I know there will be no doing so. My sister is stubborn as they come, nearly impossible to sway from the decisions she makes. Still, I must try.

"This isn't something you should be a part of, Em," I say, her eyes flashing dangerously at the statement. "With town the way it is, we have to keep things quick and quiet. It should just be us three. Less moving parts, less to worry about."

"First off, you don't have to worry about me: I can take care of myself," she says. "Second, you two aren't the only people who care about Felix." She rolls up her sleeve and shows the deep scar she received on the trail. "When I was lying helpless, gripped in fever dreams from an infection, where was Felix?" Her stare is piercing. First on me, and then on Leon. "He was with you two. Risking his life to save mine. I haven't forgotten. So if I can help him now, nothing either of you says is going to keep me from doing so."

I nod, accepting what I should have accepted the moment I heard her voice. Besides, she makes a valid argument. My father must feel the same, for he makes no further attempt to convince her to stay. As much as he may hate her choice, he accepts it. With that squared away, I now force myself to face the girl I've been avoiding since I broke the news. The moment her eyes meet mine I know she has decided. The words she speaks are for the benefit of everyone else.

"If you go, I go," Lauren says.

I don't reply. Don't argue. I stay still and silent, wishing I could change her mind if I just stared into her eyes long enough. The promise I made to her comes back to me, as I feel it is destined to do so time and again in moments such as this. I thought I knew then what I was promising. I was a fool. I could never have guessed it would be this difficult to keep. This isn't lost on her either. I can see it buried in her eyes: a soft, almost apologetic glint, as if she knows exactly how difficult her decision is for me to accept. Perhaps she does.

"I know," I finally say. I tear my eyes away from her and look around the room once more. The faces of those I love stare back at me, tense, worried. I wish I could say something, do something to alleviate their concern. More than that, I wish I didn't have to leave them, not now that things are finally looking up for us. But it's the way it has to be.

"You may not agree with what we go to do," I say. "That's ok. But please know, I didn't make my decision lightly. Everything I do is for this family. I wouldn't have agreed to this if I didn't believe this was the best choice for all of us."

Slowly the kitchen empties. Both mine and Leon's parents stay with us, as do Ray and Grace. The time passes quietly as we prepare for tomorrow: sorting food, loading bullets, discussing our options once we reach town. Felix joins us eventually, eyes red, voice hoarse. His aunt took the news worse than my father. It's not difficult to see why. Her husband left this farm in search for his family as well. For weeks she hoped, prayed, waited until the night she and Rob were forced to flee. Now Felix intends to do the same. The fear that she might lose him too must be overwhelming. We can't let that happen.

Conversations fall silent as I enter the living room, the subject of our departure clearly being discussed. I pay it no mind. I've already said all I can on the subject. Avoiding eye contact, I force a smile and enter the small bedroom in the hallway beyond. Inside is our armory, each weapon and bullet meticulously counted and sorted by Richard.

"We need another three-hundred rounds each of the 5.56 and 9mm," I tell him as he enters the room behind me. "It's a lot, I know, but we might need it if things go south."

He brushes the numbers aside. "Take what you need," he says. "I'm not here to monitor you."

Strange. I know he's against this move of ours. Why then is he so willing to let another six-hundred rounds of ammo walk out this door without opposition? Stranger still is the stare he fixes me with. These past months, dozens of emotions have filled his eyes as he's looked at me, most falling somewhere between hostile and mocking. This is different. He looks troubled, concerned even. I don't know what to make of it.

"Is it to tell me that I'm making a mistake, then?" I ask. "That only a fool would take a risk like this?"

He shakes his head. "No, Morgan. I understand Felix is like a brother to you. I know you can't turn your back on that." He pauses, searching my face in quiet calculation. I wait for him to continue, more curious than ever to his appearance.

"We've had our differences, you and I," he says. "No sense in pretending we haven't. And I'll admit, a lot of that was on me. There were times I couldn't stand you. I hated how outspoken you were, how much you challenged me. I hated the sway you had over the others— the way they looked at you, listened to you. I thought I had everything figured out better than you did, that I alone knew what was best for us, and that you were just an obstacle standing in my way. But I was wrong, I see that now. I learned that after what happened with TJ.

"It wasn't your fault, what happened, but I was happy to let you believe so—happy to seize the opportunity to discredit you while you beat yourself up over it. I don't know if it was because of guilt or stress or whatever, but you stopped challenging, stopped speaking your mind. It's like you were just going through the motions, determined to keep your head down and mouth shut. Truth be told, I wasn't all that concerned; it's what I had wanted since the start of this after all. But things didn't fall into place like always thought they would. And the further you retreated into yourself, the worse things became.

"Then the whole situation with Mitch happened, and as ugly as all that was, it seemed to snap you out of whatever it was you were dealing with. And what you said to everyone after he left, about family being everything? It was exactly what we needed to hear to begin the healing between us. You made that happen, not me."

He sweeps his hand about the room. "Everything we have, everything we've built, we've done together, as a family. But you and I both know this is far from over. If this family's going to survive the long haul, we need you at the center of things—engaging, innovating, leading. I realize that now, accept it. I need you to do the same."

I'm lost for words. Never would I have expected Richard to admit even half of what he just did. It's not his way. But when I look back on the past couple weeks, things begin clicking in place. The lack of hostility, the respect that has grown between us. Suddenly it all makes sense.

"That's why you came with us to the ranch," I say. I always knew there had to be a reason, a motive for his involvement. And now I know that reason.

He nods. "You were hellbent on going," he says. "Didn't matter that you had no clue what waited for you, I knew there was no stopping you then, just like I know there's no stopping you now. I also knew what it would do to the family if the five of you rushed off and never came back. Joining you was the only way I knew how to help you."

There's no reason for him to lie to me right now. I know that. But what he's just confessed is difficult for me to wrap my head around. Had I not heard it first hand, I might not believe it.

"I don't know what to say," I admit.

"You don't have to say anything," Richard says. "Just understand that I'm telling you this for a reason. When you leave for town tomorrow, make it mean something. Follow every lead, act on every hunch, flip the town upside down if you have to. Find them. Save them if you can. Just be sure you take care of yourselves first. We still have too much work to do, too many things to accomplish. This family still needs you. So whatever happens, you get your ass back here. Understand?"

It's in this moment that the magnitude of what we're facing fully hits me. All this time I've been focused on the obstacles, the dangers. What fear I've felt has been for the lives of those who'll accompany me, for the fate of those we search for. But there's so much more at play. So many factors, so many variables, so many lives intertwined in this vast, cosmic web. I can't lose sight of that.

"Understood," I say. He searches my eyes for a long moment, more piercing and intense than he ever has. Without breaking eye contact, he reaches into his pocket and withdraws a knife sheathed in leather.

"I'm fourth generation military," he says. "Did you know that?"

"I didn't," I admit.

"This was my great-grandfather's, issued to him during the first world war," he says, unsheathing it. It's a simple blade, thin and wickedly sharp, the handle bound in leather the same shade of brown as the sheath. "Four generations it's been in my family, passed from father to son. My grandfather carried this knife as he charged the beach of Normandy. My father carried it for over a decade in the jungles of Vietnam. Twenty-two years of service I gave my country. Tours in Iraq and Afghanistan. I handled this knife every single day during that span.

"I always imagined I might give this to my own son one day. As it is, I was blessed with daughters, and after my wife passed, I knew that day would never come. Since then, I've raised my girls the best I knew how. Tried to teach them how to be independent, self-reliant. They're strong, both of them. But the thought of this knife in either of their hands makes me sick to my stomach. I can only pray they never know the burdens the men who've carried it have endured. Which is why I'm having this conversation with you, and not them."

I'm stunned, understanding now what he intends. To admit the things he did earlier is one thing. This is quite another.

"For over one-hundred years this knife has been in my family. I won't see that tradition broken. You may not be blood, but you are family; may not be military, but you know what it means to fight for something bigger than yourself. If I can't give this knife to my own son, I will at least have it passed into the hands of a man strong enough to carry it."

He extends the blade to me, handle first. I take it into my possession carefully, the weight of its history impossible to ignore. Pressure builds behind my eyes, stunned he would give me an heirloom that means so much to him.

"Thank you," I say. "It's an honor, truly. I only hope I can carry it as well as those who did before me." I'm not sure I deserve this knife, but I will not insult him by questioning his decision. If I know one thing, it's that it wasn't made lightly.

I extend my hand to shake and he clasps it in a tight grasp. "You'll do fine, Morgan," he says. "I wouldn't have given it to you if I didn't believe that."

Chapter 21: (Lauren)

"I don't want you to worry about me. I'll be fine...Just promise me you'll keep yourself safe."

Grace's voice trembles slightly as we say our farewells, the fear she tries so hard to hide from the world revealing itself in our moment of departure. I hate the sound of it, hate that it's there because of me. I don't want to leave her. But the days of staying behind while others risk their lives has passed. Whatever future we build, I will have my hand in molding it.

"I promise," I say, squeezing her in a tight embrace. "You're the most important thing I have in this world, Gracie. I wouldn't be leaving now if I didn't believe it was the best thing for us."

"I know," she says. "That's why I'm not asking you to stay. Everything good I've ever had in this life is because of the choices you've made...I won't stop believing in you now."

I blink back the tears pooling in my eyes, desperate to maintain my composure. "Thank you. You have no idea how much that means to me." I hold her close for as long as she'll let me, savoring each second with her as if they were our last. *Please God, don't let them be our last.* When we part, there's a moment where I see her not as she is, but as she once was: the little girl I have loved and protected from the moment I held her in my arms. My sweet girl. She's grown up so fast. This world has made sure of it. I can see it in her eyes as she stares at me now, wisdom far beyond her years filling their depths. Young as she is, she understands the world as well as any of us.

"Stay safe," I say. "I'll be back before you know it."

"I know," she says. "I love you, Lauren."

I squeeze her close one last time. "Love you more."

I turn toward the rest of the group who are busy finishing their own quiet goodbyes. Most of the family sleeps in the living room. Only the parents and siblings of those leaving tonight join us. Nervous energy lingers among us, but never is it mentioned. Tears build in the eyes of many, but few are shed. Everyone does their best to keep up the morale, sharing words of encouragement and positivity. It helps to some degree.

"Take care of my son, won't you?" Mr. Taylor asks me, squeezing me in that fatherly fashion of his. He jests, but there is no hiding the worry in his voice. His heart is big as his son's. Like with Morgan, that heart is both a gift and a curse, the capacity of its love at once his biggest strength and weakness. Already he struggles beneath the weight of it. And I'm afraid it's only going to get worse for him.

"I will," I promise. I squeeze him back, putting as much love as I can into the gesture, hoping it helps him cope in some small way.

Softer hands hold me now, Mrs. Taylor's touch warm and reassuring. Undoubtedly she has her own fears, her own misgivings about what we set out to do. How could she not? Yet one would never guess so by looking at her. Her ability to remain cool and collected despite overwhelming circumstances is one of the things I've come to admire most of her. Even now she remains resolute, unflappable: an island amid a storm-tossed sea. Being held in her arms I feel my fear lessen, my confidence swell, emboldened by this woman's quiet strength. It's with a pang I recognize the sensation for what it is. The warmth. The comfort. It's all part of the ineffable influence of a mother's embrace—a feeling that lingers even after we have parted.

"I was right," she says, a small smile on her face. "My son is lucky to have you." My breath catches, surprised at her sudden praise. She reaches out and brushes a stray strand of hair from my face. "Take care of yourself. Morgan isn't the only one who needs you."

"Thank you, Marie," I say. "I'll do whatever I can to get us back."

"I know you will," she says.

Footsteps sound on the back staircase, their tread slow and heavy. Felix enters the kitchen a moment later, eyes red, voice hoarse. He's only just finished saying his own private goodbye's to his aunt and cousin. Mrs. Taylor pulls him now into her arms, whispering words of comfort into his ear. He nods, closing his eyes as she kisses him atop the forehead. He shares quick words with Mr. Taylor and Leon's family before finally turning to us.

"If anyone has changed their mind, I won't blame them," he says.

Morgan snorts in false offense. "Ducks fly together, Chavo," he says. "You know this."

An incredulous smile splits Felix's face. "Really?" he asks.

"And just when you think they're going to break apart, ducks fly together," Morgan continues.

"And when the wind blows hard and the sky is black, ducks fly together," Leon adds in amusement.

They look to Felix expectantly, twin grins on their faces. He shakes his head once, before eventually obliging. "And when the roosters are crowing, and the cows are spinning circles in the pasture, ducks fly together."

The three of them can no longer hold back their laughter, sharing an inside joke lost on the rest of us. Where the hell ducks and roosters and cows came into this conversation, I haven't a clue. But it has the three of them smiling, laughing. It eases the tension hovering over our departure. That's all I need to understand.

"And when everyone says it can't be done... ducks fly together," Morgan finishes. "We know what we agreed to, Chavo. We're with you. No matter what."

Felix nods, accepting what Morgan is telling him. "Thank you," he says. "All of you...it means more than I could ever explain." He pauses, another smile splitting his face. "Excellent reference by the way," he says. *"D2: The Mighty Ducks?* Probably the most motivational speech ever written."

"It felt appropriate," Morgan says.

"Quack, quack, quack," Leon adds, drawing another brief round of laughter between them.

The laughter soon fades, leaving us in a peaceful silence. The moment stretches on, none of us speaking or moving. Soon as one of us does so, the moment will be broken. Our goodbyes have been said, our hugs and kisses given. All that's left is for us to take our leave.

It's Felix who moves first, strapping up his hiking pack and shouldering his rifle. "We should get going," he says. The four of us mimic his action, strapping our packs and shouldering our weapons.

"Lead the way," Morgan says.

The further we travel, the more I am reminded of why I feared the arrival of winter. The warm house and sudden surplus of food have made me forget. Removed from those walls, I remember. Each step through the snow is a battle that must be won, each gust of frigid wind a slap across the face, bringing me jarringly back to reality. To conserve our strength, our pace is slow and measured. There's no telling what surprises town may hold for us. We need to arrive with enough energy to face it.

The back-country lanes we travel show little signs of disturbance, the snow as untouched as that blanketing the fields and forest. That changes once we reach the highway. Here there are footprints, tire tracks. They weave between the snowy mounds littering the road's expanse, abandoned vehicles buried beneath the snow like the rusting relics they've become. I think of our own vehicles safely tucked away on the farm, wishing I was inside the cab of a truck, warm and comfortable. But to bring a vehicle with us would be far too dangerous. Stealth is the name of the game, and rolling through the streets with a loud, half ton target doesn't qualify.

As we come upon the outskirts of the town, I notice a trend among the tracks and prints we pass. Though it's difficult to tell in the dark, nearly all of them appear to be moving away from town. And here we are, entering the place people are so desperate to leave that they would risk exposing themselves to the elements rather than stay. I don't mention it to the others, but something about the tracks feels ominous to me. What could have changed to make these people finally abandon town after so long? It makes me fear things may be even worse than we thought.

We break beside a jack-knifed semi, it's bulk an effective windbreak from the icy gales that have plagued us since leaving the farm. Morgan points to a massive, sprawling building to our right, more shadow than substance from this distance.

"That was the hospital," he says, capping his canteen. "Roughly the halfway mark between the farm and town." He speaks casually, but there's a note of regret beneath his words. He grows quiet, and I recall the conversation we had earlier.

"What about the hospital?" Leon asked. "It's possible he got injured and went there for help."

"You really think the hospital would still be operational?" Emily argued.

"Not fully, but there could easily have been some who stayed behind to help. At least in the beginning."

"They're not at the hospital," Morgan said. "That man and boy we caught stealing? They were hiding out inside when they were attacked. If there are still people in there, it's nobody we want to meet."

That same note of regret filled his voice then as it does now—regret over what he witnessed that night—at what he refused to stand up and stop. I take his hand and squeeze, drawing his attention away from the shadowy building.

"C'mon," I say. "Let's keep moving."

The wreckage grows as we enter the outskirts of town. The most congested areas of which, I notice, have been cleared to one side or another. It's not a straight shot, but there is room enough to accommodate large vehicles if need be. The Animals have been busy it seems. Who else has both the vehicles and manpower to take on such an undertaking? But though they have the lanes open, they have yet to clear them of snow. Apparently, the fringes and countryside don't fall high on their priority list. One can only hope that continues.

Past the vacant Walmart, we veer right onto a smaller, two-lane highway. A rocky face leers to my right, protective netting, and concrete barriers in place to shield the highway from falling rock. A guardrail runs along the left-hand side of the highway, the steep embankment beyond leading to the river below. Twice the railing is sheared through, cleaved, no doubt, by EMP affected vehicles the day everything went black. My eyes linger on these patches longer than they should, wondering about those who were lost that day. It's not pity or compassion I feel in these moments, but rather a morbid curiosity about the dead—about their lives before, and the lives they might have had if they survived. Then again, maybe it's better not to know. Makes it easier to absorb to think of them as statistics: faceless victims of the greatest tragedy the world has ever known. Makes you almost forget how easily it could have been us in their place.

The highway slants downhill, at the bottom of which lies the dark mass of the first true neighborhood we've come across on this venture. My stomach clenches nervously at the sight of it. I adjust the sling of my AR, feel the weight of the Glock holstered on my hip, their presence only a small reassurance against the enormity of our task. Deserted as this place appears, life remains in the homes and buildings, danger lurking in the shadowy pools below. Weapons be damned. Should the shadows shift against us, we won't have the firepower to turn them. All I can do is pray it doesn't come to that.

We veer left onto a narrow side-street soon as we reach the bottom, keen to avoid the major thoroughfares as much as possible. Squat little houses fill the blocks, their darkened windows like the eyes of ghosts, leering as we pass. I stare back, searching their depths for a hint of movement, a flicker of a flame, anything that might alert us to the presence of others. But the layers of darkness remain, the quiet unbroken. If our progress is noticed, it goes unchecked. For now, at least.

Deeper we enter this residential labyrinth, the disturbed snow and lingering smell of wood smoke the only evidence we are not alone. I study my surroundings the best I can, mapping our route in case I am somehow separated from the others. It's a difficult undertaking, the streets we pass indistinguishable in the darkness. Only a few landmarks stick out to me: a church; a school; an apartment building; all meaningless if I can't find them again. Still, I try. It makes me feel calmer, as if by doing so I somehow have more control over my fate. But deep down I know that's folly. Truth is, I know my fate is tied to those I travel with. If I walk out of here alive, it won't be alone.

We enter the mouth of an alleyway, a feeling of anticipation rising among us as we do so. Morgan's quickened breaths. The edginess in Felix's movement. We've nearly arrived.

"This is it," Morgan whispers as we come to a stop at the end of the alley. A wooden fence fills my vision, the skeletal branches of a tall tree the only thing I can make of the home or yard. Felix tries the gate. Locked. Wordlessly, he hands his pack to Morgan, grips the top of the fence, and is up and over a heartbeat later. There's the sound of shifting snow, a scrape of a bolt, and the gate swings open.

The anticipation I felt at the mouth of the alley multiplies with each step we make across the snowy yard. Weapons are drawn. Flashlights at the ready. Felix tries the door. Open. He shares a wary glance over his shoulder and then disappears inside. Morgan and Leon follow, Emily and I bringing up the rear. A cramped laundry room opens to the kitchen, cabinets and drawers flung open or else ripped out entirely. Broken dishes and cutlery crunch underfoot as we pass through. The living room. Two bedrooms. Bathroom. We find each in its own state of disarray, long ransacked of anything valuable. What's more important is what we don't find: people, Felix's family or otherwise.

"It was always a long shot they would have stayed here," Felix says. "But it was the logical place to start." Long shot or not, the disappointment in his voice is noticeable. Then again I can't blame him for hoping. I had my hopes up as well.

"Would have been too easy," Leon says. "Where's the fun in that?"

He smiles, and I find myself returning a tired grin. Tired as I am, I can appreciate the attempted humor. Felix must feel the same, a small smirk crossing his lips before replying.

"True," he says. "Since when has any of this been easy?"

"It doesn't have to be easy," Morgan says. "It just has to be worth it."

Felix nods once but doesn't reply, perhaps wondering if this trip will indeed be worth it. If he does, he doesn't mention it, taking the opportunity to change the subject.

"Sun will be up in an hour," he says. "I'll take first watch. The rest of you should get some sleep."

It's an offer I can't refuse. I take the smaller of the two bedrooms, an audible sigh escaping me as I sink onto the bed. I stack my pack and AR beside the bed, ready to grab at a moments notice. My Glock remains in its familiar position beneath my pillow. Morgan enters a minute later.

"How's he doing?" I ask.

"He'll be fine," Morgan says, settling himself on the bed beside me. "He just needs some time to collect himself."

"At least there's no blood this time," I say, recalling the gory mess we found when we first arrived at the farm.

"Yeah, there's that," he sighs. He wraps his arms around me, pulling my body closer to his. "Let's hope that trend continues."

Chapter 22: (Morgan)

I sit on the edge of a bare mattress, stained and torn bedding lying in a heap at my feet. Like all the homes we've searched, the place has been trashed and looted, long stripped of anything valuable. Slowly, the room comes into sharper detail, the early morning sunlight revealing more and more of the debris left behind. What draws my attention most, however, isn't the wreckage, but one of the few features that remains intact.

Across from me, above an upturned desk, hangs an artistic rendition of the sci-fi series *Stranger Things*. In the depiction, four youths stand on a desolate highway, their bicycles stalled as they face a sinister storm brewing in the distance. Thunderheads the color of blood and fire consume the sky, flaming bolts of lightning dancing across its expanse. And in the midst of it all, an unearthly creature of mountainous proportions, its form more shadow than substance, looming over the quiet town below. It's the Upside Down they face: an alternate dimension where the towns and cities of earth have fallen into darkness and menacing creatures rule the land. Gripped in shadow though the print may be, the images no more than dark outlines from where I sit, it remains as vivid in my mind as the day I hung it upon the wall.

I don't know how long I've sat here, staring at the print without truly seeing it, my mind beyond these walls I once called home. I thought I was prepared for this, that I knew what to expect by returning here. I was wrong. This town has fallen so much harder than I would have thought possible. Waste fills the streets and gutters. Gunshots echo through the air. The smell of death is not uncommon as we search, often warning us of the grisly scenes waiting around corners and behind closed doors. Perhaps the best illustration of how dire things have grown came within minutes of leaving Felix's cousins house, when, in the very next alleyway, we came across the corpse of a man lying face down in the snow, his frostbitten hand frozen around a single can of cat food. I wish I could say it was the only body we've found, but it was only the first.

Five days we have scoured this forsaken place, following every lead, every hunch in our search for Felix's family. So far nothing has come of it. Making contact with others has proven difficult, most of those we've come across preferring an exchange of bullets rather than words. Only the night before last we were shot at while passing Riverview Elementary. That nobody was hurt is nothing short of a miracle, the attack itself clumsy and desperate. Soon as we took cover and returned fire they fled, leaving us whole but shaken. For Felix, we didn't let the incident scare us away from our task, but another encounter may change that.

The few occasions we've actually managed to parley with others have been tense and brief, hands hovering over weapons in case discussions turned south. Most of the town's residents have either fled or died. Those who remain are deeply guarded, mistrustful of our intentions. Can't say I blame them. Surely they've seen things that warrant such mistrust.

I wanted so badly to find solidarity among the survivors—some small semblance of the community I grew up in. I realize now how foolish of a hope that was. This isn't the town I know and love. It's only a broken reflection of what once was. The Upside Down.

A sharp throb beats at the back of my scalp, drawing my focus away from the conversation taking place around the table. Not that it much matters, it's the same conversation we've held since the night we left the farm: where do we look next? But after nearly a week of searching our ideas are growing thin, each location we search more far-fetched than the last. It won't be long until one of us mentions that unasked question hanging in the back of our minds: when do we call off the search? I look across the table at Felix, the stress eating away at me reflected ten times in his troubled eyes. He knows that time is nearly upon us.

"Museum, hotel, what does it matter?" Leon asks. "Can we risk either of them after last night?"

For the first time, my attention is focused entirely on the conversation that has suddenly grown quiet, the room tense and alert. Last night we crossed a church, a daycare, and a house of our search list, all of which had at least some connection to Frank or his girls. As has been the norm, all three were found stripped and abandoned. What set last night apart however wasn't something found, but something felt. Goosebumps. Hairs rising at the back of the neck. From the moment I entered the church, I was overcome with the inexplicable feeling of being watched.

At first, I attributed the feeling to the church itself—to the figures etched in the stained-glass windows and the statues lining the walls around me. Even in the world before, churches made me edgy in a way I could never quite explain. Only that edginess persisted, stalking us as we hit the street and searched the daycare where Lena was employed. By then I wasn't the only one who felt it. Unnerved, we retreated to the house I shared with Leon and Felix before the collapse, and which has served as our base of operations these past few days. Once this was a place of peace, of safety. My home. Now it's no different than the other derelict buildings on either side of it.

"We don't know for sure that we were followed," Emily says. "If we were, they were damn stealthy about it. Doesn't sound like AA."

"Agreed," Felix says. "No need for stealth when you're the one running the streets. And in any case, they would have sent in a raiding party by now."

Yes, they would have. The Animas Animals have descended on this town like a plague of locusts, devouring people and material in their bloody campaign to claim this place as theirs. The rifles and packs we carry would have been too much enticement for the greedy bastards to resist.

"You don't have to be AA to pull a trigger," Lauren says.

"Exactly!" Leon agrees. "In a way, that would make them more dangerous. They have less to lose."

"What do you suggest then?" Felix challenges. "We can't stay here forever."

"No, we can't," Leon says. "But we also can't head out with a half-cocked plan just because we're running out of time."

Felix has no response to that. None of us do. For the first time, our ticking clock has been mentioned. Leon's expression softens as sees the effect this truth is taking on our friend.

"Look, all I'm saying is we need to think this through," he says. "If we were followed last night, whoever it was could have a trap waiting for us the moment we leave here." He meets my eyes. "We've been blindsided before...we can't let that happen again."

Maya.

I thought the pain of losing her might dull with time. It hasn't. Even now, remembering that night is like a knife to the heart. I can still see the smile she wore before the light left her eyes—before she left this cruel world for whatever lies beyond. My sweet, brave girl. So full of love and loyalty that she didn't hesitate to sacrifice her life for mine. It was her choice, I know that. Still, there's guilt in surviving, in owing your life to another. It's a burden I carry with me each day. I don't want my friends to know this guilt, this burden. More than that, I don't want to add to my own. Leon's right, we can't let it happen again.

"We won't be," I say.

Hours later we make our leave. Despite my assurances, I'm shot through with nerves as I step into the fading twilight. The shadows seem deeper. The sound of our footfalls overly loud. The feeling of being watched returns tenfold as we proceed down the block, Felix at our lead. It's only with the greatest restraint that I resist the urge to look over my shoulder for pursuers. If there are eyes watching us, it's best to let them believe we're oblivious.

Night falls fast, the light growing darker with each block we pass. By the time we reach the maze of crushed and twisted metal that has become Main Ave, the sky has turned to black. We cross quickly onto another side-street, careful to remain in the center of the lane. To our left sits a hotel, and beyond that, a snow covered trail and footbridge spanning Junction Creek, no more than a bed of frozen rock and snow right now. We turn left, the trail a deeper shade of darkness than the street. Pass the bridge the trail splits, the left side leading toward the high school, and the right to Rank Park. We turn right. A dozen paces later we make our move.

We melt into the shadows off the side of the trail, the dense foliage keeping us from view. My heart beats hard inside my chest, adrenaline flooding my veins as it always does in moments such as this. I remind myself to breathe, to remain focused. My eyes close as I drink in the sounds around me: the wind's howl sweeping in from the south, the creaking of branches overhead. I'll hear any potential threat long before I see it. The seconds stretch like minutes and still, no one approaches. Then, just as I allow myself the possibility that we were not followed, I hear it. The slight shifting on my left and right tell me my friends notice as well.

The footsteps are feather light, noticeable only for the soft crunch of snow accompanying each step. I strain my ears for more information, a scrap of conversation, the tread of a second pair of feet. Nothing. Only a solitary pursuer then. I track his progress as he approaches the fork in the trail and veers right. I shift my weight, ready to explode from the brush the moment he comes into view. But then the feet come to an abrupt halt. A pause. One second. Two. Then without warning, our pursuer is in full flight back the way he came.

I drop my pack and tear after him, no fear or hesitation in my movement. The moment he fled he became prey, and I, a predator. My eyes zero in on him as I round the corner, his retreating form nearly at the bridge. He's fast. I'm faster, the anger and frustration I've felt propelling me forward. I'll catch him before he reaches the street. He knows this too, altering his course by hurdling over the side of the bridge, landing with the grace of a cat on the snow-packed creek below. Without thinking I plunge after, ignoring the shouts from above. He can't escape. We need to know why we're being followed.

My landing is less graceful, the force of the drop sending me to my knees, buying my target precious seconds. I continue my pursuit but the gap between us only widens. My target's no fool. He chose this route for a reason, his lighter build allowing him to skim atop the deep snow instead of sinking through as I do. He continues to pull away, rounding a bend in the creek bed, momentarily blocking him from view. I reach the bend just in time to see him scamper up the creek's right bank. My stomach drops. Main Ave lies just beyond the bank, its minefield of wrecked vehicles the perfect place to lose us and disappear into the shadows. And I'm too far, too slow to catch him. He's going to get away.

Still, I try, pumping my legs for all they're worth even after he disappears from view again. I'm almost to the bank when I hear Felix shout, not from behind, but ahead. I burst through the brush and emerge at the entrance to the high school parking lot, our purser subdued by a panting Felix, his knee between the man's shoulder blades and his pistol to the back of his head.

"I'm going to let you up," Felix says as the rest of the group joins us. "Do as I say. Try anything stupid and I won't hesitate to shoot."

Felix stands. "Lace your fingers behind your head and get to your knees." He does. "Now, on your feet." He stands. "Turn and face me." He turns. No, I realize. Not he, but she.

"Lylette?" Emily asks

The girl's eyes fix on my sister. "Emily?"

"You know this girl?" I ask, turning to Emily.

She nods. "I tutored her my senior year. Algebra and biology."

It's then I notice just how young she is, her face youthful enough to have still walked the halls of the school behind her had the world not gone to shit. But I know looks can be deceiving. She's out here on her own after all. That alone tells me she can take care of herself. I won't make the mistake of underestimating her.

"You check her?" I ask Felix.

"Haven't gone through the bag, but I found these." From his coat, he withdraws a switchblade and a snub-nosed pistol. In the small sports bag, we find nothing but a protein bar, two water bottles, and some matches. No wonder she kept her distance. A confrontation was the last thing she wanted. Still, she followed us. She must have had a reason for doing so.

"What were you planning on doing with this, then?" I ask, holding the pistol.

"Wasn't planning on doing anything," she says. "It's only for protection."

"How's that working out for you?" Leon asks.

She eyes him with distaste. "You would rather I have used it? Killed one of you perhaps?" That shuts him up

"Why didn't you?" Felix asks. "You didn't even know Emily was with us at the time."

She shrugs. "Gunshots attract attention. I'd rather stay under the radar." She pauses, looking over the wreckage filling the street. "Besides, this town has seen enough bloodshed."

I hear the dejection in her voice, the bitterness of her words. Of course, she's survived this long. We've all seen things, done things since the collapse. We've all suffered losses. Pain is the universal language in this new world. The price of survival.

"How long have you been following us?" I ask.

"Since last night," she says. "You were crossing Main onto 17th St." Just before the church, I think to myself.

"Why?" I ask, no elaboration needed on my part.

"To observe," she says.

Her response is purposefully vague, testing my already thin patience. Lauren must feel the same. "Lylette, is it?" she asks. "How about you cut the shit and just answer the damn question?"

There's a fire burning beneath this girl's cool exterior. Defiance that flashes in her eyes in moments such as this: first when Leon mocked her, and now with Lauren. She's quick to tame it though, answering the question with a deep breath rather than push the issue.

"Let's just say you caught my interest," she says. "It's clear you haven't been in town long. You're too armed, too well supplied. Nobody outside of a gang would have loadouts this nice, and there's not a chance in hell you're with any of them."

"How can you be sure of that?" Felix asks.

"Because no gang would send soldiers out with that much supplies to search buildings that have been looted for months. Even if they did, you would have returned to your base last night instead of camping out in no man's land."

She's sharp, I'll give her that. But that still doesn't explain why she followed us.

"You're right," I admit. "We've been in town less than a week. What I don't understand is how that's of interest to you."

She takes her time replying, her eyes looking us over as if appraising our worth. "It's of interest because it means you know how to take care of yourselves—that you're survivors." She looks to the wreckage once more and shakes her head. "Look at what's happened to this place. Sickness. Violence. People killing each other over scraps of food. Blame the blackout all you want, but we didn't lose our ability to think, to reason. It's our choices that led us here, just as it's our choices that will determine where we go next."

She's getting close now, the real reason she would risk traveling these cold streets alone. And I must admit, I am curious.

"Somewhere along the line, we got it in our heads that this is what it takes to survive—to only look out for ourselves, damn everybody else. We flocked together in little bands and gangs, drew lines in the sand, made it so that it's me against you, us against them. Don't you see how foolish that is? Making enemies of one another instead of working together? Destroying what's left of this town instead of building toward a future? Something needs to change. If it doesn't there won't be a future worth being a part of."

Her words are an echo of my own thoughts, the future she speaks of the same future I've long dreamed of for my family. I meet her eyes and I see that same fire I saw earlier, burning with conviction now rather than defiance. I want to trust her, to believe she wants the same things as I do. But I'm hesitant. I've been duped into trusting others before. I can't make that mistake again.

"And that's why you followed us, is it?" Felix asks skeptically. "To recruit us to your cause?"

"What alternative was there?" she asks. "I couldn't just approach you from the start, I had to see the kind of people you were first."

"And what was your verdict?" I ask.

"Do you think I would have told you all this if I didn't believe you were good people?" she asks.

I look to my friends, each of them struggling with the same uncertainty I feel. I catch Felix's eye, that silent question passing between us. He nods his head, giving me his answer.

"We should talk more," I say.

She nods, a small smile of satisfaction finding her face. "I have just the place."

Half an hour later, we stand at the gate of what was once an upscale bed & breakfast, the feeling of being watched returning tenfold as we enter the enclosed yard. Three stories of blackened windows stare down at us, unseen eyes surely hidden in their depths. Halfway through the yard, Lylette withdraws a small flashlight, clicking it in on and off in a quick pattern. Our entry code, the front door swinging open as we approach.

The grip on my Glock tightens as I enter, my eyes scanning every detail I can make of the dark room. Movement ripples around me, the darkness shifting into shadows, the shadows solidifying into the forms of men. The clicking and clacking of chambered bullets and lifted safeties fill the air, the sound colder than the icy winds howling outside.

"Easy," Lylette says. "They're friends.'

A low hiss issues from the dark, quickly followed by a click and a sudden whoosh of light. A blade of a man holds the lantern aloft, face nearly as dark as the coal colored eyes that stare at each of us in turn. Three men and one woman are also revealed, their weapons lowered but not forgotten. I don't spare any of them a second glance. It's clear to me who the leader here is.

"That, we'll find out," the lantern bearer says. "Let us talk." He gestures for us to enter the next room. I feel his eyes on me, looking for signs of hesitance, of fear. I show none, walking forward as if my heart does not beat so hard it hurts, and I don't grip my Glock like a vice inside my coat pocket. My friends follow after, taking seats on either side of me at the wooden table. The man joins us, hanging the lantern above the table before sitting next to Lylette on the opposite side.

"So, *friends*, what exactly has Lylette told you about us?" he asks. He addresses the table, but his eyes are quick to settle back on mine.

"Enough to catch our interest," I say.

He nods once. "And what are your interests?"'

"My family. Keeping them safe, provided for. Doing everything I can to create a life of peace for us. From what Lylette's told us, I believe we may have that in common."

I watch him consider my words, face stoic as a stone, giving nothing away. "You certainly seem to be doing well in terms of providing for them," he says, eyeing our packs and weapons. "Not many remain so well supplied. How have you managed it?"

"Sweat and blood. Scavenging. Defending what we have by any means necessary. How have you managed?"

His mouth twitches, more of the impression of a smirk than anything else. "In a similar fashion." He pauses. "I am curious though, what are your reasons for entering town? Surely you had an idea of the state this place would be in. Why take that risk?"

I knew this question would be asked at some point. I look to Felix. It's his story to tell. Slowly he reaches into an inner pocket of his coat, drawing sharp looks from the men who flank the table.

"This is why we're here," Felix says, passing him a picture of his uncle and cousins.
"Have you seen them?"

The man surveys the picture a moment before passing it to Lylette, who then passes it along to the rest of their people. One by one they shake their heads, giving us their answer. "I'm sorry," he says. "How long have they been missing?"

"Since the start," Felix says.

I can sense their pity. It flashes across their faces, the same look one might give a stranger in mourning. They don't need to say they believe our mission is foolish. It's obvious   A fact that's not lost on Felix.

"Think what you like, but for months I gave up hope of ever finding my family alive. I believed them dead just as you believe now. But two weeks ago I was reunited with my aunt and cousin, freed them from a man we thought a friend. So here we are. I won't make the same mistake twice."

A brief silence follows as they absorb this information, Felix's stare fierce, as if daring Lylette and her colleagues to contradict him. They don't.

"So now you know our reasons for being here," Emily says from Felix's other side. She looks not to the man who's acted as their speaker, but to her former pupil, Lylette. "What are yours?"

She shares a quick look with the man beside her before replying. "I meant what I said earlier. We have to stop seeing everyone we come across as enemies. All that does is alienate ourselves even further. If we don't learn to give people a chance, to work together, we're going to end up destroying ourselves."

"You said something earlier about defending what you had by any means necessary," the man beside her continues. "I understand— everyone who still has something worth protecting does. That's why we're here. The community we're part of has a lot worth protecting."

"And you need help protecting it," I say, connecting the dots.

"Yes," the man says.

Leon scoffs. "Not asking much are you?" he says. "I mean what would you have us do? Abandon our home, everything we've built just to join you?"

"No," he answers. "I'm not suggesting anything at the moment. You must understand that you are a surprise to us. This is our third scouting trip, and we've yet to meet a group even half as equipped as you are. There's a handful of gangs left, but we've stayed clear of them for obvious reasons. Filter out those too violent, too ill, too untrusting, and it doesn't leave us with much in terms of prospects."

I see their dilemma. To trust these people enough to abandon everything with only the prospect of joining their camp would take a huge leap of faith. One would have to be desperate indeed.

"So what are you suggesting exactly?" Felix asks.

"That you stay with us while we're here," he says. "We're looking for people, the same as you. We can help one another. We'll let you know more about us, about our operation, and you can do the same. Let's see if we can't figure out a way forward, together."

It's an intriguing offer. Since returning home, these are the first people I've met who've spoken of helping one another, of building a future. I want to believe him just as I wanted to believe Lylette. But trust is a precarious proposition these days, and I'm terrified of making the wrong call. I look to my friends, the same indecision I feel staring back at me. I find Felix's eyes again, that silent question passing between us for the second time tonight. Only now he doesn't nod, instead, raising his eyebrows and tilting his head slightly, deferring to my judgment. Of course. He's said since the beginning that these calls would end up falling on me.

I look back now to the man sitting across from me, searching his face, his eyes for any signs of duplicity. I find none. He truly seems sincere.

"If we agree to stay, we're going to need to know your name," I say.

The man smiles, nothing like the ghost of a smirk he gave earlier. "Name's Byron," he says.

I stand and reach out my hand. "Morgan," I say as he stands to shake. We both sit once again. "Now, tell us more about this community of yours."

Chapter 23: (Lauren)

A frigid wind rattles the window pane, the sound of its cruel howl filling the kitchen where we sit. Even now, the feel of its icy breath lingers against my skin, the chill nothing compared to the cold dread coiled in the pit of my stomach. One way or another, things will change after tonight. We all knew that coming into this. The only question that remains is how.

Morgan's fingers tap a quick rhythm against the tabletop, his nerves through the roof since our arrival. I take his hand and his eyes find mine, a wealth of emotion and unspoken words passing between us. He squeezes and I exhale a slow breath, this moment a brief respite from my rampant thoughts. But like all moments it isn't meant to last.

"Tony's back," shouts a voice from the front of the house. Seconds later the door opens and closes, quickly followed by the sound of several people approaching from the hall. Leon and Emily enter the kitchen, their faces falling as they note our number.

"Nothing?" Leon asks, eyes on his best friend.

Morgan shakes his head slowly. "You?"

"Not a trace," he says. He looks to Lylette and her companion. "Tony wanted to see you two. We picked up another couple people for your camp."

Her companion is up and out with a curt nod, but Lylette is slow to follow. At the door, she pauses and looks back hesitantly, as if debating whether to say something. In the end, she chooses silence, leaving us alone in the semi-darkness. Leon and Emily take their seats and the waiting recommences, time even slower in its movement now that only one pair remains unaccounted for. Anxious faces fill the table, each of us lost in our own minds. It's the curse of this waiting, of the uneasy silence filling the space between us. Too much time for our thoughts to eat away at us, to take us places we'd rather not go. Nothing to be done about it. All any of us can do is hope for the best.

Lylette does not return to the kitchen, nor do her companions or any of their new enlistees. They have the tact to give us space during this time, something I couldn't be more grateful for. Because though they search this town as we do, our reasons couldn't be more different. They're recruiters, searching out those they think might help them build a better future. Our aims are less grandiose. We're just searching for a miracle, our entire rational based on the fact that they can happen. Felix's aunt and cousin are proof of that. But as the hour grows late, the window for miracles grows smaller.

"Dawn's not far off," Emily says. "Shouldn't they have been back by now?"

Yes, they should have been back over an hour ago. Though it's hardly surprising they have yet to return. With this being our final night here, Felix would want to be as thorough as possible.

"It's his last search," Leon says. "He won't come back until he has no other choice."

"Or he's found them," Morgan says. Even as the words leave his mouth, it is with no real hope behind them. Whatever optimism he may have held when we arrived has left him, the state of this town stealing that hope away. It's a feeling we all share but won't admit aloud. Better to pretend. If not for our sakes, then for Felix's.

The black of night slowly ebbs from the sky, a deep indigo taking its place as the sun prepares its rise. Shapes assert themselves out the kitchen window, trees, patio furniture, a tall wooden fence. Then there's movement, the gate swinging open to reveal two figures enter the yard. I recognize one and my stomach flutters, my eyes instantly looking past them to see if others follow. They don't. Just as quickly my stomach drops. The time for pretending has ended.

Lylette joins us once more as Felix and Byron enter from the back entrance, limbs frozen, faces somber. Felix quickly scans the table, our own solemn expressions enough to tell him what he needs to know. I want to say something, anything that might comfort him in this moment. But for the life of me, I can't think of a single thing.

"Felix..." Morgan says, the name stretching long and thin until it dissolves back into the quiet of the room. He's as lost for words as I am.

Felix shakes his head. "We did everything we could," he says, voice hoarse. "It's not the outcome I wanted, but at least I know I tried." He and Byron move forward, taking seats at either head of the table. "What we need to figure out now is how we move forward."

He's hurting more than he lets on. Later he will mourn, breakdown. But for now, he buries the pain, distracting himself with planning our next move. And we'll let him because everyone grieves in their own way, on their own time. Who are we to deny him that? In any case, this conversation was always going to happen.

Felix turns to Morgan, the first of us whose eyes he meets since walking through the door. Morgan holds his gaze, the look stronger than any words that could pass between them. Morgan nods and shifts his attention toward Byron and Lylette.

"Yes," he says. "We've worked well together these past few days. We owe it to ourselves to explore all our options."

"I'm glad you feel that way," Byron says. "From what you've told me so far, I think we may have a very unique opportunity to help one another."

Unique indeed. A secluded ranch over seventy strong and sitting on one-hundred acres of land. Cattle and horses. Fresh water. Access to a nearby creek and surrounded by prime hunting grounds. Such a place would be in an ideal position to weather the storm; to build a future. Still, all we have is his word this place exists. And perhaps my past has left me biased, but I've always been of the notion that if something sounds too good to be true, it probably is.

"By now you know everything I could think to mention," Byron continues. "You know our number, our resources, our general location. More importantly, you know our aims—why we would risk so much in coming here. The time for standing alone has passed. We need others. We need the strength, the security that only comes from a community. And we don't get that without a leap of faith. Granted, I realize that leap will be much greater on your end. But the fact that we're having this conversation at all has me hopeful you might consider following us tonight. I think seeing the place with your own eyes will go a long way."

The invitation has been extended. An expected move, but one that now puts the ball in our court. Fortunately, we've already discussed this among ourselves.

"Undoubtedly it would," Morgan agrees. "And I admit, I am eager to see your operation first hand, but I'd like to offer an alternative."

Byron shares a quick glance with Lylette, before focusing again on Morgan. "What do you propose?"

"That one of you accompany us to our place first." He pauses, allowing them a second to process. "You must understand, we never intended to be gone as long as we have. Our people have to be as worried for us as we are for them. Going to your place puts us at the very least a full day away from them. Not to mention, I doubt our word alone will be enough to convince everyone to uproot all we've built. They'll likely want to see the place themselves. I know some certainly will. That's a lot of back and forth between us. We can eliminate that by returning to our farm first and informing our people of what's going on. Whoever accompanies us can guide a small group of us back to your place, and we can decide where we go from there."

Byron considers this, his face impassive as he surveys Morgan quietly. He looks to Lylette, a conversation passing between their eyes. After a moment she nods, and he acknowledges it with one of his own.

"We can agree to that," he says. "Lylette will join you tonight. From what I understand of your location, you should make it to your place by sunup, yes?" Morgan nods. "Good. That will give you the day to talk to your people, gather those who will help you make your decision. All goes well, we'll see one another again the following day."

Morgan and Byron both rise and clasp one another's hand, an act more binding than their words could ever be. Around the table, I feel a cautious optimism rise. A feeling of hope. I can see it in my friend's faces even as the weight of our failed mission lies heavy on our shoulders. Leaving this town without Felix's family won't be easy. That's what makes this moment all the more meaningful. Now when we leave we'll have a reason to look forward instead of looking back.

"It's been a long night," Byron says a minute later. "I think we'd all bene—"

His words are cut short, a frantic yell sounding from the front of the house. Guns fly into hands as we rise to our feet, the sound of breaking glass and splintering wood reaching our ears before we can so much as move or shout back. Byron and Lylette are the first out of the kitchen, two gunshots in quick procession reverberating through the air as they disappear.

"Backyard!" Felix yells, stopping us from pursuing. Several figures rush toward the house, aiming for different points of entry. Felix breaks a window with the butt of his rifle and starts shooting, the sound deafening in such an enclosed space. One goes down. Two. Leon takes aim at a third and misses, the man streaking past and disappearing around the side of the house.

"Don't let them breach!" Felix yells over his shoulder.

Morgan turns me around to face him, his eyes wide and fearful. "Stay close," he says. The words are barely past his lips before he pulls me forward. Breaking glass sounds from behind the first closed door along the hallway. Morgan wrenches it open and quickly flattens himself to the side, a hail of bullets flying through the doorway and into the opposite wall a moment later. I withdraw a small compact mirror from my coat and scout the room through its reflection. I nod and Morgan acts, taking the man out as he attempts to climb through the window.

"Smart think—"

"Down!" I shout, pushing him out the way as two figures, a man and a woman, spill into the far side of the hallway. My Glock is out and firing, catching the woman twice in the chest but missing the man completely who flings himself into the next room. Morgan and I duck into the bathroom they just vacated, desperate for cover from return fire. It doesn't come. A thunderous shot comes from the room and the man falls back into the hallway, screaming in agony as he clutches his stomach which has been reduced to shredded meat. Lylette enters the room and finishes him off.

"There's too many of them!" she yells. "Scatter and regroup at the safehouse." She disappears and charges toward the front of the house where the shooting is most focused. We leave our cover and bolt down the hall to warn the others. Bullets tear through the kitchen's shattered windows, Felix, Leon, and Emily barely able to keep their advance at bay.

"We're scattering!" Morgan yells as we take cover behind the kitchen island.

Felix curses. "Yard's a no go. We have to push toward the front."

"We'll lay cover."

The three of them crawl toward us, our bullets flying over their heads and into the yard. We stop firing as they reach us and dip out the kitchen, Morgan and Leon toppling over the fridge and a heavy bookcase at the entrance to slow pursuers. I jump over the faceless corpse at the end of the hall and enter one of the two connected living rooms. Through the shattered window figures dash across the yard in all directions, the sound of gunfire filling the air like cracks of thunder. A closer crack goes off and my ears begin to ring, forcing my attention away from the window. I turn in time to see an attacker dive behind an upturned table in the adjoining living room, a second attacker dead at its entrance. And still they come, two more entering from around the corner.

"Second floor!" Felix yells, taking the stairs to his left. Emily and I are on his heels, Leon and Morgan keeping the trio of attackers at bay with several shots before following. We duck into a small office, Felix already flinging open the window.

"You two first. Garden sheds onl—"

He stops mid-sentence, drawing his gun as a huge crash sounds from the hallway. Leon and Morgan have been taken to the ground, each of them struggling against separate attackers. I pull my own gun, their twisting bodies making a clear shot impossible. Felix takes a step forward and stops dead before he can take a second,

Morgan's attacker subduing him in a chokehold with a gun against his head. Using Morgan as a shield he turns toward us, his face twisted in a feral snarl. Then his eyes go wide as they find Felix, the snarl disappearing from his quickly paling face.

"Tio?" Felix asks, voice barely above a whisper.

Everything clicks into place in that moment, leaving me stunned. His is a face I know but have never seen outside of photographs—the face we've scoured this town searching for. Frank Chavez: Felix's uncle.

"Mijo?" Frank asks in confusion.

They stare at one another as if the other were made of smoke—a mere apparition of the men they knew rather than the men they've been shaped into. Frank opens his mouth and then whips his head to the right, the sound of approaching reinforcements reaching us over the grunts and labored breaths of Leon and his attacker.

"Matador caught another!" shouts a voice from down the hall, triumphant cackles following the announcement.

"A traves de la ventana. Ahora!" I don't know what he says, but the urgency in his voice tells me there's little time. And yet none of us move. "Confia en mi," he adds, voice softer than before.

His words are enough to uproot Felix, who turns and physically moves me and Emily toward the open window. Emily is first, her face tortured as she leaps out the window. Felix goes next landing beside her atop the snow-packed garden shed, looking back toward me expectantly. But I can't force my feet past the ledge outside, every instinct I have at war with one another. I look back through the window, a third man now visible, helping Leon's attacker finally subdue him.

Emily and Felix yell my name from below, their pleas barely reaching me from over the conflicting voices in my head. I turn to Morgan, his face purpling from the chokehold he's held in. But when his eyes meet mine they're filled with a burning intensity, begging, pleading with me to jump, to save myself. He tries to yell, and though the word never makes it past the air trapped inside his chest, I can't pretend I don't see it: *Please.* Tears spill from my eyes as I force myself to look away—to heed his plea and leap off the edge.

I hit the garden shed and scamper off into the neighboring yard. Felix leads us around the side of the house, bullets at our heels as we round the corner. We hit the street and Felix sets a blistering pace, dipping in and out of backyards and alleys to throw off any pursuers. Each stride feels like a betrayal, the blocks passing by in a blur through my tear filled eyes.

Don't think. Just run. Don't think. Just run.

The mantra plays over and over in my head, the words giving me something to focus on, distracting me from the poisonous thoughts plaguing my mind. I don't know how far we've traveled or how long it's taken, but it's only once Felix leads us up the front steps that I recognize the bed and breakfast Lylette first brought us to. That night we were greeted by armed men and women, eyeing us with that open wariness that comes with meeting new people. Now, there is no armored guard. No eyes watch us. The place is completely deserted.

"What the hell just happened?" Emily pants.

I don't answer nor does Felix. I have an idea, suspicions, but no more than that. And with Felix's uncle somehow involved, I don't want to put my foot in my mouth and say something I regret. As for Felix, he doesn't look as if words will find him any time soon. He sits heavily, his head hung, face ashen. Meanwhile, Emily paces the length of the parlor, nerves and adrenaline forcing her to keep moving.

Who were they? Have they been following us? Why did they attack?

Questions pour out of Emily as she continues her pacing, none of which we can know for certain. Her breathing grows labored, her pacing turning into a stagger, feet unsteady.

"Are you alright?" I ask, seriously concerned now.

She turns and sways alarmingly, my arms reaching out just in time to keep her from hitting the floor. Felix curses and helps me guide her to the couch.

"This isn't happening; this isn't happening; this isn't happening." She repeats the words over and over, her voice faint, breathing erratic.

"It's alright Em," Felix says, kneeling so his eyes are even with hers. "It's going to be alright. Just breathe with me. Just breathe." He takes her hands in his as he begins a series of slow, deep breaths. Every several breaths he reminds her it's going to be alright and to just keep breathing. After a minute or so her breathing returns to normal, though her eyes remain as flooded with tears as ever.

"What are we going to do, Felix?" she asks. She sounds hopeless. Lost. So unlike the girl I know. Though to be fair, I'm feeling every bit as lost as she does.

Felix looks away briefly and shakes his head. "I don't know, Em," he says. "None of this makes any sense to me. But they're going to be alright. My uncle—" He pauses, angry tears leaking from his eyes as he works past the lump that's risen in his throat. "My uncle said to trust him...that's what I'm going to do."

I want to trust him too. I want to believe that the good man I've heard tales of still exists inside him. But I can still see the cold gleam which shone in his eyes as he used Morgan like a human shield. It's burned into my mind.

"These weren't just some desperate scavengers," I say. "They were AA. Had to be." This fact isn't lost on him. Yet he stares at me in defiance all the same, as if he already knows what I'm about to ask. "You know what they are—the things they do. And he's one of them...how can you still trust him given all that?"

"An answer I'd like to know myself."

I jump at the voice, not expecting it to sound so suddenly behind me. I turn to find Byron enter the room, face furious as he stalks toward Felix, gun drawn. Two of his men enter behind him, their guns trained on me and Emily. None of us make for our own weapons. We'd never draw them in time.

"What the hell is this?" I ask.

He ignores me, not even sparing me a glance as he continues to advance toward Felix. "Your uncle sure seems to be in good health. But I suppose that'll happen when you run with thieves and murderers." He stops feet from Felix. "Was anything you said real? Or have you been playing us this whole time?"

Felix doesn't flinch, not at the accusation nor the pistol aimed between his eyes. "Everything I said was true," Felix says. "I haven't seen my uncle since before the collapse. I have no idea how the AA found us, or why he was with them. But I know there's a reason. He would never join them otherwise."

Byron scoffs. "Survival is a big motivator. Makes men do things they would never normally do. Like raiding a house at dawn— like killing others for what they have and taking prisoners to exploit. It's not a stretch to think one might gain the trust of a group of survivors only to turn around and sell them out."

Emily snorts contemptuously. "Great theory, genius," she says, her anger propelling her to her feet. "Only you've failed to notice one thing: Leon and Morgan were taken too! If we were in league with the Animals why the hell would they have taken them? For that matter, why wouldn't we have joined them during the raid and helped take you in? You're paranoid. I get that. But you need to think twice before you start throwing accusations you can't take back."

Byron looks hard at Emily but has no response. Felix takes the opportunity to push the matter.

"She's right, Byron. We were as blindsided this morning as you were. You have to believe us."

For the first time, the anger and fury leaves Byron's face, tears pooling in his eyes as the gun shakes in his hand.

"Gary and Kathy are dead: gunned down not five feet from me. Lylette and Tony? Captured. Saw it happen and there wasn't a fucking thing we could do about it. God knows what happened to our recruits. Dead or captured most likely. And all because of those bastard's greed—bastards your uncle is involved with. How can I possibly trust you after all that's happened?"

"Because those bastards have taken people I love too, and there's nothing I wouldn't do to get them back. I know you feel the same. We can help each other. Isn't that what we agreed to before they came? To help each other? But it's like you said, we can't do that without taking a leap of faith. I can't take that leap for you. That's something you have to decide for yourself."

Byron breathes heavily through his nose, eyes never leaving Felix as he considers his words. I can only imagine the flood of thoughts and emotions trapped inside him. Friends dead. Friends captured. And now being asked to trust when every instinct must be telling him not to.

"And what if your uncle isn't the man you remember?" Byron asks. "What happens if he tries to stand in our way?"

Felix is silent a moment as he considers this, face unreadable. But when he answers, his voice is unwavering.

"Then I'll put him down myself."

Chapter 24: (Morgan)

Bound and beaten I sit in the hold of a metal box truck, Leon beside me, Lylette and Tony beside him. Across from us sit three of Lylette's recruits, two of whom were brought in only this morning. Poor bastards. For months they've survived this cesspool of a town only to end up here, their chance at a better life slipping through their fingers just when it seemed within reach. I want to say something, anything that might keep some flicker of hope alive inside them. Without it, they might as well have died alongside those who fell during the raid. I can still smell the blood, see their broken bodies. But what haunts me now isn't the dead, but the living. I close my eyes and I can hear my sobbing sister, can see the blood drain from Felix's face. I see the torture in Lauren's eyes before she leaped, and I bang my head against the metal wall in anguish. I always knew coming here was a risk. For Felix, I accepted it, knowing he would do the same for me. But for all the worst case scenarios I prepared for, this wasn't one of them.

For most of my life, Frank Chavez was like a second father to me. As far back as I can remember, my memories are filled with his easy smile and booming laugh. His spirit was infectious: a genuine love for life like few I've ever met. I remember the graduation party we threw at his farm—a massive, three-way celebration for Felix, Leon, and myself. At one point it was just the two of us, both of us deep in inebriation. We talked for a long while, about the past and future both. Much of the conversation is lost to time and the alcohol I consumed, but I'll never forget what he called the true keys to happiness:

"Family and friends," he said. *"Nothing else in this life matters without them."* I remember smiling and asking if he was sure there wasn't anything else. He thought for a moment until a smile split his lips and he raised his cup in toast. *"Well, a man can never go wrong with a cold beer."*

A pang goes through me at the memory. How can the man who told me that be the same man who gave me these injuries? Even now, I'm struggling to come to terms with it. All this time I prayed to find him alive—that somehow he found a way to survive. But to join the Animas Animals? To raid and kill? To blackmail and coerce? I would never have thought him capable of such things.

Our ride is a short one, the trucks in our convoy coming to a halt not ten minutes later. Engines go silent. Doors open and close, jeers and taunts reaching us through the truck's walls. There's a metallic scrape and the doors open to reveal a line of five men, each with their guns pointed inside.

"Out," barks the thickest of them.

Clumsily we climb out, our hands restrained behind our backs. A girl, one of Byron and Lylette's recruits, slips upon exiting and faceplants hard onto the icy parking lot. A low whimper escapes her as the men laugh.

"Get up you stupid hatchet wound," sneers the man who ordered us out. He grabs a fist full of her hair and pulls her to her feet, making the woman yell out in pain. "Quit your crying," he says yanking her hair further so she's bent backward, staring up at him.

"Enough!" I shout.

The man's eyes snap to me, his torment of the girl forgotten. A sudden hush falls as he advances toward me, every guard within earshot stopping to watch.

"What did you just say?" he asks, so close the sourness of his breath fills my nostrils. He's bigger than me. Armed and clearly callous. But I stand my ground all the same.

"I said, enough," I answer. He stares down at me long and hard, face angry. Then, slowly, he smiles.

"You have fight in you," he says. "That's good. It'll be fun taking it away."

He watches me close, looking for signs of intimidation, of fear. I show him none. Instead, I smile back, aiming to antagonize, to unnerve him in some small way.

"You have no idea what I fight f—"

His strike is fast and hard, catching me on the side of the head completely unexpected. Another strike lands and I'm forced to a knee. A third strike, and I'm flattened to the frozen ground. Damn he's strong, my face aching from where his fist connected. I look up and Leon's face swims in and out of my vision, his shaking head warning me to stay down. But then the sound of that bastard's laughter reaches my ears, and I feel the rage rise within me.

"Like I said," he cackles. "It's going to be fun tak—"

I sweep out his legs in one smooth motion, the air leaving his lungs as he lands flat on his back. I roll over on top of him, knees pinning him to the ground. Hands bound behind me, I rear my head back and bring it down hard onto his. Pain erupts from the moment of contact, my vision going black. I'm violently ripped off him, the hands restraining me the only thing keeping me from hitting the ground.

"Get off me!" I hear the man yell.

I open my eyes at the sound of his voice, the world a blurry mess. He swats away the men trying to help him and rises violently to his feet. His nose is broken, dark rivers of blood flowing freely down his chin and staining his shirt. My head throbs and aches, but this site makes it all worth it.

"You stupid son of a bitch!" he seethes, withdrawing his gun and leveling it between my eyes.

"ENOUGH!" yells a voice I know. The man looks angrily to his left and I follow suit. Frank marches toward us, brow narrowed in disdain.

"Lower your gun," he orders. "I won't ask you twice."

The authority in his voice is unmistakable, enough so that the man bottles his anger and lowers it resentfully.

"But he attacked me, sir," the man spits. "That can't go unpunished!"

Frank looks at the man in disgust. "I saw," Frank says. "And if a bound grunt flat on his face can do that to you, you deserve the injuries he gave you. Now go get yourself cleaned up! I'll take it from here."

The man looks mutinous, but he doesn't challenge the order. "Yes, sir!" he says, shaking in fury. He spares me one last glance, and if looks could kill I'd be dead where I stand. Then he turns and walks through the guarded front entrance. It's with a sinking stomach that I finally realize where we are: The DoubleTree. I haven't forgotten the night we freed my cousins. The security was lax then, and still we needed every bit of luck on our side to succeed. Things have tightened considerably since then. I'm afraid luck won't be enough this time around.

"Leave him be," Frank orders. I nearly buckle when the guards let me go, only just managing to keep my feet. I straighten myself out, fighting through the throb beating inside my skull.

"Try that shit again, and you'll regret it," Frank says

His eyes meet mine and it's as if I'm seeing him clearly for the first time. Did we never laugh together, joke together? The early morning hunts and fly fishing trips—the ATV adventures and nights around the campfire—did they never happen? Or did the man I know die sometime between then and now?

"Sorry sir, but she's a friend of mine," I say. "A man I once knew said nothing in this life matters without family and friends."

Something flashes behind his eyes, a flicker of emotion so quick I can't decipher. But when he speaks, it's with the same cold indifference as earlier.

"Sounds like the kind of bullshit people used to believe," he says. "But it's a new world, and the only thing that matters in it is power: those that have it and those who don't. The sooner you realize things have changed, the better off you'll be."

My eyes never leave his, searching for the flash of emotion I saw only moments ago. I find none, his stare as cold as his words.

"Yeah, I'm starting to realize that," I say.

"Good. Now fall back in line." He waits until I've done so before addressing his men. "Let us show these grunts their accommodations."

Frank leads us around the north side of the building, my eyes soaking in as much detail of their fortifications as possible. The windows and sliding glass doors have been boarded all along the first floor. Lookouts have been posted at intervals along the top floor, their decks barricaded in the event of a shootout. One shifts his gaze from the highway and spots me, a grin splitting his face as he puts me in his crosshairs and mimes taking a shot.

A sharp smack hits the back of my head.

"Eyes ahead of you," one of our escorts warns. I glare at him but raise no more issue. I don't need to give them any more reason to injure me further. We reach a side entrance, the door opening at our approach.

"Inform Captain Barr of our arrival," he instructs one of the men standing guard.

"He's already sent word, sir," the guard replies. "He asked that you begin overseeing the interrogations without him."

This catches Frank by surprise. "Did he specify why?"

"No, sir. Only that he had other matters to deal with."

"Very well," Frank says. "As you were."

We continue past the guards, a small flashlight in Frank's hand the only light in the dark hall. Frank opens a door at the end of the hallway and steps back.

"This will do for now," he instructs the men. "I don't want them speaking with the others before interrogations." One by one we file in, but just as I'm about to enter, Frank throws out an arm to stop me.

"This one likes to talk," he says. "I'll start with him. In the meantime, .keep the rest quiet. I don't want any collaboration on their part."

"Do you need assistance, sir?" one of the men asks.

Frank just smirks. "That won't be necessary. If this grunt tries anything stupid, I'll show him what real pain feels like." His men nod their approval, leering grins splitting their faces as Frank leads me to another room several doors down. I enter the room, Frank lighting a lantern just inside the door.

The room is as sparse as it is bleak, a quick survey of the place telling me all I need to know. Splatters of dried blood stain the carpet. Metal hooks hang from the wall. In one corner sits a metal tub filled with jugs of water, a black tool chest filled with God knows what sitting in the other. How many have suffered within these walls? How many wills broken, secrets spilled? I think back to the night of Richard's interrogation, of the tactics he used to ensure that father and son were not a threat to us. Perhaps I'm about to receive my penance for my part in it.

"You truly have become an Animal, haven't you?" I ask with as much bitterness as I can manage. Frank sets the lantern down on the room's lone table, his back to me. If ever there was a prayer of a chance of me overtaking him, it's now. But then he speaks, his voice filled with such pain that it freezes me where I stand.

"No, Morgan," he says. "I'm afraid I've become something far worse."

He turns, and the resentment inside me dies at the sight of him. Gone is the cold-hearted tyrant who brought me here. In his place, a man who is the embodiment of misery and torment, as if the dark energy within this room has taken over him.

"Frank..." His name leaves my mouth before I can think of anything to say, the sudden change in his demeanor leaving me lost for words.

"Don't," he lashes out. "I'm not worthy of your sympathy." I watch him for a strained minute. I thought outside I saw Frank at his worse. But this is something else entirely.

"What the hell are you doing here, Frank?" I finally ask. "How could it possibly have come to this?"

He violently wipes the tears from his face, steeling himself the best he can with a steadying breath.

"I've asked myself the same question a thousand times," he says. "But in the end what does it matter? Regardless of my reasons, there's no justifying the things I've done."

His eyes meet mine for the first time since entering the room, the remorse and self-hatred so potent it's all I can do but not look away.

"Maybe not," I say. "But that doesn't mean your reasons are irrelevant."

He shakes his head slowly. "I'm here because I'm a fool. A fool who's made more mistakes than I could name. Worst part is I didn't even realize it until this morning."

He pauses, a visible tremor rocking his body. I have the sense to wait, to give him the time he needs to gather his thoughts. It's his story to tell after all. He deserves the right to tell it in his own time.

"When the pulse hit, I knew the world had just gone to hell," he says. "Knew it the moment everything went black. But that doesn't mean I had a clue on what to do, how to handle it. All I knew was that I needed my family together. That was the most important thing. I could figure out the rest after we were all under one roof. Felix was in Denver of course. Nothing I could do about that, except pray he could find his way home...and he did."

His voice breaks, and he has to pause for a moment. He works past the lump in his throat and continues.

"That left my girls. I hated the idea of leaving Christina and Rob alone, but I couldn't justify taking them with me. So I had them lock the place down, and told them I'd be back by nightfall, morning at the latest. I had my old Polaris, after all. I figured even if I lost the thing after arriving in town, we could make it back by then, no problem. But when I got to their place, they weren't there. That put a hole in my plan, basically leaving me with only two options: either stay and hope they returned, or else leave and try and find them through chaos. I chose to stay.

"I waited all afternoon, all evening. I fell asleep at some point, woke up just as the sun was rising. I couldn't wait any longer. I left a note behind telling them I was there and to stay put, that I would return to the house if I hadn't found them. I searched everywhere I could think of, any place I thought they might feel safe. No luck. And when I returned to their house, they still hadn't returned.

"I can't even begin to describe how worried I was by then—literally sick to my stomach, my mind filled with every vile scenario imaginable. I knew first hand how bad things had turned. The things I saw searching broke my heart, made my skin crawl. Two days and the town didn't even resemble itself. No law, no rules, it was an open free for all, everything up for grabs. And my daughters were somewhere in the middle of it, my wife and son on their own, wondering why the hell I hadn't made it back.

"I set out the next morning the same as the last, searching anywhere I could think of. I was driving down 3rd Ave when I noticed a truck pull up next to one of the houses. I knew what was going on, this wasn't the first raid I had seen since I'd been in town. Even if it was, the tied and gagged women in the truck bed were clear enough. They hadn't seen me though, and I had enough sense to keep out of sight until they passed. I waited, did my best to block out the gunshots and the screams that followed. I hated myself for doing nothing. But I couldn't risk my life if my girls were still out there somewhere. The truck started again, and I could hear it draw nearer. Finally, it came within sight of my hiding spot, and my heart stopped. They were there, both of them, gagged and bound to the girls on either side of them."

A shadow crosses his face as he says this. A dark menace filling his words as he continues.

"I never knew hate like I did at that moment. Never felt rage so pure. I didn't even think, just acted. I took out the driver easily enough. They were barely moving, and I had a clear shot. The two in the bed were next, dropped both of them before the truck had even rolled to a stop. Without the guards, the girls were frantic. Half tried to flee, the other half were too afraid to do anything but try and find cover. Tied as they were, nobody could make a run for it. This all might have turned out differently if they could.

"I had three down, but there were still three inside the truck, and they were smart enough not to give me a target. I emptied two full magazines into the side of the truck. Managed to get one, but the bodies kept the other two safe until they crawled out the back. I hoped they would make a run for it, try to escape. Instead, they flipped the script on me.

"They took cover behind the girls, using them as human shields so I couldn't take a shot. They told me I had ten seconds to lay down my guns and show myself. If I didn't, one of the girls would die. I couldn't show myself, it was the one advantage I had. So I called their bluff, and ten seconds later they put a bullet through one of their heads. They gave me another ten seconds. I didn't need half that. When my girls saw me, they lost it. I don't blame them, but that gave those bastards all the explanation they needed. I expected them to kill me then and there...hell, part of me wishes they had. But they had other plans for me.

"They had their fun humiliating me in front of my girls, beating me till I lost consciousness. I don't know how long I was out. By the time I came around, I was chained to a metal support beam In some garage, tied so tight I couldn't move a muscle. I tried to break free, but all I managed to do was make enough noise to let them know I was awake. Three men entered, the two who beat me and a third. One look at the third man and I knew he was the shot caller of the bunch, and he didn't waste any time letting me know so. He introduced himself as Boss—a vain, narcissistic name if there ever was one—and handed me this."

Frank reaches into his pocket and withdraws a wallet, empty but for several photographs of his family. But from the back, he takes out a single photo that stands apart from the other, one that makes my stomach churn and horrifying understanding blossom. Brianna and Lena, two girls I love as if they were my own sisters, kneel in the photo; hands bound, mouths gagged, cheeks slick with tears as two men hold guns against their heads. It all makes sense now.

"He told me he was planning on building something, and that I had just been recruited to his cause. He would keep my girls safe, unharmed, so long as I did as I was ordered. Then he went on some about his vision for the future, how we would be the kings of this new world. It was all bullshit. All that mattered was that he had me by the balls and that so long as he had my girls, I would do whatever he asked."

I search his eyes, the self-loathing I witnessed earlier as potent as ever.

"I don't blame you for hating me, Morgan," he says. "But trust me when I tell you that it will never be more than I hate myself."

The room grows silent. He's right, I think to myself: I do hate him. At least, I hate the things he's done. But where there is hate there is also sympathy. Understanding. I know what it means to do things for those you love. Had I been in his shoes, I don't know that I'd have done any different. Even so, his story doesn't explain everything.

"You claim you were coerced into this, and yet you walk through these hallways, unchecked, unchallenged. You have men calling you *sir,* obeying your orders without hesitation. How have you not figured out a way to get you and your girls free form this?"

He laughs, a dark cackle of a sound, so unlike the one I remember.

"Do you know where my girls are at this very moment?" he asks. "On the third floor, in a block of suites that have been sealed off from the rest of the hotel. It's where Boss keeps high valued hostages—wives, children, whoever he needs to keep people like me in line. There's a squad of soldiers he's handpicked whose sole responsibility is keeping the area secure—nobody enters, nobody leaves without his approval. I can visit, but only under the supervision of the guards, my weapons stripped before I'm even allowed to see them. They are allowed time outside, but only within sight of the snipers, and never without accompanying guards. But yes, I've planned ways to free us of this hellhole, each one less likely to succeed than the last. We would be caught, and we would die a traitor's death. I couldn't risk it, Morgan. Not when I know the sick things that son of a bitch would subject my girls to. I already failed my wife and son...I couldn't fail them too."

The anguish lacing his final words is undeniable. How long has he tortured himself over leaving his wife and son—how long has he mourned them, ignorant to their survival? He's no longer the man I once knew. This place, the deeds he's committed have changed him. But one trait that has endured is the lengths he would go through to keep his family safe.

"They're alive," I say. He looks up sharply at my words. "Christina and Rob, they're alive."

He shakes his head, his voice a low growl. "You lie. It took nearly a month, but finally Boss let me scout alone. First chance I got I went back to the farm, but it was too late. They were gone, and the place had been taken over by a roaming gang. I lost it, seeing them in my home like that. I attacked. The place was a bloodbath by the time I was finished, but not before I learned the truth: my wife and son were dead, killed by those pieces of filth the night they took the place. One of the men confessed before he bled out, gloated about it. So don't paint me a fantasy, Morgan. Not when I know the truth."

I lean forward. "That man lied to you," I say. "I don't know why. Maybe he just wanted to torture you. But it's not true. I've known you over half my life, Frank. I wouldn't lie to you about your family."

His stare is piercing, brows narrowed in mistrust. But slowly, my words sink in, his features softening as he realizes what I say is true.

"They're alive." The words are hardly more than a whisper, his face one of stunned disbelief. His eyes settle on mine once more, desperate now for the information I have. "Tell me everything."

I oblige, my turn now to explain the events that led me here. I start with our arrival at the farm, and the challenges we've faced to ensure our survival. I explain how Rob found us and told us of the conditions he and his mother were subjected to while being kept on the Sawyer's Ranch. Rescuing Christina; killing Pete Sawyer and his lackeys; allowing the few survivors of the ranch to join us; I include it all. I speak of Felix's guilt, and our decision to help him search the town despite so many risks. I tell him of Lylette and Byron and sparing as many details as I can, tell him of their vision of building a community.

"We were planning on visiting their operation first hand," I say. "We'd already searched everywhere we could think of. It killed Felix, but even he knew it was time to move on—to accept he wasn't going to find you...and then there you were. Can't say the universe doesn't have a sense of humor."

Frank has not interrupted me once since I started speaking, soaking in my words in an almost manic intensity. Still, I can tell that learning these truths is as much a burden as they are a relief. I saw it in the way his face lit up after hearing of Rob's arrival, and in the shadow that fell upon learning of the suffering he and his mother received at the hands of a man he once considered a friend. Now that I've finished I see the longing in his face—the desire to see them, hold them in his own arms. It's a desire I know will not fade. Justifying the deeds he's done for the survival of his girls is one thing. But knowing now that the rest of his family still lives? He'll put everything he has into making his family whole. At least, that's what I'm counting on. Because if I know one thing, it's that I won't make it out alive without his help.

"I've always thought of you as family," I say, pulling him away from his thoughts. "The things you've done, what's happened this morning, doesn't change that." I pause, taking the opportunity to lean closer, guaranteeing I have his full attention. If I'm going to make a play for his help, now is the time.

"Nothing in this life matters without family and friends," I say, speaking the words for the second time today. "Do you still believe so? Or is that man truly gone?"

A fire burns inside him—that wild, unchecked courage that only burns inside the young. He's not the first to enter here with such spirit, resolved to withstand the horrors that would soon follow. A chill runs down my spine as I think of those poor souls—of the flames that were snuffed within these very walls. I should know. For months, my job has been to mold the soldiers of this army. But to mold them, first, I had to break them. It's why this room exists, everything within it a tool for me to use. Some lasted longer than others, but eventually, all who've entered this room have been broken, molded into something else. Me most of all.

Every scar I inflicted, every scream I extracted, every moment spent within these cursed walls have taken their toll. I feel it in my very soul—a darkness born of the sins I've committed. Frank Chavez vanished months ago. In his place as has risen El Matador, *one of Boss's three captains, charged with managing the army he's amassed.*

I hate him, but out of necessity, I've lost myself in him. Now I stand at a crossroads, either path irrevocable in the course they will send me.

We had heard rumors of the community he spoke of, of their recruitment inside the town. It's the reason behind our raid this morning, why I was tasked with leading it. Their growing numbers, their proximity to the town, it poses a threat. And now I have proof of its existence. I could force the truth out of his companions, use the tools at my disposal to break them as I have so many before. I would report to Boss, and he would order a strike force large enough to crush their fledgling community. It would be massive, and it would be complicated, and I could use the ensuing frenzy to sneak my girls away. I could return home. I could make my family whole again.

"Nothing in this life matters without family and friends." His words echo inside my head. "Do you still believe so, or is that man truly gone?"

It's not a question I can so easily answer. But in my heart, I know that if I do this, if I torture the truth out of his companions and leave him behind to suffer Boss's wrath, Frank Chavez will cease to exist. El Matador will be all that I am. The realization hits like a slap in the face. Suddenly, I know with complete certainty the path I must take. There will be risks. Danger. But it is the only way my family can ever truly be whole. I turn toward the fiery young man before me, a rush of affection I have not felt in months blooming inside my chest.

"I don't know if that man still exists, Morgan," I say. "But we're going to find out."

We discuss all of the options available to us. I draw out a map of the hotel, going into as much detail as I can. I mark hallways and stairwells, exits and areas most occupied with soldiers. I walk him through our security: snipers, patrols, barricades. I include anything I can think to mention, anything at all that could help us figure out a way out of this. In return, he gives me information, telling me of those left at the farm, and the kind of firepower they have stockpiled. When the time comes, we'll almost certainly need outside help. Which means I have a house call to make, a prospect that gives me goosebumps just thinking of seeing my wife and son again. We continue as long as we can so as not to arouse suspicion.

I return him to the holding area, faking cosmetic injuries lest the guards grow suspicious. I expect to continue onto the others when a runner informs me that Boss has requested my presence in the War Room. Climbing the stairs, I feel only a fragment of the hatred which usually consumes me at Boss's summonings. Perhaps because I am finally working against him as I've always wanted to.

I enter the War Room to find everyone already seated around the table. At the head is Boss. To his left, sits Captain Vonn. To his right, sits his brother and second in command: Captain Barr. Beside Barr is an unfamiliar man, his clothing ragged, his hair and beard a matted mess. He casts me a quick, furtive glance, our eyes meeting long enough for me to discern the shameful resolve in his stare. I know that look well—a look I've seen in my own reflection too many times to count. Whatever's brought this man here, it can't be anything good.

"Matador," Boss says, tipping his head in greeting. "Congratulations on this morning's raid. I knew I could count on you to get the job done." I hate hearing the approval in his voice, seeing the cold satisfaction in his eyes. I hate knowing that I'm the reason for both. I want so badly to reach out and wipe the smirk from his face, to hurt him the way I've hurt so many on his orders. Soon, I tell myself. Soon you'll have your chance. For now, I bottle my emotions, acknowledging his words with a nod as I take my place at the table.

"Thank you, sir," I say smoothly. "I've already begun the interrogations."

"Glad to hear it," he says. "But for now, they can wait."

Boss shifts his gaze to the man on my left. My eyes follow, alarm bells ringing in the back of my mind. Boss has been after the community Morgan spoke of for some time, ever since we learned of their presence and recruitment within the town. What could this man possibly have to offer that would make him cease the interrogations?

"Do you recall the break-in we had at the end of summer?" Boss asks.

As if I could forget. Nearly a dozen of our soldiers killed, grunts escaping in every direction, Molotov cocktails exploding against our first responders. It was chaos. We were the predators who stalked at night. To have the tables flipped on us was not something we were prepared for.

Naturally, we retaliated. We hunted down as many of the escapees as we could, bringing them back alive whenever possible. Some chose to fight back, to attack us with whatever they could get their hands on. They were killed of course, put down as if they were pets who had turned rabid. In truth, they were the lucky ones. At least they were spared the days that followed, the pain and suffering those we captured were subjected to, a warning to the remaining grunts. In the end, they too met their deaths. They begged for them.

"Of course, sir," I say, anxiety rising inside me.

"We found them!" Barr speaks in place of his brother, unable to hold back his excitement any longer. "The bastards who did it."

"You're certain?" I ask, nodding to the unnamed man. " He has proof?"

Barr looks to the man, a twisted leer on his face. Wordlessly, he snatches an upturned photo from the table and hands it to me. I stare at it for what feels like an age. My face doesn't betray me, the emotionless mask I've earned after months of servitude hiding the current that ripples beneath the surface.

A family stands captured in time, their smiles grand and true, assembled around an elderly man who sits before a giant cake, two numbered candles lit, marking his 90th birthday. Far to the left, almost out of frame, stands the man at our table. Three of the faces have been circled in pen. A boy and a girl who look to be in their mid-teens stand just behind the old man, their faces more youthful than I ever saw them in person, but no less recognizable. And they are not the only faces I recognize.

"I never forget a face," Barr says, his words a low growl. He reaches and taps his finger on the third person circled. "He was behind it, I'd bet my life on it. That makes it twice he's gotten the better of us. It won't happen a third."

"Captain Barr and yourself will lead the engagement," Boss says. "Bring him in alive. I want his screams to echo down every hallway, up every stairwell. I want to make an example of him: a warning to anyone foolish enough to cross us. I wouldn't task this on anyone but you. I know you'll get the job done."

Details of the engagement follow: men, resources, firepower. The scope of the operation is massive, larger by far than any we've ever attempted. It's proof of how badly Boss wants the man who attacked us. Only the plan won't work. It can't because the man they seek isn't there. He's here, two floors below our feet. Now everything he and I discussed before this meeting is for naught. And if I don't figure out something in the next few hours, both of our families will feel the full extent of Boss's cruelty.

Chapter 25: (Lauren)

The sun fades at our backs, the temperature dropping as the light grows weaker. Not that I feel the cold. My anxiety keeps me numb from such things. The wait was torture, the walls around me like a cage I couldn't break free of. Only through sheer force of will was I able to resist the urge to leave, to throw caution to the wind and return to the farm alone. But after the fiasco this morning there was bound to be patrols in the area. Getting caught wouldn't help anyone.

We make up for the hours lost, covering the snowy terrain as fast as we can manage. It's still too slow. Already Leon and Morgan have been at the Animal's mercy for too long. Just thinking about it fills me with dread. Surely they were taken for a reason. And knowing what they're capable of, I know it can't be anything good.

I push myself harder, desperate to move faster, to outrun the thoughts plaguing my mind. No such luck. I've not felt fear like this in some time; not since Denver, not since the journey home. Memories of the trail return to me: of the night Morgan was captured in Salida, and the unrelenting worry that followed. I remember waiting with Maya as Emily fought off her infection, waiting to learn of Morgan's fate. In so many ways this situation reminds me of then. Only this time I will not simply sit and wait. I will do everything in my power to free the man I love. I don't care about the odds, the danger. I won't give up on him. He would never give up on me.

Night has fallen in earnest by the time we reach the driveway, the house standing like a darkened shadow at the end. A voice rings out of the shadows, warning us of our trespassing.

"It's us, Richard," Emily yells out.

A spotlight shines down, scanning each of our faces in turn.

"Where are Morgan and Leon?" Richard asks. "Who the hell are these people?"

"They're friends," she says. "Look, we have a lot to discuss, and it's freezing as hell out here."

Richard is silent a beat. "Come inside. But your *friends* hand over their weapons or they don't enter."

"Then we don't enter," Byron says.

"Byron—" Felix is cut off before he can even get a second word out.

"No!" Byron says. "We're not handing over our weapons. We may be here, but make no mistake, that doesn't mean that I trust you! If we didn't need help getting our people back—people captured by *your uncle*—we wouldn't be here at all. So we enter with our weapons, or we take our chances alone."

Felix stares at Byron for a quick moment and nods. "They keep their weapons," he calls up to Richard.

"The hell if they—" it's my turn to cut someone off.

"They're keeping their Goddamn weapons!" I shout. "If you want to shoot us, shoot us, but we're wasting time we don't have. We're coming in." I march forward, the others following close behind me. From above I hear Richard curse, but he doesn't try and stop us. We walk around to the back entrance, the door opening for us as we reach the porch.

The moment I enter I am nearly tackled to the floor by Grace, her thin arms squeezing me for all they're worth. I squeeze back even tighter, barely able to keep the tears from falling as she sobs silently into my chest.

"I'm here Gracie," I whisper. "I'm here."

I needed this more than I realized—a moment where all the pain of the outside world cannot touch me—where nothing exists but Gracie and me. Just the two of us. Like it used to be. I fight to hold onto the moment as long I can, but already I feel it slipping away. It's in the swell of voices, the movement of those around us. It reminds me that it's no longer just the two of us. It hasn't been for some time now.

Finally, I break the moment, untangling myself from Grace's arms. I scan the faces before me, my eyes drawn to Mrs. Taylor's like a pair of magnets. I know those eyes well, seen them in her son every day since this all began. I search them now, hoping they might settle my nerves as they so often have before. But it doesn't help. If anything they grow worse, weighed with what I must tell her.

"Morgan and Leon were captured earlier this morning," I say. I nearly have to shout to be heard over the others. When they hear me, they grow quiet. I shake my head, dreading this next line most of all. "They were taken by the Animas Animals."

The noise returns. Curses and questions sound from every corner of the room, everyone vying for their voices to be heard over the others. I hardly hear them, my attention still on Mrs. Taylor whose eyes close at the news, the composed facade she normally maintains betraying her as it all hits home. Beside her, Mr. Taylor steps forward and wraps his arms around Emily.

"It's going to be alright," he says, voice cracking with grief. "It's all going to be alright."

I don't know if she believes him. I don't know if he even believes himself. But in her father's arms, she comes undone, no longer holding back the flood of emotions she's fought so hard to repress. Mrs. Taylor moves forward and I shift to the side, certain she too wishes to embrace her daughter. To my surprise, however, it's me she reaches for, wrapping me firmly in her arms.

"Thank God you're alright," she says, the relief in her voice genuine and heartfelt. Hearing it, feeling the warmth of her love as she holds me close, it's all too much for me to handle. I break. The guilt, the worry, the hate—it all comes pouring out of me.

"I'm sorry," I say, barely coherent. "I...I should've—"

"Shhh..." she breathes into my ear, the sound low and soothing. "If there was anything you could have done to bring my boy home, you would have. I know that as certain as I know anything."

Fresh tears squeeze past my eyelids at her commendation. The woman is amazing. Embracing me as if I were her own, easing my pain with words of comfort when inside her own pain must be agony. It's proof of her enduring strength. I lean on that strength now, feeding off it until I feel it in myself. I don't know if there was anything else I could have done. In any case, it's too late. Nothing I or anyone else does can change what's happened. But I didn't come here to mourn and grieve. I came because I'm not the only one who cares for them. And if I'm going to stand a chance in hell in getting them back, I'm going to need some help.

"Thank you," I say, breaking the hug and quickly wiping my eyes. I don't even know what I thank her for. For the hug? For her words? For actually caring whether or not I live or die? Perhaps for all of it. And from the way she looks at me now, I know she understands all the same.

To my left, Felix is all that stands between Richard and Byron, both of whom seem a split second away from tearing into one another. And not only those two. Hands hover over weapons behind each of them, each side eying the other with mistrust. The situation needs to be defused before something happens.

"Enough!" I have to yell at the top of my voice, but thankfully, it has the effect I had hoped. The room quiets, their attention drawn to me. I take advantage of it. "We have to keep it together." I turn to Byron and his men. "These are good people. We've spent the past few days together, getting to know them and the settlement they're part of. We were discussing a possible alliance when we were attacked. Some of their people were taken. Others were killed. That's why they're here. Neither of us can get our people back unless we work together."

"Get them back?" Richard scoffs. "Wake up, girl. There is no getting them back. If we try, we'll either end up dead or captured ourselves."

Emily steps forward, wiping at her eyes which have turned fierce at his words. "So what are you saying, that we should leave them there?" she challenges. "We've broken in and retrieved our people before."

"Yes, we have," Richard says, cutting her off. "And the Animals won't have forgotten. We won't be facing the same lax security we did last time. They'll have tightened things up tenfold, you can count on it. And their prisoners? They won't be in the same location. They'll have them locked up somewhere more secure. No amount of stealth will matter if we don't know where they are. We'd need an army to even stand a chance."

I can see the effect his words are having on the family. I can see it in their somber faces and gloomy eyes. What's worse, I know there is truth in what he says. The Animals are not the type of people to make the same mistake twice. Whatever means they used to rescue Trent and Julia will not work a second time around. But I refuse to believe there is no hope for them.

"We wouldn't need an army if we had a contact on the inside," I say. That gets their attention.

"What do you mean?" Uncle Will asks from beside Richard. "What contact?"

I turn to Felix. I hate putting him on the spot so abruptly, but the family needs to know the truth. Felix knows this too, nodding once before settling his eyes on his aunt.

"My Uncle Frank," he says. Surprised murmurs immediately follow, the family completely taken aback at the revelation.

"The uncle you went to find?" Uncle Will asks incredulously.

"Yes," Felix answers, never looking away from his aunt. "He was part of the raiding party that took Leon and Morgan."

The surprise quickly turns resentful, angry. Many look to Felix as if in betrayal, as if he approved his uncle's actions. I doubt he hears any of it. His whole focus remains on his aunt, holding her hand as they speak in rapid Spanish. I don't understand a word she says, but her tears tell me how painful this is for her to hear. The last thing she needs is to be heckled right now.

"Inside man?" Richard asks. "How the hell can we trust this man if he was the one who captured them in the first place?"

"You weren't there," I say. "It was chaos, everything happening so fast. One second I'm running into an upstairs bedroom, Leon and Morgan behind me, and the next they're taken to the ground just outside the door. We couldn't even react before Frank had Morgan in a chokehold. But as soon as he saw Felix, his whole demeanor changed. Still, we were surrounded by Animals, and they were moving our way fast. Frank let us go, shouted at Felix to run. We made it out because of him. I think that garners some trust, don't you?"

"For sparing his nephew?" Uncle Will asks. "Hardly. He still took Morgan and Leon didn't he? Why not let them go too?"

"Because the other men had already seen him," Emily says. "Or do you think they wouldn't have found it suspicious if he just let them go?"

"In any case, we can't be sure of his reasons," Richard says. "And I think it would be foolish to assume we can trust him based on that alone."

"I think it would be just as foolish to write him off for the same reason," I counter, unable to keep the heat out of my voice.

"She's right," Felix says, ceasing his exchange with his aunt. He steps forward, holding his ground against the skeptical faces aimed his way. "I don't know why my uncle was with the Animals. I don't know why he let us go. There are a dozen questions I don't have an answer to. But I do know that my uncle has a reason for everything he does. If he's with them, there's a reason, a reason other than just trying to survive. He would never have abandoned my aunt and cousin otherwise."

That gives people pause, reminding them of what Frank left behind by failing to return. Everyone here knows the value of family. Because of that, they can imagine the circumstances it must have taken to keep Frank away from his wife and son. Still, the skepticism lingers.

"I understand you want to believe the best of your uncle, Felix," Richard says. To my surprise, his words spoken with care, free from his usual edge. "And I'm inclined to believe you. To abandon your children..." His eyes sweep briefly over his two daughters. "It can't have been without reason. But let's say we can trust him, that he can help us. He's still only one man. One man among hundreds. How many lives will we have to risk so that we might free two?"

He looks now toward Emily, and then to me. "Believe me, I want them back," he continues. "Morgan and I have had our disagreements, but that doesn't mean I don't respect him. He's a good man. But is his life worth more than any of our own? You know him as well as anyone: would he even want us to take such a risk?"

A pang goes through me at the question. No, of course he wouldn't. This is the man who gave himself up in Salida so his friends could escape and get his sister the medicine needed to save her life. The man who faced a firing squad outside Rockridge on the smallest of hopes that doing so might save the rest of us. I remember the fierce look in his eyes this morning, begging me to run, to leave him and save myself. The lives of those he loves have always mattered more to him than his own. If he were here now, he would side with Richard, would tell us to leave him. But he's not here. I am. And I won't give up on him so easily.

"No, Richard," I say. "He would never want any of us to risk ourselves on his behalf. He would want to keep us safe, protected. I know because since the collapse, that's all he's ever tried to do. But I also know what he would do if the tables were turned—if he stood here now and it was one of us who were taken." I pause, taking a moment to look about the room. I watch them visualize such a scenario, imagining the things Morgan might say. It's easy enough to imagine.

"He would never abandon someone he loved, not if there was even the smallest hope of saving them. Do we not owe it to him to at least try?"

Slowly, I feel something stir in the air around me. A buzz. A spark. Hope. It's not just me either.

"I will help," Vince says. He looks to his fiance, eyes pleading for her to understand. "He would do the same for me."

"Me too," Trent says, stepping up. "He got me out of there once. I owe it to him to try and do the same."

More voices chime in, pledging to help if they can. Richard listens to each person speak, his face unreadable as he does so. It's only after the voices go quiet, and everyone has had their chance to speak, that he weighs in.

"Very well," he says. "So long as there's a chance that we can retrieve him, I will help."

The relief that floods through me is overwhelming. This is only the first step, of course. We will still need help from Byron's people, from Frank himself, neither of which are guaranteed. But for now, I will allow myself to hope.

I open my mouth to speak, ready to iron out the plan moving forward, but the words never leave me. The shrill blast of a whistle from our lookout stops them in their tracks. From the top of the back stairwell, our lookout yells down, his message turning my blood to ice.

"Trucks. Incoming."

Chapter 26: (Morgan)

In darkness I wait, feet bound, hands tied and looped through a metal ring bolted to the wall above my head. Makes my arms ache something vicious, the spasms increasing as time goes on. Worse is the throbbing at the base of my skull; the slow torture of thirst as your mouth and throat grow dry. It feels like an age since Frank delivered me here, my spirits bolstered by the conversation we had. I try my best to hold onto that feeling, telling myself I can trust him, that the man I knew still lives beneath the Animal. But the longer I wait, the more I question. The more I doubt. It's as if the shadows of the room seep into my mind, making my thoughts as dark and bleak as this wall of black before me.

He told me of the layout of the hotel. The security measures they have in place. All of it taken on his word alone, impossible to verify. And in turn, I told him everything about the farm. His farm. Our resources and fortifications; the guns and ammunition we've amassed, he knows of it all. More importantly, he knows of the people we left behind. In short, I've told him everything he needs to know to take the place.

He wouldn't, a voice inside me says. *Not with his wife and son on the farm. He would never risk it.*

I nod, agreeing with the voice, convincing myself of what I need to believe. But before it can take root, a second voice sounds in the back of my mind.

Wouldn't he? The voice challenges. *If he thought he could keep them safe from it. He's already proven the things he's capable of.*

The debate rages back and forth between the two voices, and I don't know which one to listen to. What's more, trying to understand Frank's intent is only part of my concerns. Relieved as I am that Lauren and the others escaped from the house, worry fills me as I think of them. Are they safe? Do the Animals still hunt them? If so, is it only a matter of time before they join us? Just as terrifying are the thoughts of what they might be planning. I know my friends. With Leon and I captured, they will feel worry. Fear. Those feelings will eat away at them, making them restless, making them want to act. It's what frightens me most of all: the thought of them being killed or captured in some desperate bid to free me. I don't know how I could live with myself should it come to that.

Beside me, Leon wakes in a dry, hacking fit that leaves him breathless. It's a minute before his breathing returns to normal.

"No sign of our *friend*?" he asks.

Friend. He makes a mockery of the word, his mistrust for Frank running deep. I filled him in on everything after we were separated from Lylette and the others. His reaction was not a pleasant one:

You told him of the farm?

How can you trust him? He's one of them!

What's to stop him from getting Christina and Rob, and then sending in the hounds to wipe us out?

I had no answers then, just as I have no answers now. The truth is, nothing is stopping him from carrying out such an assault. And as the hours pass, I half expect Frank to return with the remnants of my family—those who managed to survive his attack, anyway.

"No," I say, choosing to bury those thoughts, adding to the teeming mass constantly threatening to break the surface. "Nobody's come."

He lets out a frustrated breath but says no more. The silence returns, nothing for us to discuss that hasn't been beaten to death already. In any case, there's no sense in planning given the state we're in. Even if we weren't bound hand and foot, there are still locked doors, a maze of hallways, soldiers manning the exits and snipers overlooking the perimeter. And those are just the challenges we know of. Surely there are more. So whether we can trust Frank or not makes no difference. He's the only hope we have of escaping. That's all we need to know.

Time trickles slowly forward, impossible to gauge without a point of reference. Sleep claims me, my mind no longer able to resist my body's demands. In and out of nightmares I drift, each so vivid I can hardly distinguish between the dream world and my reality. I see my mother and father in chains, their warm eyes turned cold, angry, asking me how I could betray their whereabouts. I see the farm, once our great chance at a new life, now no more than a graveyard. I walk through its haunted grounds, the smell of blood and death potent as ever, the broken bodies of my family as real as my own skin.

I watch Lauren appear at the room's entrance, gun drawn, relief warming her face at the sight of me. She's come to free me. Then the shadows behind her shift, materializing into Frank's lowering form. I yell, I scream, I rage against my restraints in a futile attempt to warn her. But she doesn't turn, doesn't make a single motion to defend herself. The smile never leaves her face, her eyes never leave mine, that spark of life I fell in love with burning in her stare. And then it's gone, snuffed out with the crack of exploding thunder.

When I wake, it's in a blind panic, my heart beating so hard and fast it hurts. I don't sleep again after that.

The tread of approaching footsteps sound outside the room, drawing our attention. They grow closer, a strip of light now visible beneath the doorway. The footsteps halt, followed by the jingle of keys and scraping of a lock. The door opens, the light spilling into the room blinding to my cave eyes. I squint against it, unable to make out more than the outlines of several people moving forward.

"Uncuff them, quickly!"

Frank's voice is immediately recognizable, as is the urgency of his words.

I blink and the face of a middle-aged woman comes into focus, sparing me only a brief glance before setting to work on my restraints. Once free, I make my way shakily to my feet, groaning against the stiffness that has settled in my joints. She sets to work on Leon, his expression shrewd and suspicious over our sudden turn of events.

"What's happened?" I ask. Certainly, something has. Frank wouldn't come here like this if he could avoid it.

"They know of the farm," he says. "We move on it within the hour."

My stomach drops, my blood freezing in my veins. Around me, everything falls away. The people, the voices, the light shining in my eyes, it all disappears. Through the nightmarish graveyard I walk once more, the ground littered with fallen loved ones. I see their sightless stares, fear still etched onto their faces, and I know it is my fault. I should never have left them. I should never have let us come to this hellhole of a town in the first place. If we hadn't, none of this would have happened.

An angry roar sounds beside me, bringing me back to this cold reality. Leon lunges forward, uncaring of the weapons Frank and his soldiers carry. Rationality left him the moment Frank spoke. Frank, it appears, does not need weapons to handle himself, blocking Leon's attack and locking him in the same chokehold he held me in this morning.

"Quiet, you fool!" he seethes. "Do you think I would have uncuffed you if I meant to go through with that plan?" He releases Leon who doubles over and coughs but makes no other attempt to attack. Frank continues. "I know what you must think, but I didn't speak a word about what we discussed, Morgan. Your uncle, Mitch; he's the one who sold you out."

"How do we know he won't want revenge? We'll be looking over our shoulders for the rest of our lives."

Richards warning echoes back to me. This is the fear he spoke of, this retaliation Mitch has taken against us.

"That bastard." Leon's words are strained, equal parts hate and anger. "That dirty, piece of shit! We never should have let him go."

No, we shouldn't have. We should have let Richard deal with the situation when we had the chance. Now it's too late. Yet even as the news sinks in, something about it all seems off.

"But why attack us?" I ask. Mitch left us weeks ago, before the rescue of Felix's aunt and the influx of food and supplies from the Sawyer's ranch. We were only hanging on by threads at that point. Factor in the snow and the defenses we've raised, and it makes less and less sense for them to risk the manpower and resources needed to attack us. I mention this to Frank.

"It's not the farm they want," Frank says, his eyes falling heavily on me. "It's you."

He fills me on the meeting he had after our conversation this morning. I shouldn't be surprised. After that night with Lauren, I should have understood what he was capable of. But turning us over to the Animas Animals? Not just Lauren and me, but the entire family? His sisters. My Aunt Virginia who practically raised him after my grandmother passed. My Aunt Claire who paid his way through multiple rehabs. My mother who never left his side no matter how hard he relapsed. I would never have thought his hatred for me ran so deep that he would condemn them.

"So be it," I say.

"So be it?" Frank asks.

"You said it yourself, it's me they want," I remind him. "Well, they can have me."

Mitch would sacrifice my family in order to get to me. I would sacrifice myself in order to protect my family. They won't suffer because of me. Not if I can help it.

"I'll turn myself in, now, before it's too late," I continue. "There will be no need for them to attack because they'll have already gotten what they want."

Leon lets loose a breath of frustration. "There it is, right on cue," he says bitterly. "What is it with you? Why are you always so quick to play the martyr?"

"Play the martyr?" I ask, taken aback. "Is that really what you think I'm doing?"

"It's what you always do," he says. "Salida. Clovis. Now, this. See a pattern? You're always throwing yourself into the fire without considering the alternatives."

I open my mouth to reply, the anger that's been building inside flaring bright and hot. But before I can speak, Frank cuts me off with an irritated hiss.

"Enough!" he says. "We don't have time for this." He turns to me. "I respect what you're willing to do for your family, Morgan. But turning yourself in won't stop anything. You weren't the only one who broke in that night. They'll raid the farm to find the others. They'll never let it rest. Not after what you did."

The reality of my situation settles in my stomach like a block of ice. The Animals have their sights set on my family, and there's not a damn thing I can do to change that. All our guns, all our defenses, will any of it even matter? Likely not. When it comes to their revenge, they won't take any half measures. They'll come in hard and heavy. My family won't stand a chance. Not on their own.

I look to Frank, the dread I feel mirrored on his face. My family aren't the only ones the Animals have their sights on. And from the look he gives me, I know things are as dire as I believe them to be.

"What do we do?" I ask. It all comes down to this. Any plan, any action, starts and ends with the man standing before me.

"Do you remember when I told you that every plan I made was more desperate than the last?" he asks.

I nod. "I do."

"This is more desperate than all the rest combined."

Leon laughs, short and bitter. "Of course it is," he says.

"But it's also the only chance we have to save our families."

Leon and I share a look, the resolve in his stare telling me we are aligned in our thinking.

"We can handle desperate," I say.

I pace about the room, the adrenaline coursing through my veins not allowing me to sit idle. I'm a nervous wreck, my anxiety reaching its breaking point. I feel it in the thumping of my heart, in the cold sweat breaking across my forehead. My stomach is clenched in an impossible knot, making me nauseous. I said we could handle desperate. Now, I'm not so sure.

The waiting is the worst part. Analyzing the plan. Weighing the odds. Thinking of all the ways things could go wrong. It's hell. I'd rather be in the thick of things—would rather risk my life instead of dreading the prospect of doing so. At least then there's no thinking, no dwelling. It's all momentum. Action and reaction. Each move a precursor to the next.

I glance at Leon who's slipped into his own zone, the sound of his tapping foot reaching my ear with a sense of nostalgia. It's a sound I grew up with, a beat, more often than not, I would pace along with during times of great stress. At least, what was considered stressful at the time. Hard to believe some of the things we once worried over, back when tomorrow seemed all but guaranteed. So much has changed. But seeing my friend, pacing along with the beat he plays, I realize some things remain the same. Some things always will.

The sound of distant shouting reaches our ears. It has begun.

"I believe that's our cue," Leon says as he joins me.

"Sounds like it," I say.

We stand side by side, both of us gripping the handguns Frank managed to smuggle us as the shouting grows louder.

"Do you think we can actually pull this off?" he asks.

I feel his eyes on me and I turn my head to meet them. Sixteen years of friendship reflect back to me from those deep, brown depths. The joys. The tribulations. All the milestones shared as we grew from boys to men. I feel my mouth twitch into a ghost of a grin, the knot in my stomach unwinding.

"I don't know, Lee," I say, honest. "But whatever happens, I'm glad you're with me."

He stares at me for a moment, emotion swelling in his eyes. With a nod, he works past the lump in his throat and extends his fist. I extend my own and knock it against his.

"Always, brother," he says. "Always."

The shouts and screams intensify, accompanied by the pounding of dozens of feet. Then, finally, our door bursts open. Val, the middle-aged woman who uncuffed us earlier, stands in the doorway, her form obscured by deep smoke.

"It's go time!" she yells.

Chapter 27: (Lauren)

Fear is a dangerous thing. The way it can consume a person. Make them freeze up. Make them hysterical. More dangerous still is the effect it can have en masse—the way it spreads from person to person, filling the air like a bad odor. I feel it's suffocating presence press heavily upon the room. It's in the frantic faces, in the clamor that rises as everyone fights to be heard. There's a mad rush to the sniper-holes built into the boarded windows, the family pushing and shoving each other out of the way to see the convoy with their own eyes. Myself included.

I stand beside Felix on the second floor, watching the trail of lights snake their way up the road. The sight steals the air from my lungs. There must be a dozen vehicles at least. I share a look with Felix, his expression cold and disbelieving. He knows what this means as well as I do. The Animas Animals. They're the only gang big enough to have this kind of fleet. Which means there can be no doubt of where they are headed. And if that's true, it also means that someone sold us out. Leon and Morgan would rather die than betray us. Which only leaves one person who could have known. Frank. Neither of us says it. But we both know it to be true.

Someone curses, loud enough for me to hear from the next room. I don't need to ask why. I watch as the trucks come to a halt at our main gate. All that holds them at back are two padlocks and several rows of spike strips laid out on the driveway. Neither will hold them back for long I feel the fight or flight response overcome me, every instinct I have telling me to flee: to grab Grace and run off into the night. But as strong as the feeling is, I know there is no running from this. Already the Animals have broken through the gate. Even if Grace and I manage to escape, most of the family would not. The farm would be raided, picked clean of everything of use. And then what? We would have survived only to suffer a worse death later. If there's one thing I've learned, it's that nobody can survive in this world alone.

We need others. This family has accepted me as one of their own. I won't abandon them now.

"Let's go," I say, grabbing Felix by the elbow and pulling him forward. "We can't let them take the place."

We race out of the room and down the stairs where most of the family still wait. Richard descends after us, barking orders as he goes.

"Arm yourselves," he shouts. "Ted, Will, Julia: man the sniper holes in the master bedroom. Kelly and Colton: the office sniper holes." For maybe the first time, I'm glad to hear him take command. He's no stranger to battle. Here, now, with the enemy knocking at our door, he's in his element. Nobody questions the instructions he gives. Even those barely holding it together hurry to their tasks, readying themselves for a fight even as they're filled with dread.

"We're going to need every gun we can get," he says, stepping up to Byron. He doesn't elaborate further, nor does he need to. The two share a hard look, each measuring the other up. Finally, Byron nods.

"We're with you," he says.

Richard returns the nod, then quickly divides us into two groups. The old and young are stationed inside to man the remaining sniper holes. The rest of us are to hold the wall outside. Fleeting, fierce embraces are shared throughout the room. Siblings. Lovers. Parents. Children. I'm overwhelmed with emotion at the sight of it. It's in the darkest hours that love shines brightest. I feel that love in every fiber of my being as I hold my sister in my arms.

We've been through so much together, Grace and I. Our mother, the journey to Durango, everything that's happened since; we've survived it all. For a long time, I felt as if that was our destiny: to fight, to scrape and claw all so we might see another day. It wasn't until I met Morgan that I believed there could be more for us. I believe it still. It's why I'm still here.

My time is up. I unwrap my arms and lay my hand against her tear soaked cheek. There's so much I want to say to her: *stay safe, be brave, everything is going to be alright.* I want to tell her that she means more to me than anything in the world and that I'm so, so proud to call her my sister. Instead, I lean close and kiss her lightly upon the forehead.

"I love you, Gracie." It's all that needs to be said. She knows the rest already.

"I love you too," she says.

With that, I fight the tears threatening to fall and hurry past Grace to join the stream of bodies heading for the wall. I don't look back. I only tighten the grip of my rifle. Let the love in my heart feed me the strength I need for what is to come. And step into the cold dark night while adrenaline spreads like fire through my veins.

Headlights creep up the driveway as we move into position, the sound of their engines reaching our ears like the growl of an approaching beast. I reach the cover of the wall: a barricade made of upturned vehicles, sandbags, and frozen snow. It spans the driveway, from the front corner of the house to the pasture fence. It took over two weeks to complete. Long hours spent filling and hauling sandbags, mile after mile of pushing stalled vehicles toward the farm. It was hell. But from where I stand now, staring down the sights of my rifle as the headlights reach us, I'm thankful for every blister and aching muscle I received while building it.

The headlights fan out, facing the house and wall in one straight line behind the barbed wire fence we erected. We debated extending the wall but ultimately decided on a fence. It's less laborious for one. And unlike a wall, the fence gives a layer of protection without providing a potential shield for would-be attackers to use against us. It also gives us open sightlines both at the wall and from the house.

The engines cut off almost instantaneously, their sudden silence a harbinger of the battle looming over us. I can feel it—that controlled adrenaline I've grown accustomed to. Yet even with the battle fast approaching, it's as if time stands frozen as the ground beneath my feet. The adrenaline. The fear. The glare of headlights. It all brings me back to that night, months ago, when we took refuge behind a parked SUV as these same Animals bore down on us. Only now there's no Morgan to risk his life for us. There's nobody coming to our aide as Richard and Vince and Jerry once did. We are on our own.

Doors open. Bodies pour out of the vehicles, the light in my eyes hiding their features. They move like shadows, using their fleet as cover rather than step out in the open. Smart on their part. Even so, there is no mistaking the size of the force. It's massive. The Animals easily outnumber us two to one. More, most likely. I glance to my right where Felix stands, a scowl on his face as he stares ahead. He claims he trusts his uncle, but surely he must have his doubts. Indeed. To have prayed for months for his uncle to return home, only for him to return like this? I can't even begin to Imagine the thoughts running through his mind.

"Stand strong," Richard says. He speaks from the center of the wall, his voice low, but easily carrying to us down the line. "No matter what happens, remember why you're here."

His message is simple yet I feel its impact ripple along the wall, strengthening the resolve in all of us, especially those who need it most. We are all here for the same reason after all: a reason that means so much more than our own lives ever could. We are here for each other. We are here because we are family. If we survive this, it will be for that same reason.

"Richard Davis!"

The voice cracks the quiet like an icy whip. A voice I recognize: heard in the streets outside Rockridge as he faced off with Morgan, and in the glow of the inferno he set to William and Claire's home. I scan the fleet until it lands on a face half covered in shadow, his sneer more obnoxious than I remember.

"Vince Morris!" He continues listing names. "Jerry Morris! And last, but certainly not least: Morgan Taylor. These are wanted lives. And one way or another, we *will* have them."

Like with Richard, this man's message has a rippling effect along the wall. I feel it sweep over me, a foreboding sense that something's off about all this. The coordination. The knowledge of our people and defenses. Even if Frank betrayed our whereabouts, he couldn't have possibly known all of this. And if that were the case, surely he would have turned Morgan over by now. Doesn't the fact that they are looking for him here prove Frank hasn't betrayed us?

"Never heard of them," Richard yells back. "You obviously have the wrong place."

The man's sneer deepens. "No. I don't think I do." He looks over his shoulder and beckons somebody forward. Surprise. Disbelief. Anger. I feel all of these at once as Mitch steps into the light. Judging by the curses of those beside me, I'm not the only one.

The man pats Mitch's back in greeting. The weeks since he was exiled have not been good to him. Desperately thin. His clothes dirty and ragged. He looks not at us, but at the ground, his face haggard and solemn. In comparison, the sneering man looks positively buoyant.

"What say you, Mitch?" the man asks. "Are we at the correct location?"

Slowly, Mitch nods.

The man laughs. "Yeah, I thought so," he says. "Now, back to the reason for this little visit..." He pauses, his flippant attitude disappearing in an instant.

"Truth be told, I don't want to be here at all right now. This isn't how things should have been. We could have been friends. We could all be back at the base right now, warm and comfortable, but you ruined that chance by shitting all over our invitation to join us. Not only that, you had the nerve to come into our home and create a goddamn mess of things! Eight of our men died that night, one of whom I watched burn to death in front of my own eyes! That's something that can't be forgiven. So here we are: the big bad wolves ready to blow your fucking house down! And you have nobody to blame but yourselves."

He starts cool. Calm. But each word grows colder, louder, fueled by deep-seated anger. His sneer twists into something dark and feral, body shaking with barely suppressed rage. He takes a deep breath and exhales as if to calm himself.

"That being said, we are not unreasonable," he says. "Not all of you have to die tonight. Only four: Richard, Vince, Jerry, and Morgan. The four of you turn yourselves over, here, now. You do that, and the rest of your family will be spared. We'll have our vengeance, burn this place to the ground, and we can all move on from this mess, together. The way it should have been from the start. You have sixty seconds to decide."

Not unreasonable. All we have to do is allow them to kill four of us and agree to become their captives. The fact that this man can stand there, acting as if he offers us some golden opportunity speaks volumes. He's a sociopath in every sense in the word. I doubt the soldiers he spoke of have crossed his mind even once since they were killed. It's power he cares about. I heard it in his voice the first night we met, just as I hear it now. This isn't about revenge of the dead. It's about reclaiming the power he feels stolen from him.

"Our lives are our own!" The words leave Richard's mouth as a defiant roar. With the battle only a breath away, the warrior in him fully awakens. "They will never be yours!" And though his words are his own, they speak for all of us.

The man scans the wall and house coldly. "I'm disappointed, Morgan," he says. "I wanted to see the light leave your eyes before you died." He takes a deep breath. "But I guess we don't always get what we want, do we? So be it."

He turns to his right. "Ready Matador?"

A man steps forward from the shadows, the glow of headlights illuminating his face for the first time: Felix's Uncle Frank. I don't need to search Felix's face, I can all but feel him tense beside me. Inside the home, I imagine his wife and son do the same. He stops beside the sneering man, sparing only a slight glance our way before returning his attention to him.

"You have no idea," he says.

The man smiles, mistaking the rage that burns inside Frank's eyes for excitement. In the span of a breath, the smile leaves his face, experiencing that rage first hand. Frank moves with speed and violence, disarming the man and maneuvering him into a chokehold effortlessly. His gun rests against the man's head, reminding me, vividly, of this morning: when it was Morgan he held at gunpoint, his face turning blue, eyes pleading with me to run. I cursed him then, certain the man Felix knew was dead and gone. But in an instant, he's crossed that invisible line in the sand—choosing us over them. It's like seeing a man come back to life.

"The hell...you...doing?" the man chokes out, his voice a mix of venom and betrayal.

Frank ignores him, addressing, instead, the ranks of Animals who have drawn their guns on him.

"This isn't how things have to be," he yells, backing away till he reaches the boundary of the fence. "Aren't you tired of this? We raid and kill and do whatever we're told because we're terrified of what they might do to us and our families if we say no. I'm done being a pawn in their game. If we would just stand together, we could take back our lives. We could find a new way forward. And it all starts here."

Of the faces not hidden by shadow, most are full of indecision. I'm caught off guard. All this time I've thought of the Animals not as individuals, but as a collective. I modeled them all after the sneering man who leads them: bloodthirsty and callous. It never occurred to me there might be more to them. But seeing them waver, caught between their desire to join Frank and their fear of the man he restrains, I realize how wrong I was. They're just people, filled with good and bad like all of us.

"Anyone... against...slaughter...entire family," the man spits.

There it is, the fear that holds them back. It's a dangerous thing. And the Animals are no more immune to it than we are.

"No, you won't," Frank says. With his gun still in hand, he reaches toward his shoulder. "Matador to base."

The words hardly leave his mouth before there's a reply. *"Where the hell have you been?"* a staticky voice replies. *"Return immediately! There's been a breach. Grunts are escaping left and—"* He silences the voice just as quickly.

If Frank meant to assure them, he was mistaken. Instead, there's an outcry of mutinous dissent. He's put people's families at risk with whatever he's done. And though they may hate what they do, they never would have taken such a risk themselves. Now their fear turns to panic, to anger, all directed at the man who put this in motion.

"I did what I had to," Frank yells over the tumult. "I told you, I'm done being their pawn. Now you must make that choice for yourselves. Join me and take back your freedom, or choose to be a puppet for them to control!"

Chapter 28: (Morgan)

Smoke fills my lungs and stings my eyes the moment I enter the hallway, so overpowering I almost miss the tinge of chemicals and gasoline rolling off our guide. Almost. I realize then what she has done. *A distraction.* That's what Frank had told us. That they would create a distraction to cover our escape. I had been skeptical, wondering what could possibly distract over three hundred soldiers at once. Now, I have my answer: fire. A desperate plan indeed.

Without so much as a nod, Val turns and we follow her down the hall, away from the orange glow at our backs. She stops at a door halfway down, a second key already working at the lock. The door opens and there stand Lylette and Tony, the rest of their recruits fanned out behind them. By their confused faces, I gather they were not informed of the plan. Val makes no attempt to do so now, her message short and blunt: "Move your asses unless you want to burn to death!"

Val doesn't wait to see if they comply, already turning and continuing down the hall. If Lylette questioned her intentions, it disappears the moment she sees me. I forestall any other questions she may have by matching Val's urgency.

"We're breaking out. But we have to move, now."

It's all the assurance they need. They file behind Leon and me, all of us fighting through coughs to hurry after Val. The end of the hallway comes into view, the light of a single lantern revealing the form of a solitary figure standing at the exit. It's not until we are feet away that I make out the three bodies heaped on the floor.

"Nice work, Mack," Val says as we reach him, eyeing the bodies.

"You too," he says, glancing at the approaching inferno. He considers the rest of us. "Our backup?"

"Just these two," she answers, pointing out Leon and me. She addresses Lylette and the others now. "The rest of you, this door leads to the river trail. Take it and run before you're burnt or caught."

The three recruits don't hesitate, bolting through the door a split second later. Only Lylette remains unmoved, Tony stopping halfway through the door as he realizes.

"What the hell are you doing?" Tony asks her.

"I'm not leaving," she says.

"That's not an option," Val says. "Run, now, while you still have the chance."

"No!" Lylette says, defiant. She points to the guns in our hands. "Give me a gun. Whatever you're planning, I want in."

"This isn't some game, girl," Val says.

"Don't talk down to me like I don't already know that," Lylette says, the fire in her voice as heated as the one behind us. "I watched your people murder mine. I won't just let that go. I'm staying."

It's then I notice how red and swollen her eyes are. My mind has been so consumed with worry over my family and whether or not I can trust Frank, that I barely gave the people she lost a second thought. How easy it is to forget that others feel just as much pain as we do. I see that pain now, and I know there will be no swaying her. There would certainly be no swaying me if it were the other way around.

Val huffs in exasperation and turns to her partner, Mack. He considers a moment and then nods. From his waist, he unholsters one of two pistols and hands it to her. "You follow our lead, understand?" he says.

"No problem," she agrees. She turns to Tony who looks as if he's on the verge of tears. He grips the crucifix hanging around his neck tightly, shaking his head as if in shame. He doesn't need to speak for me to know his decision.

"I'm sorry," he says. He's out the door before she even has the chance to reply. If Lylette is surprised by his exit, she doesn't let it show, turning back to Val and Mack as determined as ever.

"We proceed to the top floor," Mack says. "Right now the fire is concentrated on the bottom two levels of the south wing, but we don't know how fast it might spread. We need to free the hostages before they have the chance to organize. Keep your heads cool and only shoot if necessary. As far as they know you're one of us. We'll play that card as long as possible, got it?" He surveys us briefly as we nod and give our understanding. "Alright then, on me."

Slices of moonlight filter through the windows of the stairwell. Through them, I spot figures darting through the parking lot and toward the river trail, accompanied by the sound of gunshots muffled by the walls and thick glass. There will be lives lost tonight, just as there was the last time I carried out a plan within these walls. There's guilt in that, knowing they die because of our actions. But more than anything there's anger that we were forced into this position in the first place. The Animals made nights like this inevitable. And so long as they hold power, more nights will follow. I lost sight of that on the farm. I won't do so again.

We reach the top floor and pause at Macks outstretched hand. He peeks around the corner, his rifle held at the ready. "Only two guards. The others must have left to see what's going on." he turns to us. "Watch my back."

He enters the hallway at a run, catching the guards' attention instantly. They raise their guns defensively, yelling at him to stop. He doesn't.

"Boss sent me you fools!" he says. "Did you not notice the smoke and gunshots? There's a massive fire burning in the south wing. Grunts are escaping left and right. We need to corral the hostages and get things under control."

He sells the bit well, his voice frantic and impatient. The guards buy it. They lower their weapons.

"How did—" The guard is silenced before he can finish his sentence, Mack bringing his gun to bear in one quick motion. It's over in two shots, each guard dropping with a bullet through their head. He swipes a set of keys from one of them and gets to work freeing the hostages as we run toward him.

Mack makes quick work of the locks, the freed hostages spilling into the hallway confused and frightened. A girl of maybe eight spots Val and rushes into her arms, tears streaming from her eyes. "Momma," the girl says, the word softening the gruff woman.

"Lena, Brianna." I turn at Leon's voice. I spot them, their confusion quickly turning to surprised disbelief. They rush toward us, Brianna into Leon's arms and Lena into my own. I exhale a long breath of relief. Just as Felix is a brother to me, these two are my sisters. After so many months I feared the worse. Holding them in my arms now, whole and unhurt fills me with relief.

"How?" Lena asks.

So much is asked with that one word. I can see the questions burning in her eyes. I want to answer them all, to tell her everything. But now is not the time.

"It's a long story," I say. "I promise to tell you once we get you home to your family." A dozen more questions arise at the mention of her family, but she doesn't voice them. She's smart enough to know we're far from safe.

"Settle down," Mack barks. "You're not free—*DOWN!*"

I follow his horror-struck gaze and feel the same horror wash over me as I see what he sees. Animals have entered the hallway, anger flooding their faces as they survey the scene, guns already rising in retaliation. I don't think, just move, pushing Lena into Leon and Brianna and all but tackling them to the ground as the hallway erupts in a storm of bullets and cracking thunder. We scramble into the room they just vacated, others tripping and falling over us in panic.

I turn around just as Mack sinks to his knees surrounded by the bodies of three hostages who have already fallen. His back is turned on the Animals, his arms outstretched wide on either side of him. His eyes click to mine and it's then that I understand what has happened, what he's done. He was the first to notice the Animals, the first raise the alarm. Yet rather than save himself, he used his body to shield others. And though his thin frame is no match against the vastness of the hallway, there's no doubt more bodies would litter the floor had he not done so.

In his eyes there is no fear, no regret. There's only peace, arms still open as if ready to embrace someone waiting for him on the other side. A half second later his body jerks, more bullets hitting their mark. His eyes close not in pain, but release, a ghost of a smile on his blood coated lips as he falls forward and his soul is put to rest. I don't know him; don't know why he chose to help us or why he would sacrifice himself for others. But I know I won't forget this moment, his tranquil face and open arms seared forever in my memory.

"Plan B," Val shouts, unearthing a length of rope from her pack. No, not just rope: a ladder. "Hold them back as long as you can."

Lylette reaches the door first, peaking quickly into the hall and firing off several shots before they return fire. I go to one knee and use the same technique, peeking in and out, firing a burst of bullets each time. One goes down by me. Another by Lylette. But a half dozen remain, using the recessed alcoves for cover as they push forward.

"We have transport waiting at the TBK," Val says, the ladder attached to the patio railing. "Get there at all costs." She's the first one down the ladder, the girl she held in the hall clinging to her back with tears streaming down her terrorized face. I turn from the sight, focusing the anger that rises toward the bastards who've forced us here.

I empty the clip and reload my one spare. I glance back at the balcony. Only a handful of hostages remain. I want to scream at them to move faster, the need to escape an overwhelming force. But I resist the urge, knowing that doing so will only make matters worse. I shoot off another burst of shots, clipping one guard on the shoulder and just missing a kill shot on a second. Movement flutters just out of the corner of my eye. More Animals rush from the opposite end of the hall, their weapons rising as we come into their line of sight. By the collar of her shirt, I yank Lylette to the ground, bullets hitting the door where she stood not a split second before. I fire off my last three shots into the chest of the closest attacker before slamming and locking the door shut.

The room is nearly empty, most of the hostages already on the ground and running toward our transport. "Lylette, you're next," I say as the final hostage mounts over the railing and begins to climb down. It takes all my self-control not to follow immediately after. But this ladder isn't the strongest. At most, it can hold two of us at once. From this height, a fall could be fatal.

The Animals are at the door, the loud *thump-thump* of them trying to breach flooding my ears. "Now you, Lee." He opens his mouth to argue but I cut him off, already knowing what he's about to insist. "Just go! I'll be right behind you."

He curses but brokes no further argument, mounting the railing and beginning to climb down. No sooner does his head clear the patio that a tremendous crash sounds behind me. I turn to find the door swung open, a huge Animal shouldering his way into the room with more pouring in behind him.

"Show me your hands!" barks one of the Animals.

I raise my hands, my mind frantically thinking of a way out of this. I have no ammo, no cover. The second I make a move I'll have a dozen bullets in me. Even if I could make it over the railing, I couldn't climb down without getting shot, and all jumping would accomplish is either a quicker death or severe trauma. None of these options end with my escape. But there is still a chance for the others. All I can do is buy them as much time as I can.

"Now, on your knees and hands behind your head." I comply, hating the vulnerability of such a position, but knowing resisting will accomplish nothing but a bullet through my head. Death might be coming for me, but I'm not ready to meet it. Not yet.

Two Animals come forward at the leader's command, one stripping me of my pistol and the other to check the balcony. The Animal at the balcony curses. "They climbed down," he says. "Heading north around the side of the building. Couldn't get a shot off before they disappeared."

I let out a breath of relief. They still have a chance.

"Hunt them down!" barks the leader. "Every single one of them, understand?" Like a chorus, they all reply with the same two words: "*Yes, Boss*". Most of the Animals leave to do his bidding, only three staying behind with him. His honor guard.

"So, you're *Boss*," I say. Hatred flares hot inside me. All the pain and suffering the Animals have inflicted, all the lives they've destroyed and taken, it all stems from the callous man before me. My hope of survival leaves me, a new hope rising in its place.

"And you're the infamous *Morgan*," Boss replies. His eyes are dark pits, fixed on me in undeniable malice. He doesn't say how he knows me. There's not a single mention of Mitch or the raid, and I don't question the matter. The less he thinks I know, the better. He walks forward and unholsters a revolver at his hip, making a show of placing it slowly against my forehead. My pulse quickens at the touch of the cold metal, my adrenaline off the charts. But as it was with his brother, I don't let it show. And though I'm on my knees, I have no intention of living here.

"This was your doing tonight," he says. It's not a question and I don't deny the fact. Better that the blame is put on me.

"It was," I say.

He surveys me for a cold minute, the same hatred burning inside me burning in him as well. I can feel it rolling off him, can see it in the rage that fills his eyes.

"You have heart," he finally says. "That's good. Soon we'll find out just how much." He withdraws the revolver from my head and my hand drifts toward my boot. "Take him."

He turns toward the door and I rise, all my hate, all my anger adding speed and violence to my movements. Out of the three guards, only one reacts quickly enough to fire off a shot. It misses, sailing past my ear by less than an inch. There is no second shot, the three guards freezing as I hold a knife against Boss's throat—a knife that has known over one hundred years of warfare.

"If I can't give this knife to my own son, I will at least have it passed into the hands of a man strong enough to carry it."

Richard's words echo in my mind as I use the knife to disarm Boss and force his men back. Boss drops the revolver and I kick it to the side.

"What are going to do, Morgan?" he asks. "The second you use that knife, my men will kill you."

"I'm dead either way," I say. "Rather it be a bullet than whatever you have planned for me."

"Plans can change," Boss says. "Tonight doesn't have to be the end of either of us. It can be the beginning of something new."

He speaks without panic, without fear. It's as if the knife I hold to his throat weren't there at all for all the concern he shows. It's unnerving.

"I was offered to join you before," I say. "My answer hasn't changed."

"Why?" he questions. "Because you think what we're doing is wrong: that we're just a bunch of scumbags doing what we please?"

"You think differently?"

"Of course," he says, a dark humor filling his voice. "It's a new world, Morgan. Everything we do shapes what kind of world it's going to be. Most people are sheep. Left on their own they're helpless, just easy prey for the wolves. They need shepherds to guide them, lead them."

"And that's you?" I ask.

"You're damn right," he says. All the humor has left him. When he speaks, it's with pure conviction. "We bring people together. We make the choices they're too afraid to make—do the things they're too weak to do themselves. Our methods might seem extreme, but they are necessary."

"Killing and ransoming are necessary?" I challenge, unable to keep the disgust out of my voice.

"And how many have you killed tonight, Morgan?" he asks. "Demonize me all you'd like, but those bodies in the hall are on you. They were safe, provided for until you came along. You'll rationalize it of course—tell yourself it was *necessary*. Doesn't change the fact that you have blood on your hands the same as me."

His words hit hard, a wave of guilt boiling in the pit of my stomach. I know he's trying to rattle me, but I can't escape the truth in what he says. There is blood on my hands. The bodies in the hallway, the captives who are gunned down trying to escape, at least part of their deaths are on me. But it's as I reminded myself earlier: they are the ones who made nights like this inevitable. They're tyrants. And as with all tyrants, there will come a time when they will fall. Rebellion is the natural counterpart to oppression. All it takes is a spark.

"We're more alike than you would like to admit," he continues. We're both—"

"We're nothing alike," I cut him off, tired of hearing his attempt to sway me. "And I'd sooner die than join you."

He laughs, the sound amused and mocking. "If you can, keep him alive." Boss speaks not to me, but to his men. "I want him to know what it means to suffer before he dies."

There is no fear in his voice. No attempt to sway me further. Even now, he commands an air of authority. I've dealt with my share of wicked men since this all began. Unconsciously, I regarded him the same as those I've met before him. I was wrong. He's something else entirely. Killing him could be the spark needed to bring them all down.

This is it, I realize. After everything I've fought for, this is how it ends. They won't take me alive. If I am to die, it will be on my terms, not theirs. My grip tightens around the knife, my resolve hardening. I don't think of the pain to come. I don't ponder what happens after my heart has beaten it's last. I think of those I love most. I see their faces, hear their voices, and I feel blessed to have lived the life I have.

I'm so absorbed in my thoughts, that it's with a jolt I realize one of their faces is more than just a memory. Boss notices too. He shouts a warning but already it's too late. The sound of thunder cracks within the room, followed by the thud of falling bodies. One, two, three guards hit the floor, none of them so much as able to lift their guns before they're killed. I keep my hold on Boss as he howls in rage and struggles against me, utterly lost for words.

"They almost have the fire contained," he says. "We need to move."

His voice helps me find mine.

"Lee?"

An irritated look crosses his face. "No, Moe," he says. "I didn't leave you to die. Now deal with him and let's be done with it."

"You fools," Boss says. At some point his snarls turned to laughter, dark and manic. "You've no idea the hell in store for you. My brother will find you. You'll beg for death before—"

Blood soaks my hand as I drag my blade across his throat, his wrathful words replaced with choking and gurgling as he falls to his knees.

"You talk too much," I say.

Leon and I arm ourselves with fallen weapons before hurrying to the balcony. Behind us Boss slumps to the floor, his choking falling silent as his life's blood bleeds out of him. We don't look back. I signal for Leon to go, but he shakes his head, the corners of his mouth lifting with the hint of a grin.

"Oh no," he says. "After you."

Chapter 29: (Lauren)

Growing up I never knew what to expect from my mother. At times she was warm and caring. At others, cold and violent. But mostly, she was sedated and quiet, lost in a gray fog of drugs and alcohol. I remember walking home from school full of dread at what I would find at home. The first step through the door was always the hardest. My heart would stop mid-beat, my stomach churning like a restless sea. My eyes would seek my mother and then time would all but stop, the world holding its breath as I held mine, waiting to see if the ax would fall. That's what I'm reminded of as I stare out at the line of Animals, waiting to see which way they lean.

A large, bearded man is the first to step forward. "You're a fool," he says, lifting his rifle to his shoulder. "I won't risk my family over you."

Others follow his lead and shoulder their rifles, stepping toward Frank menacingly. Not all do so. Several look unconvinced, their hesitation easily transparent. So is their fear. As much as they may hate what they do, they're terrified to back Frank.

"Our families are already at risk," a woman speaks up, drawing glares from those who raised their weapons. "We can at least make it mean something." There are nods at that, her words a reflection of what many are too afraid to speak themselves.

"All it will mean is death," another man snarls. "If you can't see that, you're as big a fool as he is."

She doesn't cower. Doesn't back away. There's a fire to the woman that isn't so easily snuffed. I hear it her voice as she speaks again.

"If death is all that's left for me, so be it," she spits, raising her own rifle in the process. "At least I'll die free instead of a soldier for the likes of him!"

It's a chain reaction of yelling and cussing and drawing weapons. Sides are taken. Lines, drawn. Many back away from the thick of things, back into the shadows where there is more cover. Part of me prays for a pulled trigger. It would only take one for things to spiral out of control. Let them finish one another off. I look again to the fiery woman and feel a twinge of guilt. They are not saints, but they are not all like the sneering man Frank holds hostage either.

Still, it's easy to see the tide is against Frank and the woman. The other side has more guns, more hate. They close ranks and advance. Frank steps back until the fence stops him, his gun darting from person to person.

"Vive libre o muere!" he yells. As if on cue, several canisters fly through the air and land around them, thick clouds of red smoke billowing from their ends. There's a split second's confusion. Hesitation. And then all hell breaks loose. One of the men charges Frank who levels his gun and takes him out with one quick shot the head. More shots follow, the booms and muzzle flashes reaching us through the smoke like violent fireworks. Two more charge, smoke so thick now I can barely see the outlines of their bodies. Frank takes out one, but only manages to clip the second, his body barreling into him, sending all three of them to the ground.

I lose track of them in the bedlam. Gunshots continue to rip through the air, accompanied with the sound of screaming and guttural howls. Shadows ripple through the smoke as the Animals attack one another. I aim into the cloud of smoke, searching in vain for a target to reveal itself. It's impossible, each shadow indistinguishable from the next. Through the smoke, I hear the sneering man, his voice rising above the clamor of battle, hoarse and full of undiluted rage.

"SEND IT!"

At his words, the roar of a powerful engine sounds into the night. The roar grows louder, louder; like a caged beast snarling and straining against its enclosure. And then the beast emerges from the smoke, flames spouting from the engine and licking inside the cab. It hits the fence with a clang, cleaving through it like a scythe through chaff.

"Clear the house!" Richard yells, the truck gaining speed as it barrels forward. "Everyone, out!"

I move toward the house on instinct, desperate to get to Grace. Felix reaches out and stops me, his arms wrapping around me in a tight grip. I curse and struggle to free myself, yelling in panic for him to let me go. He doesn't. His hold on me grows stronger, forcing me to my knees, his body wrapped around my own. There's a second, maybe two, and then the world explodes around me. It's deafening. I feel the shockwaves of the blast even through the metal wall and Felix's body. He doesn't let go, continuing to shield me as debris fall around us. Eventually, his grip eases and I find my feet. I turn toward the house and nearly fall back to my knees.

It's devastating. A crater has replaced the living room wall, the explosion leveling the room and collapsing much of the second story above. Inside is nothing but rubble and spreading fire, the open air fanning the flames that twist and leap in search for fuel. Family members pour out of the back of the house in wild disarray. It's chaos. Shouting. Coughing. Crying. I search each face for Grace, growing more and more frantic when I don't find her among the crowd.

"They're leaving!"

My eyes flick back to the smoky battlefield, my panic driving the threat completely from my mind. Headlights flash through the smoke where several shadows still stand, continuing to fire shots at the retreating vehicles. I feel no relief, no joy at the sight; just a brief flash of anger before the panic overwhelms me once more. The family stops streaming out the house. Grace isn't among them. I don't think, just act, running into the darkened doorway with reckless abandon.

The kitchen is thick with smoke, burning my lungs and making me hack the second I enter. I stay low and cover my mouth the best I can as I move forward. The swinging door to the living room has been blown open, revealing the orange glow of the fire inside. I enter the inferno. Flames consume furniture and debris, lick up the walls and what remains of the ceiling. The heat is overwhelming, reaching through my layers and prickling my skin. My eyes stream and burn, the smoke so dark and thick I can barely see at all. Every instinct I have screams at me to leave this place, but I force my feet forward. I'll never be able to live with myself otherwise.

I skirt a flaming heap and my heart stops. On the floor, pinned down by a wooden beam, lies a body. I'm on my knees beside them a moment later, only recognizing Virginia's face as I push her hair back. My heart starts again, beating so hard and fast I fear it might rip from my chest completely. Not just Virginia, but Grace as well. My sister lies beneath the older woman, Virginia's body cocooned around her like a protective shell. I shout and shake them, but neither stir. Frantic, I try to free them from the beam, pulling and pushing and lifting with every ounce of strength I have. It doesn't budge.

I cough and choke. Tears fall freely from my eyes. Still, I don't give up, blindly attacking the beam with a wild fury, animalistic screams drowned by the roar of flames circling closer. A hacking fit overwhelms me, sending me to my knees. I break down, sobs reverberating not from my chest, but from my soul. My hand reaches out and cradles Grace's face.

"I'm scared." It was the first words Grace said to me after we left my mother behind for good. We were on a bus, all of our worldly possessions stuffed into the backpacks at our feet. I remember being scared for different reasons. I hid it well, but I was terrified Steve would call my bluff and track us down. I could handle anything he did to me, but the thought of him touching my sister was paralyzing. I remember looking at her, my ray of sunshine in a darkened world, and feel my heart harden. For her, I couldn't let myself feel that fear. I had to stay strong for the both of us.

"Don't be," I said. I brushed the hair from her eyes and cradled her face as I do now. *"I'll always protect you, Gracie. Always."*

Only there is no protecting her from this, everything I have done burning to the ground before my eyes. Even so, I will not leave her. Her fate is my fate. I burrow closer to her side, my hand never leaving her face. Unconsciously, I begin to hum a soothing melody, the sort of which I would use to lull Grace to sleep once upon a time. My mind is sluggish. Body heavy. I feel the darkness deepening behind my closed eyelids. I welcome it. I'd rather not feel the pain of what is to come.

I've nearly passed through the door of oblivion when I'm wrenched back to the present. First, there is a voice, soft and urgent, like a plea shouted from a great distance. Then comes the shaking, the feel of hands roughly rousing me from those dark depths. My eyes open and deep, painful coughs rack my body. My lungs burn. Hot bile scorches my throat and pushes past my lips. I hear the voice again, clear and familiar.

"Can you stand?" Felix's face draws level with mine, searching my eyes intensely. Before I can respond, movement behind him catches my attention. Vince stands, fire extinguisher in hand, fighting the flames circling closest to us. No sooner do I spot him that the extinguisher sputters and then dies. He tosses it to the side and turns toward us.

"We have to move! Now!"

Shakily, I make it to my feet, Felix and Vince already in motion. Felix works a piece of metal between the floor and beam trapping Virginia and Grace, using it to lift it off of them. Together, Vince and I grab hold of Virginia and Grace, a violent scream sounding throughout the room as I pull my sister free from the wreckage. The moment they are both freed, Felix lets go, the beam crashing back to the ground with a thump. Wordlessly, he pulls Grace into his arms and rushes out of this hellhole. I follow at his heels, Vince behind me with Virginia slung across his shoulders.

I don't make it three steps outside before I collapse in the slushy snow. The fire remains in my lungs, in my throat, each cough flaring through me like streaking flames. I feel a presence beside me, feel a hand pull my hair away from my face as I empty my stomach for a second time.

"It's alright, Lauren." My eyes shut with pain, it's not until she speaks that I recognize the voice of Leon's mother. "It's alright."

I don't know how long we remain like this: me hacking and coughing, Mrs. Thomas brushing my hair back and soothing me the best she can. Long enough for the pool of sick to ice over before I open my eyes again. Mrs. Thomas helps me unsteadily to my feet, my legs so numb I can't even feel them. I meet her eyes.

"Grace?" It's all I can manage.

Her face turns grim. "I don't know," she says, eyes darting toward the barn where most of the family gathers around the glow of a fire. I make my way there as quick as I can, slipping and sliding on uncertain legs. I push past the throng of people, terrified of what I might find. My heart stops, the entire world paused and muted in space it takes to inhale. Exhale. My heart restarts, pounding now against my chest.

I'm on my knees once more. I can't stop shaking. Not from the cold, but overwhelming emotion. Words fail me, all I can do is sob, thick tears making the world a blurry mess. Her hand finds mine.

"It's alright, Lauren," she says. "It's alright."

I squeeze her hand and hastily wipe the tears away. The world refocuses and there lies Grace, awake and alive. A shaky laugh escapes me, the sound closer to a sob than anything else.

"I know, Gracie," I say, brushing the hair away from her face. "I know."

A whisper of a smile graces her lips and her eyes slowly close. I turn to Felix who kneels opposite me.

"She should be fine," he says, not needing me to ask. "No signs of a concussion. Nothing broken. She's lucky."

The relief is a physical thing, as if a great weight has been lifted from my shoulders. Even so, I feel another weight settle in its place. I hear it in the flatness of his voice, see it in the somber lines of his face. Grace was lucky. Her body was sheltered from the beam and debris. But she was not the only one trapped.

"Virginia?" I let the word trail, dreading the answer. Emotion swells behind his eyes, but he doesn't look away. He shakes his head and what small hope I held is gone. I follow Felix's gaze and spot what I had missed in my haste to find Grace. Deeper into the barn gather several family members, their lamented cries hitting me with the force of a tidal wave. How did I miss it till now?

Mrs. Taylor kneels by Virginia's side, clutching her hand as silent tears trail down her face. Her sister does not squeeze back. She gave her life so my sister might squeeze mine. Grief and guilt consume me. I grew close to Virginia, her kind heart and warm smile a rarity in this cold world. Seeing her lifeless body, watching Mrs. Taylor weep beside her, it breaks my heart. But though I mourn her, there's a small, guilty part of me that is thankful it was not Grace, that it is not me clutching a hand whose grip has left it.

Heavy footfalls sound behind me, giving me an excuse to look away. Richard comes into view, closely followed by Jerry and Mr. Thomas. Richard eyes Grace, his features softer than I've ever seen them.

"Is she ok?" he asks.

"She is," I say. "She was lucky."

He nods solemnly as the other two walk past. "Your uncle is alive," he tells Felix. "Your aunt and cousin are with him."

Emotion flashes across Felix's face, a lump rising in his throat. "And the others?"

Richard drops his eyes to the floor with a slow shake of his head, the same kind Felix gave when I asked about Virginia. "No sign of them."

I cast a questioning look at Felix. "Ted and Heath are missing," he says. I turn toward the house. It's only gotten worse. Fire consumes most of it, flames spreading from the living room to the kitchen, dancing and twisting through the darkened windows. Missing. A gentler word than dead, but no less despairing. We all know the truth.

"What about the Animals?" I ask.

His eyes harden. "Four alive," he says. "The rest are either dead or retreated."

There's a silence. None of us ask the obvious: *"what now?"*. The remaining Animals might have taken Frank's side, but does that negate what they came here to do? Had Frank not baited them with their families and their freedom, I have no doubt they would have followed any command the sneering man gave. Where does that leave us? How can we possibly trust them?

Richard glances at the vigil around Virginia with a heavy sigh. "I need to pay my respects," he says, excusing himself.

"I can watch over Grace," I say. "You should see your uncle."

He looks quietly toward the car-wall where his family stands. He watches them for a long moment and then shakes his head.

"I can't," he says. "Not right now."

I'd be lying if I said I understand. To finally have his uncle back after so long is one thing. The circumstances involved are quite another. I can only guess at the range of emotions he must feel right now. Relief, yes. But also anger and a dozen others as well. It's not surprising he needs time to sort through them.

My arms wrap around Mrs. Taylor sometime later, her tears wringing out some of my own. The guilt I felt returns in her embrace. I tell her how sorry I am, how Grace only survived because of what Virginia did for her.

A sad smile appears on her face. "That's who my sister was," she says. "She would have done the same for any of us."

Time passes slowly. The fire has claimed the entirety of the house, the flames drawing our eyes to the sad scene like moths. Though we gather around Virginia, there are words and mourning for Ted and Heath as well. The Sawyers stand among us, sharing in our collective grief. They've grown closer with the family in our absence. It's a good thing, we need each other now more than ever. Frank and the remaining Animals remain apart, perhaps knowing their presence would only be a complication. It's not until the sky has lightened a shade and the flames have died down to a low smolder that we hear from them. It comes as an alarm, Frank's voice shouting of an incoming truck.

Anger, cold and vicious erupts inside me. The Animals have destroyed our home, killed our people. Have they not taken enough from us? I sprint toward the wall along with a dozen others, the anger I feel shared by the surging mass around me. A single truck pulls into the driveway as I reach the wall. The headlights shine along the wall and we raise our rifles in warning. Still, it creeps closer, slowly coming to a halt some fifty feet away. The engine dies and the headlights are cut off. The passenger side door opens and I adjust my aim, my need for vengeance as real as my need for air. A man steps out and all thoughts of vengeance vanish, the air in my lungs lost in a sharp exhale.

I vault the wall without a second thought, filled with a new need. The distance shrinks between us in quick strides, each of us moving toward the other as fast as our feet will carry us. And then I'm in his arms, my tears soaking his chest, his falling into my hair. I don't know how long we stand here nor do I care. In this moment nothing else matters, the pain and grief of the real world unable to touch us. Would that I could reach through space and time and keep us here forever. But such moments are not meant to last.

He pulls back to look at my face, the flicker of fire reflected in his eyes. I don't need him to ask, the questions are clear as day. I don't inform him of all the details, only those that matter right now: Virginia's sacrifice, Ted and Heath missing, Frank and the Animals who have stayed behind. He rests his forehead against mine, eyes closed as if afraid to see the world now that he knows what has left it. I try and repress it, but with him here I give voice to the question that has plagued me since I spoke with Felix and Richard.

"Where do we go from here?"

Chapter 30: (Morgan)

My heart breaks. At least it feels as if it does—as if it sits in the grasp of an angry beast, its grip growing tighter, claws digging deeper, leaving my heart twisted and shredded. It's devastating, the pain so crushing I can barely stand against the weight of it all. I close my eyes and rest my forehead against hers. I think of my Aunt Virginia, of her warm smile and kind words and innate ability to see the good in others. I think of Ted and the son he leaves behind—of TJ. having to move forward from today without a father. I think of Heath, of his determination to distance himself from his family's legacy and prove himself to us. It's not right that they are gone. All we've ever wanted was peace, yet violence and conflict seem intent that we should never find it.

"Where do we go from here?"

I look toward the flaming house, unable to meet her eye. I don't have an answer for her. Never have I felt so lost, so hopeless as I do now. We've accomplished so much since we arrived here. Tears and sweat and blood. We gave everything we had to make a future for ourselves. Now it feels as if that future is lost, gone, turned to ash the same as that which falls around us. I can't see the way forward.

"Look at me," she says.

I force myself to meet her eyes, a fire of a different sort burning inside those depths. She takes my hand and lays it against her chest, the gentle beat of her heart drumming against my fingers.

"We're still here, Morgan," she says. "As long as our hearts still beat, there is reason to hope."

It's as if my own heart thrums to life inside my chest, her words a salve on the wounds left by the beast which gripped it. They will never heal entirely. Tonight has left scars that will forever be a part of me, a reminder of what was lost. But I need look no further than the girl before me to know how much there is still to fight for. All is not yet lost. Not even close.

I cup the nape of her neck and draw her closer, kissing her softly atop the forehead. My arms wrap around her once more, the warmth of her body dispelling the cold that has settled over me.

"You're my reason," I whisper against her ear.

A circus of emotions greets us as we join the others. Grief and anger, joy and relief. There are tears of mourning, tears of gratitude. Half of the hostages have been reunited with Animals who fought beside Frank, their elation completely at odds with their counterparts. A young girl kneels in the snow beside one of the fallen Animals, her deep sobs punctuated with a single word: *"Papa."* A rail-thin woman kneels feet from the girl, silent tears trailing down her face as she holds the hand of another of the fallen.

For so long I couldn't think of the Animals without hate filling my heart. Given our history, it was impossible not to. Since I was taken, things have changed. They are not the bloodthirsty villains I painted them as. At least not all of them. They are people, flawed and broken just like the rest of us. Cut them they bleed. Take away their loved ones, they mourn. Ransom their loved ones and they are yours to command. Is it so outlandish to think we might have done the same in their position? Witnessing their teary reunions and grieving vigils, I don't feel any of that old hate rise to the surface. But not all feel as I do.

The family makes no attempt to mask their contempt, wearing it as boldly as the blood frozen upon the snow. I understand it, the anger, the rage every bit a part of me as it is them. I'm just not sure these people warrant it. They backed Frank, risking their lives in doing so. Regardless of their reasons, the fact remains that had they not acted, more of my family would be dead right now. That doesn't make them friends, but it seems foolish to assume them enemies.

My eyes move toward the barn, and all other thoughts are pushed from my mind. I was a child when my grandmother died. I have no true memories of her, only vague impressions: a warm smile, the smell of cinnamon and vanilla, a gentle hand in mine as we strolled to parts unknown. I remember nothing of the funeral, not the songs that were played or the words that were spoken. I only remember after, walking past my parent's bedroom and hearing the muffled sobs through the gap in the door. I remember the fear that swelled inside me as I witnessed my mother breakdown, face buried in her hands, body shaking and chest heaving as she struggled to draw breath. I remember her suddenly looking up, her eyes snapping to me as if she sensed my presence. Her face was twisted in pain, eyes puffy and swollen. I remember her reaching out and pulling me into her arms, only realizing I was crying once nestled safely in her embrace. She rocked me and held me and whispered soft words until I fell asleep. When I woke, the tears were gone, but that image of my mother remained. That's what I remember most of all.

The moment I meet my mother's eyes I am transported back to that day, her face a mirror image of the face I saw all those years ago. I wrap my arms around her and hold her tight, whispering soft words as she once did for me. It's all I can do but not breakdown myself, memories of my aunt flowing hot and fast as the tears trailing down my face: camping trips at Navajo Lake, when she and Uncle Joe would steal me and my cousins away for weekends full of sunshine and aquatic fun; catching me and Vince sharing a joint one Thanksgiving, the fear I felt when she pried it from my fingers and then the shock when she took two puffs before passing it along to Vince, her finger pressed to her lips as she winked and walked away; the smile she greeted me with whenever I stopped to visit, and the question that always followed: *"So, how is my favorite nephew today?"*

I'll never see that smile again. Never hear that voice. It's one thing to know a person you love is gone. It's quite another to kneel beside their still body, to hold their hand and feel nothing but cold emptiness where once there was warmth and life. Overwhelmed, I have to look away, my eyes landing on Lauren kneeling beside her sister's sleeping form. I feel my stomach clench. The girl came too close to death this morning. Lauren told me she couldn't believe what Virginia had done—that she would sacrifice herself to protect Grace. She doesn't know my aunt as I do. She wouldn't have even needed to think twice about it.

"I don't even remember the last words she spoke to me," I say.

My mother lays her hand on the back of my neck, drawing my attention. Looking into her eyes, I know what my own must look like, the pain and heartbreak we share greater than our shape and color.

"The words don't matter, my son. What matters is the love that filled them."

My chest tightens at that. She's right of course. There is power in words, but more powerful still is the feeling they leave you with. Death may have stolen her smile, her laugh, her voice, but the love I felt for them survives. So long as I remember her, honor her, they will never leave me.

I wipe my face gruffly and take a deep, shuddering breath. Heavy as my heart is, there are matters that must be resolved. Leaving Grace in my mother's care, Lauren and I make our way to the others. Things have only grown tenser. Richard and Frank are locked in an argument, the family and the Animals around them facing one another with cold stares. There's no pushing, no shouting. But the air is charged, taut as a rubber band stretched to its limit. It won't take much for it to break.

"There is no *we*," I hear Richard say as we come within earshot. "There is *us* and *you*."

"Nevertheless, *we* are in the same boat," Frank says. "I know Barr. His brother was the only thing keeping him in check, the only shred of humanity he had left in him. Now that he's dead, none of us are safe. He'll never rest until he finds us."

"We'll be ready for him," Richard says.

Frank laughs, no humor at all in the sound. "Trust me, you won't be."

Richard sneers as well as Barr ever has. "Trust you?" he asks. "Why the hell would I trust you?"

"Because without him, most of us would be either dead or worse right now," I say, finally joining them. "We at least owe it to him to hear what he has to say."

I expect Richard to scoff, to roll his eyes and call me a biased fool. But he does nothing of the sort. Instead, he stares at me for a long moment, his face deep in thought. Then he nods. "Fine," he says, turning once more to Frank. "What exactly is it you propose?"

"An alliance," he says. Cries of protest sound from the family, but Frank barrels forward. "I understand your misgivings. Given your past with the gang, I wouldn't expect anything less. But they want our blood as much as they want yours. More even. We betrayed them...please believe me when I say you don't want to know the things they do to traitors. Even if we captured every single one of you and delivered you to his doorstep, Barr would never forgive what we did. There's no going back."

"And that's supposed to comfort us?" Richard asks. "That you wouldn't sell us out to the Animals because you couldn't get away with it?"

"No," Frank says. "I'm merely making it clear that whatever ties we had to them are completely severed."

"Even so, you're not addressing the biggest issue," Leon says, stepping up beside Richard. "I've known you over half my life, Frank. I trust you, trust your family. But how the hell am I supposed to trust them?" He gestures to the Animals who stand behind him. "They've already proven the lengths they would go to survive. How can we be sure they wouldn't betray us if the opportunity arose?"

"How can we be sure of anything in this life?" Val argues. "You look at us, and all you see are the things we've done, the blood on our hands. I won't make excuses for either. There's no taking them back. But all any of us have tried to do is protect our families. And the simple truth is that on our own, none of us have a chance. Making this work is our best shot at keeping our families alive. Why would we want to mess that up?"

Her argument doesn't sway the family, but it does give them pause—makes them consider the proposal instead of dismissing it outright. There is still skepticism. I feel it myself. But this Barr is a special sort of beast. I believe Frank when he says he will not rest until he finds us. Boss himself died laughing, warning me of his brother's vengeance. If he does find us, my family can't hope to stand against the full might of the Animals. Not alone.

"Even if we agreed, we don't have the resources to spare," Richard says. He gestures to the smoldering house. "Most of what we had was in there. Unless you have a stockpile of supplies hidden somewhere, we won't have nearly enough to go around."

"We might." All of us, family and Animals alike turn toward the voice. Lylette makes to move forward but Byron sets his hand on her shoulder, stopping her.

"Lylette, no," he says.

She shrugs his hand off her. "Why are we here?" she challenges. "Why risk our lives if we're going to balk at the first real chance we have to make a difference?"

"We're talking about close to forty people," Byron says. "And when you consider the situation...they'd never approve it."

"Are you on the council?" she asks. "No? Then how can you be sure of anything? They sent us out to make these contacts. We need to at least bring it to their attention."

It all comes rushing back to me: their ranch, the whole reason for recruiting. I had completely forgotten with everything that's happened. Since we first met Lylette, the community she spoke of intrigued me. The idea that we could be part of something bigger, that we could work together to create a future for ourselves is something I've dreamed about. Yesterday I was cautiously hopeful, reassured with the knowledge that if it didn't work out, we still had a place to call our own. Now, I have no such reassurances. If they don't take us in, I don't know what we'll do.

"Whose attention?" Richard asks, breaking the silence. "Who are you people?"

Byron breaks his staredown with Lylette and turns toward Richard. "We're recruiters," he says. "Tasked with finding others to join our community."

"Really informational," Richard scoffs. "Care to elaborate further?"

"No, I don't," he says.

"Byron, we had an agreement only yesterday," I say. "Can't we—"

"No, Morgan!" he snaps. "Whatever you're about to ask, we can't! It doesn't matter what we agreed to, things have changed. Yesterday might as well have been another lifetime."

His voice is harsh and cold, effectively shutting the door on any plea I might have made. Lylette, however, is not so easily dissuaded.

"You don't speak for me," she says. "Let us make that perfectly clear. And if you refuse to take them to the council, then I will."

Byron's eyes widen and narrow in the span of a blink, his surprise quickly giving way to anger. He stands rigid, his entire face flushed.

"You would really risk everything we have for *them!*" He points to Frank. "*He's* the one who led the attack on *us!* Gary, dead. Cathy, dead. Tony? I can only pray he escaped. Do you forget your friends so easily? Do their deaths mean nothing to you?"

Lylette doesn't move, doesn't speak, it's as if Byron's words have frozen her in place. Only her eyes give her away. There's undeniable hurt, betrayal even. But it's the anger that shines the brightest. I can feel it emanate through the air, not in rolling waves of heat, but an icy coldness that stretches and spreads from her to Byron. I can tell the moment it hits him, the way his stony mask fissures and cracks with unease.

"I forget nothing." She doesn't scream, doesn't even raise her voice, yet the power behind her words is unmistakable. "They were my family before they were yours. I'll *never* forget them. But they died believing in something. They knew our only chance at a future lied in finding others. The world's too brutal for us not to. I'm not doing anything for *them.* I'm doing it for *us.* All of us: everyone who would help build a future the others died believing in."

As she finishes, Frank takes the opportunity to press his own luck.

"I won't insult you by claiming I only did what I did to protect my daughters," he says. "It was still a choice, one I will own up to. But you should know that the Animals have been aware of your operation for some time."

Byron and Lylette share a startled look, neither able to mask their fear at this mention. "What do you know?" Byron asks.

"Nothing concrete," he says. "They know you're recruiting within in the town. They know you have resources: supplies, livestock, access to clean water. What they don't know are your numbers or location, though that's not from lack of trying. They've had scouts searching for you for weeks. I'll give you credit, you do some stealthy work. But eventually, you slipped up. A scout tracked two of you back to that house two nights ago. He stayed, casing the place. When he saw you leave the next night in two's and three's he reported it back. Boss ordered a strike team right away. And well, you know how that turned out."

Lylette curses. "You're absolutely sure they don't know of our location?" she asks.

"Positive," Frank says. "Boss would have moved on the place if he knew. That's why he was so desperate for information. You are a threat to the little kingdom he's built."

"You mean the kingdom *you* built?" Byron asks. "We may not have the resources the Animals have, but even we've heard of *El Matador!* You're as responsible for what the Animals have become as much as anyone."

The truth hits Frank hard. I know the guilt and self-hate inside of him. I saw it firsthand as he broke down inside the Doubletree, confessing to all the vile things he was forced to do while under Boss's control. I see it rise in his eyes now, his shame as easy to see as Byron's scorn.

"You're right," Frank says. "I've done things that can never be forgiven, sins I will one day have to answer for. I don't expect to ever be absolved of the things I've done, but I will make it my life's work to undo the damage I've caused."

He takes a step closer to Byron who takes a step back and half raises his gun.

"I know this all means very little coming from me, but consider this: if I meant you or your people harm, would I be here now?" This gives Byron pause. "I had your people in my custody, had the tools to make them spill their darkest secrets. Believe me, if I wanted to find your location, I would have. Setting your people free, coming here and doing what I did, it was a choice that can never be taken back. I don't expect you to like us, but it's as the old saying goes: the enemy of my enemy is my friend. And make no mistake, the Animals are very much your enemy.

"If you take us to your people, I will place myself entirely at their mercy. I will tell them every shred of information the Animals have on you. I'll feed them anything they need to know on their operation: supplies, people, tactics, anything. If they ask me to help secure your land in case of an event like tonight, I will. If they ask me to lead an attack on the Animals directly, I will. If they ask me to leave, and never come back, I will. Anything they need, I will do it."

Neither moves or speaks for the longest time, their focus entirely on each other's eyes. I can all but feel the tension between them, the sort of charge that fills the air in the moments before lightning strikes. Not the raw, kinetic energy of the strike itself, but it's potential—the sense of what might come. Byron's the first to break the stare, shifting his gaze from Frank to Lylette. She stares back at him, an unspoken dialogue held between them. Finally, he nods.

"So be it," he says. "You may accompany us to our settlement, but I make no promises. Our council will be informed of what has happened, and they will make the final decision. I want your word on the lives of those you love that you will abide but whatever they decide."

His eyes move from Frank to Richard to me. All of us accept.

"Very well," he says. He turns his attention to Frank once again. "How long do you give us before the Animals return here?"

"Night at the earliest," Frank says. "Barr's blood is up, but he's no fool. He won't run blindly in here without a plan."

"Good," Byron says. "We need to be gone long before then."

The husk that was once a home smolders behind me. Charred wood and plaster, smoke and ashes, it's all that remains of the place we worked so hard to make our own. Most of our food was lost, as was our entire store of medical supplies. The arsenal we amassed has been reduced to a single crate of ammunition and what we carried on our person, everything else buried under layers of debris. More important is the security we lost, the feeling that we had a place where we belonged. And yet none of these come close to the biggest loss of all: that of our own people.

I feel it deep inside me, a gnawing absence as if something vital has been lost. With time, that feeling will lessen, but I know from experience it will never fade entirely. But that's a good thing, a blessing hidden inside the pain. To grieve, one must have loved. So long as that feeling remains, those we lost will never truly have left us.

I fight to keep the notion in my head, but the grief is still too fresh, too raw to be consoled by logic. I stop fighting, letting the tears fall as Jenna steps toward her mother, a lone torch in her hand. Behind her is Trent, his face a mask of pain, eyes so red and swollen It's a wonder he can see at all. Abigail stands by his side as confused as anything else. It breaks my heart seeing her like this, today's events so much more than someone her age should ever have to suffer. I wish I could shelter her from such things, that she didn't have to witness this sad scene. But if my aunt loved anything in this world, it was her. It's only right that she should be here.

Jenna leans down and kisses her mother once atop her head, tears leaking past her closed eyes. When she straightens up she looks us over. Only the family has gathered, the Animals and Byron's people at work loading the trucks with what we will be taking with us. Her eyes settle on mine and I brace myself, half expecting to see blame in those hazel depths. Instead, there's a softness I've never seen from her—a vulnerability she's never let me witness. She holds my gaze a moment, clears her throat, and finally begins her eulogy.

"My mom was the best person I ever knew," she says. "She was kind and brave and stronger than I could ever hope to be. Her capacity for love was..." She has to stop, a deep sob ripping through her chest. She sniffs and takes a shuddering breath before continuing. "Her capacity for love was truly amazing. It was the force that drove everything she did. It's only fitting that her final act was made out of that love."

Grace coughs beside me, working past a sob of her own. I put my arm around her and squeeze her tight, trying to comfort her the best I can. She sniffs and nuzzles closer and all I can do is thank God she survived.

"I hope you're at peace, mom," she says, her voice shaking. "I hope Ted and Heath are with you too, and that you all know how much you are missed. Watch over us...I have a feeling we'll need it now more than ever. This isn't goodbye. If you taught me anything, it's that this life isn't the end. We will see each other again. Until then, know I love you, and that I will do my best to make you proud. Rest easy, mom. I love you."

She takes a step forward, a look of great determination upon her face. I know how hard this must be. If she asked, I would carry out this final task for her. But as much as I loved my aunt, it's not my place. It has to be her.

She raises the torch, her hand strong and steady. For a moment, she holds the torch aloft, the cackle of the flickering flame the only sound and movement among us. And then she lets go. I find myself holding my breath as it falls, slowly, slowly, until finally, it hits the pyre. The flame spreads quickly, the torch itself lost as the bed comes ablaze. Soon even my Aunt is lost among the flames, her body turning to ashes before our eyes.

I don't know how long we stand here, watching the flames dance and twist in cadence with the shifting wind. I only know when the time comes for us to make our leave. In truth, we should have left already, our duty to pay our final respects to Virginia keeping us here longer than is safe. And though I feel that urgency, I'm reluctant to leave this place. Things were never perfect. Hunger. Strife. Betrayal. We faced these and so much more in the months we've been here. At times it felt like we were only hanging on by a thread, as if at any moment it might sever and our plight would end. But always, we pulled through. We did it together.

When we leave here, it will no longer just be us. We will no longer have the comfort of being surrounded by those you love and trust. Everything will change. I turn toward Lauren who meets my eyes expectantly. I once told her everything I wanted in this life was reflected in her eyes. So long as I draw breath, I won't stop fighting till I make that a reality. She tilts her head slightly and I nod my understanding. It's time.

With one last glance at the burning pyre, I turn and take that first step forward, Lauren and Grace by my side. Wordlessly, the others follow. Emily. Leon. Felix. My mother and father. Everyone I hold dear in this world with me as we travel forth into the unknown. Like all such journeys, there is fear and uncertainty among us. I feel it myself—the same fear which gripped me the day this all started. I didn't know what lay ahead of me then either. All I knew was that as dark as the prospect looked, I didn't face that darkness alone. I had those I love to help guide me through. I have that still. So long as I do, I can withstand whatever this world has to throw at me.

Epilogue

I sit alone, gripped in an icy fury the likes of which I've never felt before. It fills every part of me—in the air I breathe into my lungs and the blood flowing through my veins. I breathe deep, the smell of smoke and gasoline stinging my nostrils, reminding me. The flames are gone, but the damage has been done. Twice now we've been attacked on our own ground. After the first incident, I saw to our security arrangements myself. I doubled the patrols, assigned more men to the entrances. I ordered the fortifications along the lower levels be strengthened tenfold and had sniper nests built on the top floor which were to be manned at all times. The place turned into a fortress, and I felt confident no party could breach it. But for all my planning, what I did not anticipate was an attack from within.

Frank Chavez's face flashes across my mind and the icy fury turns into a murderous rage. Everything that happened tonight stems back to him. My eyes survey the body lying atop the table. My brother looks peaceful in death. Ironic. If there is such a place as hell, he's there as surely as I'll be when my own time comes. He was a bastard, yes. But he was my brother all the same. I stare long and hard, searing the image of his slit throat and blood-drenched shirt into my memory. He will be avenged. Frank will beg for such a death by the time I've finished with him. They all will.

"Sir?" The voice is hesitant, fearful. I turn toward the soldier standing at the door, his unease readily apparent.

"What?" I ask, irritated. I made it clear that I was not be disturbed unless absolutely necessary.

"I'm sorry, sir," the soldier says. "But I found this as I was clearing out the trucks." He holds out the family photo Mitch gave us as proof of his story He points to Morgan. "I recognize him. Matador brought him in yesterday after the raid."

I propel to my feet, my pulse doubling with anticipation. "You're sure?" I ask. "Is he accounted for?"

"No, sir," the man says. "I checked myself. He must have escaped during the fire."

I wrench my chair off the ground and slam it against the wall, my rage finally boiling over. It breaks apart in my hands and I throw it across the room in disgust. Morgan was here, under my very nose. He had a part in this. I feel it in my bones. Somehow, he and Frank are connected. It's too much for it to be mere coincidence.

"Sir?"

I almost forgot the soldier was here, consumed as I am in my hate. He blanches as I turn to him, his words tripping over one another.

"I'm s-sorry, sir," he says. "We will, of course, continue the search, and I will let you know immediately if he is apprehended. But you should know we have caught another man. He isn't in the picture, but he was part of the same group Matador brought in. He might—"

"Bring me to him," I bark, already level with the soldier. He flinches out of my way and hurries to do my bidding.

"Y-yes, sir!"

He leads me down the stairwell and out into the main lobby of the hotel. My soldiers have the place cordoned off, the captured grunts on the floor bound hand and foot.

"That's him, sir," he says, pointing to the young man at our feet. The man stirs at being addressed. His lip is busted. His nose, broken. Clearly, he put up a fight. He stares up at me, eyes narrowed in hate. I match it, my anger beyond anything this man has ever felt before. I squat down so we're at eye level.

"Tell me everything you know about this man." I hold out the picture and point to Morgan. He surveys it briefly before glaring back up at me.

"Fuck you," he says and spits at my feet.

I smile. Finally, I have an outlet to channel my rage. I snatch the crucifix hanging around his neck and hold it out to him.

"You can pray," I say. "But know there is no saving you from me." I straighten up and turn to a pair of soldiers. "Bring him. There is work to be done."

Acknowledgments

It has been said that to write well, you must write what you know. True, I know nothing of living in a post-EMP world. I have never faced starvation, or been hunted by men out for my blood, or been forced into a situation where it's either kill or be killed. The burdens my characters carry have never been placed upon my shoulders. But for everything in this book that I do not know, the one thing I do is the immeasurable power of a family's love. Above all else, it is the inspiration behind my writing.

Thank you to those who fill my heart with such love. To my mother who played *Simple Man* for me as a child and told me to listen to the wisdom in the lyrics. I am following my heart and doing something I love and understand. To my father who taught me that anything great in this life must be earned, and to take the time to "fine-tune" my work. To my sisters, nieces, and nephews, who literally give me a reason to laugh and smile every single day. Gallaghers for life, lol.

And of course, thank you to the reader. It's still surreal to me that so many of you actually like what I have written. Your kind words, both in person and online mean more than I can say. I look forward to continuing this journey with you into book 3.

Lastly, if you could please leave a review on Amazon I would greatly appreciate it. They help self-published writers such as myself immensely. Thank you.

Made in the USA
San Bernardino, CA
19 February 2019